THE PRIESTLY SINS

**Center Point
Large Print**

**This Large Print Book carries the
Seal of Approval of N.A.V.H.**

ANDREW M. GREELEY

THE PRIESTLY SINS

CENTER POINT PUBLISHING
THORNDIKE, MAINE

For June Rosner, who suggested it

This Center Point Large Print edition
is published in the year 2004 by arrangement with
Tom Doherty Associates, LLC.

The text of this Large Print edition is unabridged. In other
aspects, this book may vary from the original edition. Printed in
Thailand. Set in 16-point Times New Roman type.

ISBN 1-58547-443-6

Library of Congress Cataloging-in-Publication Data

Greeley, Andrew M., 1928-
    The priestly sins / Andrew M. Greeley.--Center Point large print ed.
        p. cm.
    ISBN 1-58547-443-6 (lib. bdg. : alk. paper)
    1. Clergy--Fiction. 2. Whistle blowing--Fiction. 3. Catholic Church--Fiction. 4. Child sexual
abuse by clergy--Fiction. 5. Large type books. I. Title.

PS3557.R358P75 2004b
813'.54--dc22

                                                    2003027141

Every high priest is chosen from his fellow-men and appointed to serve God on their behalf, to offer sacrifices and offerings for sins. Since he himself is weak in many ways, he is able to be gentle with those who are ignorant and make mistakes. And because he himself is weak he must offer sacrifice not only for the sins of the people but also for his own sins.

—Epistle to the Hebrews 5:1–4

Any organization whose leaders are guilty of such knavish imbecility must have the special protection of God merely to survive.

—Hilaire Belloc

Author's Note

Plains City and Prairie County and the Archdiocese of Plains City (lat. *Urbsincampuensis*) are all imaginary places that exist in my world but not in God's. Also imaginary are all the hierarchy, clergy, and laity of the Archdiocese. While the sexual abuse story in Plains City is similar to that in many other American Archdioceses, the similarity is due to the discouraging pattern of the Church's failure to deal with the problem and should not be taken as evidence that I am writing about a specific Catholic place in God's world.

All the events narrated in the story, however, have happened somewhere or other in the United States, including the incarceration of whistleblowers like Herman Hugo Hoffman in mental institutions. Let no one say that the Chancery office depicted in this book is an exaggeration. It may not be typical, but there are many like it around the country. One who is dubious that these things happen need only read *The Boston Globe* book or the report of the Grand Jury of Suffolk County. The setting, then, is fiction, the horror of sexual abuse by men called "Father" and the deadly cover-up by Church authorities real.

The statistical data that Dr. Liam Shannon quotes is based on my own research as reported in *Priests* (University of Chicago Press, 2004).

THE University that Herman Hugo Hoffman attends occupies the same area in my world as does the institution in God's which my esteemed colleague Stanley Lieberson has always called the University of South Cook County. However, the characters who inhabit my University are not based on any real people in that institution.

I am aware that Illinois is the Prairie State in God's world; it is not in my world.

PROLOGUE

(PRINTED IN THE *PLAINS CITY PLAINSMAN AND GAZETTE*)

(PARTIAL TRANSCRIPT OF HEARING IN RE THOMAS PATRICK SWEENEY V CATHOLIC BISHOP; SUPERIOR COURT OF PRAIRIE COUNTY, JUDGE ARTHUR STURM PRESIDING. MR. VANDENHUVEL FOR THE PLAINTIFF, MR. KENNEDY FOR THE DEFENDANT, MR. HELLER FOR THE WITNESS.)

JUDGE: Just what kind of priest are you, Mr. Hoffman?

REV. HOFFMAN: One that tries to be a good priest, Your Honor, not always successfully. I suppose I would say that I'm a sinful priest like all the others.

JUDGE: I will not play word games with you, Mr. Hoffman. Are you a Jesuit or a Dominican or a Franciscan or a Clementine or what?

REV. HOFFMAN: I am a secular priest of the Archdiocese of Plains City, Your Honor. I do not belong to a religious order.

JUDGE: Not smart enough to be a Jesuit, huh?

REV. HOFFMAN: I'm afraid not, Your Honor.

MR. VANDENHUVEL: Let the record show, Your Honor, that Father Hoffman has a doctorate from the University of Chicago in history and in addition to his pastoral work at St. Cunegunda parish teaches courses at State U.

JUDGE: A lot of education for a simple parish priest, isn't it, Mr. Hoffman?

REV. HOFFMAN: One might well think so, Your Honor.

JUDGE: Very well, Mr. Vandenhuvel. You may continue your questions.

VANDENHUVEL: Where were we, Father? Oh yes, you

heard Todd Sweeney screaming in Father Lyon's quarters. You ran into the room and pulled Father Lyon off of Todd, is that correct?

HOFFMAN: Yes, sir, though I didn't know it was Toddy at the time, only a child in great pain.

VANDENHUVEL: Did you experience any difficulty in separating them?

HOFFMAN: Some difficulty. Father Lyon is not as strong as I am but they were stuck together pretty tightly.

VANDENHUVEL: Did you notice any discharge of semen at the time?

KENNEDY: Objection! Irrelevant and prejudicial.

JUDGE: Overruled. Continue, Counselor. I urge you to try to stay out of the gutter.

VANDENHUVEL: Yes, Your Honor. I would observe that it is not my client or Father Hoffman who created this gutter.

KENNEDY: Objection!

JUDGE: Sustained. No more program notes, Mr. Vandenhuvel.

VANDENHUVEL: Yes, Your Honor . . . Father Hoffman, did Father Lyon say anything to you at that time?

HOFFMAN: Yes, sir. He said he would kill me if I told anyone about what I had seen and ordered me out of his room.

VANDENHUVEL: Did you leave immediately?

HOFFMAN: No, sir. Toddy was still on the floor and still screaming.

VANDENHUVEL: What was he screaming?

HOFFMAN: He was shouting, "Father Lyon hurt me.

Father Lyon hurt me."

VANDENHUVEL: Was he bleeding, Father?

HOFFMAN: Yes, sir.

VANDENHUVEL: From his rectum?

KENNEDY: Objection! Unnecessarily vivid question!

JUDGE: Shut up, Counselor. We are not talking about a Ping-Pong game in a rectory basement. Witness, stop sitting there like a bump on a log and answer the question.

HOFFMAN: Yes, sir. Yes, Counselor. He was bleeding from the rectum.

VANDENHUVEL: Copiously?

HOFFMAN: Yes, sir.

VANDENHUVEL: What did you do then, Father?

HOFFMAN: I lifted Toddy from the floor and helped him to pull his pants up.

VANDENHUVEL: Was Father Lyon still in the room?

HOFFMAN: Yes, sir.

VANDENHUVEL: Did Toddy say anything to Father Lyon?

HOFFMAN: Yes, he did.

VANDENHUVEL: And that was?

HOFFMAN: "Father Lyon, you did a bad thing to me!"

VANDENHUVEL: Did Father Leonard Lyon say anything in reply?

HOFFMAN: Yes, he said, "If you tell anyone, I'll come to your house at night and slit your throat with my big hunting knife while you're asleep and kill your father and mother too."

KENNEDY: Objection, Your Honor! Witness would have us believe that a priest made that threat in the presence of another priest!

JUDGE: Shut up, Joe, and sit down! You'll have your chance on cross.

VANDENHUVEL: What did you do then, Father Hoffman?

HOFFMAN: I helped Toddy down the stairs to the door of the rectory.

VANDENHUVEL: Did you take him to the hospital?

HOFFMAN: I'm afraid I didn't think of that.

VANDENHUVEL: Why not?

HOFFMAN: I guess I was emotionally numb. I was a farm boy six weeks into his first assignment. I'd never been out of the state . . .

JUDGE: Mr. Hoffman, may I remind you that this is a hearing on plaintiff's motion *in re Sweeney v Catholic Bishop*. Court is not interested in your excuses.

VANDENHUVEL: Did you say anything to him?

HOFFMAN: Nothing. I didn't know what to say.

VANDENHUVEL: And Toddy?

HOFFMAN: He begged me to say nothing. "Father Lyon will really kill us all at night. He has secret powers."

VANDENHUVEL: What did you do then, Father Hoffman?

HOFFMAN: I went to my room to think.

VANDENHUVEL: Had you ever seen anything like that before, Father?

HOFFMAN: I had not. I knew there was such a thing as rectal intercourse, but I had never seen it.

VANDENHUVEL: You were shocked that a priest would engage in it with a child in his rectory room.

HOFFMAN: Yes, sir, overwhelmed. It was all so ugly.

KENNEDY: Objection! Witness is embroidering his testimony.

JUDGE: Sustained. Strike the words "all" and "so" from the record.

VANDENHUVEL: Did Father Lyon speak to you at that time?

HOFFMAN: Yes, sir. While I was trying to sort it out he came to the door to my room.

VANDENHUVEL: What did he say?

HOFFMAN: He waved a large knife at me, and said, "No one will believe you if you try to tell them. If you do, I'll slit your throat too."

VANDENHUVEL: Did you reply?

HOFFMAN: No, sir. I was too confused. I just sat there, Your Honor should excuse the expression, like a bump on a log.

JUDGE: Order! Order in the courtroom! Witness will restrain his attempts at humor.

HOFFMAN: Yes, Your Honor.

VANDENHUVEL: What did you do next, Father?

HOFFMAN: I finished my record keeping, ate supper, did a wedding rehearsal, and tried to sleep.

VANDENHUVEL: Could you sleep?

HOFFMAN: No, sir.

VANDENHUVEL: And the next morning?

HOFFMAN: I made up my mind to tell the pastor, Monsignor Flannery. The door to his suite was closed. So I had to wait.

VANDENHUVEL: Anything happen while you were waiting?

HOFFMAN: Yes, sir. A young woman came to the rectory office, a seventh grader. She said that Father Lyon had told her he needed help in his room and she should go right on up.

VANDENHUVEL: And what did you say?

HOFFMAN: I said that she looked uneasy about his request and she said she was. I told her that she should never go to his room and that she should tell all the other girls that I said they should never go to Father Lyon's room.

VANDENHUVEL: And what did she do?

HOFFMAN: She said, "Yes, Father," and ran away. Happy to be excused.

KENNEDY: Objection. Witness speculates.

JUDGE: Overruled. I think we can concede witness's ability to read the emotional reaction of a junior high school student.

VANDENHUVEL: Do you recall the young woman's name?

HOFFMAN: No, sir, I do not.

VANDENHUVEL: Do you think you saved her from sexual assault?

HOFFMAN: I hope I did.

KENNEDY: Objection. Witness is speculating again.

JUDGE: I'll let it stand.

VANDENHUVEL: Subsequently you talked to the Monsignor?

HOFFMAN: Yes, sir.

VANDENHUVEL: And what did you say to him?

HOFFMAN: I told him what I had seen in Lenny's room.

VANDENHUVEL: And he said?

HOFFMAN: Monsignor Flannery was very angry at me. He said that he was sick of hearing accusations against Lenny. He was a good priest who had been slandered in the past by false accusations. There would be none in this parish. Lenny had been cleared both by the police and the psychiatrist. He was a popular and effective priest. I was neither. I couldn't preach and I was—his exact words, Your Honor—nothing but a damned German bump on a log . . .

JUDGE: Order! Order! I'll tolerate no more outbursts!

HOFFMAN: He also said I was jealous of Lenny's success in the parish and that's why I made up such stories . . . I think he meant envious.

JUDGE: Witness, it is not necessary to correct the Monsignor's grammar . . . How do you know word for word what he said?

HOFFMAN: I wrote it in my diary, Your Honor.

JUDGE: Ah, how long have you kept that diary, Mr. Hoffman?

HOFFMAN: Since my senior year in high school.

JUDGE: Interesting—and in the present circumstances how convenient.

HOFFMAN: In my culture we're paper savers, Your Honor.

VANDENHUVEL: Was this the first time you heard the implication about other charges against Father Leonard Lyon?

HOFFMAN: Yes, sir.

VANDENHUVEL: Were you surprised?

HOFFMAN: At that time, sir, nothing would have surprised me.

VANDENHUVEL: What did you do then?

HOFFMAN: That afternoon I went to visit Dr. Sweeney at his home down the street. I told him what I had seen.

VANDENHUVEL: And his reaction?

HOFFMAN: He threw me out of the house. He said I was a lying Dutch dolt, that everyone in the parish loved Father Lyon and despised me. If anyone was a threat to his son, it was me.

VANDENHUVEL: Were you surprised by this reaction?

HOFFMAN: I knew Dr. Sweeney had a temper, sir.

VOICE: The Dutch bastard is lying, Arthur. He never came to my house, never!

JUDGE: Timmy, I'd suggest that you sit down and shut up. Witness is appearing in support of your family's suit. It is not wise to impeach his testimony as well as making a damn fool out of yourself. Not for the first time, either. Proceed, Counselor.

VANDENHUVEL: Nonetheless, Father, you swear under oath that you did call on Dr. Sweeney?

HOFFMAN: Yes, sir.

VANDENHUVEL: Did you try again to awaken someone else to the danger to the children of the parish?

HOFFMAN: Yes, sir. I walked over to the police station to report the incident to the chief of police.

VANDENHUVEL: You were aware, Father, that even then there was a requirement to report the abuse of children to civil authorities?

HOFFMAN: I was not aware of it at that time. I thought a priest ought to report a rape that he had observed.

VANDENHUVEL: What did the chief say?

HOFFMAN: He was very upset, sir.

VANDENHUVEL: At what you described?

HOFFMAN: No, sir. He was upset that people would come to his office to complain about the misdeeds of priests. He said that it was the Church's problem, not his, and that the Church better straighten itself out now and not expect the police to do their work.

VANDENHUVEL: Did you do anything more?

HOFFMAN: Yes, sir. I asked to see the Archbishop personally. He had said that the door was always open to his office for any priest who wanted to see him personally. His secretary gave me fifteen minutes for a week from Thursday.

VANDENHUVEL: What happened during those ten days?

HOFFMAN: It was very awkward in the rectory. Neither Monsignor Flannery nor Father Lyon would talk to me.

VANDENHUVEL: Did you see any more children go to Father Lyon's room?

HOFFMAN: I did not.

VANDENHUVEL: Did you hear from any priests?

HOFFMAN: To my surprise, several of my classmates called me. They warned me about Lucifer Lenny as he was called in the seminary . . .

KENNEDY: Objection! Your Honor, this is absolutely outrageous! It is hearsay, prejudicial, and completely irrelevant!

JUDGE: Counselor?

VANDENHUVEL: Your Honor, our case argues that the diocese has systematically covered up sexual abuse and punished those who tried to report it: the victims, their families, eyewitnesses. We have here an example of a good priest who is trying to do what is right being systematically harassed by his fellow priests. It is entirely appropriate that he report the words of the conversations.

JUDGE: Which he happened conveniently to note in his journal, I suppose . . . Well, I'll overrule the objection for the present. Proceed, Counselor.

VANDENHUVEL: "Lucifer Lenny"? Father?

HOFFMAN: Yes, sir. They called him that in the seminary because . . .

KENNEDY: Objection!

JUDGE: I'll sustain that.

VANDENHUVEL: All right, Father, can you tell me the substance of these conversations?

HOFFMAN: They warned me that Father Lyon had influence Downtown, that the past charges against him had been dropped, and that the police and the psychiatrists had cleared him, and that I was only making trouble for myself. They told me that I should stay out of it. Most of the guys thought Len was a good man. He denied anything had ever happened. You'll make enemies for yourself. There's no point in upsetting the Downtown.

VANDENHUVEL: How did you respond?

HOFFMAN: I told them that I had personally witnessed the rape.

VANDENHUVEL: Did that have any effect on the callers?

HOFFMAN: No.

VANDENHUVEL: Did they seem to know that you had

an appointment with the Archbishop?

HOFFMAN: Yes, they did.

VANDENHUVEL: So someone must have told them both about your claim and that you wanted to see the Archbishop?

HOFFMAN: Yes, sir.

VANDENHUVEL: Who might it have been?

HOFFMAN: Anyone to whom I had made charges, then someone at the Chancery.

VANDENHUVEL: So you thought that the Archbishop might be prepared for you?

HOFFMAN: I didn't know, sir. I always felt that the staff tried to protect the Archbishop from bad news.

VANDENHUVEL: And when you arrived at the Chancery?

HOFFMAN: I was not permitted to see the Archbishop. Monsignor Meaghan, Father Peters, Dr. Straus, and Mr. Kennedy were waiting for me.

VANDENHUVEL: Now, help me to understand this. What are their roles in the Archdiocese?

HOFFMAN: Monsignor Meaghan was the vicar for the clergy, now he is the Auxiliary Bishop and the Vicar General. Father Peters was the victims' advocate, though that was not his title in the Archdiocesan Directory. Mr. Kennedy was and is the lawyer for the Archdiocese. Dr. Straus does psychological examinations for the Archdiocese.

VANDENHUVEL: Father Peters is also a civil lawyer, is he not?

HOFFMAN: I believe so.

VANDENHUVEL: Are they all in court today?

HOFFMAN: I believe that Mr. Kennedy, Dr. Straus, and Bishop Meaghan are present, sir. I don't see Father Peters.

VANDENHUVEL: Are you aware that Father Peters has been suspended from the diocese because of credible charges of sexual abuse?

HOFFMAN: I have read that in the papers, sir.

VANDENHUVEL: Thus the victims' advocate seems to have abused victims himself?

KENNEDY: Objection! Your Honor, counsel is leading the witness.

JUDGE: Sustained.

VANDENHUVEL: Did you know then that Dr. Straus is not a board-certified psychiatrist?

HOFFMAN: I did not, sir.

VANDENHUVEL: You have read in the papers, I presume, that he is a family practitioner and not qualified to do psychological evaluations?

HOFFMAN: Yes, sir.

VANDENHUVEL: All right, what happened when this foursome confronted you at the Chancery?

HOFFMAN: They did not give me much chance to speak, sir. They dismissed my story as a fabrication. Before I could say anything, they accused me of being a homosexual and reporting a homosexual fantasy as a fact.

VANDENHUVEL: How long did the discussion last, Father?

HOFFMAN: A lot longer than the fifteen minutes. An hour and a half perhaps.

VANDENHUVEL: Did you think they were sincere in

their charges against you?

KENNEDY: Objection!

JUDGE: I'll let it stand.

HOFFMAN: I can't be certain, sir. They seemed to be sincere. I don't have the gift of reading human hearts. I suppose they were trying to protect the Church from scandal.

VANDENHUVEL: Are you a homosexual, Father Hoffman?

HOFFMAN: No, sir, not that I think homosexuality is sinful. I think the Church should leave them alone.

VANDENHUVEL: Have you ever had homosexual intercourse?

HOFFMAN: No, sir.

VANDENHUVEL: What happened then?

HOFFMAN: I drove back to Green Island, that's where St. Theodolinda parish is. I was troubled and confused. I couldn't understand what was happening. I was the only one in the rectory. The cook had not prepared supper for me. I scrounged some food from the fridge.

VANDENHUVEL: You did not sleep well that night, I presume.

HOFFMAN: No, sir.

VANDENHUVEL: Then?

HOFFMAN: The next morning, Monsignor Meaghan, Dr. Straus, and Father Peters arrived in a large Cadillac—the Monsignor's, I believed. They told me to pack a bag. They were taking me to St. Edward's Center for treatment. They said they believed that would help me to straighten myself out.

VANDENHUVEL: You went along with their proposal?

HOFFMAN: I would never have thought in those days of challenging authority.

VANDENHUVEL: Dr. Straus signed you in?

HOFFMAN: Yes, sir.

VANDENHUVEL: A physician without any credentials as a psychiatrist signed you in to a mental institution?

HOFFMAN: A mental health center, sir.

VANDENHUVEL: Very well. A mental health center.

HOFFMAN: I believe he's on their board of trustees, sir.

JUDGE: Sit down. I'm going to strike the question.

VANDENHUVEL: How long were you incarcerated in that place?

JUDGE: Counselor, before our learned colleague has a heart attack, I'm going to ask you to reword the question.

VANDENHUVEL: Very well. How long did you remain there, Father?

HOFFMAN: Six months, sir.

VANDENHUVEL: Did Dr. Straus interview you during the course of, ah, treatment?

HOFFMAN: I believe twice.

VANDENHUVEL: Of what did the treatment consist?

HOFFMAN: Medication to calm me down and tests.

VANDENHUVEL: Did you take the medicine?

HOFFMAN: Not usually, sir, not after the first couple of months.

VANDENHUVEL: And the tests?

HOFFMAN: They were designed to determine whether or not I was a homosexual.

VANDENHUVEL: How was that done?

HOFFMAN: That's a little embarrassing, sir.

JUDGE: We're all adults here, Mr. Hoffman.

HOFFMAN: I wouldn't bet on that, sir.

JUDGE: Order! Order! Contain your sense of humor, Mr. Hoffman, and answer the question!

HOFFMAN: I don't believe you have the right to order me to, Your Honor, but I will anyway. For example, they would show me photos of women and of men in various stages of nakedness and engaged in various sexual situations. They would monitor my reaction.

VANDENHUVEL: Would you not say that was a terrible way to treat a priest, Father?

HOFFMAN: What I said was not relevant, sir.

VANDENHUVEL: And what was the nature of your reactions?

HOFFMAN: Embarrassingly heterosexual, sir.

VANDENHUVEL: What did those who were testing you say?

HOFFMAN: Not much. They were very apologetic . . . One of them whispered to another, but loud enough so I could hear, "I don't care what Straus says. This poor guy is not gay."

KENNEDY: Objection! Hearsay!

JUDGE: Sustained. Strike it from the record.

VANDENHUVEL: How long did this treatment last?

HOFFMAN: About two weeks.

VANDENHUVEL: And then?

HOFFMAN: Nothing at all.

VANDENHUVEL: Nothing? You did nothing?

HOFFMAN: Oh, no! I presided over the Eucharist, anointed the sick, visited the troubled, preached every day on the closed-circuit TV, talked to my folks once a week to calm them down, read the history books one of my classmates brought to the door, and prayed. It was kind of like a long retreat.

VANDENHUVEL: No visitors and only one phone call a week?

HOFFMAN: That's right.

VANDENHUVEL: You like being a priest, don't you, Father?

HOFFMAN: Always have, always will.

VANDENHUVEL: You were finally released after six months?

HOFFMAN: Three days short of six months. Monsignor Meaghan and Father Peters drove me back to Plains City and to the Chancery. They told me I had been cured, and they were very proud of my efforts.

VANDENHUVEL: Cured of homosexuality in six months?

HOFFMAN: That's what they said.

VANDENHUVEL: And you met with the Archbishop?

HOFFMAN: Yes, sir. For about a half hour. He was charming as he always is and vague as I have come to expect he will always be. He praised my patience and virtue, my strong willpower, and my excellent ministerial service to the people at St. Edward's.

VANDENHUVEL: And then?

HOFFMAN: Then he said that he didn't think I'd really be happy in ordinary parish ministry so he was sending me to graduate school—any school of my choice, any subject of my choice. I said that I enjoyed parish work very much, but, if he wished, I would like to study immigrant history at the University of Chicago. He said that was fine. The Archdiocese would pay my tuition and living expenses. I thanked him and said I was sure I could get a fellowship eventually and would live in a parish in the Chicago area and be little if any drain on my home Archdiocese. He seemed quite relieved when I left.

VANDENHUVEL: Glad to be rid of you?

KENNEDY: Objection! Speculative! Irrelevant!

JUDGE: Oh, all right, Joe, I'll sustain that.

VANDENHUVEL: Let me rephrase it: Did you feel that you were railroaded out of your parish and out of town by your Church?

HOFFMAN: At first I was just glad to escape all the mess, all the foolishness, all the dishonesty . . .

KENNEDY: Objection . . . !

JUDGE: In a case like this, Joe, a witness's feelings are not irrelevant, the witness may continue.

VANDENHUVEL: All the corruption?

HOFFMAN: I almost said that, but I didn't.

VANDENHUVEL: And later?

HOFFMAN: Later, when I regained my confidence, I realized what they had done to me. I was furious; then I calmed down and worked on my research.

VANDENHUVEL: Yet you returned.

HOFFMAN: Plains City is my home.

VANDENHUVEL: That's all, Father.

JUDGE: I'm going to declare a recess, Father Hoffman. I'll turn you over to Mr. Kennedy on Monday morning. Before the recess I want to ask you just one question: After all you allege was done to you by your Church, your Archdiocese, and your Archbishop, why

25

the hell did you stay in the priesthood? Surely with a degree from a great university you could have obtained a better job, perhaps married, and had a happier life?

HOFFMAN: I'm Volga Deutsche, Your Honor.

JUDGE: So?

HOFFMAN: You remember what they say about us Russian Germans? We combine the worst traits of both cultures?

JUDGE: Stubborn like the Germans and crazy like the Russians?

HOFFMAN: I like being a priest. I like being a Russian German. I like Plains City. No one is going to take any of those away from me.

I

"You're not going to wear that Roman collar much longer, Herman."

I looked around for the origin of the nasal whine. Then I looked down and saw the ferret face of Josh Reynolds, almost a foot below me. I was worn-out from my time on the witness stand and still on edge. So I said something that I perhaps shouldn't have said.

"When this is over, Josh, you'll trade your three-piece black suit for prison orange."

Then I saw Todd Sweeney, a tall, lank young man with a haggard face, blank eyes, and long, unkempt hair. He was only twenty-three or twenty-four years old, but looked forty years older, like a man who had spent his life in prison or maybe even a concentration camp. Ten years ago he had been the brightest kid in the class and a charming little guy with a great jump shot. Now he was a thief, a drug addict, a homeless derelict.

Another one of Lucifer Lenny's accomplishments. He always destroyed the best. There were at least twenty other charges against the Archdiocese. It would be surprising if there were not many more.

"Hi, Toddy," I said to him, extending my hand.

"Hi, Father Hoffman," he said, accepting my hand with a wan smile.

"You goddamn lying bastard!" Dr. Sweeney, a bald little man with a crimson face and tiny eyes, rushed up to me. "Get away from my son! Haven't you done enough harm to him already!"

27

"Don't pay any attention to him, Father," Toddy said with a weary shrug of his thin shoulders. "He's always been an asshole . . . thanks for trying to help."

Dr. Sweeney pounded on my chest with his tiny fists. "Leave him alone! I'll see you in jail before this business is finished! You're a fucking faggot!"

The media vultures gathered around.

I should have walked away. Instead, I lost it again, and said something I should not have said.

"More likely I'll see you in court for a slander suit!"

I was sorry at once. A priest should not make threats like that. Then I turned and walked away, much too late.

Outside the courtroom a woman reporter from the local news pushed a microphone at me.

"Why are you choosing to attack your own Archdiocese, Father Hoffman?"

"I was subpoenaed to testify at this hearing because I was an eyewitness to the crime. Under oath I have no choice but to tell the truth."

"Don't you think this is an attempt to make money by attacking the Church?"

"Whatever the motives, the issue is whether Todd Sweeney was raped by a priest who had often been reassigned by the Archdiocese."

I walked away from her.

A male reporter from a national medium cornered me next.

"How many abusing priests are there in the Archdiocese, Father Hoffman?"

"Only a very few. Ten, fifteen at the outside. Out of four hundred and fifty. Most priests are not abusers. It doesn't take very many to give the rest of us a bad name, especially when the Chancery routinely reassigns them so they can do it again."

"Why aren't other priests speaking out like you are?"

"They have not been subpoenaed."

"Do you think they are silent out of loyalty to the Church and to the priesthood?"

"I don't know."

I did, of course. The silence of my fellow priests was as irresponsible as the Downtown's policy of reassigning men like Lenny.

Then a young woman with horn-rimmed glasses and a large notebook cornered me.

"I'm from *The Drover*," she informed me—a far-right-wing Catholic paper. "Don't you think, Father Hoffman, that it is time for healing in this crisis?"

"I certainly do. Healing, however, can only occur in the wake of truth."

"Wouldn't it be better for the Church to admit it made a mistake in ordaining all those homosexuals in recent years?"

"Many of the men charged were ordained long before the Church began to ordain more admitted gays. Most gay men, most gay priests are not abusers. I don't think that charge helps the cause of healing."

"What does?"

"Truth."

I almost said, "and new bishops," but that would have been a terrible mistake.

The religion writer from the *Plainsman and Gazette* shouted after me, "Are you worried about cross examination Monday, Herman?"

"Not in the least. I will simply tell the truth."

There were two more reporters in the gauntlet I had to run. The first was a nun (or a former nun, I have a hard time telling the difference) who worked for the *National Catholic Inquirer*.

"Don't you think, Herman, that you're really defending a fraternity that is collapsing from the inside?"

"Meaning?"

"The all-male celibate priesthood?"

"I wouldn't know. I have not been a part of that fraternity for a long time."

Finally, Timothy Hawkins of the *Prairie Reader*, the weekly paper that had first hunted down the story of Lenny Lyon and from which the TV stations picked up the story, asked, "Off the record, Hugh?"

"Sure."

"What was Lucifer really like?"

"He was a very gifted man, God be good to him, brilliant, charming, hardworking. He knew the name of every kid in the school and of the parents of each one of them. He taught every day in the school, talked to them in the schoolyard, and told them wonderful stories. He was a model of what a parish priest should be. I think he became a priest so he could work with kids."

"So he could rape them?"

"No, I don't think that was his original intention. Unfortunately, in their presence he became sexually aroused. He resisted it as best he could, then the attraction was too much, and he went wild."

"You visited him before he died?"

"I did."

"Was he penitent?"

"I can't judge that. He continued to deny that any of the charges against him were true."

"Was he lying?"

"I don't know."

"He was gay, of course?"

"Surely not in the ordinary meaning of that word. Even in the seminary he seemed to enjoy tormenting people. Later it would appear that the gender of the person tormented didn't matter."

Kathleen and Liam Shannon collected me at the door of the courthouse. As usual my throat tightened with affection and desire at the sight of my former lover. She was wearing a short-sleeve, blue pastel dress with a vee neck and a white belt. It left little doubt about the shape of her body or the elegance of her breasts.

I sighed mentally.

"We'll take you to supper, Father Hugh," Liam ordered. "Wouldn't you be needing a good thick steak and a small sip of the creature?"

The tightness went away. Mostly. As it does. Usually.

The thunderstorm in Kathleen's green eyes and the frown on her forehead told me that she was in one of her angry moods, much rarer now than they used to be when we were kids.

"Your wife needs a sip or two also. Isn't she in one of her thunderstorm moods?"

"And haven't I noticed it too?"

The thunderstorm abated, and Kathleen laughed. The

31

storm could come back later as a tornado.

"You were wonderful, Huey!" she said, squeezing my arm lightly.

We walked out of the decaying redbrick Greek Temple that was the ancient county courthouse into a perfect spring day on the prairies, clear blue sky, gentle sun, budding trees and flowers promising that winter was finally over, often on the prairies a false promise.

"As an expert on body language," Liam Shannon observed, "I'd suggest you tied them all into knots today, not that it was difficult."

I was led across Rutherford B. Hayes Park to the new Prairie County Bank skyscraper, at the top of which was the city's most exclusive eating club. I began to whistle "It Might As Well Be Spring." Kathleen joined me in her pretty soprano tones. Singing again like we had at my house out in the Russian German prairies when we were both just friends, untouched yet by the demands of puberty. Liam hummed along with the tune. For a moment I thought we'd break into dance. However, if any one of the media vultures saw us . . .

The Plainsmen Club was complete with an idealized painting of Wild Bill Hickok in its lobby. The frontier days were more than a hundred years ago, yet this moderately sophisticated city still treasured the myths and the legends of its past. As well it might. The meat-packing yards, the grain elevators, the railroad yards across the river and the interstate beyond were proof, if any were needed, that the city still lived off the plains. The heavy maroon drapes were open in the club. In the distance the winter wheatfields glowed in the setting sun. Beneath us the Prairie Square stood immobile, unshaken by the conflicts of the day—the Mormon Temple, the courthouse, the Masonic building, the Cathedral, River Bank (once called Volga Bank), which was far too thrifty to build a skyscraper, the decrepit two-story redbrick offices of the *Plainsman and Gazette*.

On the two, sometimes three, days a week Liam saw patients in his office lower in the building, he ate lunch in the club because it was "quiet and there's always a bottle of single malt Bushmills for me to drink a tiny sip to steady me nerves. Being a psychiatrist is no easy task at all, at all."

For Liam, unlike most Irish, including in the past his luscious red-haired wife, a tiny sip was no more than a tiny sip.

"I hate Judge Sturm." The tornado now lurked in Kathleen's eyes, ready to sweep across the dining room and destroy its complacent peace. "He is a mean, nasty, corrupt old . . ."

"German!" I finished her sentence.

She broke up in laughter.

Her husband rolled his eyes in approval.

"Fair play to you, Huey!"

"I mean the Archdiocese couldn't ask for a better judge. He's on the board of the two hospitals, Bellarmine High School, Clementine College, St. Edward's asylum . . ."

"Mental Health Center," I corrected her.

"Regardless." She waved me away impatiently. "Catholic Social Services, the Pastoral Council, Mercy

Hospital, whatever. They must have really tilted the playing field to get him."

"I'm sure they did," I said calmly. "They made a big mistake, though they're too dumb to know it yet."

"Huh?" She sipped a bit from her tiny sip.

"What Huey means," Liam explained, "is that if one watched the reactions of media people today, they were on his side all along, as the judge wanted them to be. You noticed how he called him 'Father' at the end? The press did."

"Oh." She sighed and began to carve the small fillet with which she had been served. The staff of the Plainsmen Club understood that Ms. Shannon ate a small steak and her big Irish husband the largest in the house.

"The Chancery people," I said, "typically have forgotten what's at issue now. All they want at this hearing is to destroy me. I don't think they will. Joe Kennedy is not a very good lawyer; otherwise, he wouldn't be working for the Church. However, they should forget about me and settle the Sweeney suit tomorrow. This isn't a trial, just a hearing on a motion. My testimony is supposed to support Vandenhuvel's motion to open the Archdiocesan file. Their real worry should be that Arthur Sturm will order them to turn over all their records of past abuse cases. Then they'll leak the worst to the media, and there'll be a lot more suits. Sturm might be angry enough to turn the records over to the media."

"You think he might do that?" Liam asked.

"He's the only judge in town who has the prestige to take that risk."

Kathleen was silent for a moment, digesting this idea as well as her steak.

"What will happen then?"

"They'll appeal on the grounds of separation of church and state, and their appeal will be slapped down. They're finished, poor men," I said. "The Archbishop will never become a Cardinal. Bishop Meaghan will never become Archbishop here. Father Reynolds will never make monsignor. The Vatican might make them all resign, though I don't think so. Best of all, the whole culture of denial, stonewalling, and cover-up will collapse."

"And you'll be vindicated!"

"Whistle-blowers are never vindicated, Mavoureen." Liam took her hand. "For those who know Hugh, he doesn't need any vindication. The rest will say that, well, maybe he was right, but he went about it the wrong way. Since he's a historian as well as a priest, he knows that history will say that he was a hero. I don't even think that's important."

What's important, I thought, is winning.

Kathleen's gorgeous shoulders sagged.

"You're both right. You always outnumber me. Anyway, Hugh, you just have to win!"

"He will, Mavoureen," her husband assured her, and extended an arm around her shoulder.

They would make love tonight, I thought, in part because they both loved me more than I deserved.

Well, he never had her when she was a sex-crazy teenager.

Then I mentally apologized to God for such a terrible

thought. I imagined that God told me he didn't believe my apology.

"Why haven't they destroyed their records?" Liam asked. "They could have before the suit was filed."

"Because they're dumb, Liam. They never thought a judge in Prairie County would even consider a motion to disclose them. When Art Sturm took plaintiff's motion under consideration, they just about died. My sources tell me that there's a big debate over there about what to do. Meaghan and Reynolds want to destroy them. Straus and Kennedy are afraid to do that—contempt of court, you know. The Arch dithers, as he usually does. Truth to tell, they probably would have a hard time finding the records."

"I don't like that lawyer either," Kathleen persisted.

"Joe Kennedy?"

"No that Vandenwhatever."

"He's a typical tort lawyer, Kath," Liam pointed out. "Smart, effective, more greedy than some of them."

"He pays the witnesses and the traveling tent show of victims that mill around outside of the court looking for someone to comment to."

"Did he try to pay you?"

"He spoke to me about reimbursing expenses. I told them that I didn't have any. He may be on the sleazy side, but it takes someone like that to blast the Downtown crowd out of their dreamworld."

"What ever has happened to our Church, Hugh?"

"Jesus shouldn't have turned it over to humans."

They drove me home to Prairie View and my parish of St. Cunegunda.

I shook hands with Liam and brushed my lips against Kathleen's. There were no particular memories. Well, maybe a few. "Do me a favor, Liam?"

"Sure, aren't you talking like one of us now?"

"I learned that in Chicago . . . Do you think you can get Todd Sweeney into your program?"

"Hadn't I already thought of that? It won't be easy, but we'll do it. It will be a tough case. Maybe we can make life a little easier for him."

Joachim Binder was on the phone as soon as I entered the darkened rectory.

"Well, you really shit in your pants today, Hermie. Did you see the six o'clock news?"

"No."

"Boy, they really nailed you. Josh Reynolds was so happy he almost had an erection. They'll wipe you out on Monday morning."

"Perhaps."

"The guys are all saying that you're dumb even for a Russian German. Why did you go after poor Lucifer Len now that he's dead?"

"Dead of AIDS," I muttered.

"What does that matter? He was a priest, wasn't he?"

"Yes, he was . . . Look, Jock, as I told you before, I didn't volunteer. Dr. Sweeney knew I was an eyewitness. They subpoenaed me. I had to tell the truth."

This was an argument, I had learned, that did not satisfy my fellow priests—or anyone else. Perjury had apparently disappeared from the list of sins.

"About another priest? You gotta be kidding."

"I don't hold with the morality," I said pompously,

"that if you lie to protect a priest, it's no sin."

I hung up before I lost my temper completely.

And I had made fun of the thunderclouds in Kathleen's eyes.

I noticed a note from Megan, the porter person, on my desk.

"Father Hugh, the Manzio called. You should call back no matter how late."

Manzio? What was a manzio?

I looked at the area code—202?

What was that? New York was 212. Chicago 312.

I opened the phone book. 202 was Washington, D.C. Ah, Nuncio.

So it might sound to a sixteen-year-old at the edge of the prairies.

I dialed the number.

"Nunciature," a sleepy voice informed me.

"Father Hoffman from Prairie View."

"Ah, yes, Father Hopman!"

So, a German secretary at the Nunciature. I was tempted to go into German. He might laugh at our dialect.

"The Nuncio is very interested in the trial out there. He will send a certain major prelate to observe discreetly. He will arrive late Sunday. We trust you will receive the prelate and provide housing for him."

"There's plenty of room for him here in the rectory."

"Yes, yes. All will be good."

"Ja, ja, alles gut."

He laughed, a papal diplomat actually laughed.

He did not tell me who the major prelate was or why

he would stay with me. Perhaps the Archbishop had complained. The man would probably try to tell me what to say. No way.

I spent a restless night, haunted by Todd Sweeney's tortured face. Later, dreams about Kathleen arrived. They were quiet and peaceful, then so was I.

II

FROM THE *PLAINSMAN AND GAZETTE*

"GAY" PRIEST ATTACKS CHURCH
CALLED LIAR IN COURT

Rev. Herman Hoffman, an allegedly gay priest exiled from the Archdiocese of Plains City for five years, attacked the Catholic Church for its response to sexual abuse charges in superior court today. Under fire from fellow priests for selling out the Church to appear in court, he was also denounced as a liar by Dr. Thomas P. Sweeney, the father of the alleged victim.

Monsignor James Reynolds, Vice Chancellor of the Archdiocese, commented after the trial was recessed until Monday that the Archdiocese was confident that it would refute Hoffman's testimony on Monday.

"He's a Judas Iscariot," Reynolds said. "He's betrayed the priesthood and the Church for his own financial gain. We have solid evidence that Vandenhuvel is paying him to testify. We deplore all sexual abuse. This case, however, is against a dead man who cannot defend himself. We must defend his memory. Sexual abuse has happened in the priesthood. It is very rare. We have it under control here in Plains City. In this case, nothing ever happened, and Father Hoffman knows that."

Hoffman is pastor at St. Cunegunda Church in Prairie View. He also lectures in the History Department at State U. There are already demands from trustees of the university that he be dismissed from the department. Trustee Arnold Bruckner said late today, "We should get that pervert out of there before he harms any of our kids."

Dr. Burke Crawford, a specialist in priest abuse cases and himself a former priest, said that he did not find Hoffman's testimony persuasive. "This is a most unusual case. The alleged victimizer is dead. The testimony comes from a fellow priest whose credibility is dubious. It is not unusual for a priest to blame someone else for what he has done."

Jeff Simmons, chairman of the Plains City chapter of CATH, Catholics Against the Homosexuals, told the *Plainsman*, "That man should never have been ordained. The Holy Father has warned us against gays."

However, Clara Kean, of the Woman's Ordination Movement, disagreed. She said, "If they want to stop all this abuse they should let priests marry and ordain women. It's going to happen eventually anyway."

40

REPORTER: (Standing in front of Dr. Sweeney's home in Green Grove) Sophia, there has been an interesting development in the Todd Sweeney suit against the Archdiocese. Ms. Clarissa McNamara, the next-door neighbor of Dr. Thomas P. Sweeney, told KOPC News this morning that she saw Father Herman Hoffman go into Dr. Sweeney's home the day that his son was abused by the late Father Leonard Lyon.

MS. MCNAMARA: I remember the day very clearly because it was my sister's birthday. Father Hoffman, who is a darling priest, stopped to talk to me. He always stopped to talk to people. We loved him. He was so shy and sweet. I was outside watering my rose plants. He asked me if I knew whether Dr. Sweeney was home. I said that he was. I had seen his Italian car, a Ferrari I think it was, go into the garage just a half hour before. I then said that he should be careful because Dr. Sweeney had an ungovernable temper. Because he was a surgeon, he thought he was God's gift to the world.

REPORTER: What did Father Hoffman say?

MS. MCNAMARA: He just smiled sadly.

REPORTER: Were you there when he came out?

MS. MCNAMARA: I sure was. Poor Father Hoffman's shoulders were slumped. I asked if he had any luck. He just shook his head.

REPORTER: So Father Hoffman was telling the truth yesterday?

Ms. McNamara: He sure was. Tommy Sweeney has always been a liar.

Anchor: So we have another controversy in this most unusual case.

Reporter: That's certainly true, Sophia.

III

My priest "friends" called all day Friday about the article in the *Plainsman*.

They wanted to know how much Vandenhuvel was paying me, accused me of disloyalty, warned me that Ferret Face was out to get me, told me I was endangering the Archbishop's chances at Philadelphia, advised me to retract and get out of town.

A couple encouraged me, Dave Winter, even Matt McLaughlin. Lucifer had done that at every parish he'd ever been in. High time that someone spoke out. Still, I was finished in Plains City.

Then my "source" at the Chancery phoned.

"Hermie, you got them all running to the can to crap. Their bowels are in an uproar."

"Are they going to settle the case before it's too late? That's the smart thing to do. Otherwise, Judge Sturm is going to demand all their papers."

"They don't believe he'd dare, not in a Catholic city like this."

"Then they didn't study the judge very carefully yesterday."

"They think they have him in their pocket. That's why they tilted the playing field to get him on the case."

42

"Reynolds's idea?"

"Who else? He wants to be a bishop so bad that it hurts. He's in the can more than any of the others."

"So what are they going to do?"

"Go after you, what else?"

"Figures."

"They're going to get a letter from the hospital saying that they treated you for homosexuality and released you after you had controlled your impulses."

"No doctor would sign a letter like that."

"Old Man Geneva up there would do anything to keep the Arch happy."

"That's crazy."

"Sure it is. But they figure they've kept the costs low and the publicity nonexistent for such a long time that they're infallible."

"That's crazy too. Vandenhuvel has twenty cases lined up because of Lenny."

"They figure that they knock you down on Monday, Vandenhuvel leaves town with his tail between his legs. So you're the big target."

"We'll have to see what happens. Thanks for the warning. Stay in touch."

"I sure will . . . You're one tough son of a bitch, Hermie."

"Russian German son of a bitch."

We both laughed.

Monday would be a very interesting day. I still had a card or two up my sleeve. That's an unusual phrase for me. I never gamble.

Except this time I was gambling for very high stakes.

I had two funerals that day and three wedding rehearsals after supper. The next morning I presided over the weddings and attended the receptions at the Prairie View Country Club, not the most elegant venue in the state for receptions. However, it was transformed by the joy of the six young people. I prayed to God, not that they would be spared troubles—they go with the territory—but that surmounting the troubles together would deepen and enhance their love.

I was exhausted when I pulled up to the rectory. Megan gave me slips with more calls from my priest friends. I threw them in the wastebasket, put on old clothes, and went out to battle with some of the local teens who hung around the courts all day Saturday. I was never much of a hoopster, but I was better than the kids, or at least bigger.

Back at the rectory, Father Retramn, my weekend help and sometime spiritual director, was drinking a 7Up and chatting with Megan. He was arguing that 7Up was the best possible thirst quencher. Megan was asserting it was yucky. Retramn was always arguing. No one minded because with his long white beard, bushy white hair, and monastic robe, he charmed everyone.

"Out pretending to be a teenager, Father Herman?" He cocked a dreamy eye on me.

"The boys," Megan came to my defense, "are really bummed that they can't beat Father Hugh. 'Course he's extremely bigger than they are."

From the kitchen, the aromas of Mrs. Smid's "good German cooking" wafted into the front of the old wooden rectory. She cooked for us every Saturday night when Father Retramn came out for supper. He was my weekend help. He heard confessions, after supper, such as they were. And said the 8:00 Mass on Sunday before he drove back to the Clementine monastery. I said 5:30 Mass on Saturday and the 9:30 and the 11:00 on Sunday. By the 11:00 my homily was on automatic pilot.

"You better get ready for Mass, Father Hugh," Megan informed me. "You only have an hour."

"Yes, ma'am," I said, and threw up my hands in mock exasperation at my teenage porter person.

After Mass, the people were supportive, as those at the wedding receptions had been.

"It's high time someone spoke out," was a common enough remark. So too was, "Don't pay any attention to those ass lickers at the *Plainsman*."

At supper Retramn, who had supported me through thick and thin at the seminary and after, sighed loudly.

"Well, Hermie, it looks like you have the tiger by the tail."

"The ferret, you mean."

He laughed loudly at this. His laughs came in two kinds—loud and louder.

"We should never have ordained Lucifer. Everyone knew what he was, but they were afraid to ban him. The then Archbishop liked him."

"A lot of people liked him. He was a charmer."

"A driven man . . . Thank God we're more careful whom we ordain these days. A lot of them are creeps looking for certainty and respect but not predators."

45

"Or torturers like Lenny."

"But you're the big surprise, Hermie. No one in those days would have thought of you, of all people, as the one who would stand up and say that it's time for all this shit to stop."

"Is that what I've done?"

We both dug into Mrs. Smid's pot roast.

"Oh, yes . . . Some of us are very proud of you. What's more, the ordinary people believe you. They're fixing to get angry. When that happens, the idiots in Rome will have to take notice and Slippery Louie will never go to Philly."

The Archbishop always signed his letters, "S. L. I. P. Louis." The S. L. I. P. was for "Simon Lazarus Isidore Peter." Louis had been Ludwig a couple of generations back when his family still identified with their German origins. Naturally the clergy had taken to calling him "Slippery Louie."

"I don't think the Archbishop is as much slippery as just not very bright."

"Oh, that too. Yet you don't have to be too bright to play the Vatican game. I think you have done him in, which makes me say that I'm proud of you. You've grown up a lot since ordination . . . No, that patronizes you. You've become the person you always really were . . . I don't know. Maybe that young woman did something for you."

"Kathleen? That's a change in your stand, Retramn."

"Not the first time I've changed my mind. Maybe, God willing and the creek not rising, I may do it again."

I had expected that when Kathleen had come back

into my life along with Liam, he would object strenu-
ously.

Instead, he had said thoughtfully, "God usually
knows what he's doing."

"How could they be so dumb as to put Judge Sturm
und Drang on the case?" he asked.

"That's the one thing I'm hoping for."

"That and your ace in the hole."

He was the only one who knew about my ace in the
hole. I had told no one, not even Liam and Kathleen.
Also the one who had told me to be sure of the secret
knew that I would probably follow his advice.

"You got a secret," my father always said, "keep it
secret."

After most of the people had cleared away from the
back of the church on Sunday, I heard a soft voice say,
"Father Hoffman, could I talk to you for a minute?"

I turned around. It was Todd Sweeney.

"Sure, Todd, for as long as you want. Do you want to
come over to the rectory for a cup of coffee?"

Something like a smile flitted across his face.

"I try to avoid rectories, Father."

"We could sit on the swing on the front porch."

Help me to do this right, I begged God.

"OK," he said, doubt in his voice.

We sat on the swing in silence for a couple of eterni-
ties as Todd tried to figure out a way to start.

"I don't think I'll accept Dr. Shannon's invitation," he
began. "I don't much like doctors anymore."

"I can understand that."

"My father is such an asshole. You can't talk to him.

He kept asking me what was wrong with me for the last ten years. I tried to tell him, and he wouldn't listen. It just got worse and worse . . ."

"Dr. Shannon specializes in treating victims."

"That's what he said. He seems like a real nice man. Talks kind of funny."

"He's from Ireland."

"Yeah, that must be it . . . I'd like to visit Ireland someday. Guess I never will."

I remained silent.

"I'm doomed, Father. He doomed me that day at St. Theodolinda. Just as sure as if he threw a switch on an electric chair. I don't have a chance. I'll never make it back."

"Never is a long time, Todd."

"Yes, I know that . . . Dr. Shannon said the same thing."

More silence.

Then tears streamed down his face, and his poor, frail body shook with sobs.

"He still comes after me in my dreams. With his knife. I know he's dead, but his ghost haunts me . . . Why did he do it, Father? Why?"

"Because he was a very sick man, Todd. A man who found pleasure in humiliating and destroying other people, especially talented and special people like you."

"I hope he's in hell!"

More tears.

"God decides those things," I said cautiously.

"God didn't protect me that day at St. Theodolinda."

"God's giving you another chance now, Todd."

"God can keep his fucking second chance!"

I wasn't doing very well.

"Maybe I should have rushed in earlier."

"Don't blame yourself, Father. You did all you could . . . I wanted to kill him. I still want to kill him. I'm sorry he's dead. I'd kill him now if he were still alive."

I said nothing.

"You see, we all thought he was the greatest guy. He took us on trips and gave us presents and told us stories and played basketball with us. Kids that age need idols I guess. And he was the idol of all of us. We would do anything for him. Anything."

I knew.

"He was our priest. The eighth grade priest. He had us in the palm of his hand. Sometimes in his room we had kind of horseplay. It made some of the guys uneasy, but I said he was a priest, he wouldn't do anything wrong. Only he did."

He sobbed hysterically again.

"He would have gone after the girls too, if you hadn't stopped him. They liked him too. He was so cute, they used to say, but some of them didn't like him at all. When you sent the message through Mary Jane Dooley they all agreed. It was too late for me—and for a couple of other guys he'd messed around with . . . I should have killed him then . . . We should have killed him. We talked about it. Maybe we could get away with it . . . We all thought he was our friend!"

"I understand."

"We liked you too, despite what my asshole father

said. But you weren't one of us. You weren't our own special, personal priest, our own 'father.' "

"That's what makes what he did so hurtful."

"I didn't fight back when he started. I couldn't believe what was happening. That a 'father' would do that to me . . . It had to be a dream . . . an ugly nightmare . . . I've run out of tissue, Father."

"Just a minute."

I dashed into the rectory and removed our rectory box of tissue from Megan's desk. She looked up at me quizzically, but wise young woman that she is, she didn't say anything.

"Thanks, Father . . . I haven't broke down this way for a long time."

"It's all right, Todd."

"Before I knew what was happening, he had me on the floor. He turned into an ugly, panting monster. He shouted at me to shut up. He punched me when I wouldn't lie still . . . I still don't understand it. I hate him. I hate him even worse than my old man."

He sobbed again and wiped his nose.

"I wish I could kill him. He ruined my life. He and my asshole father."

"He's dead, Todd . . . I think what Dr. Shannon wants to do is to help you kill the Father Lyon that is still hurting you even now."

"Yeah? That will never happen. I wish it could."

I realized that Liam, with his easy charm, had opened a possibility for Todd, a fearful but attractive possibility.

"You know him for a long time?"

"Four or five years. He's the best there is."

"I suppose so . . . My asshole father would never let me see a shrink . . . How come you know this guy?"

"He married a woman I went to school with."

"Your sweetheart?"

"For a time."

"I've never had a sweetheart . . ."

More tears.

"I never will . . . What kind of woman would want a wreck like me . . . He made me a wreck, Father. A Catholic priest made me a wreck that could never love a woman or be loved by one."

"That's not a life sentence, Todd."

"Yeah . . ."

What do I say now? Dear God, please help me.

"Well, thanks for the tissue . . . Thanks for listening too."

What to do now?

Keep your big mouth shut.

"I don't think I'll see Dr. Shannon, Father. He's a good guy, I'm sure. I don't think I could stand the hell I'd have to go through all over again."

"It might be better than the hell you're trapped in now."

"Yeah, maybe . . . Anyway, maybe I'll see you later."

I wanted to walk down to the car with him. Something told me that I should leave him free to go. No way I could beg him.

Should I call Liam and tell him what had happened? No way, idiot! Priests must respect the confidentiality of their people.

I put the tissue box back on Megan's desk. She was studying for her geometry final. Neither of us said anything.

I fell on my knees on the prie-dieu in my room and begged God and the Blessed Mother and all the angels and saints to help Todd to go over to State U and see Dr. Shannon. I wasn't demanding an instant cure. I just wanted him to enter a process towards health.

Then I got pretty blunt with God.

Look, it's Your fault you know. You gave him an idiot father who was afraid of his handsome son and probably envied him. You sent Lucifer Lenny to our parish. You sent me there to protect the kids. I was too green and too unsure of myself to know what to do. So I blundered. OK it was my fault and I know You don't like excuses . . . What the hell, You're not a Russian German, You don't mind excuses because You love us . . . Anyway, You should have sent some one better and tougher to St. Theodolinda . . . But You sent me, and You knew I couldn't cope . . . Or maybe that I wouldn't cope . . . So now I can cope a little better, and You had Kathleen drag over my replacement to show me that someone could love her . . . It looks to me like a plot, and You'd better get on with it.

The bell rang from downstairs. I jumped a half foot in the air. Like a phone call in the middle of the night. It rang again. Megan was not the most patient of porter persons.

"Yes, Megan?"

"Father Hugh, there is a cute little priest down here.

At least I think he's a priest because his eyes are so kind, though he's not dressed much like a priest."

"Ah," I said.

That was a quick answer, I told God.

"And Father Hugh?"

"Yes."

"How did he know my name was Megan?"

"He thinks all teenage women who work in rectories are called Megan."

I hung up the phone and rushed down the stairs.

"He's out on the porch, Father Hugh, staring at the prairies."

"Figures."

IV

"ARGUABLY, HUGH," THE "CUTE LITTLE PRIEST" MUSED as I dashed out on the porch, "I sent you a letter praising your book on the Russian Germans. It is possible that I may have called it magisterial. But I do not do all the virtuous things I think of. Mostly because of the demands of my e-mail."

"You did both."

He was wearing his usual garb, black jeans, a black clerical shirt without the Roman collar, a Chicago sports jacket (White Sox this time), and a sports cap that said "North Wabash Avenue Irregulars."

He was an insignificant little fellow, the kind, as he often said, you would not notice if he was on an elevator with you—short, slightly pudgy, with thick rimless glasses behind which pale blue eyes blinked. It was a disguise that he believed made him invisible.

Yet he could walk into any rectory in the city of Chicago, and indeed now into almost any rectory in the country, and be recognized immediately, even if he had left behind the ring and the pectoral cross of his office.

"In that book," he continued, "you described the delight of your forefathers who came, and organized villages and communities as you remarked, from the banks of the Volga River where they had been invited in the early eighteenth century by the illustrious Catherine of Russia. They came out to the prairies and reacted to them with the same joy and perhaps more reason than did Brigham Young when he came to the Great Salt Lake. They saw prairies that were almost the same as the steppes along the Volga. If there was one thing they knew about, it was how to farm prairies. So they turned what was tall grass and cornfields and rice fields into what would become one of the two main breadbaskets of the world."

"You did read the book!"

"Patently and not just on the plane coming out either. I suppose that's winter wheat out there. I must say for all the beauty and the political correctness of prairie grass, I prefer to see winter wheat."

I sat on the swing next to him for a moment. We shook hands briskly. If he were German, I would have embraced him, but the Irish are much less demonstrative than we are.

"Prairie grass is important," I said. "Out at the edge of the state in Lincoln County where I come from, we actually have set aside some fields along the roads where it can flourish. We get a lot of environmentalist tourists. It's the only tourist attraction in the county. We Volga Deutsche don't believe in wasting anything . . . Want a beer?"

"Better an iced tea and assure the Megan that I am Father Ryan. I am here incognito, if such be possible."

"Megan," I said to that prairie charmer, "would you mix up a glass of your special iced tea for Father Ryan while I get myself a beer."

Megan's iced tea was saturated with fruity tastes. Great for other teens and for bishops who liked teens.

He pronounced her work as "brilliant!" which made her blush happily.

"They said they would send an important prelate to monitor the situation."

"Patently they were unable to find such, so they sent me instead. Actually, Cardinal Cronin is behind it all. He called a certain ally of ours in the Eternal City, a man not without substantial clout. He confirmed that the papers had already been prepared for Archbishop Louis to translate to the City of Brotherly Love. Milord Cronin suggested something inappropriate to the effect that the assholes were still making the decision over there and wondered if they knew *Urbsincampuensis* was about to become another Boston. He promised to call back, which he did in a half hour. They have a holy and wholesome fear of another Boston. So the appointment is on hold. They wanted the Cardinal Archbishop of Chicago to send a monitor out here, our contact suggested *faute de mieux* that I might do."

"They must really be scared."

"Oh yes, so Milord Cronin in his full robes said to me, 'Blackwood, go out there and find out what demons your good friend Huey Hoffman has stirred up. See to it.' "

"As I remember your Cardinal is not an admirer of Slippery Louie."

"I have that impression . . . In any case I am sitting here in awed admiration of the agricultural revolution that your careful and thrifty ancestors worked out here in the nineteenth century and for which they have yet to receive full credit, pending the issuance of the paperback edition of your book."

"You want me to tell you about the situation out here?" I asked, embarrassed by these compliments.

He searched in his pockets and found in the pocket of his clerical shirt a crumpled clipping of the transcript that the *Plainsman* had printed that morning.

"What I want to know is if this is the same able, intelligent, and charming young priest whose presence in Chicago I authorized ten years ago? He was not the kind of man from whom this assault on authority might be expected, as admirable as it may be."

"Probably not."

"Then what happened to him?"

"It's a long story. Would you not rather hear about the trial?"

"I probably know enough about it."

I decided I would not tell him my secret. There was no one I trusted with a secret more than John Blackwood Ryan, particularly this secret. Yet it could wait till tomorrow in the courtroom.

"I've been keeping a journal since my senior year in high school, Blackie. A couple of months ago I extracted the entries that seem to have been decisive in my life. Then I wrote an introduction describing my life up to the senior year. I wanted some kind of record in case anything should happen to me. For the distant future, that is."

"Admirable."

"I think you'd find it rather dull."

"I will have to judge that."

"There's a red-haired woman in it."

"There usually is."

"Irish-American."

"The worst kind . . . Does she play an important role?"

"My spiritual director thinks she does."

"Capital."

"I'll go get it."

Later that evening Horst Heller called.

"Catch the ten o'clock on KOPC, Hermie. Good stuff."

Blackie and I sat in my crowded study and watched the program.

ANCHOR: There's been a surprising new development in the sexual abuse crisis. A nurse at University Hospital has spoken up in defense of Father Herman Hoffman. Renaldo Cruz is on the story at the hospital.

CRUZ: That's right, Sophia. Mary Anne Dooley was in seventh grade at St. Theodolinda school in

Green Grove when the late Father Leonard Lyon allegedly abused Todd Sweeney in the parish rectory.

(Scene is at a hospital. Dooley is a pretty, fast-talking blonde in nurse's white.)

DOOLEY: I was the one Father Hoffman was talking about on Friday. He didn't want to, like, embarrass me by mentioning my name. I was totally afraid to go up to Father Lenny's room because he had seemed kind of weird, you know, the last couple of weeks. Father Hoffman, who was a dear, sweet young priest, told me that if I didn't want to, then I shouldn't. He also told me to warn the other girls. When we found out from the boys a couple of days later, like, what Father Len had done to Toddy, were we ever glad that we had stayed away from him!

CRUZ: What did Father Lyon do when the kids avoided him?

DOOLEY: We weren't kids. We were in seventh grade. He was very angry at us. Finally, some of us decided, you know, we'd better tell our parents.

CRUZ: What happened then?

DOOLEY: Some parents, like, didn't believe us. Some, like my dad, you know, did, so a few of them went down to see the Archbishop. At first he wouldn't talk to them. Then he screamed at them that they would destroy the Church. My dad, and was I ever proud of him, he was like a Marine and a lawyer, goes that he would sue the Archdiocese if they didn't get that pervert out of St. Theodolinda.

58

CRUZ: Then what happened?

DOOLEY: Well, Father Peters said that poor Father Lyon was having a hard time and they were going to send him away to, you know, New Mexico to help him get better. He promised that he'd never be sent to a parish ever again. He like lied, you know. Father Lyon was in another parish three months later and poor Father Hoffman was locked up in a nuthouse and sent away and Father Peters turned out, you know, to be like a child abuser himself.

CRUZ: So you see, Sophia, the controversy about sex abuse by the Catholic clergy grows more intense.

ANCHOR: It certainly does, Renaldo. KOPC news caught up with Joseph T. Kennedy, an attorney for the Archdiocese later today. Steve Cooper reports.

COOPER: Sophia, Mr. Kennedy was very angry when he heard about Ms. Dooley's allegations.

KENNEDY: Well, that stupid young woman will have a defamation suit on her hands before the week is out. Her father is a lawyer; he should have taught her to keep her mouth shut.

SOPHIA: Sounds like the Archdiocese is still playing hardball doesn't it, Steve?

COOPER: Peter Dooley, Mary Anne's father, didn't seem very worried when we talked to him, Sophia.

DOOLEY: We've always been proud of Mary Anne. She tells it like it is. There was a time when lawyers here in Plains City would tremble when Joe Kennedy would threaten suit. We knew that the Archdiocese had deep pockets. Now they're so discredited that we laugh at them.

COOPER: You're not afraid of a suit?

DOOLEY: If Joe is dumb enough to file one, we'd welcome it. We'd depose the Archbishop for at least a week.

COOPER: Do you see any solution to the controversy, sir?

DOOLEY: Sure, send Slippery Louie off to Philadelphia where he wants to go and give us a new Archbishop, one without a negative IQ.

I turned off the television. Blackie searched in his pockets for a cell phone and on the second try found it.

"The father of the redoubtable Ms. Dooley is, I presume, not a practicing Catholic?"

"Every Sunday."

"Indeed. And without prestige in Prairie County?"

"President of the county bar."

"Fascinating."

He punched a number into the phone, canceled it, and tried again.

"A sin against nature that a Cardinal Prince should have to answer the phone on Sunday night . . .

"Ah . . . I thought you might want to inform our mutual friends in the Eternal City that the president of the bar association in this county informed the denizens that the solution to present problems is to translate your good friend Slippery Louie to the City of Brotherly Love and send a new Archbishop here. Granted the historic fate of said city to be unfortunate in such matters, it still would not be wise for the new man to come with such a recommendation . . ."

He paused for a moment to listen.

Blackie sighed.

"Given the fallen state of humankind, it is a matter of certainty that remark is already on the wires."

Another pause.

"Tomorrow's contretemps before Judge Arthur Sturm, as in *Sturm und Drang*, could have decisive impact . . . Indeed, I will."

He clicked the phone off.

"Milord Cronin sends his greetings, best wishes, and promises of great events."

"I don't want any great events, Blackie. I just want to keep working in this parish."

"I'm glad to hear it. I am reassured that it is unlikely that the Pope is going to join the Church of Jesus Christ of the Latter Day Saints."

V

I'LL BE CANDID ABOUT IT AT THE BEGINNING OF THIS memoir. I am a peasant. A bumpkin. A hick. I may have a Ph.D. and teach at a university. I may be able to speak two languages rather fluently. I may read *The New York Times* every day and listen to the *Lehrer Report* every evening. I may play the piano by ear and sight-read notes for choir music. Yet I have never been east of Chicago or west of Denver, south of Little Rock or north of St. Paul. I am the son of a farmer and a farmer at heart myself. You wouldn't have to talk to me more than five minutes to know that I'm a hayseed, a big, broad-shouldered bumpkin with a round Teutonic face, sleepy blue eyes, and straw-colored hair.

I was born in Lincoln County in 1967, at Mercy Hospital in Lincoln City. My father Franz Hoffman was a farmer, a descendent of the Volga Deutsche who had settled here a hundred years before and revolutionized American agriculture. My mother, Trudy Vogel, was the daughter of a similar Russian German (as we now call ourselves) who lived less than a mile away from our farm. I was the youngest of three children, born when they were both twenty-eight years old. My older brother was also a Franz, though often Franky. My sister was Hildegard after the famous German Abbess and musician Hildegard of Bingen, who had become fashionable again. I was Herman Hugo after my two grandfathers, who were very much alive.

They're still alive. We Russian Germans live long lives.

I am told that the extended family choir sang a Bach cantata at my baptism. Hicks all right, but not the kind you'd expect.

Franky is now in charge of the farm. Hildegard and her husband Frederick teach at the Lincoln Township High School, which we all attended.

And I am a priest.

I think it had been decided before I was born that I'd be a priest if I were a boy. It was time the family had one, my mother assured me. Yet it was never mentioned when I was growing up. I was afraid to tell them about my vocation when I graduated from State University with my degree in history. Both my parents wept with joy.

I guess they prayed me into the priesthood. At times I have resented that.

Let me tell you about Lincoln Junction. If you leave the interstate at the last stop before the new bridge over the big river and head south you will come upon a sign that says LINCOLN JUNCTION TEN MILES—REAL PRAIRIE GRASS. You continue on that road and you indeed come to a succession of fields of the six-foot-high grass that covered the plains from Lake Michigan to the Rockies two hundred years ago, with exception of a few "groves" or thin forests along the riverbanks. A sign tells you that if you are interested, you should visit the Prairie Museum in River Grove. It is in fact the Russian German museum, but the canny burghers of the Junction figured that potential tourists would be more interested in prairies than in Russian Germans.

Lincoln Junction hasn't been a real junction since 1950, when the Plains City and Denver Line stopped running. Passenger service died five years later. If you want to go somewhere from the Junction you either drive or take a Greyhound bus. However, a transcontinental freight line still runs through the Junction and during harvesttime stops to pick up wheat from the spanking new grain elevators that the Verein (co-op) has built along the tracks. All year round, however, the freights still roar through town, whistles blowing. I always liked waking up in the middle of the night to the sound of the whistle. It was somehow reassuring. There was still order in the world.

As you drive down the highway, you may notice that the farms are not like many of the others you might have seen as you drove across the country. There are no broken-down cars or pickups in front of the houses. The homes are big and solid and freshly painted. Around the houses there are white picket fences and neatly land-scaped yards. Farm equipment seems not only cleaned but freshly polished. TV dishes decorate most of the roofs. This is a land of successful and compulsively neat farmers.

You leave the railroad yards on the outside of town and enter the town limits. As you turn the corner and drive down the main street, you may gasp just a little. You have entered what seems like a Swiss village though there are no snowcapped mountains in evidence. If there is snow on the ground, it may even seem like a winter wonderland. There are huge and very old trees on both sides of the street and carefully maintained lawns. The homes are painted in bright colors, the shops have vivid window displays. There are three ice-cream shops, two music stores, and a couple of coffee shops with outdoor tables and chairs. The old station is now a restaurant, called Bahnhof Grill. Just beyond the only stoplight there is a small park with a bandstand in the center, a small concert hall on one side, and on the other side a church with an onion-shaped dome—St. Killian's Catholic Church, the oldest building in the whole of Lincoln County. Next to it, stands a Catholic school, the oldest west of Plains City. Next to the concert hall there is a three-story brick building, the Lincoln Junction Museum, filled with archives of Lincoln County history and indeed the principal archive of the Russian German migration to

Kansas, Nebraska, the Dakotas, and Colorado, in addition to Prairie State. There is no movie theater in town. There used to be, but it lost out to television and the addiction of the Volga Deutsche to music. As you drive on to the big river ten miles away and turn north towards the Theodore Roosevelt Bridge, you might ask yourself how such a quaint little European village managed to appear, perhaps only as a mirage, in the midst of the American prairies.

That's Lincoln Junction. Those of us who grew up there know it is a very special place.

Most of us are parishioners of St. Killian's, an Irishman who brought the Good News to Bavaria, from which kingdom, as it was then, our remote ancestors migrated to the Volga. Our family was Catholic before it accepted the invitation of Catherine the Great to move to the steppes in 1737. It was Catholic when we left for the plains of America in 1866. It's still Catholic and shows no signs of being anything else. It's still taken for granted that all the Russian Germans who are not confined to bed will be at Mass every Sunday at St. Killian's Church in Lincoln Junction. We marry our own kind, and some of us stay in Lincoln County all our lives. We are loyal to the Church. Does it tell us that we must have Mass in English? We go along, though we wish it could also be in German. We sing enthusiastically at Mass— often in German-language hymns. We obey the Church, though, to tell the truth, only when we think it is right. There are few couples in Lincoln County who do not practice birth control of one kind or another. "It is the only thing that makes sense," my mother says.

Also we are perhaps more tolerant of gay men than are other American Catholics. My mother's late uncle, Wolfgang Vogel, was thought to be "strange." He lived with another man, Henry Schultz. Together they worked their small farm with considerable success and were active members of the Verein, the local German Russian fellowship. There may have been some whispers in back of the church when they appeared for Christmas and Easter, but no one, not even Monsignor O'Brien, the pastor, presumed to say anything out loud.

"Poor man," Mama would say. "It's not their fault. It's the way God made them."

Yes, the pastor was Monsignor Francis O'Brien, a long-lived Irishman exiled for some reason (perhaps what his own people would call "too much of the drink taken") to Lincoln County and the Deutsche. Somehow or other he got along with us, though he couldn't sing a note.

"The Irish can't sing," Mama would say.

"What about Kathleen Quinlan?" Hildy would demand.

"*Ja,* she was born here," Mama would answer.

One Saturday morning in autumn we were engaged in a family singspiel. Kathleen, who must have been about eight and who rode all over the county on her bike, showed up at our front door.

"Mrs. Hoffman, may I sing with you?"

There was a moment of silence. The farm on which she lived was only a mile closer to town than ours, but neither she nor her father had ever appeared at our door.

66

He was our doctor and a recluse. She was reputed, quite properly I thought, to be a wild child.

"Of course, dear," Mama said. "Please come in."

I hated her because she was the leader of those who taunted me for my clumsiness.

"Kathleen can't speak German," I pointed out.

"Well," Mama said, frowning at me because I had not shown courtesy, "when Kathleen is here, we will sing mostly English."

So we sang mostly English.

"You have a lovely voice, dear," Mama said after our first song. "Now we have an alto as well as a soprano."

"Danke," Kathleen said with her impish grin, which usually meant trouble for someone, normally me. "Why don't you sing something in German. I'll try to vocalize."

She did it very well, imitating even our facial expressions.

She also stayed for lunch, bratwurst, zwetschkenknödel, and beer, though for her only Coke because, as Papa had said, "You're driving."

Much laughter. We Deutsche laugh easily.

"Schweinehund," she whispered to me as she slipped out of the door.

"Poor little motherless child," Mama sighed.

Little bitch, I thought but did not say.

We were all authentic bilinguals, though for my parents and me English was our first language, the one we usually thought in. We could switch back and forth easily. Saturday, when Kathleen had left, we shifted into German because the weekends were German days.

Hildy said that the Germans from Germany thought we were very funny because we spoke a very old-fashioned form of German, kind of like Shakespeare's English.

"*Ja,*" Papa spoke up. "It's been more than two hundred years since we were real Germans."

We always insisted that we were Russian Germans. During the two World Wars this meant that we were good Germans. We managed to carry it off when much of German culture was purged from American life— and the frankfurter became the hot dog.

Thus did Kathleen, with her long red hair and her green eyes and her laughter and her furious temper and her foul mouth become part of our family on Saturday mornings. Even in the winter, Dr. Quinlan would deliver her at our doorstep (though he would never come in), and Mama or Papa would drive her home. She changed her relationship with me at school. I was no longer an overgrown lump of shit. I was a nice boy the others should not pick on.

"You changed your mind," I said to her one day when she chased a group of sixth graders who were chanting, "*dummkopf,*" at me, one of the favorite amusements in the schoolyard for those who could not pick on those their own age.

"You have nice parents," she replied. "Besides you're not clumsy, just a little shy."

"Oh," I said.

"Besides, my daddy says that in a few years, you'll be a real big kid and you can beat up on those assholes."

I knew I'd never beat up on anyone, no matter how big I might become.

"You're too pretty to use that language, Kathleen," I blurted.

I felt my face heat up as I became aware of what I had said.

She turned scarlet too.

"I'm sorry, Hermie."

"You don't talk that way when you're at my house."

"Your mother wouldn't like it."

"It's none of my business."

"It is TOO your business . . . I won't do it anymore."

We were both aware, I think, that we had crossed some invisible line with one another.

"What about *schweinehund* and *dummkopf?*" she asked anxiously.

I wanted to hug her and reassure her.

"Mama says *dummkopf* all the time. I don't think she'd like the other word, but it isn't a dirty word."

"Thank you." She turned and ran away, crying, I think.

I filled up with sweetness, which lingered all day. Our little red-haired hellcat, as one of the teachers had called her, wasn't a hellcat at all. How mysterious. In February she sent me a valentine which she'd made on her computer. It surrounded "Hermie" with "Love." I told no one about it and hid it. Later I must have lost it because when I look for it now I can't find it.

Another time in the schoolyard she was running towards a fight, like the morning freight steaming through the Junction. It didn't matter who was fighting, she'd pick a side and furiously punch and claw. I reached and grabbed her arm. The engine lost its steam.

The fury drained from her body. Momentarily, she leaned against me.

"All right, Hermie. I suppose I have to give up fighting too."

I released her immediately. I was too shy to permit myself even for a moment to enjoy the sensation of a girl surrendering to me.

"I wish you wouldn't."

"Then, *dummkopf,* I won't anymore."

Shy and awkward I was. I took refuge in reading, even the leatherbound German classics from our family library. That's right, we had a library. Plains peasants with a library. We Volga Deutsche are different. I was different from the rest of them. I went to the boisterous picnics where my family and our neighbors sang loudly, drank beer, ate wursts, and argued, mostly about farm prices and politics. However, I sat quietly on the edge of the fun with a wurst in one hand and a book in the other. Some of our relatives called me a bookworm. Mama said, "*Ja ja,* there are worse things a boy could be."

The politics we argued about was always Democratic politics, another difference between our kind of Russian Germans and most other farmers. Later I would learn that we had become Democrats long before FDR and the New Deal, part of the populist surge on the prairies that produced the Progressives and the Non-Partisan League and the Farmer Labor Party. We didn't like Richard Nixon or Gerald Ford very much. We thought Jimmy Carter was wonderful because he was a farmer like we were, though we eventually soured on him.

Later, we took an instant dislike to Ronald Reagan.

"Never trust an Irishman who smiles that way," my father observed, nursing his beer, "especially if he is an ex-actor."

We had a big farm—a thousand acres—and all the expensive equipment that you had to have for a spread like that. We usually made more than enough money, though, as is required for farmers, we always complained. I loved working on the farm, looked forward eagerly to the day when I could drive a tractor, and loved to swing the pitchfork, which we rarely had to use.

At the end of the day—hot, tired, satisfied—I would find a shady spot under one of our apple trees and, beer in one hand, scrawl poetry in a spiral notebook with a blue cover. Mostly it was in English, but when I was reading Rilke, I tried to write some verses in German. They were even less successful than my English poems. Many of them were about Kathleen, even some of the German ones. Naturally, I showed the poems to no one, especially Kathleen.

She came regularly to our singspiels though not to our picnics. My family, sensitive to my shyness, never razzed me about her. When she went off to Europe before seventh grade with an aunt and uncle from California, I was miserable all summer. The family continued to leave me alone. When she returned, Kathleen, always deft in avoiding the label of "stuck-up," told us very little about her trip. "The real Germans," she whispered to me, "are not as nice as you Russian Germans."

I was fascinated—obsessed might have been a better

71

word—by the changes in Kathleen's body over the summer. And troubled by the changes in my own. Farmer that I was, I knew what was going on, but I didn't understand it.

While she was away there was a scary incident at St. Killian's that in a way was a foretaste of what would happen later. Those of us who were faithful acolytes were asked to volunteer for one week in the summer. I always seemed to draw the hottest week in early August. Monsignor was away on vacation, and a visiting priest, name unknown, was saying the 8:00 Mass.

Kathleen was a mass server too, a smooth and efficient presence who managed to efface herself in the ceremonies while still being present—strikingly so. However, those who made the decisions about such things were very careful not to schedule us at the same time.

"They're afraid you'll stumble more than usual because you'll be gawking at me."

I almost said that she was worth gawking at.

Anyway, the first morning of my week with the visiting priest I bicycled into the old wooden church, thinking neither of Kathleen nor of the odd, fussy priest who had said Sunday Mass and preached incoherently about the "grave sin of abortion," a subject which, I realized even then, priests choose for their homilies when they can't think of anything else to preach on. Rather I was thinking of how hot it would be out in the fields as we harvested the spring wheat.

When I walked into the old wooden church I felt I had walked into a furnace, a stagnant one at that. No one had opened the windows in the Monsignor's absence to make room for the slightest touch of summer breeze. It didn't matter. There hadn't been any breezes for a week.

Father smelled of cigar smoke and alcohol and strong aftershave. His fingers trembled. He seemed unsure of where he was. Yet he smiled pleasantly enough and knew my name.

"Good morning, Herman," he said, as though he were reciting carefully memorized words. "It is good of you to rise so early and come here to help an old priest."

He didn't seem that old, not as old as my grandfather, certainly not as old as my great-grandfather, Pa, as we called him.

He said Mass slowly and carefully, like he was trying to make sure he did everything right. I felt sorry for him. It must be very difficult to be a priest who was worn-out and not quite sure of what to do next.

"You are a very serious young man, Herman," he said to me one day as he was removing his vestments.

"Only in church, Father."

He chuckled, a dry rasp.

"Very wise."

As the week wore on I realized that he was strange, really weird, actually. I still felt sorry for him, but I couldn't wait for the week to be over. I understood that he was in some sort of deep pain, but I didn't know what it was, and I didn't like to be around it.

On Saturday morning as I was hanging up my sweat-drenched cassock, I suddenly smelled Father very close to me. I turned sharply and realized that he was about to kiss me. I stumbled away and put up my hand to shove him off. My heart was pounding furiously.

He collided with my hand and fell backwards into the big chair that was reserved for the eventuality that the Bishop might come someday. He was weeping.

"Promise me one thing, little Herman," he begged through his tears.

I was standing with my back to the sacristy counter, breathing heavily, frightened and confused. I could not find words to speak.

"Promise me that you won't kiss a girl until after your twenty-first birthday."

I wasn't going to promise that. I hoped to kiss Kathleen when she came home from Europe. I scrambled out of the sacristy, jumped on my bike, and pedaled away into the rising sun.

That night after supper I cornered my father and told him my story.

"*Ja.*" He sighed heavily. "He did not kiss you, Herman?"

"Certainly not!"

We were sitting in the parlor of our newly air-conditioned house. The next thing, Franky had said, we'll have to air-condition the fields.

"Only today?"

"After Mass, when I was hanging up my cassock."

"How did you feel?"

"Disgusted," I replied, "and frightened. He was a pathetic and scary guy. So I ran outside and got on my bike and raced home, where the world was normal."

"*Ja, ja.*" He smiled. "Smart young man . . . There are

74

some priests like that . . . Only a very few . . . You did well . . . I will speak to the Monsignor about it when he returns . . . You should not worry."

"I won't."

"You did not make the promise he requested?"

"No way."

"*Ja,* it would be a shame to make poor Kathleen wait that long," he said, and grinned broadly. *"Nein?"*

"She's stuck-up!" I insisted hotly.

"No, she's not, Herman. She's a beautiful child who has no mother and not much of a father, poor man. And no brother either."

The voice was Papa's, the thoughts were Mama's.

"You should be kind to her . . ."

"I always am."

"And realize that you are both very young."

"Too young to worry about kissing her," I said firmly.

That was simply not true; both of us knew it, but neither mentioned it.

That night, as I twisted and turned and tried to sleep, I was tormented by the smell of the priest trying to kiss me and the realization that my parents both approved strongly of Kathleen. They must have known that I was a brother, but also more than a brother, and they didn't mind.

I still wanted to be a priest. I never gave much thought to how my crush on Kathleen, a word I wouldn't have used in those days, might fit in with that. The idea of a "vocation" originated with Kurt Manders, a young priest who was an associate pastor in our parish, when the Archdiocese still had enough priests to be able to send someone to help the Monsignor.

He was articulate, charming, more like his Irish mother, someone said, than his German father. (He was not a Russian German, which made a big difference.) He was a brilliant preacher, a hard worker, and a sensitive counselor. What more could you ask of a priest—though these days especially the poor laity have to settle for a lot less. I identified with him completely. I wanted to do what he did. He taught me how to serve Mass, which increased my hero worship. I finally found the nerve to tell him I wanted to be a priest someday.

"It's a good life, Hermie, so long as you do it right. A lot of guys are leaving now because they're not happy as priests. I don't blame them. If you're not happy, you're no good to yourself or to others. But if you like what priests do, then you'll love being a priest."

"I think I like what priests do," I said, with a firmness that surprised me.

"Sometimes," he said, "it's a lonely life. No wife, no family. You're by yourself in a rectory these days with the next priest forty-five miles away. Other times, most of the time I think, you're so busy that you wish you had a little more time to yourself."

I nodded as if I understood, but I really didn't.

After Father Manders had been transferred to the other end of the Archdiocese—amid grief and some anger at the old Archbishop, an Irish-American who had never come to Lincoln Junction or to any of the parishes in the Russian German belt—I relied on Sister Angela for advice.

"The Monsignor would tell you that you should go to

St. Clement's for high school and preparatory seminary," she said once. "What do you think about that?"

"I couldn't go that far away from my family or the farm."

"When you're a priest, you'll have to do that."

"It will be different. I'll be an adult then."

I had no idea that ordination didn't necessarily make one an adult.

"It might be better if you attend Lincoln Township and even State U to find out if you like women. A lot of men are leaving the priesthood these days because they only discovered after ordination that they like women."

"How could any man not like women?" I replied, showing a good deal more wisdom than my thirteen years.

Sister nodded solemnly.

"A good point, Herman. You already like Kathleen, perhaps more than you should at your age."

I felt like I had been hit over the head by a hammer. How could people know about my intense fantasies about the hellcat redhead? Much less how could they think we might have gone too far?

"We haven't done anything wrong," I said, stumbling over the words.

"I know that, Herman. Yet your feelings for each other are very strong . . ."

"Not strong enough to prevent me from becoming a priest," I said, stubbornly.

"She will make a good wife and mother."

"For someone else."

I remember the words of that last exchange very

clearly. They echo and re-echo in my head.

One cold winter night in seventh grade the two of us stayed after school to practice the Bach song based on the old German hymn, "O Sacred Head" (written by Martin Luther), in the decrepit auditorium/school hall in the basement. We had S'ter's permission, though she told us we had to leave by five o'clock. Hildy had promised to pick us up when she was finished with her basketball practice at Township High. Kathleen wanted to be able to sing the alto part in German. I was to help her in the pronunciation.

Was it an unintended assignation? Did we both want a chance to be alone with each other, an opportunity we had rarely experienced? Even today I'm not certain about that. However, I'm pretty sure we were in love even then, not the puppy love of junior high school students, not an early adolescent crush, but authentic and powerful love, checked only by morality, and undisciplined by either experience or wisdom. Our love was shallow, but not any less potentially overwhelming.

We snapped nervously at each other, uneasy in the intimacy of our unaccustomed privacy. I insisted that she wasn't reading the notes properly. Close to tears of rage, she charged that I wasn't hitting the right notes on the school auditorium's creaky old piano.

"It won't work," I shouted once as I pounded the piano impatiently, "unless you understand that you cannot pronounce the German words like they're English."

She drew in a deep breath and exhaled slowly, an exercise she had insisted was the only way she could control her temper. In the process her budding young breasts pressed against the fabric of her uniform blouse, and I was suddenly dizzy.

"Play it again, Sam," she laughed.

I played it again. This time it all worked.

"What are you two doing?" Monsignor O'Brien, hobbling on his cane, came into the auditorium.

"We're practicing this song from Bach's *St. Matthew Passion* to sing at Hermie's house on Saturday," Kathleen said smoothly. "I have to learn to pronounce the German properly. S'ter said we could use this piano. Hildy Hoffman will pick us up in a few minutes on her way home from Township."

"She's getting there," I said lamely.

"Why don't you sing some of it for me?" the Monsignor asked, leaning on his cane.

So we sang a long passage where the alto and tenor voices have important contributions to make. For two kids in the winter darkness at the far end of the prairies with a blizzard about to move in, we weren't bad.

O haupt voll Blut und Wunden/ voll Schmerz und
   voller Hohn,
O haupt, zum Spott gebunden/ mit einer Dornenkron
O Haupt, sonst schoen gekroenet mit hoechster Ehr
   und Zier,
jetzt aber frech verhoehnet: gegruesset seist du mir.

Du edles Angesichte,/ vor dem sonst alle Welt/
erzittert im Gerichte,/ wie bist du so enstellt.
Wie bist du so erbleichet,/ wer hat dein Augenlicht,

79

dem sonst ein Licht nicht gleichet,/ so schaendlich
  zugericht'

Tears streamed down the old man's face.

Hildy bounced down the stairs, then stopped in her tracks, caught up in the magic of that moment. She clapped when we finished. The Monsignor embraced both of us and told us what wonderful young people we were. Caught up in the solemn magic of the moment, we joined in his tears. As did Hildy.

"Why was he weeping?" Kathleen asked in the car as we drove down the road, windshield wipers whizzing back and forth against the first snowflakes.

"Probably because he was so proud of two of his children?" Hildy suggested.

"You Krauts are sentimental all the time." Kathleen dismissed the incident.

"Monsignor *O'Brien?*" Hildy asked.

Hildy, a senior then, was tall, and blond like me, only on her it was lovely.

"You're crying more than anyone else," I pointed out.

"That's because I cry all the time," Kathleen admitted, beginning to weep again.

Thus our first kiss was postponed till graduation day. Then it was a brief touch of lips that filled my soul with unbearable sweetness.

If it were possible, I became even more of a romantic that year. I discovered *Parsifal*—not Wagner's opera, but the medieval romance by Wolfram von Eschenbach, which has a happy ending. I tried it in the original Middle High German and couldn't get very far until I found a Modern Library translation tucked away in a corner of our library. In my fantasy life, I became the true and perfect knight, and Kathleen became my lady. The daydreams were pleasant. As my lady she never gave me a hard time, which she did constantly, or so it seemed to me, in real life.

She was a mystery to me. She was bright and received good grades. Yet she didn't study much and pretended to be flighty much of the time. Boys don't like smart girls, she insisted. I like smart girls. You're different. And that was that.

Like most of the girls our age she freaked out over rock and roll. I tried to talk her out of it without much success. Then one day when she was hanging around our house, I put on the record of Arnold Schoenberg's *Transfigured Night*.

"This piece," I informed her, "created so much controversy that people rioted after it was performed."

"German stuff?"

"Sort of . . . First modern German romanticism."

"Sounds gross."

However, she became silent as the music began, strangely, bafflingly silent. She stared out the window, as though she saw something far away, a vision perhaps. I began to worry. Was she going into a trance?

After the music ended, she remained silent.

"Kathleen . . ."

"Hmm . . . Is there a story behind it, Herm?"

I glanced at the record liner.

"A man and woman walking around a lake. She tells the man that the child she is bearing is not his. He tells

81

her that he has so much love for her that it will embrace the child too. Real German romanticism."

"Can we listen to it again?"

"Sure."

She closed her eyes for the repeat playing. I worried. She was a strange little girl. Or, I corrected my thoughts, a strange young woman.

"Ja, ja." She sighed. "Love music, Hermie. German love music. If I live a long time and experience great love, maybe I'd be able to understand it."

I gulped. What makes a junior high school girl think such things? What was a junior high school boy to say in response?

Nothing.

St. Killian's, small school that it was, with a cracker box gym, usually provided a good account of itself in the Lincoln County basketball playoffs. When my brother Franky played for the team, they actually reached the quarterfinals which was considered a big victory. The parish celebrated much of the night with the usual ebullient German mix of songs, band music, beer, and wurst.

In my eighth grade year we lost in the first round to an even smaller Catholic school—SS Perpetua and Felicity in the minuscule hamlet of Prairie Springs. We should have beaten them. I was a good five inches taller than their center.

Every time I tried to score a demon appeared and put a lid on the basket. I was worse than terrible. From being short and clumsy I had become tall and gawky. My limbs did not operate properly. I was as tight as a piano wire. I knew I would disgrace my family, my school, and my town. It was written in the stars from all eternity that I would. I made only six points and missed ten free throws, most of them air balls.

Even some of the St. Killian's cheering section booed me. As they should have. Worse still, when I fouled out at the beginning of the fourth quarter, our half of the gym at Township (where the playoffs were staged) booed loudly. Kathleen, a dispirited leader of our dispirited cheerleaders, was unable to rally any applause.

It was my fault. I should not have gone out for the team. I should have known that I was an oaf and buried myself in my books back at our house. I was talked into it because I was by then the tallest player in our division. I had even scored twenty points one stormy March afternoon against Miller's Crossing, a school twice as large as St. Killian's and a basketball power in the county. Expectations were high that we would knock off SS Perpetua and Felicity without any trouble.

However, we had beaten Miller's Crossing at their gym. Only the cheerleaders accompanied the team. Family, neighbors, classmates were not there to watch me. In their presence, as Coach said sympathetically after the game, the fire in my belly went out.

I never had any fire in my belly. I wasn't a competitor. I did not belong on the basketball court. Give me a pitchfork or a tractor or a copy of Rilke, and I'd know what to do. Give me a basketball, and I'd probably drop it. Then I'd foul the player who had picked it up.

"You were just flat, Herman," said my brother

Franky. "That can happen to anyone."

"As flat as the prairie," I murmured. "Face it, Franky. I don't have it."

"Wait till next year." He slapped me on the back. "We'll show them."

Next year I'd be a freshman at Township. I would not go out for the team.

Kathleen and I huddled at the Dairy Queen, drowning our sorrows in chocolate malts—three of them because I consumed two.

"This has to stop, HHH," she said to me.

"Only one malt?"

"Don't be silly," she said, pounding my arm. "This geekiness of yours is becoming pathological."

A term she had doubtless heard from her father.

"How do we stop it?"

"You have to build up your self-confidence. You're a good hoopster, not the greatest, but good enough. You freeze when anyone important is watching."

"You were watching me at the Crossing."

"I don't count."

"Yes, you do."

"Yeah, I know." She shrugged her shoulders, a movement that sent an electric current through my body. "But I'm different."

"How?"

She shrugged again.

"You know that I love you, whether you're geeky or not."

So did my parents. Yet I was so pleased with her statement of love that I didn't argue.

VI

THE YEARS AT TOWNSHIP WERE TERRIBLE. I HATED EVERY minute of them. No, I overstate the case. Generally I was unhappy, but there were bright moments, mostly Kathleen.

Perhaps half of the eight hundred kids in the school were townies, the rest were farmers like me. The former ran the school. The latter stayed out of the way. I signed up for the choir and the German club, which should have been popular in our part of the world but wasn't because many of my contemporaries were revolting against the family culture and purported to be sick of it.

"Ja," Mama said, "we were that way once too."

Because Kathleen promised she would never speak to me again if I didn't, I signed up for the basketball team, where I instantly became a figure of fun to the coach and the other players. I would never live down the incident with Prairie Springs. To nobody's surprise, I was the first one cut, an event that caused me to sigh with relief and Kathleen to rage against the coach.

I played a lot of schoolyard ball that year, till winter came to the plains, then the next summer, when my farm neighbors would come over to our house for beer and basketball in the parking space in front of our barn. I felt my body slowly become accustomed to the rest of me.

In class I played my usual role of the *dummkopf*. I asked no questions, proffered no answers, and got A's on all my tests and papers. When I was forced to answer a question, I usually gave a jejune answer.

As in, "John Brown was an abolitionist."

"What did he do?"

"He killed slaveholders."

"Why?"

"Because he believed that by killing people you could free slaves. Mr. Lincoln thought the same thing later on, so that made it all right."

That was an unnecessary slur on a man that all we Russian Germans admired. I was in a bad mood that day.

"What happened to him?"

"Mr. Brown?"

"Yes!"

"He raided the federal arsenal at Harpers Ferry to find guns for a revolution. The government sent General Robert E. Lee to put down the rising. Mr. Brown was hung . . . They wrote a song about him."

I then sang the song—on key—about Mr. Brown's body mouldering in the ground. I added, "You'll recognize the music. 'The Battle Hymn of the Republic.' That came later. Nice irony, huh?"

Then I relapsed into silence, more than satisfied with myself.

"Nice voice too," said the teacher.

Or:

"Wagner wrote an opera called *Parsifal*."

"What else do you know about it?"

"It was based on a long poem by Wolfram von Eschenbach, which, unlike the opera, had a happy ending. There's a difference of opinion about whether the Percival in the Arthurian saga first set down by Chrétien de Troyes is the same character. I don't think he is."

Dead silence from the pretty twenty-five-year-old teacher.

"You sound like you've read it."

"I have."

"In German or English?"

"German. With some help from the Modern Library translation."

"You like the poem better than the opera because it had a happy ending?"

"Yeah."

I could hear Kathleen sniggering.

We went on to something else.

"Why didn't you tell me about this Wolfgang von Achingback?" she demanded of me after class.

"I didn't think you'd be interested."

Lie. Terrible lie. I didn't want the real Kathleen to elbow her way into my fantasy.

"I want to read it."

"In German?"

"No, *dummkopf*. In English."

"OK. I'll bring it along tomorrow."

"Well, you showed that stuck-up bitch. I really hate her. She thinks she's so gorgeous."

"There you go again, Kathleen. Why do you have to be so nasty? She's a nice young woman who is scared of her first year of teaching."

My ladylove's shoulders slumped.

"I really am a terrible bitch, aren't I?"

"Not always."

For the rest of the semester she was best friends with the new teacher.

It was the only class we shared. She was very busy with her computer graphics work with which she impressed the teachers. By midyear she was doing graphics for the whole school. Even I was impressed.

She also read von Achingback over the weekend.

"Hmpf," she said, giving it back to me. "You think you're *Parsifal*, don't you, Hermie."

"No, I don't," I said, feeling my face warm up.

"Yes, you do. And in some ways you are . . . What do you think they were doing in their chamber when the priest delayed Mass for them?"

I knew what they were doing, but I didn't want to say. "Praying, maybe."

"You're such a prude, Herman Hugo Hoffman. They were screwing, which is what husbands and wives do."

She stalked away as she did when she was impatient with me.

High school is hellish. The only ones who don't know that are those whose nostalgia dims their memories once they escape it. It's a zoo that the animals run, to use a hackneyed metaphor, even when the animals are mostly farmers and small-town kids who in my era knew no other drugs besides alcohol and pot.

Like I say, the townies ran it. As did the jocks, especially the football stars and an occasional basketball star and their women. They were all nasty people, I realize in retrospect, because they were worried about their status like everyone else. A couple of athletes made moves on Kathleen and struck out.

The then quarterback decided it was my fault. He figured that big, lanky farm boy that I was, I'd be a pushover.

"I hear that Quinlan is your woman, *dummkopf.*"

"Who?"

"You know, the whore with the red hair who fucks everyone."

"Don't know anyone like that."

"You don't know much of anything, do you, asshole?"

"Nope."

He shoved me. I turned my back and walked away. He spun me around and tried to punch me. I ducked. I think he saw the look in my eye and realized that I might be dangerous in the fight.

"Coward!" he sneered, backing off. "Afraid to defend your whore."

I walked away again. He didn't follow me.

Our quarterbacks don't come that big or that strong. I would have picked him up and carried him to the swimming pool and thrown him in. I didn't want to do that, however. It would mean playing their game. I didn't like the game.

"I hear you defended my honor," Kathleen said later, not sure whether she was angry.

"Kathleen," I said solemnly, "your honor doesn't need any defense."

"What would you have done if he was dumb enough to fight you?"

"Thrown him in the pool."

She giggled. "That's my Parsifal!"

As much as I tried to stay on the fringes of Township, she threw herself into it—yearbook, paper, computer club, cheerleader, softball, computer art. She still came around to our singspiel some of the time.

"Sometimes I think you're right, Parsifal." She would sigh wearily. "All this activity is silly. Better to stay on the fringes and take an occasional sniper shot."

Kathleen was a bundle of contradictions, an increasingly attractive bundle, I have to add.

She was always enthused, but the enthusiasms changed. After my mini-lecture about Parsifal she consumed all the books on the Arthurian saga she could find, and even listened to the opera, which she informed me was dull, BORING, and much too German.

"I have a hard time figuring out which Knight of the Round Table you are."

"Maybe Sir Gawain," I suggested.

"Don't be silly." She waved off my suggestion. "You're either Lancelot of the Lake or Galahad. I'd like you to be Lancelot, but I'm afraid you're Galahad."

Oh.

I didn't want to know what she meant.

Then her interests turned to Jane Austen, whose stories made her angry at men.

"You guys are all creeps!" she thundered at me.

"I'm not English," I argued.

"Germans are even worse."

Before she left for her European trip—Austria and Switzerland—after our freshman year, she left me firm orders to work on my free throws.

"No more air balls."

"I'm not going out for the team next year."

"Yes, you are," she said, kissing me good-bye. "Oh, Hermie, I'll miss you so much. I'm sorry you're not coming along."

We kissed infrequently, but it was always wonderful. I would drift dreamily for a week on the strength of one kiss. The memory of her fervent farewell sustained me through several weeks of no postcards. Then seven or eight would come the same day. Her scribble was unintelligible, but the word LOVE in big bold letters at the end was clear enough.

For anyone in the family who might get to the mail before I did.

I did practice my free throws. In one contest with Franky, who was perhaps distracted by the courtship in which he was engaged, I made twenty-one in a row. I didn't tell her when she came home. Despite the excitement in her cards, she assured me that she had not enjoyed the trip.

"I guess I belong in the prairies too," she admitted.

The first time she appeared at our Saturday singspiel, Franky told her.

"Hermie made twenty-one free throws in a row while you were away, Kathleen."

"See"—an imperial finger pointed at me—"I told you you could do it if you really worked at it!"

"It's different in a game," I said.

"All you have to do is concentrate!"

She kissed me often during our sophomore year. Occasionally, I would kiss her, and she would purr contentedly, like a temporarily appeased bobcat.

I wasn't cut from the team that year, but I didn't play much because there were two junior centers ahead of me. Kathleen was furious at the coach, because "he *knows* you're the best."

"I don't think I am."

As the season wound down in February, I had my chance. One of the juniors was sick, and the other fouled out with ten minutes to play.

"Don't take any chances, *dummkopf,*" Coach said to me as he sent me in.

I didn't score any baskets because I was fouled almost every time I had the ball. The coach from River City must have remembered my eighth grade performance. I made ten straight free throws, the last with five seconds to play. We won by those two points. The Township crowd went crazy.

Hermie as hero.

"Don't think you're going to get any more minutes," Coach warned me, "just because you had a lucky night."

"No, sir," I said meekly.

"You were sensational!" Kathleen screamed.

"You showed them Hermie," Horst Heller, from the farm next to ours, who had become my best friend, said. Best male friend. Horst was a little wisp of a guy, maybe five-foot-nine, with blond hair like mine, quick eyes, a quicker tongue, and a very quick mind. You wanted Horst on your side, all the time.

For a couple of days Hermie was the toast of the school and received much attention from the young women. Kathleen was furious.

"I'll make those bitches leave you alone!" she whispered.

"You're face is too beautiful to be angry," I told her.

"All right," she said with one of her wondrous deep breaths. "I'll just smile at the little bitches."

"That will make them more angry," I observed.

She laughed at me. "You're a bad man, Herman Hugo Hoffman!"

During our sophomore and junior years, as I look back on them, my relationship with Kathleen changed. She was no longer a pretty little girl or a luscious young woman. She had become a friend, like Horst perhaps, only a lot more appealing than Horst. I gradually recognized that she was very intelligent and that I could learn from listening to her. She was also artistically gifted. Her computer art, which she had started as a game, was extraordinary.

I heard two women faculty discussing her one day around the corner from my locker.

"She is a little bitch, but I've never seen such gentle and sensitive art from a teenager."

"A little bipolar, I think. One moment she's laughing and the next moment crying."

"She doesn't have a mother. Not much of a father either."

"She has to settle for that goofy giant Hermie Hoffman."

"He'll never do anything to hurt her."

"Not deliberately anyway."

I hurried down the corridor in the opposite direction.

No, I would never hurt her.

But later I did just that.

We listened to opera records together at her house.

"If you weren't a *dummkopf* Deutsche, you'd know that Wagner is a boring pig!"

"You don't understand his spirituality, Kathleen."

"Let's play *Traviata* again. That's the kind of spirituality I like. Everyone is saved at the end."

"Italian sentimentality!"

"Better than German sentimentalism!" she would say, kissing me.

We kissed a lot in those days, nothing serious I thought. I would come to realize later that affection between a boy and a girl whose bloodstreams were drenched with hormones could quickly become very serious.

It didn't help much that I was immersing myself in German romantic literature, either in German or English, depending on how difficult the German text was. I became not only a goofy giant but an awkward *dummkopf* whose head filled up every morning with dizzy romantic daydreams.

"The difference between Italian sentimentality and German sentimentalism," I told her one day, "is the Italian is shallow, and the German goes to the heart of the soul."

"Only if you're a dumb Deutscheman!"

Maybe she was right.

I wouldn't admit to her that I liked *Traviata* too. If she were Violetta, I would take much better care of her than did that jerk Alfredo.

When she turned legal her father gave her a brand-new Fairlane. Every Saturday afternoon, except when I was working on the farm, we'd drive down to River View, a small city beneath the bridge across the big river, to buy records and books and see a movie.

"You two are going steady," Horst would accuse me.

"Do you see a ring on her finger?"

"No, but I see the look in your eyes."

"She's special."

"I won't argue about that."

"I think Hermie is in love," Franky said one Sunday, when I was looking for Kathleen in the crowd after Mass.

"*Ja,*" Mama agreed. "It happens."

"I'm not in love," I insisted. "We don't act silly like everyone else our age."

"Maybe," Papa observed, with his usual boisterous laugh, "that's because you are more in love than they are."

We all joined in his laughter, as we usually did.

Papa's laughter usually accompanied an insight.

Although I would never have admitted it then, we were crossing the border that separates puppy love and adolescent crushes on the one hand and intense adult passion on the other. We weren't adults, however, and would not be for a long time.

Lincoln Junction, like all such towns, had a swimming hole. It was a tiny lake in a small grove of trees near the bank of the little river that rushed down towards the big river ten miles away. In big rainstorms, the lake overflowed its banks and carved its way to the river.

I stayed away from it because I did not know how to swim and was afraid to learn.

"Do you want to see me in my new red bikini?" Kathleen asked one Sunday after Mass.

"No," I said firmly, though of course I did.

"Then you'll have to come down to the lake with me. Everyone will be there."

"Then you won't need me to join the admiration society."

"I'll pick you up at one."

"You're going out this afternoon with Kathleen?" Mama asked when the Fairlane rolled up to the house.

"Only to the lake."

"To swim?" Hildy asked in disbelief.

"Maybe."

"Swimming holes are dangerous places," Papa said. "Aren't they, Mama?"

"And not because someone could drown there either," she agreed.

They both laughed.

"What kind of swimsuit does Kathleen wear?" Hildy demanded.

"I hear she has a new red bikini," I responded. "Nothing very interesting I'm sure. You see one belly button, you've seen them all."

They all pretended to be horrified at my gross disrespect.

None of them was mean enough to ask whether I'd seen Kathleen's belly button yet.

We were the first ones to get to the swimming hole, something she had deliberately planned.

She threw off her terry-cloth cover-up and faced me, hands on her hips.

"Well, *dummkopf,* what do you think?"

My love was so beautiful that I was unable to say or think anything. Long, slender legs, flat belly, breasts that were not big but elegant and graceful, gently curving shoulders, defiant posture—a water nymph spoiling for a fight.

I reached out, put my hands around her bare waist, and lifted her off the ground.

"HERMIE! What are you doing!" she said, flustered and a little scared.

"Just admiring."

"Oh," she said, relaxing. "Well, I guess that's what you're supposed to do."

"You're gorgeous, Kathleen," I said, my voice choked.

"When you're ready, you can put me down."

"No rush?"

She gulped. "Not particularly . . . except I think that another car is coming down the road!"

"OK."

I placed her, very gently, on the minute pier, which extended out to the swimming hole. She rushed to the end and dove into the water—a graceful dive, of course.

"Come in, Hermie, the water is warm."

"As warm as the Mediterranean?"

"Oaf." She splashed me with water.

I was in those days still a shy, overgrown oaf, with a voracious mind, a rampaging imagination, and maybe more than the usual quotient of male hormones. Yet at that point my love for Kathleen had helped me to mature. I wasn't in love with her for the purpose of maturation. That excuse would never have occurred to me. But in the glow of our love I was beginning to understand how a man should relate to a woman. I still had a lot to learn.

"I learned to swim this afternoon," I reported to my family when I returned to the farm. "It's easy."

"What did Kathleen look like in her red bikini?" Hildy demanded, not looking away from the TV, where the Cardinals were playing the Cubs.

"She was OK," I admitted. "Nothing really special, but this is Lincoln County, isn't it?"

I lied. Lincoln County or not, Kathleen was the most beautiful woman in the world, and she was mine. Kind of.

The following spring we had a brush with death that sobered us just a little but not for long.

The Palace in River View had expanded to two screens. That weekend we could see *Ordinary People* or *Coal Miner's Daughter*. Kathleen decided that we would see both even if it meant that we'd not leave River View till almost midnight. She warned my parents we'd be late getting home, and they could blame her, not me. It was a measure of how much they trusted Kathleen that they did not object.

"If we're not home by one," Kathleen continued, "the only reason will be that Hermie is acting up."

They all laughed, knowing that Hermie would never act up.

In fact, our love was remarkably chaste even for our time and place. We kissed, we embraced, we cuddled in each other's arms. But we did not play with each other. Kathleen showed no signs that she would welcome such affection. Despite all my fevered fantasies, in real life, I would not, could not do anything that might hurt this beloved and fragile child.

Or so I thought.

When we left the Palace, arms around each other, occasional snowflakes were falling in the silent darkness of the city.

"Hey, what happened to spring?" I asked.

"We'd better drive right home," Kathleen said. "I don't want your parents to worry."

"We don't have blizzards this late."

Kathleen turned on the radio as soon as we were inside her Ford.

"Winter is not quite finished with the plains," said the Plains City station. "A major snow squall is coming down out of the mountains and heading right for us. There is a winter storm warning for the entire state. As much as a half foot of snow is expected by morning. There will be dangers of whiteouts on all major highways. All drivers are urged to exercise extreme caution. The good news is that the storm center will have passed through much of the state by morning, and the temperature will have risen into the high thirties, so the snow will melt quickly. However, it will be quite a night out on the prairies."

"Oh," Kathleen said anxiously. "A blizzard."

"It will last only overnight," I said, though I knew as

well as she did how deadly prairie blizzards could be.

"I'll drive quick, so we'll get home before it catches up to us."

"Be careful, Kathleen, the road is already slippery."

She slowed down.

"OK. If we die, at least we'll die together."

"We're not going to die."

Suppose that it was a two-day or even a three-day storm. Suppose that there were two feet of snow. Suppose the temperature went down. Well, it would be a very sad funeral.

The snow fell like someone up in the sky was using a front loader to shove it down on us. Sometimes it was so thick that we could see only a few feet ahead of the car.

"We'd better stop, Kathleen."

"I know. Hermie, I'm scared. What shall we do?"

"We'll pull over to the side of the road and wait for the snowplow to come down from Lincoln Junction in the morning."

"We'll freeze to death. I can't leave the motor on. Carbon monoxide."

"We'll have to huddle together and keep warm with our body heat."

"Well, that's one way to go . . . Do you have much body heat, Hermie?"

We both giggled.

"When I'm around you, I have enough."

We had worn sweaters and windbreakers. We fashioned them into a kind of blanket and stretched it over ourselves as we clung together. We giggled nervously at this sudden intimacy.

"I'll be able to tell the girls that I slept with Hermie Hoffman with most of my clothes off."

"And Horst will ask me if I was able to cop a feel, and I'll say that since my head is still on, the obvious answer is no."

"Good answer."

"Then I'll add that it's not a relevant question when you and a woman are pressed together trying to stay warm, and she's wearing only a lace bra."

"Horst will about die." She sighed. "Hermie, sing to me please."

So we sang as many songs as we could remember, in both German and English.

"Lullabies, Hermie, I want to sleep . . . German ones."

She was deep in sleep before I had finished Brahms. I followed soon after with the thought that, while I might not be able to argue a good case for myself before St. Peter, Kathleen would get me through the gates.

I woke up much later, stiff with cold. Outside it had stopped snowing, but wind was whipping the fallen snow into drifts. Our car was mired in a deep pile of snow, nose down. There was a strange light in the air.

Where were we? Why were we here? Who was the lovely woman with wonderful nipples clinging to me?

Then it came back. Snowstorm. The light was dawn, an anticipation of sunrise. We were both terribly cold. I cranked down the window and peered back. The rear bumper was a half foot above the snow. The exhausts must be clear. I reached over Kathleen and turned on the ignition.

"Carbon monoxide," she said, waking suddenly. "Turn it off, Hermie!"

"The exhausts are clear," I said. "See the smoke coming out!"

"They may clog up! This is the way my mother died!"

"I'll roll down the window just in case."

She sobbed hysterically.

"My mother killed herself this way. She locked herself in the garage where we used to live and turned on the ignition . . ."

"We're not in a garage," I said miserably.

"We never knew why. My poor dad never got over it . . ."

I said the right thing.

"I'm in charge this morning, Kathleen. I'll take care of you."

She buried her head against my chest.

"Thank God!"

I untangled my windbreaker from our makeshift blanket and eased out of the car. I promptly slipped into a snowdrift halfway up my thigh. I struggled towards the rear of the car to make sure that the exhausts were above the drift. They seemed all right. The wind had stopped. The drifts were not getting bigger. I thrashed about and fought my way back into the car.

"Put on your sweater, Hermie. You'll freeze to death!"

We both collapsed into laughter.

She had already put her sweater on, worse luck for me.

"Did you have any dirty thoughts about me last night, Hermie?"

"I was too cold . . . Look, turn up the heat. I'll leave the window half-open on this side and check the exhausts every half hour. There's nothing to worry about."

"My mother was manic-depressive, I guess . . . What they call bipolar these days . . . I don't want to get that way and die like her . . . Sorry I made a fuss."

I put my arms around her.

"That's OK, Kathleen. Now close your eyes and go back to sleep. I'll sing some more lullabies *auf Deutsch*. We do the best lullabies in the world."

"Sentimentalism . . ." She cuddled up in my arms and went back to sleep.

Poor woman. It was all right. I would take care of her for the rest of my life. Then I realized that I still planned to be a priest. I hadn't thought about that for a long time.

Then, as though it had been planning on doing it all along, the sun rose and chased away the snow clouds. We were still marooned in a snowdrift in the prairies, but the world seemed much safer. I turned on the radio. The weather news was all about Plains City where twelve inches of snow had fallen in twelve hours. However, the surprise winter storm had already passed on, and much of the snow would melt because the temperature would be in the forties that day and the fifties the next. No serious damage was expected to the winter wheat crop.

"So it looks like we're not going to die, Hermie . . ." Kathleen woke in my arms and stretched. "Seems like I'm spending a lot of time wrapped up in you."

"Only because of necessity . . . Where's the snow-plow?"

Two hours later the snowplow did arrive, accompanied by a second plow, a state police car, and a tow truck.

"Are you Miss Kathleen Quinlan?" the state cop, who was more of a bumpkin than I, asked.

"Yes, sir," Kathleen said demurely.

"You shouldn't be out on the road in this kind of weather."

"Tell me about it."

"And are you Mr. Herman Hugo Hoffman?"

"I'm afraid so."

"Your family is very worried about you."

"I understand."

"Well, we'll have headquarters call your parents and tell them you're safe."

"Thank you, Officer."

"We'll tow you out and you can drive home, Miss Quinlan. We hope you'll both be more careful in the future."

"Yes, sir."

"Mr. Hoffman, you shouldn't have turned on the car. If the exhausts had been covered with snow, you might have asphyxiated yourself and Miss Quinlan."

I took a very deep breath.

"I checked the exhausts to make sure they were not covered with snow."

The man was implacable.

"Just so long as you remember to be careful in the future not to drive in a snowstorm."

"Volga Deutsche," my ladylove whispered.

The tow truck dragged us out. The car seemed to function well enough. We were in Lincoln Junction in twenty minutes and out to our farm in ten more.

"Hermie doesn't snore at night," Kathleen, now in exuberant spirits, told my mother and father. "And he sings wonderful lullabies! I think you ought to keep him."

Horst asked the expected question about copping a feel. I gave him my prepared answer.

She went off to Europe again with her aunt and uncle.

"Stay out of trouble while I'm away," she warned me as she kissed me good-bye at our final singspiel before she left.

"How could I get in trouble here in Lincoln Junction? You're the one who should stay out of trouble in the Greek Islands."

"You'd be surprised at how easy that is."

VII

TOWNSHIP HAD A NEW BASKETBALL COACH FOR OUR senior year. He watched me play in some practice games, then told everyone that I was his starting center and that was that.

"You're not tall enough and not nearly mean enough to take us beyond Lincoln County, but we'll take county, that's for sure."

"We've never taken county," I said.

"We'll take it this year," he said.

Kathleen was ecstatic. She wanted to join the cheerleaders again. I argued that she would have much more impact stirring up the crowd if she were in the stands with them.

We were both busy making our college plans. Her father had sold his practice, so she was going to Stanford, though she didn't seem to be very happy at the prospect. I was bound for State U, which would take me to the other side of the state and farther from Lincoln Junction then I had ever been before. She won a state prize for computer art, an accomplishment which she dismissed as "worthless" though she secretly was very proud of it.

I had become a National Merit Scholarship semifinalist, which led Papa to say that well, we wouldn't have to worry about the winter wheat this year.

"You could come to Stanford too on that kind of scholarship," Kathleen said wistfully. "But, I know, you have to go to State because you're a plainsman."

There was less time to read that year, but more time for fun, especially as the basketball team became so accustomed to winning that it refused to lose a game. I was, as the coach had said, not all that great a center. Indeed I was probably too short to play power forward against the teams from Plains City. However, in Lincoln County that year, there wasn't anyone big enough to stop me. There was talk in the school about how we might take state. I was under no illusions.

"You might get lucky, Hermie," Kathleen had argued.

"Only if I should grow another six inches, which wouldn't be luck. You know how much trouble I have now. I'd never remember to duck my head when going through doorways."

Kathleen and I were definitely an item, though everyone knew we did not sleep with each other, except for that night in the car during the blizzard. About that there was a mixed opinion.

A lot of the senior couples were vigorously exploring the possibilities of sexual love. "They're fucking like rabbits," Horst assured me.

"With about as much sense and love as rabbits."

"Some of the guys say it's really great. Others say that the chicks don't really put out the way they pretend they will."

Kathleen echoed this view, with the dyspeptic objectivity of a professional anthropologist.

"The women are finding out that men are brutes."

"What else would they expect of seventeen-year-old boys?"

"You think they'll grow up?"

"Some will, some won't."

We did win county and made it to the second round of the state playoffs where a team of African-Americans, each one of whom was taller than I, drove us off the court. They were very gentle about it, however, and congratulated us on our courage.

I ended up as valedictorian, despite my repeated assertions that there was no way I could possibly win. I don't remember what I said. I was so ashamed of myself that I threw my copy away. I suspect that it wasn't much worse than the usual arrogant nonsense that such folk talk. Look out world, here we are!

My parents and Kathleen were very proud. My classmates applauded. Many of the young women (Kathleen included of course) shed copious tears. I think I talked about not forgetting Lincoln Township and all the wonders in it, no matter how far in the world we might wander—birds waking us in the morning, the golden fields of wheat, the smell of the harvest, the sounds of the train whistles at night. I'd stand by the theme even now, though I'd probably be a lot more moderate in my celebration of my world.

As it was I had wandered far indeed—Chicago and back!

The senior prom was a week after graduation. Kathleen and I almost didn't go. We had both hated the junior prom because most everyone else was drunk—Kathleen at that time never drank when she was with me.

But everyone insisted that we had to come. Kathleen agreed, and I didn't feel strongly enough that it was a waste of time to disagree.

Actually it was a magic night. Kathleen had decorated the walls of the gym with some dazzling computer art—all soft and pastel and springlike. The theme was "It might as well be spring—because it is!"

"Prairie art for prairie kids," she said with a laugh.

"You're not a prairie kid," I argued.

"Sure am. Always will be."

I knew that was not true. She'd already been to Europe four times. She was going to Africa the following week. Then Stanford. She'd never come back to Lincoln Junction and St. Killian's parish. I'd probably never see her again after September.

Yet I hoped I was wrong.

Kathleen was also responsible for the music, mostly "Might As Well Be Spring" music, filled with gentle sentimentality.

"Irish music," I argued, "not Plains music."

"You mean not Volga Deutsche Wagnerian horrors . . . You know, Hermie"—she drew me close as I tried with only slight success to execute a waltz—"you dress up pretty well. You've also grown up pretty well. No more shy *dummkopf*."

I proved she was wrong by blushing.

"I have a long way to go, Kathleen," I said, stumbling over the words.

"Granted, but you've come a long way too."

It shows where we both were and indeed where Township was that we would rather listen to Julio Iglesias than to hard rock and that disco never came to our part of the plains. A fad had to last for a while before we caught on. Kathleen loved the old Beatles records, and I thought they were silly. Who needed rock and roll when they had Bach.

On prom night she was wearing an off-white form-fitting gown with only the thinnest straps supporting it on her shoulders. Her long red hair was piled up on her head, and the gold choker around her neck made her look like an archduchess, a smooth, sophisticated, woman of the world who had just stopped in at Lincoln Township to rusticate with the peasants. I did my best not to ogle her breasts. My best that night was not much good. Anyway, she didn't seem to mind.

"I wish prom night could go on forever, a sweet dream of spring and youth that will never end."

"Wagner wrote music for that idea."

"Heavy, grim music."

"A lot of sweetness in it."

"In the bass and the cellos, smothering sweetness."

I drifted into her dream and wished that the night would never end. Spring was all too brief on the prairies, a week or two between winter and summer, Franky used to joke. Youth was all too brief also. After that night my youth would end. Hers too probably. Summer and winter stretched out in front of us.

Most of the class planned to have their all-night party at a lavish summer house up in the hills across the river—someone's rich uncle's place. They would have to drive down to River View, cross on the interstate bridge, and then drive back up the river, almost a two-hour drive.

"That's really dumb," my date insisted. "Why waste four hours of senior prom on an idiotic drive, especially when the drivers have had too much to drink. They won't miss us."

"They'll miss the most beautiful woman at the prom."

"Hermie, you've become a courtier."

"In the presence of an archduchess."

"Grand duchess, please!"

So we were to bring our swimsuits, towels, sandwiches for breakfast, and a blanket to the swimming hole and watch the moon go down and the sun rise and thus to celebrate our graduation from Lincoln Township. Neither of us was drunk. I had a beer and Kathleen no more than two. We were, however, drunk on a more powerful addiction, a mixture of sentiment and fear, of joy and melancholy, of love and desire.

We sat on a bench and huddled in each other's arms silently for a long time, reveling in the silver glow of the moon on our absurd little lake, the warmth of the June air, the smell of the lilacs, and sweetness of life. We kissed for a while, first gently, then passionately.

Then, without a word of preliminary discussion, we undressed one another, admired and played with each other's bodies, and took possession of one another in a chocolate storm of love.

Later, wrapped in our blanket, our naked bodies pressing against each other, we both slept. Then I woke up, fully aware of what had happened. I was proud of myself. I was a man. I had made love to a woman. I was an effective lover. I had not hurt her. She had cried out with joy just as I had. Our love was special, nothing like the hasty and awkward couplings of our peers.

I stared up at the stars. I knew they were huge balls of gas like our sun, devoid of feelings and insights. Yet I imagined that they were looking down with benign approval on us, a special pair of young lovers in all the universe. Then the stars seemed to come down from the sky and envelop us in a dance, a waltz perhaps, of twinkling lights. The whole world absorbed me and lifted me out of myself. I felt as if I was enjoying Kathleen once again, only this was something much more powerful. I thought that the joy would blow me apart. I was filled with light and laughter and love. I saw the universe and my place in it and knew that everything would be all right.

Then the stars danced away and resumed their normal

place in the sky. I was so happy that I woke Kathleen and made love to her again, this time even more manfully than before. Her cries of joy shattered the night. My own triumphant scream merged with hers at the end.

"You are not all that bad as a lover, Hermie." She sighed. "Pretty good for a dumb Deutsche. Now let me sleep."

Months later, whenever I saw Kathleen and my body reacted with desire, memories of that greater love also tickled the back of my brain, or so it seemed.

Only in later years did I try to understand the mystery of the two lovers who possessed me and were possessed by me on the night of the senior prom. I read books on mystical experience, especially William James. The second lover, if it were anyone at all, was God. Why was God intervening in my love life? Why didn't He leave me alone? What business of His was it that I had just deflowered a virgin? And why did He not make me feel guilty for what was in some fashion a serious sin? Why did He use human love, probably sinful, as an occasion for interjecting Himself in my life? Was He trying to tell me that He was a more pleasurable lover than Kathleen?

I've come to realize that, while there are answers to those questions, I will never discover them in this life. The best I can do is to wonder whether God's scheme was to reveal Himself to me through Kathleen. If that were God's game, sometimes I think it was a dirty trick and sometimes a wonderful hint.

I don't know.

We slept till dawn, then swam naked in the warm waters of the little lake. Then as the sun rose we put on our swimsuits and tee shirts and ate breakfast, washing it down with warm Cokes. Then, packing my tux and her gown in the backseat of the car, we drove silently out through the wheatfields to our farms.

"Come in for some lager?" I asked hesitantly.

"Not today," she said softly.

Then she threw her arms around me. "I love you, Hermie! I'll always love you!"

"I'll always love you too," I promised.

"Incidentally," she said, as I gathered my clothes from the back of the car, "don't worry that I might get pregnant. I borrowed some of my dad's packets of birth control pills. I was not sure anything would happen. I wanted to be ready."

I was drugged with pleasure, surprise, and exhaustion. I didn't know what to make of her comment. I didn't want to know.

"*Ja,*" Mama said. "Your father said you'd probably better take the day off and sleep. You'd be a menace out in the fields today."

So I slept till about three, rose to eat a steak, and went back to bed.

I woke again about eleven at night. The moon was shining through the window, the same moon that had watched our lovemaking the night before. At first I told myself that nothing had happened. There had been no sex between Kathleen and me, no dance of stars, no devastating heavenly intruder. It was all a prom night dream.

113

Then, for the first time, guilt appeared. What had I done! I had raped Kathleen! No, that wasn't it at all. Yet it was a sin, even if most of my classmates, good Catholics that they were, didn't think that teenage sex was wrong. "No one gets hurt," they'd say, "it's just fun and games."

And exploitation, cruel exploitation.

But we were not exploiting each other, were we?

Why had she taken the birth control pills? She had foreseen what might happen, and I had not?

I would go to confession before Mass on Sunday morning.

The visiting priest, in a hurry to work through the line of sinners, urged me not to commit the sin again, probably thinking that he was wasting his breath.

I didn't see Kathleen at Mass. I knew we had to talk about it before she left for her trip to Africa with her aunt and uncle on Tuesday. Yet I was afraid to call her. Probably she was afraid to call me.

Tuesday morning early, just as we were going into the fields, her relatives' Mercedes drove up. Dressed in shorts and a tee shirt for the long trip, she rushed out of the car, embraced me, and murmured, "I'll think of you every minute, Hermie, and pray for you too."

I murmured something unintelligible about the occasional postcard. She laughed and rushed back to the car. She waved from the rear window as the car disappeared in the dust.

What had happened on prom night had been a mistake, I told myself, something that had happened without either of us intending it. Never again, I promised.

Yet all summer long when I was falling asleep or waking again I remembered the joy of our lovemaking and the greater joy of the mysterious visitor who came to me as the stars came down out of the skies and danced around me.

I worked in the fields and worked out in the little gym Franky and I had built at the back of the house. I didn't want to be a spindly geek.

And I thought a lot about Kathleen, who had become now a special responsibility. It's hard for me to separate out what I was actually thinking about her then as she slowly became a person in my eroticized adolescent consciousness and what I figured out much later in life. As best as I can remember I made a lot of progress that summer in understanding that she was more than a pesky little girl who hassled me and bossed me around, a budding young woman who had invaded my fantasies and would not go away, and a wondrous sexual partner. She was a person, a "thou" as the Jewish theologian Martin Buber would later explain to me in my seminary reading. Of course I didn't have those concepts available to me then.

Her life had been shaped by the tragedy of her adored mother's manic-depressive trouble and eventual suicide. Her father had been a rich and successful physician at the Mayo Clinic and had withdrawn from highpowered medicine to move to Lincoln Junction and devote himself to family practice. He was by all accounts very good at what he did, but a dark melancholic recluse who avoided all social contact outside his practice. I wondered what I would be like if I had grown up in such a home.

I could not imagine what such a life would be, but I knew it would not be good . . . Kathleen was also worried that she might have inherited her mother's propensities. Maybe there were good reasons for that worry. She was intelligent, quick-witted, and very creative, as her computer art showed. She could readily imagine herself turning on the ignition just as her mother had.

To make her problems worse, she was passionate, hot-tempered, outspoken, and drank too many beers. I had tried with some little success to calm her down, to make her chill out. She gave up foul language at my insistence, limited her beer consumption, and tried to control her temper—all because I told her to. Why would such a strong-minded young person become so docile at my demand?

Even more than before, it was clear to me that she needed a forceful male presence in her life, though she had looked to the wrong person for it. She also wanted a warm and affectionate family, which she had found in the Saturday morning *Gemütlichkeit* with us Russian Germans. She found the family and then she found me, nasty little prig that I was. Or maybe it was the other way around, she found the family because I was in it.

Would I have put it that way at seventeen? Not very likely, but I knew it, however dimly.

I did uncover one bit of wisdom, which I jotted down in one of the first entries in my journal: "Kathleen wants to love and be loved, more than anyone else I know and more than I do."

I know I wrote that because I still have the spiral notebook in which I scribbled it.

My adolescent ruminations were mostly stupid and insensitive, too introspective and complex for someone who was nothing more than a big lummox of a Russian German bumpkin. I was trying to take apart a vibrant young woman and put her back together again like "Pa" (my great-grandfather) took apart watches and put them back together, for the sheer fun of solving a puzzle.

It might have helped if I could have talked it over with someone. As it was I had fallen into the apparently incorrigible German habit of reducing everything and everyone to a patchwork of concepts, a habit that even today I find difficult to overcome. If the French want only to give a phenomenon a name, the Germans want only to reduce it to an idea.

No way in the world that Kathleen Anne Elizabeth Quinlan could be reduced to an idea.

It would have been helpful if she had been around that summer and we could have talked about it. Yet she would probably have been bored to tears by my plodding *deutsch* thought processes.

As it was, she never came back to Lincoln Junction that summer.

"It looks like we might not see the cute little Quinlan girl again," Mama remarked one day at the supper table. "Her father is putting their land on sale. She will move with him up in Palo Alto when she's not at Stanford."

"We'll miss her at the singspiels," Hildy said.

"I'm probably going to buy the land," Papa added. "We've been working it anyway, no?"

"Probably it will do her good to have a new life," Franky said.

"Maybe she'll come back someday," Mama suggested.

The whole scene had been arranged to capture my reaction.

"I doubt it," I said. "She is a nice young woman and a great prom date, but she's really too big for a place like Lincoln Junction."

I said it casually (and I know I said it because I jotted that down in my incipient journal too) as though I was resigned to giving her up and not suffering greatly about my loss.

I don't know whether I fooled my family about the dark pain that oozed slowly through my body and took possession of me for days and weeks after. I probably would never see her again. I told myself that it was better for both of us.

Some enchanted evening . . . across a crowded room . . .

VIII

IF LINCOLN TOWNSHIP HIGH SCHOOL WAS A ZOO RUN BY the animals, State U was a jungle in which no one ran anything. As far as the administration was concerned incoming freshmen were computer numbers to be assigned to classrooms and housing in a manner that created few problems for the university. We might be forced to live with roommates (like mine) who were interested only in drinking binges. We might have a dif-

118

ficult time finding our classrooms. We might be desperately homesick (as I was) for our families. We might not know where the mailboxes, the cash stations, the post office were. We might be stumbling around in an angry stupor. We had academic advisers somewhere, but we rarely found their offices and, even when we did, they weren't in. None of those things mattered. The university had coped with freshmen before and it would do so again. If some of them couldn't survive the strain, that was unfortunate but inevitable. When I arrived I would discover later that the hell of the first weeks of college was the norm for all big state universities.

I had visited Great-grandpa and Grandpa's house before I left for State U, a ritual we all followed. He gave me the usual envelope with the five hundred-dollar bills in it. We all liked Pa. Though he was over ninety, his smile was radiant. His nearly blind blue eyes were clear. He joked with us and laughed. He knew who each one of us was, probably because Grandpa had briefed him.

"*Ja,* Hugo, college is not easy. I had it better when I was your age. I went to war instead of school. A little wound in Belleau Wood. Never regretted it. Came home and took over the farm when my father died. He came here from Russia as a young boy. Good man. You're all good men. I met Irene at church. We were so very happy. She died too young. I still miss her. Well, I pray for you in college. You're different from the others. Just like my father."

The last two sentences were different from the usual version of his life story, at least as I had been told in preparation. I wasn't sure I liked the comparison with the immigrants. The five hundred-dollar bills did not reassure me. The old man was wrong. I was not different.

Still, I had dug out the old family photograph album and found a yellowed wedding picture of Pa's father. Someone had written on the bottom of it in ink that had almost faded away, "Hugo Hoffman and Gertrude Klein. Wedding 1885."

It was like looking into the mirror. The original Hugo was a big blond lummox with straw-colored hair and a goofy smile. His little bride looked up at him with total adoration. Good man, good father, good husband, good farmer, good patriarch. But different?

Hildy had driven me across the state to college. When we pulled up to the high-rise dorm at the far end of the college, she sighed.

"Dorm Twenty is not a nice place, Hermie. The only thing worse than a college dorm is a prison. Get out of there as soon as you can and rent an apartment someplace. The administration doesn't mind if you sneak out at the end of the first semester."

"But I'll have paid rent for the dorm."

"Forget that. Mama and Papa don't mind. Franky and I both did it. Get out just as quickly as you can."

If Pa had survived Belleau Wood, I could survive Dorm Twenty, I told myself.

The top floor of the dorm, to which I had been assigned, was Bedlam, Dante's purgatory, and a whorehouse all rolled into one. The dominant college goal of most of my dorm mates was to get drunk as early in the

120

day as possible and every day of the week. The dominant smell was a mix of vomit and urine. The loudest noise was from boom boxes and the sexual cries of young women, some of whom were either being raped or crudely seduced. The rape and seduction victims were usually drunk. The entertainment consisted of fights between drunks egged on by those who enjoyed the fun even when the combatants were slashing at one another with knives. Though the knife victims were carted off to the emergency room at University Hospital, the administration made no effort to take back the floor.

I was relatively safe because I was big and strong, though not as strong as I wanted to be. I was also sober, which is an advantage when a drunk comes at you with a knife. After disposing of one drunk, who was almost a foot shorter than I, I dragged him to the office of the resident assistant and threw him on the floor.

"He came at me with this knife," I shouted. "Get him out of here and keep him out, or I'll go the president of the university!"

I don't know how they did it, but the kid did not reappear.

No one even pretended to study. Sleeping was impossible. I could never be sure when a drunk might try to slit my throat while I slept.

It was difficult to get to classes, even when I had figured out where the class was—which required two weeks. I had to budget a half hour for the ride down one of the two creaky elevators and another half hour to walk across campus to the classroom buildings.

The classes were all on the 100 level—World Civilization, Rhetoric, College Math, and Environmental Problems. In each subject we had a large lecture hall session—some four hundred students, with the professor allegedly in charge of the course—then a "discussion group" session with a graduate assistant. An Asian of some sort—Thai I think—babbled for an hour and a half on World Civilization while the students ate breakfast, wrote mail, gossiped, read the newspapers, and fondled one another. Our graduate teaching assistant would usually begin the sessions with a question like, "What did you get out of the lecture yesterday?"

"Nothing," I would respond to the laughter of my fellow victims.

Finally, I decided I would do something about the situation. I dressed up in chinos and a blue blazer, polished my shoes, put on my only tie, and went over to the administration building and up to the president's office. My size and my clothes got me by the security guards.

"The president is busy, Mr. Hoffman," said his unhappy-looking assistant.

"I'll wait," I said, sitting down and opening my single-volume edition of *The Foresyte Saga*.

The president finally emerged from his office, a tall, lean man who looked even more unhappy than his assistant.

"Well, young man, what do you want . . . Oh, I see you're reading Galsworthy . . . What do you think of him?"

"He's a powerful writer," I admitted, "but from that

122

era I prefer Ford and Conrad."

"I quite agree . . . Are you a senior or a graduate student?"

"A freshman, sir. I'm from Lincoln Junction, and I've come to ask you two questions."

He actually smiled.

"Is that all?"

"Yes, sir. I'd like to have a meeting with my adviser because I think I have advanced placements out of all the courses I'm taking. Can you find him for me? Secondly, I'd like to suggest that you send in the campus police to recapture the top floor of Dorm Twenty. Some of the early-Victorian writers would describe it as a den of vice. The main activities on the floor are binge drinking and vomiting. There is at least one knife fight a night and a rape every couple of nights. I've been attacked with a knife twice. Fortunately, I was bigger than the attackers. All of this interferes with my studying."

He studied me intently, trying to decide whether I was joking.

"Russian German?"

"Ja, ja," I replied.

"I don't know where we'd be without your kind. Very well, I will see that your adviser contacts you, and I will instruct the police to retake the top floor of Dorm Twenty. It has a long history of trouble . . . Where do you sleep?"

"In the library till they close it. Sometimes I hide in the stacks."

"I'd advise you to stay there tonight. It would be a

shame if you got caught up in the sweep. Stop by here tomorrow morning, and my assistant will have an assignment for you on the first floor. Thank you very much for visiting me."

As I lay cuddled up in the stacks of the library that night I realized that a man could be president of a big university and have little control .over many of the things that happened in it. The sociology I would study later would explain how that happened. A man was at the mercy of the idiots who supposedly worked for him. That helped me to understand the Church, though the problem with the Church was that the man on top of our Archdiocese was an idiot too.

The next day was a good one. I received my new room assignment and transferred my things to the first floor, which was much more civilized. The top floor was virtually empty. One of my few remaining dorm mates told me that the police had arrested almost everyone.

"It was great fun watching them drag those savages out of here. Finally, you can get something done . . . You getting a new room?"

"I guess so."

"Lucky guy!" He returned to his advanced calculus book.

I found a note from my adviser, with whom I met later in the morning.

"Sorry they gave you the wrong office number. You're right; you don't have to take any of those courses. What do you want to major in?"

"History, immigration history."

He looked up at me in surprise.

"Well let's see what we can line up for you so you won't have to haul ass from the other side of campus every day of the week. It was a dumb idea to build those freshmen dorms over there by the Lake."

I had never seen the Lake, perhaps because the windows were so dirty.

I asked whether there was a workout place nearby. Sure enough there was. I found it, signed up for an hour every day and for an intramural basketball league.

"Keep an eye on the bulletin board for practice times," the young redhead at the counter said to me. "They don't come to get you."

I thanked her and smiled, the first time since I'd come to State U.

"What day of the week is it?" I asked her.

"Friday." She smiled back. "When I was a freshman I couldn't remember either."

Weekend. I had missed Mass for two weeks. I'd better show up the following afternoon.

The redhead was not as pretty as my Kathleen, but she was pretty enough.

So at five o'clock the next afternoon I entered the Newman Chapel—an old wooden church like ours in Lincoln Junction, only not as well kept up. The Archdiocese had never been particularly interested in State U since it assumed that good Catholics would attend St. Clement's. That half the students, including the drunks and the rapists and their victims, were also Catholic didn't seem to make any difference to "Downtown" as priests called the Chancery office.

A young woman, dressed in jeans and a sweatshirt, with short red hair was just ahead of me. She turned around and grinned.

"I thought I heard your big feet, Hermie . . . Everyone says you cleaned up the mess at Dorm Twenty. It doesn't surprise me."

"What happened to your hair?"

"I cut it, silly . . . You're in church, don't talk. I'll buy you a cup of coffee after Mass."

She went up to Communion, and so did I. I'm sure God had forgiven me for forgetting that the last two Sundays were Sunday.

As for my feelings about Kathleen, God was somehow involved in those too, was He not?

After Mass, she linked her arm in mine.

"It certainly took you long enough to find me, Herman Hugo Hoffman!"

"You're supposed to be at Stanford."

"That fell through," she said grimly.

"Why?"

"I don't want to talk about it."

"You'd better talk about it. Whatever it is, you're pretty angry."

"Stop bugging my soul."

We entered an off-campus coffee shop that was too elegant and too expensive for students.

"What happened?" I asked as we sat down.

"We'll have two of your special salads," she informed the waitress, a woman as young as we were, "with blue cheese dressing."

"Sure, Katie . . . Who's the big guy?"

"Oh, him? . . . He's Hermie Hoffman from my hometown on the prairies."

"The guy who cleaned up the mess at Dorm Twenty?"

"See, Hermie, you're famous!"

"I threw all the drunks out of the windows," I said. "They landed on their heads, so they weren't hurt."

"Same old Hermie." Kathleen sighed. "Always flirting with the girls."

"Is your name Kathleen or Katie?"

"Katie is my real name. Kathleen is a nickname reserved for my lovers."

"Why aren't you at Stanford?" I asked, ducking the implication that maybe I was a lover.

"You sound like you're not happy to see me."

"Certainly I'm happy to see you. But I wonder what's wrong."

"My damn fool father is marrying again, at Thanksgiving."

"Oh."

"A nurse at the hospital. Ten years younger than he is. Sexy bitch. I hate her."

"Oh."

"She hates me too. She knows I'm going to make her life miserable."

"You didn't go to Stanford because you couldn't stand the situation."

"Correct! All the silly excitement about the fucking wedding . . . Sorry, Hermie, I know you don't like me to talk that way. My dad is such a goof . . . For eleven long years he's a recluse. Then he falls for the first pair of big boobs that come by him."

"Oh."

"Stop saying that and eat your salad. It's good for you, not like the junk food they feed you inside that awful place."

"You can eat salad in there too."

"Tastes like paper with paste poured over it."

"Is your future stepmother really that bad?"

"Oh, she's sweet and gentle and kind and all that shit. She so wants us to be friends she says, but she doesn't mind if I have to hate her for a while. As if you can turn hate off whenever you want."

"We just came from a ceremony where we promise to forgive everyone, even sexy stepmothers."

"I don't want to hear any of your goddamn religion!"

"Kathleen!"

"Oh, all right! I suppose she's all right. Dad's happy again for the first time in ages. I just don't want to be around them. She's not my mom and never will be."

"But she's a lot like your mom?"

"Sure, dammit, that's the whole problem!"

Silence.

"Well, there was another reason for not going to Stanford."

"Oh?"

"You want to know what it was?"

"If you want to tell me?"

"You weren't there."

I thought my joyous heart would tear me apart.

"Oh," I said again.

"Melissa, another salad for ape-man here. And then

128

one of your steak sandwiches, medium rare. He needs more protein."

She drew her breath.

"OK, Hermie, you win. I'll get over it. I shouldn't have cut my hair just because she said she thought it was beautiful . . . What are you up to these days?"

I told her about my struggles to get my college life organized.

"Yeah, well I moved out of the dorm the second day I was there. My roommates were both whores, worse than that, giggling whores. I rented a little coach house over on Western Street. I guess they kind of expect that freshmen will do it if they have the money."

There was no hint of an invitation in that information. Or was there?

Oddly, I was so happy to see her again, to talk to her, to walk down the street with her, I hardly thought about lovemaking.

So I settled in to university life. Later I would learn that a quarter of the students would leave by the end of the first year, some of them homesick, some of them flunked out because they couldn't learn how to cope with classes and studying, some of them to dry out. The university was resigned to this erosion. Ever since binge drinking became popular with kids our age, colleges simply shrugged their shoulders and let the kids destroy themselves.

I'd send my kids to small Catholic colleges.

Except that I would be a priest and wouldn't have any kids.

IX

So my life settled into a neat routine and became the kind of orderly life that we Volga Deutsche enjoy: classes, exercise, martial arts practice, study, intramural basketball, autumn leaves and then cold rain, lunch every day with Kathleen, and an occasional visit to her computer lab to admire her most recent creations. I was happy again, as I had been during the summer so long ago.

Why martial arts? If you lived on the edge of the jungle, it seemed to me, you had to be prepared to take care of yourself.

The graduate student who was in charge of the lab assured me that she was the most gifted undergraduate that had ever shown up at the lab.

Naturally. She was my Kathleen, wasn't she?

We went to two football games, which we both agreed were "gross." However, we attended every lecture and concert on campus.

"We bumpkins have been starved for culture," I told her.

"You're not a bumpkin, Herman Hugo Hoffman," she insisted firmly. "Stop saying such stupid things."

She took charge of my life. She cataloged (in a notebook) all the mistakes I made in our intramural games. She told me what to wear, where to eat, what I should say and should not say, what I should think and should not think, what exercises I should be doing at the fitness center, what Mass we should attend on the weekend, how much time I should study. It was like having Mama around again.

One night we went to a lecture by a "distinguished theologian" at the Newman Center. He wore a thick Roman collar and an old-fashioned black vest and looked like he hadn't eaten a good meal for thirty years. The new Archbishop had sent him to warn the Catholics in the university about "erroneous interpretations" of the Vatican Council. He argued that nothing much had changed at the Council. Pope John was a nice old man, but not very intelligent. He had been deceived by the "liberal" theologians and the bishops who had listened to the "liberals." All the mistakes would have to be undone. It would take time, but the Holy Father was determined.

There were nine of us in the small hall in the basement of the old church, including Father Horvath, the chaplain, who looked very uncomfortable during the lecture.

It seemed to me that the priest had done a pretty good job attacking the Council. He was wrong, of course. We'd never go back to the Latin Mass again. Still, I was in no mood to argue. I spent most of the lecture fantasizing about Kathleen.

She was not, however, ready to accept, like a "good, docile Christian," what this distinguished theologian had said.

"Father"—her hand popped up immediately— "where was the Holy Spirit when all this happened?"

"What do you mean, my child?"

"I'm not a child, and I'm not your child. I thought the

Holy Spirit protected the Church from error. Where was She when that poor old man was permitting the Church to change?"

"The Holy Spirit blows whither He will. We cannot measure His movements."

"Sounds to me like He was out to lunch when He let the 'liberal theologians' hijack the Council."

Father Horvath did not bother to conceal his laughter.

"Surely the Spirit is behind the present movement to restore the Church to its prior glory."

"Well, shouldn't She make up her mind?"

"You should not use the female pronoun to refer to God. That's heresy."

"I read somewhere that Pope John Paul I said that God was our mother as well as our father."

"He was a very holy man, but he was not a theologian."

"Theologians are infallible and the Pope isn't?"

I would not have expected that Kathleen Anne Elizabeth Quinlan would want to argue about religion.

"Katie," Father Horvath said, "perhaps we should let someone else ask a question?"

"Yes, Father," she said meekly, but, with a crooked grin, she nudged me with her elbow as she sat down.

"Any more questions?"

I took Katie's hint and stood up to my full *dummkopf* height.

"I thought I read somewhere that all the documents of the Council were approved by overwhelming majorities of the bishops and signed by the Pope. I think that Katie's friend the Holy Spirit could not have been absent. She must have been running around all the time."

Father Horvath was startled by the apparition of a plainsman ready for battle. So was I.

"The theologians manipulated it all!"

"The bad theologians?"

"There were few good ones there."

"Father, it seems to me that you are attacking the Church because you want to return to the old ways," I said. "You'll have a hard time selling that to the laity."

"The laity know nothing!"

"They know a phony when they see one, even when he's wearing a Roman collar."

Katie, if that was her real name except to lovers, gasped. Father Horvath gulped.

There were no more questions. Father Horvath showed the speaker out to his car. We tagged along to see what kind of a car he was driving. It turned out to be a big Caddy, the Archbishop's personal limo.

Kathleen turned to Father Horvath as the Caddy disappeared around a corner. "Let's have a cup of coffee, Father."

"I need it after that guy," he agreed. "He is a real jerk. However, Slippery Louie can now write a letter to the Vatican saying that he's retaking the university from the 'liberals.' "

"Won't it make any difference that there were only nine of us here, including you?" my true love asked.

"Not in the slightest. For Slippery what matters is what he did in sending such a man out here."

We walked into the tiny kitchen behind the lecture

hall. Kathleen put the coffeepot on and rummaged in the cabinet for a few stray—and as it turned out stale—cookies.

"You don't mess with those Russian Germans, do you, Father Horvath?"

"Tough people, aren't they?"

"I hope we don't get you in trouble?" I said.

"I'm finished here, guys," Father Horvath said, "no matter what happens. Slippery Louie wants to send an Opus Dei priest here to straighten out the mess, as he puts it."

"What's Opus Dei?" Kathleen demanded, as though she were eager to fight them.

"It's an ultra-Catholic organization that has strong influence in the Vatican. Rome doesn't care who's chaplain at State U, but Slippery figures he'll get points if he turns this place over to Opus."

"Why does he need points?" I asked.

"Because he doesn't want to die in Plains City. He expected he'd get a cardinalatial see after all the ass-licking he did in Rome. They disappointed him when they sent him here, so he's still campaigning."

"What an awful man!" Kathleen poured the coffee.

"Stupid too." Father Horvath sighed.

I began to realize that night that the future of the Church depended on human politics, often of the most despicable variety. The Newman Center was an important part of the Church's work, but for our new Archbishop it was a pawn in his own personal chess game—and not much else.

At Thanksgiving, Kathleen was to fly to Palo Alto for

her father's wedding. As the day drew near she became more irritable. She dismissed all my pleas for calm.

"If your father was remarrying after eleven years, you'd be angry too."

"I'd try to face the fact that my father had the right to live his own life."

"After neglecting me for eleven years, he has no rights at all . . . Besides, I wouldn't mind if she were not such a terrible bitch."

"Takes one to know one."

She lost her temper, which she rarely did with me.

"I am NOT a bitch . . ."

"You sure sound like one."

She drew a deep breath, which didn't work.

"You don't know her. She's a sneaky, conniving adventuress! She knows Dad has a lot of money, and she wants some of it for herself and for the little bastards she plans to bring into the world . . . Dammit, Hermie, it's all about money. She's incapable of loving anyone . . . And I don't want to hear another word from you defending her."

I backed off.

She was a nervous wreck as I drove her down the freeway from State U to MacArthur International Airport.

"Hermie, you MUST drive this Mustang home for Thanksgiving. It's silly to take a bus all the way across the state!"

"I'm not about to risk a snowstorm halfway to Lincoln Junction, especially since I won't have someone in the car to keep me warm."

135

"Don't be GROSS!"

"I want a woman with pretty breasts in a lace bra!"

"HERMIE!"

At least she was laughing again.

"With gorgeous nipples!"

"You weren't supposed to NOTICE!"

"I didn't. I'm just dredging up the images from repressed memory."

She giggled, then returned to the subject.

"I'm going to really ruin her wedding. I'll sulk, I'll be rude, I'll make mean remarks, I'll get drunk."

"You won't do any of those things, Kathleen."

"YES, I will . . . Why won't I?"

"Because you're a good Catholic, and we don't do things like that."

"I will just the same."

"What do I do now?" I asked, as we approached the airport.

"What do you mean?" she demanded. "Haven't you ever been in an airport before?"

"No."

"Oh . . . well, you turn into the parking lot, try to remember where you parked the car, carry some of my luggage, help me to check in, and wait with me till the plane takes off."

"OK . . . I've told you often that I'm a bumpkin."

"You are not! . . . Now remember that you are parked in lane K-10 facing south."

"I'll write it on the parking ticket."

"No way. You leave it in the car, or you'll lose it. You'd lose your head if it wasn't fastened on."

136

She led me to the check-in counter and out to the boarding gates. I was overwhelmed by the crowds, the confusion, the unsmiling faces. I wanted to return to Lincoln Junction.

"Look," she said, "drive the car into the bus station. You can pick it up there when you come back and drive right out to the airport to pick me up. Remember, Flight 914 on Tuesday at 1:00 P.M. from San Jose— that's J-O-S-E."

"Yes, ma'am."

"Don't keep me waiting."

"No, ma'am."

"All right, I get on the plane now."

"I figured that."

"Good, Hermie, you're learning."

She hugged and leaned briefly against me.

"Remember, Kathleen, who and what you are."

"Fuck that stuff," she said with little conviction.

I watched the plane taxi away from the gate, waved at it, then, thoroughly depressed, wandered back to the parking lot. It required no more than a half hour to find her red Mustang.

The next day I drove to the Greyhound Station, remembered to lock the car, and climbed on the night bus to Lincoln Junction way over on the other side of the state. I dreamed about her all the way back to Lincoln Junction. I stumbled into the house, happy to be home at ten in the morning.

"*Ja,*" Papa observed, "that damn bus is always late."

"At least it wasn't snowing."

"Not yet."

"You'd better get a few hours' sleep. I don't want you falling asleep over my turkey and wurst."

Among us Russian Germans, you always had wurst no matter what the festival.

"Is it true that Kathleen went to State U after all?" Hildy asked, when I stumbled down to the dinner table (dinner is always at noontime in our culture).

"Her father is marrying again this weekend. She didn't want to be around for the wedding preparations, so she quit Stanford."

"Doesn't like her stepmother?" Mama asked.

"Not at all."

"They usually don't. So sad."

"Hard on her father," Papa said as he began to carve the turkey.

After dinner, I went outside for a walk. I wore my Lincoln Township jacket because the sunshine and the warmth made it seem like it might as well be spring.

Not a good memory.

However, the brown fields, the blue sky, the smell of the earth where the winter wheat had just been planted all told me that I was home again. It seemed as if I had never left.

I departed on the Monday morning bus reluctantly. Why couldn't I do college by correspondence course from home?

Because my family would be ashamed of me, though they'd never say so.

Besides, I had to pick up Kathleen at the airport.

The snowflakes had already begun to fall when I changed to the express bus at the edge of Lincoln

138

County. We don't have blizzards at Thanksgiving, my ladylove had told me. Except when we did. I left Lincoln Junction at nine in the morning and was due in at nine in the evening. I arrived at eleven the following morning. If the trip were not mostly on the interstate, I might still be out there. I cleaned the snow off the red Mustang and picked my way out of the city by guesswork because I didn't know how to get on the interstate from downtown Plains City. If I didn't find the interstate, I'd never find the airport. I'd miss the plane. Kathleen would be furious.

I did my best to find streets that had been plowed, but it was a long and difficult trip. Fortunately, though the snow was still falling, plows had cleared the interstate when I finally found it by accident. I skidded a couple of times but made it safely to the airport parking lot at one o'clock, just the time that Flight 914 from San Jose was supposed to land. I bumbled around the lobby of MacArthur until I found a screen that told that Flight 914 had been canceled.

What did I do now?

I found a helpful-looking woman in an airline uniform, smiled politely, and asked her what had happened to Flight 914.

"We had a snowstorm," she said wearily.

Then she added, "Were you supposed to meet someone coming in on it?"

"Yes, ma'am."

"Did you call to check arrival?"

"I didn't know you could do that."

She looked at me in patent disbelief, then decided I

139

was telling the truth.

Bumpkin, but with a polite smile.

"Let's see what we can find out."

She walked over to the check-in point and spoke with a harassed passenger agent.

She returned to me.

"I'm sorry, sir. That flight was canceled in Denver. The passengers have been booked on Flight 2003 which, weather permitting, will leave Denver at five this afternoon and land at seven-thirty."

"Oh."

"I'm afraid you'll have to wait or come back later."

"I'll wait," I said bravely.

"Flight 2003 is scheduled to arrive at Gate D-5. However, please keep an eye on the arrivals monitor, because the gate might change."

"Yes, ma'am. Thank you very much, ma'am."

The security system did not want to let me on the D concourse because the car keys set off the alarm. It took me a while to realize that I should take the keys out of my pocket and put them on a tray. I walked down to D-5, collapsed into a chair, and promptly fell asleep.

I woke up several hours later, stumbled to an arrivals monitor, and learned that Flight 2003 was scheduled for nine-thirty, now at Gate C-9. I sighed, bought a hot dog (promising myself that I would never admit that to my parents), and stumbled over to the C concourse. This time I remembered to put the keys in the plastic container and survived without the screening mechanism warning the world that I might be dangerous.

At C-9, they had advanced the arrival time of 2003 to ten o'clock.

"Is that a confirmed time for 2003?" I said, having learned the proper term. I also smiled at the passenger agent.

"I'm afraid not, sir. The plane is still on the ground in Denver. We hope it will be airborne in the next fifteen minutes. It has stopped snowing out there."

"It's still snowing here, ma'am."

"Some aircraft are landing however."

Then I noticed that 2003 was arriving at D-5.

"Is that for sure?" I asked an exhausted passenger agent.

She glanced at her notebook.

"I think so. The plane is airborne now. It should be here shortly."

I returned to D-5. The people at the security point knew me by then and smiled.

"She must be pretty important," a woman said to me.

"She sure is," I admitted.

I bought the *Financial Times* and *The Wall Street Journal* and curled up again at D-5 to read them. When I was finished I asked the woman behind the counter at the gate about 2003.

"We're not sure, sir. The plane is circling about thirty miles east of the airport. We hope to have it down by eleven-thirty."

"If you don't?"

"It will have to return to Denver, sir. The crew's flying time is almost beyond permissible limits."

I curled up and went back to sleep again.

141

Then someone was shaking me.

"Hermie, wake up."

"No," I said shifting in the chair. "I'm waiting for Kathleen."

"You poor dear man. I'm Kathleen . . . How long have you been waiting?"

"What time is it?"

"Twelve-thirty."

"In the morning?"

"Yes."

"Only twelve hours."

"You should have gone home. I could have taken a cab."

We were somehow clinging to one another.

"We Russian Germans obey orders. You said meet the plane. I'm here to meet the plane . . . Rough flight?"

"I was terrified. I thought we'd never land. The crew wouldn't tell us anything. Then we came down, and we couldn't see anything till we hit the runway. I was sure I was going to die."

"You're on the ground, safe, and in my arms."

"I noticed," she said, slipping away.

Then she added, "When I thought we were all going to die, I thanked God that I had listened to you and was nice at the wedding. I wouldn't have wanted to explain to God why I had been a little bitch."

"You weren't a little bitch?" I took her hand as we walked down the corridor to the baggage claim.

" 'Course not. I knew I'd have to tell you when I returned here, and I would be ashamed. So I turned on the charm and was nice to everyone, especially poor

Josie, who is such a sweetheart, really. I even called her 'Mom,' and she broke down completely."

"You DID?"

"I figured my real mom would want me to. I'm so glad you made me be nice."

"All I did was make suggestions."

"You know I always do what you suggest."

I didn't know that.

She drove skillfully through the light snow back to her house on Western Street.

"You help me inside with the luggage, and we'll make sure there are no monsters hiding in the house. Then you take the car and drive back to the dorm. I won't have you trying to walk back in the snow. You can bring it back tomorrow."

"I need the exercise."

"Nonsense. You need a good night's sleep. Airport naps don't count."

We found no monsters, embraced, and bid each other good night. I drove across the campus to the high-rise jungle and promptly collapsed into my bunk, thankful that I had the room all to myself.

The next morning, after calling my family on the public phone in the lobby to assure them that I had survived the bus ride, I walked out into the sunlight and the bitter cold for the walk across campus. Then I remembered I had a car. Blessedness!

I parked in Kathleen's driveway and rang the bell. No reaction. I rang it again and again. Finally, sleepy-eyed and in a robe, she appeared at the door.

"*Dummkopf!* What are you doing up so early?"

"Returning your car, ma'am. I have my history class in fifteen minutes. I knew you wouldn't want me to walk across campus in the cold."

She rubbed her eyes.

"You should have a car."

"Next year."

"You have to get an apartment of your own."

"I will."

I kissed her on the forehead.

"Thank you for meeting me at the airport."

"You're welcome."

"And for telling me what to do at the wedding."

"I only told you what you already wanted to do."

"And thank you for being you."

She brushed her lips against mine and gently closed the door.

Even with the smell of sleep on her lips, eyes barely open, and in a shapeless robe, she was glorious. Yet the romantic passions of prom night were no longer present. We were just good friends. That's all we would ever be.

X

AT SPRING BREAK WE WENT DOWN TO SOUTH PADRE. Both of us were shocked.

"Prairie prudes," Kathleen said sadly.

"I guess."

"Why do kids do such terrible things to one another and to themselves?"

"Hormones. We're at that age in life when we're most

fertile. So our hormones are very strong. You put people in a situation where there's no supervision and no moral restraint, you get Lauderdale and Padre and Rocky Point and Laguna. Besides, not everyone is crazy."

"Not everyone is fucking on the sand?"

"No."

"It just seems that way?"

"Right."

"Let's go home."

"Great idea."

I was not immune to Kathleen in a string bikini. However, like her, I was disgusted by the spring break binge. It was indeed time to drive home.

It was warm in University Park when we arrived, a touch of false spring before winter returned. In Lincoln Junction we were already working on the preparations to plant spring wheat and watching the winter wheat-fields for hints of what the harvest might be. I went immediately to my books and Kathleen to her twenty-one-inch monitor in the Design Center.

I called her in late afternoon and proposed supper at an elegant restaurant at Western and First.

"You're going to take me to supper, Hermie? What an original idea! Are you going to dress up?"

"Even wear my tie."

"Charming . . . Come by at seven?"

"That late?"

"We'll eat Continental style."

I wore my blazer, chinos, and tie—my only "good" clothes. She appeared in a black cocktail dress with a miniskirt, deep cleavage, and a short cape. We had no trouble, thus arrayed, in buying a bottle of Italian wine (Barolo, which she said was totally excellent, and from which we drank sparingly).

"You still dress up real good, Hermie, despite all the junk food."

"And you're totally gorgeous as always."

We toasted each other solemnly, our first toast.

"No more junk food," she said.

"Never again," I promised.

"I was so high up in Palo Alto." She sighed as we sipped our wine and dug into our steaks. "And I'm so bummed out now. I really am a bipolar personality."

"No, you're not," I said firmly. "I've read a couple of books on the syndrome, and you don't fit the paradigm."

"Syndrome! Paradigm! You sound like my father! Are you going to be a psychiatrist or something!"

"No, but if you were really bipolar and were down, you wouldn't be here eating supper with me but in your house feeling sorry for yourself."

"When a big handsome goofus actually asked me out on a date? Don't be silly!"

"See what I mean?"

"Well . . . I don't know . . . I sure have lots of ups and downs."

"Welcome into humankind!"

She reached out and touched my hand.

"It was nice of you to be so concerned about me," she said softly, her eyes shining.

"It was nothing." I felt my face warm up.

"It was wonderful," she said, touching my hand.

It was a lovely spring evening, probably the last for another month or two. We decided to take a long walk to savor every last minute. That was a mistake. Fourth Avenue was not a particularly safe neighborhood. It was a kind of border between the university and the slum. The old houses that students rented were an unreliable border. I was still too much of a hick to worry about urban dangers.

We turned off Fourth Avenue and on to Western, only a block from Kathleen's house.

"There are people following us," she whispered.

I turned to get a look at them. Three solid-looking characters, obviously drunk, just behind us.

"We want your hole, big guy," one of them said. "And we're going to take her."

While I was thinking about the dirty tricks I had learned in martial arts class, they rushed us. Two of them grabbed Kathleen and tore at her clothes.

The other jumped me.

I lost my temper.

I grabbed his right arm and twisted it. He cried out in pain. I twisted it even more, and heard it crack. Then I threw him on the sidewalk and kicked him in the groin. The other two had torn off Kathleen's dress and were pawing at her underwear. I hit one of them in the back of the neck. He fell instantly to the ground, dazed and confused. For good measure I kicked him in the groin too.

The third thug released Kathleen and tried to face me down. Then he turned and tried to run away.

"Call the cops," I yelled at her as I grabbed him around the neck.

"I'm going to choke you," I warned him. "Say good-bye to life."

I had no intentions of killing him. As he struggled, I grabbed one of his arms and broke it. I was surprised at how easy it was to ruin athletic careers. Just to be sure he wasn't going anyplace, I kicked him in the groin several times too.

"If you try to get away," I warned them, "I may break a couple of legs."

The sirens rang almost immediately. Spring break time and the campus cops didn't have much to do. Two cars pulled up in front of the house. Kathleen stood next to me, her dress in tatters, and clung to my arm. She was shivering.

"What the fuck is going on here?" a sergeant demanded.

"Attempted rape," I shot back at him. "What the fuck does it look like?"

"These guys are on the basketball team!"

"No more this season," I said. "And never again here at any rate."

"You took care of them yourself?" a younger cop said in disbelief as he considered the mess of writhing human flesh on the ground.

"I lost my temper."

"You want to come to the station and prefer charges?"

"Tomorrow . . . All I really want is to get them out of the university."

"Yeah, I don't think that will be hard. Too bad they were so dumb."

I helped Kathleen into the house.

"Don't be afraid," I told her. "I'll stay here with you."

Then we were again in each other's arms, first huddling for protection, then caught up in passion. Our hormones, which I had thought under complete control on South Padre, erupted without warning. We were having our own spring break. I carried her into the tiny bedroom of the house, laid her on the neatly made bed, and merged with her body and soul. We were swept up in waves of pleasure that made the breakers at Padre seem insignificant in comparison. No longer mere friends as we had been for almost a year, we were now lovers again. It seemed natural, appropriate, inevitable that we had crossed the line. I felt that I could never give her up again.

I try not to think of that night and the many others that would follow. Memories like that are dangerous. Yet sometimes, especially when the Archdiocese had me locked up and drugged in a mental health center and in my hazy confusion I thought I might be gay, I would remember Kathleen and laugh at the charge.

We went to the campus police station the next morning, though all either of us wanted was to continue our lovemaking.

"You certainly took care of those three guys, Mr. Hoffman," the chief of police said to me.

"I lost my temper," I admitted.

"You must have had some martial arts training?"

"Yes, sir."

"Just as well that you did. They're bad 'uns. We've had trouble with them before. What do you want us to do with them?"

149

"What are the options?"

"You could press charges against them . . . Send them to jail . . . No way any lawyer could arrange for them to walk."

"Or?"

"We could guarantee that they will be expelled from State U. Never get back in. Coach won't like it, but he knew about their characters when he recruited them."

I looked at Kathleen. She was still hollow-eyed and sleepy. She shrugged indifferently.

"Just get rid of them," I said.

"We'll have to get statements from both of you. And, Ms. Quinlan, if you still have what they left of your dress . . ."

"Of course." She sighed.

So we gave our statements. The next day I brought the remnants of her dress to the station. There was a brief statement in the sports section that three members of the team had left the school. The sportswriters did not make much of it.

Meanwhile, Kathleen and I continued to make love for the next several days. I left her house only for the first day of class after spring break. The rest of the semester we engaged in a marathon love affair—without doubt, or question, or guilt. We were in love, and that's all that mattered.

Sometimes I had regrets. It was impossible by then to return to the "good friends" mode of our lives. We had almost carried it off and would have if it were not for the three thugs. Then I told myself that some other incident would have ignited the flames. Maybe our wine and steak dinner and my search for proof that she was not bipolar would have been enough. We were doomed to love.

I won't say that it was a happy time. We were both obsessed. We indulged in experiments and explorations of various kinds of pleasure. We went to class only occasionally. Our grades slipped. I didn't read much. Kathleen forgot about her computer monitor. We ignored our friends and called our families rarely. We were drowning in each other's bodies, we barely found time to see *Amadeus*, and we stopped going to church on Sunday.

For the second time, Kathleen assured me that she was on birth control pills.

I remembered what I had said on Padre. We were in a period of our lives when our hormones, given half a chance, took charge and dominated everything we did. Yet it was not just hormones, it was also love, at least love of a sort. Neither of us would have surrendered so completely to our sexual hunger unless we also admired and loved each other.

How does one separate love and lust? I don't know, but I think we would have soon grown tired of each other if there had not been a lot of love involved. The kind of love that could have matured in time to something more disciplined and permanent? I don't know the answer to that question, and I never will.

As the semester ended we were both exhausted. We struggled to concentrate on our exams, which would compensate for our wasted half semester. I moved back to my room during the day, but we were always together at night. We managed to recoup enough so that on our records the semester would seem nothing more than a bump in our road of accomplishments. We snapped at each other often during the week before exams and didn't say a word to each other for several days. I was looking forward to the end of term when she would return to Palo Alto—where her stepmother was already in the advanced stages of pregnancy. I would go back to the farm and work on the harvest of the winter wheat. We swore that we would write to each other and not forget about our wondrous interlude, yet we both knew that life had to get on. Orgies were great, but not enough to sustain life.

I don't know whether it was odd, but not once during our ongoing orgy did we ever talk about what we were doing or what our future might be. The pleasures of the moment did not seem to require discussion. Perhaps others of our generation did not talk about what they were doing either, but simply did it and when it was over that was that till the next relationship. O slowly, slowly run you steeds of nights, as some Roman poet said.

So she kissed me good-bye at MacArthur International and promised she would write and call often. I promised the same thing, though I knew I would never make a long-distance call from our frugal German house. I drove her car back to State U, loaded my stuff into it, and drove into the city to the Greyhound bus station and checked everything for the evening bus to Lincoln County. Then I took the car to the garage where she had arranged to store it for the summer.

"You should take my Mustang back to Lincoln Junction and use it during the summer."

I knew my family would follow its tradition and provide me with a more modest secondhand car for my very own.

"Wouldn't I look great, buzzing around Lincoln County in a flaming red Mustang."

"It doesn't fit your Volga Deutsche image," she admitted with a sigh. "We have to do something about that."

As the Greyhound lumbered down the expressway, through the golden fields of winter wheat, and towards the sunset, I tried to make sense—perhaps a bad habit I was born with—of my first year at State U. I had survived a lot, learned a lot, and made a lot of mistakes. I had agreed with Horst Heller, my old St. Killian's and Township buddy, that we should find an apartment or a house for the coming year. Since his father was not a farmer and he was not needed in the fields, he was staying at the U for summer school to boost his credits for Harvard Law School.

"Ja, ja," he said, going into Volga Deutsch, "if we can't get along with each other, then there's no one that either of us could live with."

Maybe, I thought, the quick-witted, extroverted Horst and I were the perfect mates.

The word "mate" keyed an image in my brain of Kathleen in the height of sexual ecstasy. Could I really do that to a woman? It still didn't seem possible. What would happen next? It seemed to me that we couldn't continue the affair much longer. What did she think about it? I didn't know and had never asked. Nor had she asked me.

As the Greyhound caught up with night, I relaxed, for the first time since our return from South Padre. Our affair had been more stressful than I had realized. I would not have to worry about it through the summer. Was that the way to think about love? And one's beloved?

My friends who were about to break up with girls at the end of the semester complained about how difficult and demanding they were—high maintenance in the slang of a later generation. I could bring no such charges against Kathleen. Yet our love had still been tense.

If we were to break up, better that it be done sooner rather than later. Otherwise, we would drift inevitably towards marriage. Yet that could not happen because I still intended to be a priest. I hadn't thought much about it during the school year, but it still was my ultimate goal. Two years from then, when I began my senior year, I would have to begin the process of applying to the Archdiocese and to St. Clement's seminary.

The same Archdiocese that sent the idiot to lecture us during the winter.

I fell asleep on that thought.

The next day, a Saturday, we were to have an extended family picnic at our place to celebrate the return of someone after the first year of college. I would be presented with the keys to my very own car, a glimpse of which I had caught behind the house the night before—a flaming red Chevy Citation. I laughed at what Kathleen would say when I told her.

If I told her.

It was a typical Russian German weekend picnic—kegs of beer, buckets of wurst and sauerkraut, singing and dancing to the tune of accordions, fiddles, and (a recent addition) guitars.

"*Ja,*" Mama asked me. "You see the Quinlan girl at college?"

"Now and then."

"She is happy?"

"I think so. Her stepmother is pregnant already, and Kathleen will be there for the child's birth later in the summer. They have become good friends, and Kathleen is delighted at the prospect of a little brother or sister."

"That is unusual, *nein?*"

"As you know, Mama, Kathleen is an unusual young woman."

"Do you two, *ja,* date?"

That was an unusual question for one of my parents. Whatever their curiosities, they rarely probed into the love lives of their children.

"I wouldn't call it dating," I said honestly enough. "Sometimes we have dinner together or I look at her computer graphics work."

I don't think my mother believed me, but I could hardly say that we had engaged in an orgy in the last half of the semester.

I realized again that I was looking forward to summer without Kathleen and pointed questions about her. Looking back on that from my present perspective, I realize I was a heel and a cad. I should have told her that

I was maybe going to be a priest.

As the picnic wound down, Papa rose for his traditional talk. He would not compare my grades with those of my siblings or my cousins. That sort of thing just was not done in our family.

"*Ja, ja,* our Herman Hugo is back from his first year of college," he said, waving my grades. "His work has been *wunderbar*. I often thought that he was not as bright as his brother and sister. He seemed so sleepy and read so many books. Russian Germans don't read much, do they?"

General laughter. Everyone knew that we are bookworm people.

"*Ja,* but he must have read good books, because he got very good marks and we are all proud of him. *Also* we decided that he deserved the present we give our children when they return after their first year of college. *Ja,* he won't have to ride the Greyhound anymore!"

Franky drove the red Citation around the corner and handed me the keys, with his big, goofy smile. Hildy hugged me. The crowd cheered and broke into a German student song. My mother kissed me. More cheers.

I motioned for silence. I was expected to say something funny, not easy for any of us through whose veins Teutonic blood flowed.

"*Ja, ja,* I am completely surprised by this gift. I may leave it here, however, and take the Greyhound. I wouldn't be able to read if I were driving this blinding automobile!"

Much laughter.

It doesn't take much wit to make us Volga Deutsche laugh. Indeed, too much wit and we won't laugh at all.

My cousins and my classmates from Township swarmed around. They wanted to know about Horst and, cautiously, about Kathleen.

Were we still dating?

I don't think we were ever dating exactly.

Do you see much of her?

I avoided a dangerous pun.

Sure.

How is she?

Very happy. She will have a new little sister or brother soon. You know how gracious Kathleen can be. Now she calls her stepmother "Mom."

Sighs of admiration.

I had told them the truth, not as much of the truth as they wanted, but they knew they wouldn't get the whole truth anyway. As it was I had given them just enough information to keep their imaginations churning.

And mine too.

I wanted her to have been at the party and smile at our stolid *deutsch* way of expressing admiration and gratitude. I wanted her to laugh at my flaming red car. I wanted to feel the touch of her lips on my cheek. I had lost all of that because I had rushed into a love for which neither of us were ready.

Because we Volga Deutsche are also terrible sentimentalists, I cried myself to sleep that night.

Nothing much happened that summer. It was a good

crop, not the best, but that kept the prices up. Franky took over the Quinlan farm. And Father Horvath had been assigned to replace Monsignor O'Brien as pastor of St. Killian's. For the parishioners that was very bad news indeed.

The story had begun with what seemed to be good news. The Archbishop himself was coming to Lincoln Junction, something that had never happened before. We were all jubilant. Then came the rumor that a new priest would replace the Monsignor, who would be sent away to the retirement home. The new priest, it was said, was from the university. Everyone knew that they would not like him.

The Monsignor himself made no comment, but the women of the parish reported that he often wept.

Even Mama, never much of an anticlerical, was furious.

"*Ja,* he works hard for fifty years as a priest, puts up with us thick skull Deutsche, and they send him away. It is not just. We will hate this new priest."

"I'm going to call Father Horvath," I told Papa, "and tell him about the situation out here."

"Sure! Is that new Archbishop a pig?"

"An ambitious pig."

"That is so bad among priests. You give up everything to be a priest for your people, then you spoil it all."

Already I was a rebel conspiring against my Archbishop.

"Yeah, Hermie, good to hear from you! How's that gorgeous redhead?"

"She's up in Palo Alto, where her stepmother is about

158

to produce a sibling, something that delights Kathleen."

"That's the kind of girl she is . . . What's going on out there?"

"It's worse than you could imagine. They're furious at Archbishop Louis for taking away their beloved pastor and sending him to a retirement home."

"How is he really?"

"Old, but sound. Slippery Louie is such an asshole."

"Dumb, it seems to me . . . What do you think I should do, Hermie?"

"Do you know the layout in the rectory?"

"Never been there."

"It's a big old place from the days when there'd be a couple of assistant pastors, nice, comfortable rooms for everyone."

"And I start out with the people hating me!"

"Do you give a talk?"

"Yeah, at the dinner afterwards. The Boss preaches at Mass. Frank O'Brien doesn't get a chance to say a word."

"All right, this is what you do. First thing you say is that you're inviting the Monsignor to stay on in the rectory as your mentor and adviser and that you hope he keeps his old room because it is too big for you."

Dead silence at the other end of the line.

"You are a very dangerous man, Hermie Hoffman."

"Not at all."

"How will they react?"

"Standing ovation, cheers, maybe even some German student marching songs from the early seventeen hundreds."

"It will drive Slippery out of his gourd."

"Why does he want to get rid of Monsignor Frank?"

"He has this sick passion for neatness. It is not neat to have old men in a rectory. They all should be gathered in one place. He won't be able to do it in Lincoln Junction, however! It'll fry what little mind he has."

"Will he hold it against you?"

"Hell yes, but that's all right. I'm already persona non grata because some of the right-wingers say I wasn't orthodox enough here. Lincoln Junction is the worst punishment he could think of."

"It's a good parish."

"If they're that loyal to Frank, it must be. I'll be looking forward to it . . . And Hermie, I'll always be grateful. I owe you a favor."

I didn't quite know what that meant.

Simon Isidore Louis would be my Archbishop when I went to the seminary. Would he hold Lincoln Junction against me? From the way he had been described, he wouldn't be smart enough to figure it out.

He made his entrance to the precincts of St. Killian's in his very large Cadillac under the warm July sun while the spring wheat was poking above the ground. If he missed the symbolism of that, he was really dumb. The crowd gathered around the church and down the road was conspicuously silent.

He emerged from the car already in his full purple robes and waved to the crowd as if they were cheering, which they were not. He was a tall, handsome man, with carefully coiffed iron gray hair. Alas, going to fat. His pleasant smile belied the confused, vacant look in his eyes and flushed face. I had read too much history, perhaps, but I couldn't help but think that he looked like one of the British field marshals who had turned the Great War into a bloodbath—French or Haig. Or maybe a bloated British colonel in India just before the Japanese bombers hit his command.

A large phalanx of priests, gathered to gain his attention, I suppose, led him into the church. At the very end of the procession came Monsignor O'Brien and John Horvath. The latter grinned at me and winked as he passed me outside the church. Our plan was in place.

Enthusiastic applause greeted the Monsignor. Archbishop Louis thought it was for him, and he waved more vigorously at the crowd. Our disciplined, if unhappy choir broke into *"Ecce Sacerdos Magnus"* as the Archbishop entered the church. He would never hear it sung better anywhere in the Archdiocese. He should certainly praise the singing and refer to the Russian German tradition of song. I had a hunch he wouldn't notice the choir, wouldn't say anything about Russian Germans, and not much at all about the Monsignor.

He had been so kind to me when I confessed that I had committed fornication with a young woman many times.

"Love affair, huh, son?"

"I guess so."

"Is it over?"

"She's a long way away."

"Do you love her, or is it merely for pleasure?"

"I love her very much," I said, surprised at myself.

161

"Might you marry her someday?"

"I'm not sure."

"The best way to show your love now would be to suspend the affair for a while, would it not?"

"Yes, Father."

"You'll give it a try?"

"Yes, I will."

"Good, now say a rosary for your penance and a little prayer for me."

It had all been very deft. Yet he had made me think again about what I had been doing. Could I really have any doubt that Kathleen considered me a probable marriage partner?

I caught my father, just before he entered the church, a ticket clutched in his huge hand.

"Papa, when Father Horvath begins his talk, he will say something very important. You start the cheering and keep it up!"

He grinned at me. "*Ja,* sure!"

What kind of game was I playing? Who did I think I was to play such a game?

The Archbishop's talk would have been too long on a cool day. In the July heat it was a disaster, especially since he did not have much to say. He did not mention the choir, he did not say anything about the Russian Germans, he barely mentioned the Monsignor save to say he would be comfortable in the brand-new and almost luxurious retirement home that he had "caused to be built." He did not seem to remember the name of the new pastor whom he charged with protecting the faith of the "simple" people from the evils of modern secularism, consumerism, and materialism, especially "sins of the flesh" such as abortion, birth control, homosexuality, and premarital sex. Then he launched into a prolonged explanation of his personal relationship with "our most Holy Father" which created the impression that he and the Pope were on the phone several nights a week. I wasn't sure that the Pope would like the impact on his image with the angry congregation.

Downstairs in the hall, where the old man had stumbled into Kathleen and me practicing our Bach, the Monsignor was permitted to say grace before the meal. I had hidden in a remote corner to see the conclusion of our plot.

The dinner dragged on as the Archbishop chatted with his assistant, Father Peters, and paid little attention to the sullen people. Finally, John Horvath leaned over to the Archbishop and whispered something. The latter's face clouded at the distraction, but he nodded.

"As most of you have guessed," Horvath began, "I'm your new pastor. I'm Volga Deutsche like most of you. My mother was German and my father Hungarian. I know your reputation as musicians, but I've never heard the Mass sung so beautifully as it was today. I know I will love it here in the ultimate prairies."

Polite applause. Thank goodness Papa had the sense to hold back for the really good news.

"The first thing I want to say is that unlike the Archbishop I've been in the rectory here. Monsignor O'Brien was good enough to show me around. It's a wonderful place, a tribute to your generosity in keeping your priests comfortable. There is plenty of room for the Monsignor to stay here if he wants."

I heard my father's distinctive—and loud—cheer. Others joined in.

"Monsignor O'Brien, I hereby invite you to stay on as my mentor and adviser. I hope you stay in your own room. It would take the two of us all winter to move things around. You'd be most welcome. I beg you to stay and help me."

Cheering filled the hall and threatened to tear the roof off the old building.

"As you know," continued Father Horvath, "the Archbishop in his wisdom and generosity has given permission to retiring priests to choose their preferred residence. I realize that the retired priests' home is an elegant place, but please stay here with us in Lincoln Junction!"

Led by my father, the cheering went on for five minutes. John and Monsignor Frank embraced one another, and that set the applause off again. The Archbishop looked puzzled rather than angry. He didn't know what was happening, and he thought he shouldn't like it, but he understood which way the game was going.

So with only a small show of reluctance, he rose, embraced the two priests, and shook their hands. The people of St. Killian's cheered him lustily.

He had been very lucky, I thought. He would not always be so lucky.

In the reception line after the Archbishop had left, John Horvath said to me, "I want you on my side always, Hermie . . . Frank here tells me that it was your father who led the cheering."

"It might well have been; the old man likes to cheer."

"You are a wicked young man, Herman Hugo Hoffman," the Monsignor said as he hugged me. "How's the little redhead doing? Why don't I see her in church anymore?"

I explained that she was for the moment in California with her father and stepmother.

Instantly I regretted that she was not there to enjoy our victory.

The next afternoon, while we were plowing some of the fallow land, we took the usual midafternoon beer break. It was the time of the day when Papa, if he were of a mind, could be expansive.

"*Also* Herman Hugo, that was an impressive trick you played on the Archbishop yesterday."

"Trick?" I said, trying to sound innocent.

"*Ja,* you called your friend Father Horvath and set it all up. Then you persuaded me to lead the cheers, which I would have probably done anyway. You missed one opportunity. You might have had someone ring the bell in the church when the cheering started."

I thought about that.

"It would have been overkill."

"*Ja.* Maybe the Archbishop would have smelled the rat."

"He seems too dumb for that . . . Does anyone else know?"

"Sometimes we Russian Germans are a little slow. They'll figure it out eventually. You'll be the great hero . . . Why does the Pope send us such dumb people?"

"Probably someone in Rome tells the Pope that this is a good man."

"Is he a bad man?"

"No . . . Just so preoccupied with himself that he doesn't notice anyone else."

"*Ja* . . . That's not healthy in the head, is it?"

"No one ever said that you had to be healthy in the head to be a bishop in the Catholic Church, did they?"

We both laughed, finished our beer, and went back to work.

"Still," he said as we were about to enter the house, "you are a very brilliant man. You should be careful about how you use your brilliance."

I was surprised. The scheme to keep Monsignor O'Brien in the parish was a no-brainer.

XI

THE NEXT WEEK, OR MAYBE IT WAS THE WEEK AFTER— I wasn't working very hard on my journal in those long summer days—Mama was waiting for us when we came home.

"*Ja,* Kathleen called this afternoon. She has a little half brother. He is called Edward after her father. She says he is very beautiful and recognizes her already. Her stepmother is doing fine."

"Did she say 'half'?"

"No she didn't. She just said brother and mother."

"That's Kathleen for you. When she changes, she changes completely. Did she leave a phone number?"

"No . . . I thought you would have it, Hermie."

166

"She didn't give it to me."

"And you didn't ask?" Mama sound surprised.

"I figured if she wanted to give it to me, she would have."

That was not altogether true.

"You should find out."

"I'll write her a letter tonight."

Mama threw up her hands in dismay and muttered something about men.

I did write a letter to her that night, which I copied into my journal.

Dear Kathleen,

When we came in from the fields today, Mama told us about little Edward. I'm sure he recognizes his big sister already—a big blur of red with a wonderful smile. Congratulate your mom and dad for me. God bless you all, see you soon.

Love,
Herman

Not exactly a love letter, huh? And not a word about how we had saved the Monsignor and Father Horvath. What was I trying to avoid? Did I want out of our love affair? I still thought of her often and imagined her in the midst of our lovemaking. Yet somehow she didn't fit in the real world of my life in the prairies, though she had grown up just down the road.

Anyway, why had she called in the afternoon when she knew that this time of the year I would be out in the fields? She didn't want to talk to me. Or was afraid to talk to me. Maybe she was uneasy in our love affair too. Maybe she was having second thoughts over the summer. Maybe she could not see herself as farmwife in the Russian German prairies.

Why should she?

We Russian Germans with our long history of Democratic affiliation had never liked Ronald Reagan. We thought that we could see him, a hollow man and maybe already a little senile. So we backed Walter Mondale enthusiastically. He was, we thought, a prairie populist just like us. We were furious when the rest of the country did not agree with us.

As August flamed out, I saw death for the first time. It became a decisive experience in our family.

My great-grandfather, our beloved "Pa," was dying. It was a shock to all of our generation. We had assumed that, with his reasonably good health and joyous laughter, Pa would live forever.

"He can't be dying!" I exclaimed.

"*Ja,* I know," Mama said. "We've had him so long. We all must die someday. Even you, Herman."

"I know . . . We thought he'd live to a hundred . . ."

"That makes no difference to him," Papa told me. "He was never interested in records. He is ready to go now. He wants to be with Irene again. Thirty years now they have been separated."

We all went over to see him that evening. His old face was now somehow beautiful, a finely sculpted skull covered with a thin sheet of parchment. He greeted us with his usual smile and lifted his hand in a little wave. He didn't seem to be dying. Was this what death looked like?

Grandma, who had adored him from the first time she had met him, when Grandpa had returned from the war forty years earlier, held his hand and murmured to him in gentle German. Grandpa leaned against the wall, strong and straight and infinitely sad.

"Ja, "—he shrugged his shoulders as he shook hands with me—"it is time. We should all be so ready when our time comes."

Pa's face was radiant with expectation. He was certainly ready.

"Monsignor was here today with the oils," Ma told us. "We all wept."

Sentimental Volga Deutsche wept all the time. Not so the Irish. However, had not Monsignor wept when he interrupted Kathleen and me at our Bach practice? We were then his innocent children, though perhaps not so innocent even then. Would it break his heart to know what we had become?

I worried about death most of the night. I'd have to face it someday. Would I be as ready? Would I be as content with my life? Would I be waiting for reunion with a loved one? What sense did life make? Were we nothing more than bits of cosmic fluff floating along between two oblivions as someone whom I'd read during the year had argued? How long would it take before no one remembered me?

I desperately wanted to talk to Kathleen and share my pain and uncertainty with her. That's what lovers were for, was it not? What was I doing with my life? Would I be a prairie farmer just like my father and my grandfather and Pa and all the previous generations? What would be wrong with that? I loved the farm. Why not?

Somehow I knew that it might not be enough, not even with a wife like Mama or Grandma or Ma. Not even perhaps with a wife like Kathleen.

Two days later as we were finishing in the field, Mama ran out to join us.

"Come quickly! It is the ending!"

The whole clan was in the clean old bedroom with its high ceilings and furniture brought from the Volga and its toiling Sears, Roebuck air conditioner. My uncles and aunts and cousins all looked as grim as I felt. Monsignor and Father Horvath were taking turns leading the rosary. All of us were Catholics. We assumed that what we were witnessing was not the ultimate end, but only a transition. "For unto Thy Faithful, O Lord, life is changed not taken away." Yet what was happening to Pa seemed so definitive. He was unconscious, his frail old ribs struggling to move ever so slightly up and down. I wanted to scream out, Don't go, Pa! Don't leave us!

I would embarrass everyone. Pa was willing to leave us.

I glanced up at Dr. Guerin, who had replaced Ed Quinlan. He held up a thumb and forefinger, almost completely closed. Only a little time. We all had only a little time.

Then Pa's ribs gave up their useless work. A smile transformed his face. Then he sat up, as though he were recovering, stretched out his arms, and, tears of joy flowing down his face, said in a strong, full voice,

"Irene! I knew you would come for me!"

Then he fell back on the pillow and died.

Awe filled the room. Even those of us who never knew Ma could not doubt that she had been with us in the room. My eyes were glued to the empty space where Pa had seen her standing. I imagined . . . No, I must not deceive myself. I saw nothing.

At least I don't think I did.

Yet back at our house I opened the book of family photos, which had been set on the sideboard to mark continuity and change. I found a picture of Irene Kurtz Hoffman when she was twenty and already married to Pa. It seemed to me that she looked a lot like the face I had seen for an instant in the death room.

It couldn't have been, could it?

When I was doing parish work later at St. Praxides in Chicago I encountered the Irish way of death. They laughed death in the face. Not so many years ago they had made love in the potato fields while the wake was going on. Screw you, death! Even in recent days a wake was a party!

There is something to be said for such a response, as there is for the Jewish practice of in effect having the wake after the burial.

For us Germans, especially Russian Germans, death is a time of deep grief. We do not sob hysterically or throw ourselves on the casket the way the Italians do. But we are somber and heavy and weep all the time. We sing sad and dark music and listen to Bach at his most melancholy.

All of Lincoln Junction gave itself over to that sort of

sadness. In the midst of it I went deep into my soul, what little of it there was at that time in my life. What did death mean, what did life mean, what did anything mean?

"*Ja,* we didn't think he meant that much to you, Herman," Mama said to me, a touch of anxiety in her voice. "You seem to be badly shaken."

"First time I ever saw anyone die," I replied. "Mama, do you think Great-grandmother Irene was really there in the room with us?"

"He thought she was. That's all that matters."

"No, it's not."

She sighed as mothers are wont to do.

"I think most of us believe she was there . . . At other death scenes the same thing happens."

"How old would Irene be if she really returned to lead Pa home?"

"The same age when Pa fell in love with her, young and beautiful like she was seventy-five years ago. Like we will be when we go home."

"Do you believe that?"

She laughed. "Most of the time, Hermie. That's enough for the rest of the time."

The woman I thought I saw was indeed young and beautiful. I had no reason to expect that because I had never reflected on what the blessed would look like.

Maybe I had seen the photo before, and it flashed into my imagination. But what if Irene Kurtz had really been in the room with us, as young and beautiful as she had been in 1910. Did she know that I had caught a quick glimpse of her? Did she care? Was it deliberate?

I don't know the answers to any of those questions.

Those may not be the right questions.

I dreamed of her often during our days of mourning. She always smiled at me as though we were conspirators. Was something trying to send me a message, someone who had earlier circled me with dancing stars? Like Mama, however, I believe now that the blessed are all young and beautiful. At least I believe it some of the time, which—as Mama said—might be enough.

We buried Pa in the old graveyard behind St. Killian's Church, next to Irene. Except now I was convinced that they were young again and loved each other not with the immaturity of youth but with the wisdom of those who really understood what love was about. I wanted to shout as we shoveled the earth in over the casket, we will all be together again.

Fortunately, I managed to control my emotions. I did not want to embarrass my parents, who were watching me closely. I would not crack up. Yet I was awfully close to it.

Two days later we went back into the fields to plow and harrow the fallow fields in preparation for planting the winter wheat. So our people had done after an agonizing loss since the beginning of agriculture in Europe—with heavy hearts and a sense that the fields wait for human grief to run its course.

"Would you mind, Papa, if I leave a week early for school? I'd like to spend some time with the Trappists trying to figure out what my life is about."

His soft blue eyes considered me carefully.

"I would never stop a child of mine from praying. Only assure me that you won't become one of those fellas."

"Not a chance of that," I said with a laugh. "I just want to think."

"You've always been a great one for thinking. Sometimes too much, *nein?*"

"More than others, but not too much, Papa."

"That is so. It is good that you visit the monks now while you're still young and have time before you must make all your decisions."

I realized that I would never have the wisdom of my father. But that was all right too. So the week after Labor Day and a spectacular extended family Labor Day picnic I piled my stuff into my car (oh wonderful words!) and drove across the state to Mallery-by-the-River, still feeling guilty about the amount of beer I had downed at the picnic, the first time in my life I was ever drunk, and so far the last time. No one said anything to me about how I had made a fool of myself, no one except Ma Irene, who by then periodically visited me in my dreams. She hassled me in German, though when she was alive she had, I was told, spoken excellent English, indeed she had attended one of the early classes at St. Killian's. She had doubtless sung the Good Friday Chorale in the little auditorium, just as Kathleen and I had.

Kathleen?

She was definitely on the back burner till I figured out other things.

I left early in the morning, drove across the state with

only one or two breaks, and arrived at the grim old monastery while it was still light. I wondered if I should have called about a reservation. How did monks arrange such things?

As I walked up to a sign that said GUEST HOUSE, I realized that I had already made up my mind during the ride I would become a priest, not because I had to but because I wanted to. I had always wanted to. Not a priest like the monks, but a parish priest like Monsignor O'Brien and Father Horvath. The matter was settled. I wouldn't tell anyone right away. However, it was essential that I become a priest.

"Good evening, Father," I said to the elderly monk inside the door on which a hand-printed sign said GUEST MASTER. "Do you think you could find room for me so I can pray a couple of days?"

He smiled, and his pale blue eyes twinkled with merriment.

"We'd be poor monks indeed if we could not find a place for a young man who wants to pray. I am Father Colm. Please come with me."

He found me a room, which made my first quarters in Dorm Twenty look like a luxury hotel—not that I had ever seen the inside of a luxury hotel, except on television—a cot with a thin mattress, a window that was hard to open and harder to close, a small table that might serve as a desk, an unsteady wooden chair, and a single lightbulb in the ceiling. Well, I wanted to live like a monk for a few days, didn't I?

"You may attend any of the monastery services or none if you wish. You may eat in the monastery refectory or in a dining room in this building. In both cases you must eat in silence. Counselors and confessors will be present in this building at times noted on this card. Please try to remember that silence is important to all of us so that we can talk with God."

"I'll try to make all the services," I said with greater courage than I really had.

"If you take my recommendation, Herman," he said with a smile, "you will not try to make Matins at three A.M. You are a young man, and you still need your sleep."

"I'll try. No promises."

"That is wise."

I ate two of the Hershey bars I had brought along, collapsed on my cot, and slept through till the bells rang in the morning sunlight. Too late for Matins, probably too late for Lauds too.

Yet within a day I fell into the routine of monastic life. During my four-day retreat, I attended all the hours every day, even Matins one day. I decided rather quickly that my vocation, whatever it might be, was not to the Trappists. Work in the field wouldn't bother me at all. I would get over the heavy male smell that permeated the monastery. I liked the silence. However, Matins wouldn't work for me. I'd fall asleep every morning.

It was clear to me, nonetheless, that I was called by God to be a priest, a parish priest, to work and pray for and with the people in a parish, to share my life with them and their life with me. While there was much discussion about permitting marriage for diocesan priests,

I wondered whether you could work like Monsignor O'Brien and Father Horvath if you had a family of your own. I'd commit myself to celibacy because there was no choice at the present. If that changed, then I would, as they say on television, review my options.

As I walked along the riverbank in the shattering silence of the monastery, I planned it out with typical Germanic efficiency. I would finish at State U, apply to St. Clement's seminary north of Plains City and to the Archdiocese. I would find out what their requirements for admission to the seminary might be and shape the rest of my time at the U so that I would be admitted into theology with perhaps some makeup work and be ordained six years from the coming spring at the age of twenty-five. I could hardly wait to get into a parish. That would be that. *Ja, Ja.*

There was only one problem, a shapely redhead named Kathleen. I would have to break up with her. I would tell her as soon as I saw her next week at the U. She would weep and argue, but good Catholic that she was, she'd go along with my plans bravely. We'd part in sorrow but also in hope. That would be that too. *Ja, ja.*

I was such a young idiot. I did not understand human emotions, male or female. I did not understand Kathleen. I did not understand myself.

We had been grace to one another, I told myself. Memories of that grace would shape my life in the priesthood till I was a very old man and she an equally old grandmother. She would die first because she didn't have my Volga Deutsche genes. I would never regret my decision, and, once she got over the shock, she would not regret it either. Our lovemaking would stop. And that, finally, would be that too.

It was all so simple and clear.

The trees along the river shielded me from the direct rays of the sun, but it was still hot and humid. I fought my way through great sheets of searing moisture, a hint perhaps of what hell might be like—a perpetual drought on the prairies.

I reviewed all my vices—a tendency to brood and be mean, hesitancy to act decisively in times of crisis (despite my successful plot to keep the Monsignor in Lincoln Junction), a propensity to loaf, especially with a bottle of beer in hand, an addiction to books, which often lured me away from responsibility to others, a fearsome temper when I had been pushed too hard (witness the three basketball players whose careers I had ruined), a lack of dedication to prayer, romantic German sentimentality, and, oh, yes, sensuality. The last meant, in the code of the spiritual books I had been reading during my retreat, sexual daydreaming and lust, which could possess me almost instantly if I were not wary.

As I reread these notes in my journal, I realize again what a young idiot I was. I had prepared a checklist of presumed vices I would knock off one by one in the months before I went to the seminary. If I conquered all these "sinful dispositions," God would be pleased with me (moderately) and would love me and help me to be a good priest.

I would understand much later that God already loved

me more powerfully than any human love and was pleased with me the way I was. My challenge as a priest, would be pretty much the same as the challenge to any Christian, accepting God's forgiving love and responding to it by forgiving others. Implacable forgiveness manifesting itself through flawed human forgiveness.

I talked to one of the Trappist counselors, Father Kieran, a young man under thirty, a giant man with flaming red hair and a long red beard. (It didn't flame as much as did Kathleen's.) He listened attentively as I went through the lists in my notebook.

"Ah, you're a good lad, Herman, and, sure you'll make a fine priest someday, I have no doubt about that, at all, at all. Still, maybe you should leave a little of your agenda to the Holy Spirit, couldn't you now?"

I felt my face heat up.

"What if he's overworked or is busy in some other cosmos? Can I trust him to remember me? If I don't do it all myself, how will it ever get done?"

We laughed together.

"You're one of them Russian German fellas, aren't you now? Seems to me that you are a lot like Catholic Mormons. You tamed the prairies, and so you can do anything?"

I saw the way our game was going.

"Except they have more than one wife, though in my limited observation one is usually more than enough."

"Which brings me to this young woman you've been dating."

"Kathleen."

"You'll be breaking up with her, will you now?"

"As soon as I get back to State U."

"Do it gently, lad. Don't let her think that God is a better lover than she is, if you take me meaning."

"I take your point."

"It won't be easy . . . You love her, don't you now?"

"Very much."

"Would you marry her if she were ready to marry next week?"

"I would not. I want to be a priest."

"More than you want her?"

"In a different way.'

"I see . . . you started thinking about this when your great-grandfather died a couple of weeks ago."

"No, I've been thinking about it all me, er my, life. Pa's death just brought it all to a head."

"Well, if you were Irish like I am, you'd rethink your decision a thousand times. I'd say once you Russian Germans make up your mind, it is made up."

"I'm afraid that's true."

"Well, I think you'll be a priest, and I know that if you are, you'll be a good one. Only I'm saying you have what, six and a half years to ordination. Let yourself have a bit of an escape hatch between now and then."

"Fair play to you."

"You've been to the Holy Ground, now have you?"

"Only in books."

"And another thing—don't ever forget that God meant us to be happy, not ecstatic all the time. If you're not happy in the priesthood—and most of them are despite what they'll tell you—God doesn't really want you to stay in it, if you take me meaning?"

"I hadn't thought of it that way, and I'm sure you're right, but I know I'll love it."

"I think you will too."

It was a refreshing conversation.

After a monastic supper and a promise to myself that I would have a good meal tomorrow night in University Park, I went out for another walk along the river. The temperature had dropped sharply, and the air along the bank was pleasant in a light breeze, with frogs croaking vigorously.

I studied the stars absently. The breeze had cleaned off the humidity. The sky was dense with stars. Fascinated, I stared at them. Massive explosions millions of light-years away. Then, instead of staying in their fixed places they swarmed down on me and grabbed me up in their wild dance. I should stay away from stars, I thought, as I was whirled around space. I like this dance, but it's scary.

Then they set me down on the riverbank with a thud, and the same overwhelming love seized every cell, every nerve, every idea, everything, my being itself. Everything would be all right. Everything.

I slept peacefully. Irene left me alone. She would come again, but not for a long time.

I woke up in time for Prime, morning prayers. I felt both peaceful and exhilarated. I was on the right path at last.

Then I realized that I would have to face Kathleen in a couple of hours and tell her what had happened.

XII

Horst Heller had sent me a key for our little old wooden house on Sixth Street, a couple of blocks off Western—and an easy walk from Kathleen's place. All the houses in that district, called John Barry, because a man by that name had once owned a farm there, were quaint places that looked as if they had been made by slightly tipsy elves for other slightly tipsy elves.

I pulled into the driveway, made for smaller cars than the Citation, and began to unload. As I was working away a car pulled into the driveway behind me.

"Would you look who has a flame red car?" Kathleen shouted.

My heart leaped, then sank, then leaped again.

"You didn't write."

"Neither did you."

"I congratulated you on your brother."

I found myself walking towards her car. She produced a folder of pictures.

"See! Isn't he gorgeous! Red hair and all! Looks just like me! And he knows who I am!"

The little boy was gorgeous, though there was no suggestion in the picture that he could distinguish his half sister from any other benign presence.

"And your stepmother?"

"Mother . . . She's wonderful! Isn't she gorgeous!"

"Yes she is."

"Tell you what, Hermie, it's my turn to take you to supper. I'll pick you up at seven."

"All right," I said.

"Sound more enthusiastic." She put the car in drive and swept away, a queen going down the river on her royal barge, red hair, long again, trailing behind her.

It was not going to be easy.

It was even less easy that evening. She was wearing a plain light blue sheath that was perhaps technically more modest than the black cocktail dress but still left no doubt about her appeal.

"Put your tie on, Hermie," she ordered me. "This is a big date!"

"Yes, ma'am."

All the virtue of my Trappist retreat disappeared. I wanted this woman. I must have her.

We drove into Plains City and to a place called the Beef Club, the place of choice for wealthy carnivores. She ordered a small fillet for herself and a large T-bone for me and a bottle of Barolo.

"So," I said, after we had toasted each other, "why didn't you write? I took the first step."

She sighed.

"You're going to spoil the evening with your cross-examination."

"I'm not a hostile prosecuting attorney. I'm just curious."

She sighed again.

"You know I don't like to write letters."

"I guess I could infer that."

"I'm afraid to."

"Why?"

"I'm afraid I'll reveal too much of myself. I never

want to do that, never!"

"Why not?"

"I don't want others to know what I'm really like. I don't want to know myself. Yet when I sit down and begin to write a letter—and I must have started a dozen this summer, Hermie—I babble like a spoiled, silly little fool. I guess I am a spoiled, silly little fool."

"I don't think you are."

"Whatever good things I do, you've forced on me . . . When I think what I could have done . . . almost did to Mom and Dad . . . and I would have done, if you hadn't stopped me . . . Whatever good I do you've made me do . . . and now damn you, Hermie, I'm crying like a silly sentimental German . . ."

She grabbed my hand.

"I don't want to talk about it, not tonight . . . Now I have to go fix my makeup . . . Don't let them serve the steaks before I come back."

She returned quickly.

"No more tears tonight. I don't want to become Volga Deutsche by association . . . Now tell me about your summer."

I told her about how Father Horvath and I had saved the Monsignor. I must have been saving the story to tell her because it flowed smoothly and with lots of jokes.

She thought it was a very funny story, though the radiant glow in her green eyes revealed total adoration for her Russian German love. I would have to break her heart.

Our steaks were served and we dug in—beef-eating plains persons.

"That Archbishop sounds like an evil man."

"John Horvath says that he's just stupid and ambitious."

"Comes to the same thing, doesn't it?"

"I guess so."

"Did he send John to Lincoln Junction to punish him?"

"I'm sure he did. That shows how dumb he is. John loves it, and all we thick-skulled Deutsche love him."

"He's not Irish, is he?"

"Hungarian."

"Well that's better than Irish anyway . . . What else happened at home this summer?"

Lincoln Junction was still "home." Yet this elegant, lovely woman would not flourish as a farmwife. I wonder if she had thought that future through. Probably not. When you're young, you have all the time in the world.

"Pa died."

"Your father!"

"No, my great-grandfather, we always called him Pa."

"That sweet old man with the magical smile!"

I had become sexually aroused. I should never have agreed to eat dinner and drink seductive Italian wine with her.

I told her the story of his death with as much pathos as I could muster, if only to cool my emotions and my desires.

"And he saw his wife appear to take him to heaven? Do you really think she was in the room with you?"

"His faith in her presence was so strong that for the

moment none of us doubted it."

"Oh . . . Do you think things like that really happen . . . Sometimes I think my mother comes to me . . . Not very often."

"Really?"

"She was very pleased when I made up with my new mother . . . She would be . . . As far as she was concerned, Dad could never make a mistake . . . Did anyone think they saw your great-grandmother . . . Irene, wasn't that her name?"

I drew a deep breath. My passion settled down. Temporarily.

"I think maybe I did . . . Just for moment . . . She sort of smiled at me."

"Really!" she shivered.

"I don't know. I found a picture of her as a young woman, twenty years old, right after she married Pa. It looked just like the woman that might have been with us in the death room—young and lovely and happy."

"Hermie . . ." She squeezed my hand. "Will we all be that way after we're dead?"

"I told Mama about it. She said that of course we would. She said she didn't believe it all the time, but enough of the time."

"Why would you catch a glimpse of her when no one else did?"

"Finish your steak before it gets cold."

"Yes, sir."

"I'm not sure I was the only one."

"That's true . . . But let's say you were. Why should she pick on you?"

"I didn't think she picked on me. She might have thought I was someone special. I look a lot like Pa when he was my age."

"Oh . . . You still don't see her, do you?"

I was silent.

"Hermie!"

"I'm not sure. I dream about her a lot. Sometimes I imagine that she's around watching me. As you well know, Kathleen, we Volga Deutsche are sentimental romantics."

"Is she angry at you?"

"Oh, no. Kind of caring and, well, solicitous . . . like a great-grandmother should be."

"So she's not scary?"

"Not at all. I kind of take her for granted. Don't we all have a lovely twenty-year-old great-grandmother taking care of us?"

"How wonderful!"

Did Irene, I wondered, approve of Kathleen? Surely she would, but she also knew where I was destined.

We ate chocolate mousse for dessert and sipped a Rémy-Martin cognac with our coffee. First after-dinner drink I ever had. I became woozy. Thank goodness she would drive us home.

I was in a trance, or so I told myself. I was intoxicated by wine and cognac and desire. The hormones in my bloodstream contended with the alcohol, then both of them decided it was time to cooperate. I warned Irene Kurtz to go away. I need not detail what happened when we pulled up in front of her house. She invited me in. We merged in a long and satisfying embrace. The magic was still there.

We undressed one another slowly and reverently, then gave ourselves over to the rich and powerful delights that we always experienced together. Kathleen, I thought, as we both fell asleep, was the perfect bed partner.

And one I must break away from, I thought in the last minutes before sleep.

I woke up first, probably because the effects of the alcohol had ended abruptly. Outside the birds were singing, a light breeze blew in the window of our compact bedroom. I felt satisfied and complacent after another night of exciting love. Then I realized I had a difficult task ahead of me. I would wait till she awoke.

The gaggle of schoolchildren strolling down the street to the local Catholic school (beyond the jurisdiction of the Newman Center) woke her. She smiled happily, stretched, and cuddled against me.

"You do improve with age, Hermie love." She sighed contentedly.

It's now or never, Herman Hugo Hoffman.

"You're wonderful as always, Kathleen."

"Thank you, my love."

"Yet I think we perhaps should break up for a while."

A weak, cowardly beginning.

"Why!" She sat up straight and covered her bare breasts with a sheet.

"I don't think we're good for each other at our stage in life."

"Why not!"

A thunderstorm gathered in her dangerous green eyes.

"We're obsessed with each other, addicted."

"We're in love!"

"But our love interferes with our work. Your grades fell apart last semester. Mine were so bad that I might have lost my scholarship if I hadn't knuckled down the last couple of weeks. You stayed away from your big monitor over at the Design Center. We both stopped exercising. We didn't see much of our other friends. Those things might be all right if we were planning to marry each other in a few months, but we're not."

"I'd marry you next month, Hermie," she pleaded, "if you wanted."

"We're too young to marry."

"I agree, but . . ."

"We act as if we're almost already married."

She pondered that.

"I suppose so . . . We could cool it a little . . . Cut down on the lovemaking . . ."

"Do you think we could really do that?"

"You mean we've already become so involved that we can't stop it unless we break up completely?"

"Something like that . . . I love you, Kathleen . . . But I think that our love is so intense that we might hurt each other."

"Well, we might . . ."

It was almost too easy. I realized with a powerful pain of guilt that I had enormous power over this lovely woman. Too much power.

"You will hurt me now if we break up," she said, tears flowing from her green eyes.

Then the whole ambience of the situation changed.

"It's someone else, some overweight German blonde you've been screwing all summer."

"No, Kathleen, there's no other woman."

Her eyes grew hard. She studied me closely for a moment and jumped out of bed. She dressed quickly—bra, panty, jeans, a golden State U tee shirt, loafers.

"You should have told me the truth, Hermie . . . I suppose I should have known it all along . . . I would compete with another woman. However, I'm not dumb enough to try to compete with God."

She stormed out of the bedroom. Then in a moment she returned.

"Lock the house when you leave. I have a key with me . . . and Hermie"—she looked at me grimly—"have a good life. Be a good priest. I'll look you up on Judgment Day."

And that was truly that. I did not have to tell her. Somehow she knew I was going to be a priest.

Great exit line, wasn't it?

And she hadn't even prepared it.

I put on my chinos and white shirt, stuffed the tie (still the only tie) into my jacket pocket, put the jacket over my arm, and walked out into the sunlight. The Mustang was gone.

I would look her up again soon, so that we could have some better closure to our relationship. I had assumed that she hadn't really meant her "Judgment Day" line literally. Apparently she had. There was no sign of activity around her house. Then one day when I walked by it, I saw a FOR RENT sign. I visited the computer graphics lab to find out if anyone there knew where she was. They were not very happy to see me. They assumed that I was responsible for the loss of their best student.

"She's withdrawn from State U," the lab director said. "We have no idea where she is. We thought you might know."

"Is she pregnant?" one of the young women demanded, looking for a fight.

"No," I said confidently, and made a hasty retreat.

"Where's the redhead?" Horst Heller asked me the following week. "I thought I was doing you a favor by renting a place close to hers."

"We broke up," I said.

"Yeah, but where is she?"

"Withdrew from school. No one knows where she is."

"Permanent breakup, huh?"

"Very permanent."

That was what I wanted, yet I didn't want it either. One learns how important a love is apparently only after losing it. I don't know what I expected would happen when I told Kathleen that I had made up my mind to be a priest. I must have thought that we could continue to be friends. We would return our lives to the situation when we practiced Bach in the auditorium. Now it was clear that we couldn't possibly do that. Kathleen had chosen the best possible course. She had disappeared. Definitively.

And, arrogant clumsy male that I was, I had made a terrible mess of it.

If I had wanted to, I could have found her. She had not disappeared from the face of the earth. There must be a listing for an Edward Quinlan M.D. in the Stanford/Palo Alto area. I could have contacted her by pushing a few phone buttons.

Yet what good would have come from such a phone call? She wanted out. I should respect that desire. Besides, what could I have said?

Hildy called in November to tell me she was engaged to Freddy Mueler, a classmate from St. Killian's who taught with her at Township. I pretended to be surprised, though I would have bet on the union at least five years earlier. I congratulated her and wished them a life of happiness.

"Whatever happened to you and Kathleen?"

"We broke up."

"Serious breakup?"

"I think so. She's left State U."

"I know that; she's going to Palo Alto."

"Jesuits," I said with approval.

"Her decision or yours?"

I hesitated.

"Mostly mine."

"Maybe you will get back together?"

"I don't think so."

"That's a shame."

"Maybe."

We chatted a bit about wedding plans. I told her to give my best to Freddy—called Frederick the Great in our house.

After I had hung up, I sat and stared at the phone. Now I knew where she was. I could push a few buttons . . .

192

What would be the point? I'd open the old wounds and maybe cause some new ones. What was done was done. I could have handled the problem so much more wisely. Maybe it didn't matter. Yet I had been a clumsy male and made a difficult situation messy. At least she knew she had not been replaced by another woman.

We'd have a lot to talk about on Judgment Day.

Did I miss her still? Every minute of every day. I missed her smile, her laugh, the affection in her voice when she called me "Hermie," the touch of her fingers against my hand, her contagious joy when she was joyous, her sadness when she was in a melancholy mood, the curve of her body when she was rushing somewhere.

I'd knew I'd recover eventually, but one part of me didn't want to. Moreover, as a Russian German, I had a certain propensity to enjoy melancholy.

"Negative sentimentality," Kathleen would have said.

However, our love and our friendship were over.

And, as I said to myself several times every day, that was that.

XIII

IN EARLY DECEMBER, MONSIGNOR MEAGHAN DELIVERED a tirade against a cable television channel that had scheduled a film about sexual abuse in Lafayette, Louisiana. The Monsignor was a pudgy, bald little man with a red face and a high-pitched, irritated voice.

"The film is a dishonest, I might say diabolical, attack on the Catholic priesthood and on the Church. I urge all good Catholics not to watch and call their protests into Channel Fifty-nine. They should also bring pressure on those who advertise on Channel Fifty-nine to withdraw their support or face a Catholic boycott. I can assure all good Catholics that such an abuse case, if indeed it had happened in Louisiana, which I find unlikely, could never happen here. The Archdiocese of Plains City, under the leadership of the Most Reverend S. I. Louis, has established procedures to protect the good Catholic people of Plains City from the very rare priest who might engage in such behavior. Channel Fifty-nine defames the Catholic Church. It also defames the Archdiocese and our Archbishop."

The anchor person informed us that Monsignor Meaghan refused to answer reporters' questions.

"Well," said Horst, "I guess we'll have to watch it."

"His statement is the best ad that Channel Fifty-nine could hope for. Why can't we have a more articulate spokesman?"

The film was a cautious and moderate portrait of sexual abuse by one priest in one diocese, abuse that was horrible and injured several children. I remembered the visiting priest who made a pass at me in the sacristy at St. Killian's.

"Terrible stuff, Horst," I said. "Does it happen around here, I wonder?"

"Sure it does. Lawyers are afraid to take on the cases because they know the Church has deep pockets and lots of influence. It's a joke at the law office where I interned last summer. My bosses said that someday it will explode, and the Church will be in deep doo-doo."

"They certainly manage to keep it quiet."

"That's Father Peters's job, Richard Peters. He's called the victims' advocate. As soon as there's a complaint, he visits the family and tells them that it is his job to take care of the complaints of the victims and their family. He is on their side, he explains, against 'Downtown.' He's a very charming and persuasive man. In fact he's part of the response team at the Chancery. His job is not to protect the victims and their families but to beat down their resistance. The men in our law office says he's very clever at doing that."

"He *lies* to them?"

"That's his real job. He's the Archbishop's official liar. He tells them the psychiatrist and the police have cleared the priest. If charges are brought against him, the Archdiocese might have to sue the family for defamation. He will do his best to prevent that, but he can't promise."

"That's what's diabolical!"

"Priests stand together, Hermie, just like cops and doctors and farmers. They take care of their own. People know that the Archdiocese has deep pockets. Their lawyers, afraid they'll lose a lot of money and a lot of clients if they take the case, advise them to settle for whatever they can get."

"I can't believe that, Horst . . . Do the people settle?"

"They don't have much choice. Priests advise them to settle. Other priests spread the word that they're just out for the money. They're tired of fighting the Church."

"So they settle."

"The good, kindly Father Peters, now their close

friend, tells the family that the Archdiocese will pay for counseling for their son, give them twenty-five thousand dollars for a settlement, and send Father off for treatment. He promises that Father will never be reassigned to work with young people. The family settles and signs a document that will be sealed. Father Peters and Monsignor Meaghan and the Archbishop all celebrate that they have avoided another public embarrassment and kept their expenses lower than that of any other city in the country. I think that's just talk. They don't know what other dioceses pay out. Father Peters writes out a report with the details of his brilliance and puts it in his files."

"Isn't that dangerous?"

"No judge will ever permit access to the Church's confidential files, not in this city."

"I'm shocked, Horst . . . Don't they worry about what happens if any of these stories should get out?"

"Not much. It's worked so far. Why won't it always work?"

"They don't reassign the priest do they?"

"Sure they do. They say the place they send him to has cleared him. They don't announce his reassignment, and they don't warn the pastor who finds him under his Christmas tree."

"Dear God in heaven!"

"Not all priests are saints, Hermie, you know that. Not all archbishops either."

That night as I tried to sleep I pondered the thought that I had rejected Kathleen's love to serve a Church that was so corrupt. Then I told myself that it was not the corrupt and reckless priests at the Chancery that I would be serving but God and His people. I also resolved that when I was a priest, I wouldn't let Monsignor Meaghan and his friends do that to any of my people.

It was, as it would turn out, a dangerous promise to make.

The next morning Channel 59 reported that the audience ratings were the highest ever for its movies. The Monsignor had done a fine job of advertising. The *Prairie Reader*, a weekly published by some people at the university, offered a very positive review and reported interviews with Catholics who said they were shocked but not surprised. One woman offered, "Everyone knows there are some rotten apples in the priesthood, and the Church covers it all up."

The *Prairie Reader* also provided a very cautious editorial in which it warned the Archdiocese that in many other cities around the country the cover-up strategy was not working. It pointed out that some of the people who had been involved in the Lafayette case had proposed at a meeting of bishops at St. John's Abbey in Minnesota a new program for bringing the abuse problem out in the open. The bishops had discussed it, but had not acted on it, in part because they thought the three men were merely trying to make money off the Church. At the meeting they had been told that "pedophilia" was not a spiritual problem but a psychiatric one. There was no known cure for it. No responsible psychiatrist, it concluded, could possibly recommend that a "pedophile" be reassigned to work with children. The Chancery declined to comment on the *Prairie Reader* article. "It is too small a paper to take seriously," a spokesman for the Archdiocese said.

I remembered again the visiting priest who had tried to make a pass at me in the sacristy. I wondered and worried.

My love for Kathleen persisted. I missed her. I felt guilty about the way I had ended the relationship. Sometimes I hungered for her. Slowly this messy combination of feelings declined, though my admiration for her increased. Her abrupt departure from State U showed that she meant it when she said she would not compete with God. Or perhaps she had returned from the San Francisco area only to be with me. I still couldn't comprehend my emotions or hers. Finally, I came to realize that though I might not see her again till Judgment Day (which was probably a long way off), she would always be part of my life, and I should be grateful for her. Leave it at that till later on, when I had the perspective from which to view my late teens.

That was wise self-advice. I was not always ready to accept it, however. Earthbound Russian German farmer that I was, I wanted everything to arrange itself in neat rows like a wheatfield did.

Occasionally I realized that it was probably a difficult time for her too. I prayed for her and, moved by what I thought then was great generosity, I prayed that she would find a husband worthy of her.

I prayed a lot about many things. I went to Mass every day, said the rosary, read the Bible and spiritual books, and meditated regularly. I was already beginning to live like a seminarian and a future priest. Looking back, I think that on occasion I came close to the edge of being a kind of religious nut, a person who by sheer willpower was trying to force the hand of God. Make me a saint now, please, so I can relax. Eventually I recovered from that because of sheer exhaustion and the release of working on the farm every summer.

I worked very hard on my studies. I wanted to be able to present to the Archdiocese an impressive academic transcript from both high school and college. During the summer before my senior year I informed my parents that I would attempt to enter St. Clement's Seminary the following year. They were both extremely happy.

"We have been praying all your life for this grace," Mama said when she could control her tears.

"Damn good thing," Papa said. "About time you told us."

"That's why you broke up with Kathleen, isn't it?" Mama asked.

"I guess so."

Before I returned to State U, I collected baptism, first Communion, confirmation certificates, letters of recommendation from Monsignor O'Brien and Father Horvath, and my transcript from Township. Then I had a full physical exam at the University Health Center. I waited till early in the second semester to pick up the most recent record from the registrar's office, which noted that if I sustained my work in the second semester I would graduate *summa cum laude*. That surprised and delighted me. The honor would delight my parents and impress the Archdiocese.

Horst Heller, who had figured out my vocation a couple of months after I broke up with Kathleen and whispered not a word to anyone, watched my preparations with a bemused smile.

"There are not many seminarians anymore, Hermie," he said, shaking his head. "As long as you can read and write, walk a straight line, and don't have a gay lover, they'll welcome you with open arms."

I knew that was probably true, but, Volga Boatman that I am, I wanted to do it right, *nein?*

I also applied to St. Clement's. They replied within a week. I was tentatively accepted, pending a recommendation from the Archdiocese. Finally, working up all my courage, I mailed my dossier of credentials to the Archbishop and asked that I be accepted as a seminarian for the Archdiocese of Plains City. I received no reply.

A month after my application to the Archdiocese, Tim Goodwin, the chairman of the History Department, took me aside after a presentation I had made to his graduate seminar.

"Mr. Hoffman, you're one of the best undergraduates we've had in a long time. Should you be considering graduate school, we could offer you a quite decent package here. Or, alternatively, I'm sure my old alma mater, the University of Chicago, would be delighted to have you as one of its students, doubtless with a scholarship or assistantship of some sort."

My heart flipped. I had thought often during my junior and senior years that I would like graduate school, especially in history. However, I wanted to be a parish priest, and that was that.

"Thank you very much, Dr. Goodwin. I appreciate your vote of confidence. However, I have already chosen my graduate school—St. Clement's Seminary!"

"You're going to study to be a priest?" He gasped and recovered himself. "Well, congratulations! The Roman Catholic Church needs good priests these days. In you they will have one of the best."

I thanked him and wondered why the Archbishop had not responded to my application.

Finally, I received a form letter instructing me to present myself at the office of Monsignor Meaghan, who was the chairman of the Vocations Board of the Archdiocese the next day at 3:45. The date and time had been scribbled in.

I arrived at the Chancery at 3:15. A woman in the middle years with a frown carved into her face looked at me suspiciously.

"So you think you want to be a priest, do you?"

"Yes, ma'am."

"We get a lot of nuts who want to be priests. Have to turn them down. Enough problems with the sane ones."

"Yes, ma'am."

"Monsignor is busy now. We'll try to squeeze you in before the end of the day. Wait in that room."

She gestured to a cramped little room next to her office. I waited there anxiously till five o'clock as many popes whose paintings filled the walls stared suspiciously down at me. As I waited anxiously I tried to say the rosary.

"Well, Monsignor usually goes home now. He works very hard all day. However, he has agreed to see you for a few minutes. This way please."

Later in life I would think that Monsignor Meaghan looked like a dissolute Irish Buddha, short, sloppy, fat, bald, nasty. He lacked the Buddha's serenity, however.

"Well, Hoffman," he said as he glanced at my papers, "you would have been wise to do your college at St. Clement's too. As it is, we hardly know you."

"Yes, Monsignor."

"And I'm not sure"—he sighed—"that you'd be happy in the priesthood. You're obviously very intelligent. However, we are not impressed by grades. We need good, hardworking priests, not intellectuals."

"Yes, Monsignor."

Hardly the "open arms" Horst Heller had predicted.

"Are you homosexual?"

"No, Monsignor."

"The Pope thinks there are too many homosexual priests in this country. We'll have to be sure about you."

"Yes, Monsignor."

"We'll need a complete physical exam."

"I had one recently at the University Health Center."

"Oh, yes, I see . . . Well, I'm not sure we can accept this. I'll have to talk to the rest of the board.

"No letter from your pastor . . . Young man, our checklist for applicants clearly specifies that you should present us with a strong letter of recommendation from your present pastor."

"Yes, Monsignor. There's a letter from Father Horvath in a sealed envelope as you require."

"I don't see it. What are you trying to get away with, young man!"

"I'm sure it's there, Monsignor. An envelope with the letterhead of St. Killian's in Lincoln Junction."

"Oh yes, here it is." He cast the envelope aside as though it didn't matter. "He's been out there in that hellhole for only a couple of years. He wouldn't know anything about you."

To this day I don't know whether I was being tested or whether the Monsignor was always nasty.

"I was active in the Newman Center at State U, Monsignor. He knew me there."

"Well, we'll have to judge how much trust we can put in his judgment."

"And there's another letter from Monsignor O'Brien . . ."

"I'm sure there is not." He fumbled with trembling fingers through the dossier. "No, nothing else . . ."

"It's on St. Killian's stationery . . . That green envelope in your left hand, Monsignor."

"Oh, yes . . . Well, he's a senile old man. We have to be skeptical of anything he writes."

"He is not senile, Monsignor," I said firmly.

"We'll have to see what the board says . . . You must submit to psychological screening. We can't act until we have a report from Dr. Straus . . . You should have sent your application earlier."

"I sent it two months ago, Monsignor. You'll note that my letter is dated March first."

"Young man," he said angrily, "the issue is not when you sent it, but when I received it."

"Yes, Monsignor."

My usual dormant deutsch temper was stirring. I must be careful. I didn't want to blow it. The man had all the power, and I didn't have any. I must not offend him.

"I'm not sure that we would want you, young man, and certainly not without a meeting of the board. We are all very busy men. I'm not sure when we will be able to meet again. In any event, you must call Dr. Straus and arrange for screening. We can't do anything without his report."

"Thank you, Monsignor."

"And if we do take you, you'll have to pay the costs at St. Clement's—room, board, tuition, the whole thing. No charity for you just because you're Deutsche. We're not in the business of providing seminary education for people that can afford it. Understand?"

"Yes, Monsignor."

I had every intention of paying for it. My father had begun to pay me for my work on the farm when I was fifteen. He had continued to pay me. I had more than enough to see me through the seminary, and I could continue to work during the summers before ordination.

And I truly wanted to hit him for his implication that the Deutsche had not paid their way. It was a matter of principle for us that we never relied on "Downtown." My dark side promised that someday I would get even. I told the dark side to be quiet.

He jammed the papers into my dossier, missing the physical exam report and John Horvath's letter.

"You'd better put these two documents in the folder, Monsignor," I said, lifting the documents from the floor where he had tossed them.

"I don't need any help from you, young man!"

Nevertheless, he stuffed the documents into the folder, pushed it aside, and picked up another set of documents.

My retreat was as dignified as I could make it. He was a stupid, cruel man. Had I given up Kathleen for this kind of priesthood?

I called Dr. Straus's office up in Rocky Hills—an affluent suburb north of Plains City, which could claim no hills and was not rocky. After a week of such calls, his bored secretary set a date at the end of May.

"You seminarians seem to think we run this office schedule just to suit your convenience."

"No, ma'am."

"You should have submitted your application earlier."

"I mailed it to the Archbishop on March first."

"The issue is not when you mailed it as it is when we receive it."

Right.

My appointment was at noon. Dr. Straus's office was in a bright new shopping plaza and office complex. Outside it said FAMILY PRACTICE AND COUNSELING. I began to suspect that he was not a psychiatrist. Probably a friend of someone at the Chancery. His waiting room was filled with mothers and small children in varying degrees of discomfort. I identified myself to the receptionist.

"You do not have an appointment, young man."

"I believe you gave it to me, ma'am."

"I have no recollection of your name; Hoffman, is it?"

"Yes, ma'am . . . Here it is, right next to noon."

Were all the gatekeepers for the Archdiocese stupid?

"Oh, yes, well, I'm sorry, you'll have to wait in line like everyone else."

I had brought along a book, but I found myself playing with the various kids who were sniffling and crying and complaining. I told them stories and sang songs with them, despite complaints from the receptionist. Finally, at five o'clock I was admitted to Dr. Straus's office with its oak panels, plush sand rugs, and elegant oak furniture.

"Doing a little entertaining out there, I hear?"

"Yes, Doctor. For some reason I don't quite understand I get along well with kids."

"Enough to raise prima facie suspicion that you are not emotionally mature enough to be a priest."

Dr. Straus was of medium height and movie star handsome, with tanned skin, wavy hair, a crisp little mustache, and a bright white smile. Some of these good looks might, it seemed to me, to have been artificially cultivated.

"Priests should get along with children, Doctor."

"But not if they wait till the last minute for psychological screening."

"I sent my application to the Archbishop on March first, Doctor."

"You miss the point that the important date is when I receive the request for evaluation."

Even a bumpkin like me begins to see something suspicious when everyone delivers the same irrelevant cliché. Others had been put through this process before.

Either I was being tested—which suggested a very sophisticated if cruel ploy—or the Archdiocese was monumentally incompetent. As the day had worn on, I more and more suspected the latter.

"Yes, Doctor."

"Well, anyway, go into this room and fill out these questionnaires. We get right inside of you with them, so you may as well tell the truth."

The big one was the standard MMPI, which I had taken at Township in my sophomore year. An old and oft-used instrument, it didn't tell me much about myself that I didn't already know. It certainly did not screen for the priesthood except at the lower and upper ends for any sort of mental problem. Some of my psychologist friends at State U told me with great glee how one could cheat at it in such a way as to drive the analysts crazy.

I was angry enough to think about that. However, I had to get by this fake if I wanted to be a priest, so I went through it quickly and put it aside. The other test was no more suitable for the alleged goal of testing me for the seminary. It asked about how I would interpret some twenty images and pictures, a version of what my psychologist friends would call a thematic apperception test. The secret here, I was willing to bet, was to discover whether I was dangerously creative—a trait that might fit in with my dangerously high grades. So I repressed my instinctive reactions and replied in the way that a dull bumpkin from Lincoln County might reply.

When I returned to his office, after knocking discreetly on the door, I found the doctor purring in his rich and seductive voice to someone on the phone, someone of the opposite gender I would have wagered.

"Dammit, kid!" he said, hand over the phone. "Didn't they ever teach you out there in Hicksville to knock on the door when you come into a room?"

"I did knock, Doctor."

"Not loud enough! Well, come in and sit down since you've already interrupted me . . . A patient. I'll call you back."

"Here are the tests, sir."

"Yes, well, you certainly did them quickly enough." He put them aside as though they were useless.

"Yes, sir."

"Now I have to ask you two questions. Don't think you'll get away with anything. Those tests will give you away."

"Yes, sir."

"First of all, have you ever had sexual intercourse with another male?"

"No, sir."

"Sure?"

"Absolutely. If I had, I'm sure I'd know it."

"And during the last two years have you had sexual intercourse with a woman? I don't mean fooling around. I mean full sexual intercourse."

It had been two and a half years since my last tango with Kathleen.

"No, sir."

"Are you telling the truth? These tests will trip you up if you're not."

They would not. Had he intimidated other applicants with the same lie?

"I am telling you the truth, Doctor."

"Well, we'll see about that . . . Now get out of here. You've taken enough of my time. We'll let you know of our decision after the board has its next meeting. I can't promise you when that will be. Perhaps before summer is over. Perhaps not."

"I understand, Doctor," I said, my tongue now firmly in my cheek, "how busy all you men are."

"Damn right."

A fake and a fraud and thus not a man to mess with. He was quite capable of interpreting the harmless tests I had taken as a proof of some grave psychological problem.

Outside in the shopping plaza, a warm spring sun was shining on the elegant shops, the expensive new cars, and the well-dressed women (mostly) and men who were strolling about under the shady trees lining the walks. One of the women had long red hair and a figure like Kathleen's. For a minute I thought . . . then I realized that I had given up Kathleen for a Church, which, at least locally, was run by incompetents and fakes.

Did I know what I was doing?

As I walked to my car I saw another woman, young and pretty in a pale aquamarine dress, who might have been Irene. She might have smiled at me. I almost stopped and asked whether her name might be Irene. Then she was gone. The young woman would have thought I was out of my mind. Maybe I was. It was indecent for a woman who had been dead for thirty years to wander about a shopping plaza late on a spring afternoon in an aquamarine dress. Go back to paradise with your husband, I ordered her.

I quickly apologized. Maybe heaven was not a place to go back to, but a place near us. Later, when I was working at St. Praxides, I learned that the Irish had believed that and to some extent still did. Maybe they were right. I don't know.

Anyway, I sat in the car for a few moments, trying to gather my wits together. I had moved from the unreal world of the Downtown to another equally unreal world, though far more pleasant. I told myself that Dr. Michael Straus did not really exist and my great-grandmother really did.

As I drove out of the parking lot and headed for the interstate, which would take me around the city and back to State U, I thought I saw the woman in the aquamarine dress again.

She also showed up at my graduation a few days later, again in the aquamarine dress. As always she was in the background, caught in a blink of an eye and in another blink gone. This time she seemed to have a camera with her . . .

Otherwise, it was a great event. My parents were proud that they had put all three of their children through college and that the youngest was now about to answer their lifelong prayers and become a seminarian, hopefully even a priest. Moreover, their daughter was carrying in her arms her daughter, Trudy, the first grandchild. I looked around at the family, all of us descendents of Irene Kurtz, even plump little Trudy, sound asleep. Why not take a picture of the whole crowd?

Did they have cameras in the world to come?

What did I know?

"You look mystical today, Hermie," John Horvath said to me. "Or just dreaming of ordination day?"

The question startled me.

"I was just thinking of Pa and Ma," I said, not altogether untruthfully.

"You never knew her, did you?"

Not till recently.

"She died ten years before I was born."

"Her picture is all over the parish records from the nineteen fifties, a vigorous and well-organized young woman, it would seem."

"I could easily believe it."

You bet.

Come to think of it, she looked a little like Hildy, not as tall and not as slender, but the same face.

I felt woozy.

Papa dragged us off to a *deutsch* lunch at a German restaurant in University Park, a place that Kathleen and I had not frequented during our days together.

Was she graduating somewhere that day or that week? I would have to find out on Judgment Day.

As we drank our dark beer and ate our wurst and schnitzel and rotbrat, I told John Horvath, who was sitting next to me, about my problems with the Archdiocese.

He shook his head in dismay.

"Don't worry, Hermie. They always do that. It's more

stupidity and incompetence than malice. They are frightened men, in way over their heads. They can't keep up with anything."

"Who are they afraid of?"

"Rome, the clergy who are restless under Slippery Louie, the debt that increases every year, the decisions they need to make and haven't, the pushy laity, the *Prairie Reader*, which is edited by a Catholic and has a mole inside the Chancery, the sex abuse thing, which they deny is a problem but know better, the demand for new Catholic high schools, homosexuals, Opus Dei, which watches their every move—the same fears that haunt most American bishops."

"What fun then is it to be a bishop?"

"Not much fun at all . . . You see, the old Archbishop, one of the young Turks at the Council, became very nervous when he saw what was happening afterwards. As he grew older he withdrew from most everything, with an occasional sortie to knock down someone who had annoyed him. He surrounded himself with mediocrities like Meaghan and Straus and Joe Kennedy, the in-house lawyer. Then he added a few clever psychopaths like Dick Peters. The diocese froze in winter ice and never thawed out."

"So everyone hoped that the new Archbishop would be better?"

"Right. They didn't realize that it's Rome's policy to replace a dead idiot with a live one, so nobody will notice the change. The problem with Slippery is that he's not only dumb, but ambitious. He wants the crimson for himself. He'd be afraid to make decisions in the best possible situation. With Plains City in the mess that it is, he's practically paralyzed. So we sink deeper in the mud."

"I hadn't realized things were that bad, John."

"It doesn't affect us much in the parishes, though you'd like to have a leader who is intelligent and inspiring. It's a long way from the Downtown to Lincoln Junction. Heck, it's a long way to St. Cunegunda, the parish down the interstate fifteen minutes from here. You can get in trouble if some right-wing crank complains to Rome about you. Otherwise, there's not many problems."

"It should not be that way," I said.

"Jesus should have turned the Church over to the cherubim not humans . . . Anyway, don't worry about the seminary. If you don't hear by August, I'll have a word with the abbot at St. Clement's. He'll let you in. Meaghan will get around to dealing with your application eventually. He'll find someone else to blame for the delay."

"I suppose that it's the people in the parishes that make it worth the effort."

"You got it, kid. Don't ever forget it. Too many of the guys obsess about Slippery and Meaghan and the other morons and don't pay any attention to their own people."

Later, as we were breaking up at lunch, and he was about to drive back to Lincoln Junction, he shook hands, and asked, too casually, if I ever heard from Kathleen.

"Not a word," I admitted. "Maybe she's graduating

from Santa Clara today. As far as I'm concerned she's disappeared completely."

"Maybe that's just as well. Must have been hard to lose her."

"Yes and no."

The next day I packed all my college stuff into my Citation and drove away from University Park, I assumed for the last time. Despite my Volga Deutsche propensity to *weltschmerz,* I felt little emotion at leaving State U. It had been a necessary transitional place in my life. I had learned a lot, grown up a little, made a couple of decisions, and perhaps become a man.

Perhaps not.

The harvest that summer was much smaller than the previous one. Papa had gone long at the Chicago Board of Trade, while many of our neighbors had sold short as they had done on previous summers. We made a lot of money, and they lost a lot.

"*Ja,* it doesn't seem right to make money off a poor crop," Papa admitted. "The poor farmer has no choice."

"Have you ever been to Chicago, Papa?"

"Only when I was in the Army. I didn't see much."

"So you've never seen the Board of Trade."

"*Nein.* I don't want to. It's a crazy place."

I did not tell him about the suggestion from Tim Goodwin that I might be able to make it in graduate school at the University of Chicago. That was a door God had closed on me.

Irene had the decency not to wander around Lincoln Junction.

Yet, camera in hand, she lurked in the back of some

of the photos from my graduation.

"Do you know that nice lady in the blue dress?" Ma asked me.

"No," I said. "Do you recognize her?"

"No . . . I don't even remember seeing her."

"It was a busy day."

XIV

"FATHER PLACIDUS," SAID A PLEASANT VOICE AT THE other end of the phone line.

"Good morning, Father," I said respectfully. "I'm Herman Hugo Hoffman."

"Yes, my son," he said brightly. "I have your papers here on my desk. We're looking forward to welcoming you to St. Clement's. Father Rector has studied your transcript and is looking forward to arguing with you."

"I have not received approval of my application from the Archdiocese yet, Father Abbot."

"Yes, Father Horvath has been good enough to report this to me," he purred. "I would not worry about it, my son. This kind of problem has happened before. The priests at the Chancery are overworked. They will catch up eventually, I'm sure. Just come up here, and it will all work out. You'll be most welcome."

"Thank you, Father Abbot.

"Father Placidus seems a very nice man," I said later to John Horvath.

"The salt of the earth and very smart. He's a patrologist, a man who has studied the writings of the Fathers of the Church. There's a lot of wisdom in those old fellows, and Placidus was a wise man to begin with."

I had tried all summer long to talk to Monsignor Meaghan on the phone. His secretary fended me off every time.

"Monsignor is very busy, young man. He has many more important things to do than to worry about your application."

"Do you happen to know when the Vocations Board will meet?"

"I certainly do not. If I did, I wouldn't tell you."

Finally, John Horvath had called Father Placidus, who asked him to tell me to call St. Clement's myself.

So the week after Labor Day, after yet another monumental Russian German picnic, I drove my Citation back towards Plains City, then veered north into the hill country towards St. Clement's.

It was a melancholy trip. I sensed that I was leaving the stability and the community of Lincoln Junction forever. I wept a little. In German of course. Forever would last only till Thanksgiving vacation.

The Clementines like the other monastic orders (Norbertines, Benedictines for example) came over from Europe in the middle of the nineteenth century. Like the others, they searched for dramatic places to build their monasteries, on a riverbank, on a hill, next to a lake. St. Clement's was at the top of a slight rise in the ground the people in the vicinity called Holy Hill and to which they often came on pilgrimage to celebrate or beg God for a favor. While the order was originally French, it moved to Ireland during the Revolution and sank deep roots in the bogs of that sacred land. So the foundation in our state was mostly Irish. They arrived about the same time as the Volga Deutsche. Before long the two groups of immigrants had established an informal alliance against the Bishop, then the Archbishop of Plains, who usually resented the independence of the monks and the stubbornness of the Deutsche. Their gray monastic robes appeared often in places like Lincoln Junction for missions and retreats and conferences and novenas, and some of the children of the Junction went to their colleges—St. Clement's and St. Anne's, the latter about three miles away from the monastery and the men's college. Papa sent us to State U because he was wary of "too much clericalism."

The colleges, according to John Horvath, continue to flourish, and the monks continue to recruit young members, mostly out of the college student body. The seminary was at first a scholasticate for the monks that expanded into a regional seminary for the prairies. Because the monks are smart and well educated and reasonably mature, a number of small dioceses send their seminarians there and are apparently satisfied with the products. Now the seminarians are referred to as "divinity students," the same name used for lay students who take seminary courses—including women. However, the seminarians have a house of their own as well as schedules and rules appropriate for future priests.

"It's a good place," John said. "You'll learn a lot there, even though like all seminaries these days enrollment is down and some pretty weird people show up."

"I don't think they'll bother me."

"We'll see . . . They do such a good job up there that Slippery may stop sending our men. The monks have always been in conflict with the Archdiocese because no bishop likes to have independent operators in his territory. The monks, however, are tough folks and have clout in Rome, so he has to be careful about offending them. There's bound to be a couple of crises with him while you're up there."

"I'll stay out of it."

"You might not be able to."

So it was with considerable interest that I saw the steeple of the monastic church slowly poke above the horizon line against the great autumn sky. It would be my home for four years, the place where I would become a priest. I resolved to make the best of every moment of it, so I would be prepared to be the best possible priest.

John had told me that in the old days seminarians were completely cut off from the world, no contact with laypeople, no newspapers, no television, only brief vacations. I had a hard time believing it, but he assured me that's the way it was. I don't know that I could have survived such a place.

I drove my Citation into the monastery grounds and asked an elderly monk who was walking through down the road, rosary in hand, where I should go.

"To the neither fish nor flesh building. It's that ugly little two-story brick place at the end of the road."

"Neither fish nor flesh?"

"They're neither monks, nor collegians, nor laypeople."

The brother in charge of the door smiled at me when I entered the building.

"Hoffman? Oh, yes, the rector and the abbot are waiting for you in the rector's office, Mr. Hoffman. Welcome to St. Clement's!"

A welcoming committee? I didn't like that. Maybe something was wrong.

"I'm Herman Hoffman," I said to the three men sitting around the table, which apparently served as a desk. All four walls of the room were lined with bookcases. The rector was purported to be a distinguished scripture scholar who had studied in Rome and Jerusalem. He was a vigorous, husky man in his late thirties, with piercing brown eyes, and businesslike smile, he could have been a rising associate professor at State U.

"Welcome, Herman." He reached out a strong hand to take mine. "It's good to have you with us. This is Father Abbot, and this fellow that looks a bit like an aging Mephisto is Father Retramn, who will be your director until you want someone else. He does not report to us, but only to God."

"In this and in all other matters," the abbot said with a laugh. "You are most welcome, Herman. You'll be happy to know we received just this morning a letter from His Grace the Archbishop approving you as a candidate for the priesthood."

The abbot and my director shook hands with me. Placidus was well named, a short, inoffensive-seeming man, with close-cropped hair, an easy manner, and shrewd blue eyes, the kind of person we might have elected president of the grain co-op in Lincoln Junction to bring peace among the crazy Deutsche. Retramn could well have been a white-haired Mephisto if it were not for his gentle grin.

"It's good to have Deutsche with us again," he said.

"Sprechen sie Deutsch?" I asked, emphasizing my Volga accent.

"Ja, but I can't match your glorious dialect!"

We all laughed.

They asked me to sit down, the abbot produced a tea tray with cookies. I declined them, though I was suddenly very hungry. Why, I wondered, this solemn high welcome?

"We thought you might want to look at your letter of approval," the rector said, passing a sheet of letterhead over to me.

Dear Father Abbot,

His Grace the Archbishop has directed me to communicate this decision to you which he fully approved after meeting with the Vocations Review Board.

After considerable debate the Vocations Review Board has agreed to provide tentative approval for the application of Mr. Herman Hugo Hoffman to the priesthood of the Archdiocese of Plains City. We will ask for annual reports from you of his suitability and decide upon his ordination only at the end of his years in the seminary. We entertain serious doubts about his suitability for this Archdiocese. He is obviously very intelligent. However, we suspect that, as is the case of so many young men, his intelligence and his academic performance at State University have caused him to become the victim of spiritual pride. We hope this changes at the seminary and that he comes to understand that we need in the present difficult time in the Church humble and hardworking priests rather than unstable intellectuals.

The Archbishop has asked me to remind you of the four D's which he has previously outlined to you as desiderata in young men who present themselves for ordination—Decency, Docility, Decorum, and Doctrinal Orthodoxy.

His Grace has also asked me to impart his apostolic benediction to you and all the members of the community of St. Clement's.

> *Faithfully yours in the Lord,*
> *Theodore Edmund Meaghan*
> *Vicar General*

"What do you think of that letter, Herman?" the abbot said, delicately fingering the wooden cross around his neck, the only visible sign of his abbatial authority.

"Sounds like the board was able to contain its enthusiasm about me."

They all laughed again.

"We all three have doctorates of one sort or another," Father Rector said. "I don't think the Review Board would approve of us either."

"Intelligence does not necessarily mean pride," Father Abbot added.

"And stupidity is no guarantee of virtue," Father Retramn added.

They all laughed, the abbot a little uneasily.

I should say something to ease the tension.

"We prairie folk—*Volk* if you wish, Father Retramn—get big heads over many things. The number of beers we can drink at one sitting, our singing voices, our children, the size of last year's crop, the money we made at the Board of Trade. However, on the list of things we brag about is not our academic grades nor the number of books we have read . . . I'll do my best to become a model of each of those four D's, though as I think Father Retramn would tell you, decorum comes hard when we've had a beer and a wurst and someone begins to play on an accordion."

General laughter. They seemed to be pleased that I had chilled out.

"I think we should tell you, Herman," the abbot said carefully, "that all the letters we received from the Chancery about applications for seminary training are at best unenthusiastic. We decided that we'd tell you about the letter and then advise you not to worry about it."

I grinned my best Gary Cooper grin (when playing Wild Bill Hickok) and said, "I'm grateful for your advice."

Father Retramn led me to my quarters and gave me the "horarium," the daily schedule.

"We ask that our divinity students attend Prime before breakfast in the morning and Compline before the Great Silence, which begins at ten thirty each night. We urge you to attend Mass regularly in our chapel or in the monastery church. You will usually take your noon and evening meals in the refectory in this building. Normally there will be reading at the noon meal . . . We must keep alive some of the old customs. Also there is optional noon prayer and recitation of the Angelus before the noon meal . . . You'll note, that out of sympathy with the Deutsche conviction that the noon meal is called 'dinner' I give it no name other than noon meal. However, it will be very like what the non-Deutsche call lunch.

"You need permission to leave the grounds of the seminary, though that permission will routinely be given for a good reason. The keys of your car must be left in the porter's office. In the present situation in college you will perforce mingle with the lay students who will be somewhat younger than you. We encourage you to be friendly to them, but to remember that you are studying for the priesthood and that celibacy is still a requirement in the Western Church.

"During the Great Silence it is necessary under ordinary circumstances to respect the silence of others. If you must listen to music on your CD player at that time—I know you brought one, everyone does—we ask that you use earphones . . . Incidentally what disks have you brought, Herman?"

"Bach, Beethoven, Mozart, Handel, Wagner."

"*Ja, ja* . . . Also it might be helpful for your own spirit of recollection to resolve that you will turn off your computer at that time. Television and daily papers are available in the recreation room as are pay telephones. Do you have any questions?"

"*Alles gut.*"

"I always worry about you Russian Germans"—he sighed—"so quiet, so docile, to use the Archbishop's word, so orderly. Then sometimes the volcano within . . . Have you ever lost your temper?"

I told him the story of the three basketball players whose careers I'd ended.

He was silent for a moment.

"Do you think that was wrong?"

"I'm not sure. I regret that I lost control."

"Hmm, yes . . . You loved the young woman."

"Yes."

"We should perhaps talk about her sometime, do you think?"

"I'm sure we should . . . Actually there are two of them."

"I'm sure it will be an interesting conversation."

My room was a great improvement over the Trappist monastery cell, larger, more window space, a good-size desk, an ample armoire, several lamps, a number of electrical outlets, a couple of comfortable chairs. Not unlike my bedroom back in the Junction.

All in all, the seminary setup seemed fine, the right combination of order for my German component and enough room for the craziness of my Russian component.

I walked down to the recreation room to make a phone call to my parents. Father Retramn walked along with me.

"As your parish priest has doubtless told you, the seminary was a much stricter place in the old days. However, it produced giants!"

"Really?"

"No, not at all. Diocesan priests do not, indeed cannot live monkish lives. We cannot impose artificial virtue on them here, then turn them out into a world for which they are not prepared. It does not follow that we do not keep a discreet eye on you fellows, not that it would be difficult to keep track of a big fellow like you."

I called home, and, bubbling with happiness, told them what a great place it was.

"Ja, ja," Papa said, "French and Irish. It's not a good mix."

"Papa," Mama interrupted, "you're terrible."

"I know. Irish are good people. Like poor Kathleen."

Poor Kathleen, indeed!

Yes, poor Kathleen. Well, we'd work it out on Judgment Day.

I pulled my car up to the door and began to unload my stuff. A young man, sandy hair, twinkling eyes, medium height, huge smile offered to help.

He spoke a few words to me in Volga Deutsch. I responded in kind.

"You looked like you might be one of the clan. You can always tell."

"Bumpkin look!"

"I'm Dave Winter from Falls Crossing."

"Herm Hoffman from Lincoln Junction."

"Two bumpkins."

However, Dave Winter, who became and remains one

of my very best friends, was no bumpkin.

After evening meal and a lot of exuberant hand shaking and greeting, we drifted into the recreation room, a couple of TV screens, papers and magazines, a Ping-Pong and pool table, two Coke machines, several dilapidated easy chairs.

"I've been here through college," Dave said to me. "Let me give you a floor plan. Those guys over there in the corner are called 'The Girls.' They're gay, and they hang together most of the time. They're nice enough, and I guess they have the right to be different if they want and to hang around with one another if they need to."

"They've been dealt a difficult hand."

"For sure . . . I don't think they screw. It would be curtains for them if they were caught. Some dioceses will ordain them. Some won't . . . Then the characters in cassocks and biretta . . . I think they sleep in them. They're the restorationists. They want to return the Church to the way it was before the Council, though they have no idea what those days were really like. They insist that priests are essentially different from anyone else and that the laypeople must be taught again to obey."

"Really?"

"Oh, yeah. They're totally rigid. I think they feel that they need an identity of some kind and that the old image of the priest will provide one."

"Even in Lincoln Junction we know that's not true, if it ever was."

"See that guy with the notebook? He takes notes on

everyone. He says he's preparing a condemnation of all of us. The abbot has warned him that he should modify his behavior. He took notes on his conversation with the abbot too."

"I'll be careful of what I say in his presence."

"It won't do any good. He'll make up something."

"Are the monks worried about him?"

"Not particularly. People have denounced them often in the last thirty years, and they seem to survive. Their Cardinal protector in Rome is a tough guy. The monks know how to play the system."

"And our Archbishop?"

"They won't say it in so many words, but they think he's a piece of cake . . . See that guy by himself, leaning against the wall? That's Lucifer."

"His real name?"

"No, he's Lenny Lyon, up for ordination in June. They call him that because they think he's evil. He's into torture, psychological torture. He's looking for new victims. He drove two guys out last year. He picks people he thinks are vulnerable and ridicules them till they crack. He won't be recommended for ordination by the monks, but Slippery Louie thinks there's a shortage of priests, so he ordains everyone. Lucifer has charmed him."

"He does look kind of evil."

"Watch out for him. He'll certainly go after you; a big strong guy like you will be a challenge for Lucifer."

I thought of the three basketball players and resolved to keep my dangerous temper under wraps.

Dave also pointed out the Mexicans, who, he said,

"want to return Mexican Americans to the religious ways of the old country," and some older men "who are belated vocations and don't know what to make of it all. They tend to drop out pretty early."

"Other than all the above, we're an ordinary bunch of guys who have to work pretty hard to keep up with the intellectual demands of this place."

"Interesting collection of people," I said cautiously, not sure what four years in this place might be like.

"Look out; Lucifer's coming over to see us."

He paused at the Coke machine and bought three cans of Diet Coke. He approached us and offered us each a can. Dave accepted one.

"*Nein*, Lucifer," I said.

"What's it like living up there in the rarefied air, high pockets?"

He was of medium height, well built, slicked-back brown hair, and a face that could only be called pretty.

I replied in German. "My mother told me never to speak with the devil except in *Deutsch*."

"What the hell you talking about? Why don't you take a gift?"

"From a demon, no."

"What are you talking in German for?"

"*Mit Lucifer, nur deutsch.*"

"What's wrong with this guy, Dave?"

"I don't know. He likes to talk German."

"Fucker," Lenny Lyon sneered, and walked away.

"That was well done," Dave said to me. "He'll figure out that you're a mean SOB too and leave you alone."

"*Ja, ja, alles gut.*"

228

I returned to my cubiculum, as it was called, unpacked and arranged my stuff, plugged in the computer and the disk player, and sat back in a chair to think.

Why did all the new places in my life—Township, Dorm Twenty, and now St. Clement's—seem like zoos? Was the priest shortage so desperate that this collection of strange people was the best they could do in the prairies? I could survive there if I had to, but what would the Church be like if such men would dominate it in years to come?

I dreamed about Kathleen again that night.

The next morning I woke early and walked over to the monastic church for Lauds and Prime. The church followed the medieval monastic traditions, plain, austere, big. I liked it. A jump in the lake would have awakened me more, but Lauds was a lovely way to face the day.

I walked back to the Div School, as it was called, with Father Rector.

"You like getting up early?" he asked me.

"I like chant . . . Do we have a choir at the Div School?"

"Certainly, though most of the members are scholastic monks. Should I mention to Brother Angel that you'd be interested in singing with them?"

"Please do, Father. I like the chant, but don't know much about it."

"On the basis of one day's experience, what do you think of our little community?"

"It's variegated."

He chuckled.

"Oh, that it is. If it were up to us, we would perhaps accept only a little more than half of them, for one reason or another. Bishops insist. We try to please, though we make our reservations clear to the bishops. Many drop out along the way. They find our academic demands too rigorous and too irrelevant, though irrelevant to what they are not always able to articulate . . . These are difficult times in the Church."

"I can see that."

"I am told that you had an encounter with Len Lyon last night."

"Of a sort."

"He's very gifted, quite charming too. Yet he can often be a trial."

"Father Rector, I will try my best not to be a trial."

He chuckled again, and we walked into the dining room.

I sat down with a group of younger men who seemed relatively normal, whatever was normal in seminaries these days—Dave Winter, Joachim Binder, Matt McLaughlin, Jimmy Kerr, Jake Kolokowski. I suppose we were a special group too, white, straight, and young. Perhaps like Township and State U, one could always find a group in which to belong.

The next day was Sunday. I donned my brand-new cassock, carefully buttoned it up, and joined the procession to the monastic church. Hundreds of laity from the surrounding countryside joined us and sang vigorously with the monks. I thought I saw Irene walking up for Communion. As always she was a flicker, a blink of an eye, then not there.

After the noon meal, Dave suggested we swim in the lake, which had not lost its summer warmth. A noisy mix of young people had swarmed to the tiny beach, students, men and women, from the colleges, div students, monastic brothers, some faculty—all of us seizing the last opportunities of summer before the cold Canadian air swept down to dominate the prairies.

Though Kathleen had taught me how to swim back in Lincoln Junction, I wasn't much of a swimmer. Still, I gave it a try and soon wore myself out. I had better get back in the routine of daily exercise.

A group of very young and giggly women in bikinis settled down on a blanket near us.

"Freshmen," Dave Winter observed. "They're scared stiff of college and homesick."

"Seventeen-year-olds," I murmured. Had Kathleen been like that at seventeen? I kind of doubted it.

"St. Clement would not have approved of his monks swimming, much less on a beach with that kind of person."

"Would he have been wrong?"

"Different era, Hermie. Different era."

"Better or worse?" I pushed my question.

He thought about it.

"On balance, ours is better. Different problems though. Longer life, better health, more freedom, maybe more temptations, though I kind of doubt that . . . Did you leave a girl behind?"

"Yes," I admitted.

"Serious?"

"Very . . . It's not easy."

"You're right, Hermie. Marriage isn't easy either."

The next day one of the "girls" approached me after breakfast and indirectly indicated that they would be happy for me to join "their little group of friends."

"Thanks, but no thanks," I said gently.

"No offense?"

"None given, none taken."

She smiled rather sadly and walked away.

Class started the next day. It was serious business. There were lots of signs that the seminary had seen better days, half-empty classrooms, indifferent students, run-down desks, and walls that needed painting. However, the faculty was still committed to rigorous formation of future priests and the few future laymen and laywomen who joined us.

The rector taught us Introduction to the Study of Sacred Scripture. Most of the class were literalists insofar as they had any attitudes towards the Bible. Mr. Sims, the note taker, scribbled away rapidly during the lecture, a couple of the older men snoozed. I found the discussions of the various forms of "criticism" fascinating and was challenged by the amount of work that had to be done to understand the Bible.

Mr. Sims put up his hand.

"Father Rector, why do you presume that we have the right to criticize the inspired word of God?"

The class groaned. These alarums and excursions from Mr. Sims were apparently routine.

"Criticize, Mr. Sims, means merely to search for understanding."

"If God wrote it, Father Rector, should there be any question of not understanding?"

"God works through human authors whose purposes and language are human and hence easily open to misunderstanding."

"I see. Father Rector, do you accept the decisions of the Pontifical Biblical Commission at the beginning of the century?"

"The last century?"

"Of course."

"They were supplanted by the encyclical *Divino Afflante Spiritu* of 1943."

"I see," he said, continuing to scribble. "You, of course, took the Oath against Modernism at some point in your monastic career. How dare you teach Modernism in this class?"

"I'm not teaching Modernism, Mr. Sims. I suggest you read the document on revelation from the Vatican Council."

"I don't consider that to have been a valid Council."

"We'll have to discuss that later."

Dave Winter whispered to me, "I think he wants to be dismissed so he can denounce everyone."

Father Retramn taught a class on the Second Vatican Council. Very carefully he explained how the Church had been locked into an essentially defensive position since the French Revolution. It was organized around a set of rules people believed could never change. Then at the Council some relatively moderate changes were made, and the whole rule-organized church structure collapsed. Many of the bishops didn't know what was happening, and they tried to pretend that nothing had really changed. For the last several decades there had been a struggle to try to revert to the situation before the Council, but it hadn't worked, and it couldn't work.

Mr. Sims bristled. "We don't need Councils. We have an infallible Pope."

"We seem to have had twenty of them. The Council is infallible."

"Only when a Pope signs off on it."

"Paul VI did."

"He was gay."

"You don't know that to be true. Moreover, it wouldn't make any difference if he were. A Pope convened the Council, the fathers of the Council voted overwhelmingly for the documents, and another Pope approved all the documents. It would come close to heresy to deny that the Holy Spirit was at work."

Mr. Sims slammed his notebook shut.

Were they giving him enough rope to hang himself?

The abbot taught an optional seminar on the Fathers of the Church. I chose as my paper St. Ephrem the Syrian, whose entire work was in hymns and who suggested long ago that all talk about God was metaphorical.

An ethics professor from the college, Rita Swartz, taught moral theology together with a priest from a nearby parish. She discussed theoretical principles and he had wise pastoral advice about how to deal with moral issues, not all of them, as he said wryly, sexual.

Mr. Sims turned his back on Dr. Swartz. It was not right that a woman should teach in the seminary.

A monk from the abbey taught us about Liturgy,

which somehow he made a dry and theoretical subject, which offended my Russian German soul. Another monk presided over the Homiletics course in which each of us was required to prepare and give a homily. It was a disaster.

Most of the classes, however, were interesting, some fascinating. There was so much to learn and so little time to learn it. I had to force myself to exercise and to play intramural basketball.

You see, I had to become the perfect parish priest in four years.

XV

"So," SAID MY SPIRITUAL GUIDE, "WE MUST TALK ABOUT the young woman at last, must we not?"

"Two of them," I said.

It was a bitter cold winter night in the middle of January. A prairie blizzard was howling outside, huge snowflakes were pelting the window of the little conference room, the supplemental electric heater did not keep the room warm. Both Father Retramn and I were wearing sweaters.

For much of the year our discussions about the state of my soul had focused on my obsessive work habits.

"You never relax. You dash from class to study hall to workout center to library. You stay up late to read and get up early to attend Lauds. You assume that, simply because you are a Volga Deutsche, you are indestructible."

"My great-grandfather who died a couple of years

ago at ninety-five worked in the fields during the summer till he was seventy-five."

"You never relax."

"I have to be the best priest in the world on ordination day."

"Your irony merely hides the truth that you more or less believe that. What would she think about your behavior?"

"What would who think?

"The young woman you once loved."

"I still love her. I'll always love her . . . She would laugh at me."

I had told Retramn about my two star dance experiences, but had left out the setting for the dancing stars by the lake. He had blinked only once.

"You must not think, Herman, that you're the only one who has had a mystical experience."

"I've read the books. I know I'm not."

"The involvement of the stars is not unknown in the literature . . . What do you make of these experiences of the Absolute?"

"They're grace, I suppose, that I can fall back on when I need to."

"Very good. You think you're special?"

"Not necessarily . . . I don't think about things that way . . . I think maybe that I'm lucky."

That was the end of that discussion. Retramn had been probing my spiritual insides, trying to find out what made this big lummox of a Russian German tick. Now he was inquiring about my love life.

"When did you first meet her?"

"Kathleen?"

"Irish?"

"Worst kind, red hair, pale skin, green eyes . . . She started coming over to our house when she was about seven or eight for our Saturday morning singspiels."

"Looking for you?"

"Looking for a family. Her mother had committed suicide. Bipolar. Her father was the doctor in Lincoln Junction. He'd become a recluse. We lived just down the road. We kind of adopted her. As time went on we became siblings, allies, buddies, best friends. We were a good team. She told me off. I told her off. We both changed for the better. Then puberty ruined it all."

"You made love, of course."

"Yeah. It was wonderful. Furious but kind and gentle too. Then when I decided I would become a priest we broke up."

"She was angry at you?"

"I don't think so. It was hard to tell. She said she was not so big a fool that she would try to compete with God."

"I see . . . That was all?"

"Just before she stormed out she said that we would meet again on Judgment Day."

"Indeed!"

That surprised him.

"Do you think that's true?"

"I think she meant it. She left State U and disappeared from the face of the earth. I heard later that she was attending Santa Clara, which is a long way from Lincoln Junction."

"She made no attempt to contact you?"

"No."

"And you did not try to find her? It should not have been so difficult."

"No."

"Yet you still think of her?"

"Sure, not all the time, not every day, but almost every time I see a very beautiful woman."

"Especially, I presume, if she has red hair."

I laughed.

"Certainly!"

"Would you have married?"

"Probably. My parents adored her."

"It would have been a happy marriage?"

"I don't ask that question very often . . . I think it would."

"And if you should encounter each other by chance, what would she say?"

"Probably something like, 'Judgment Day came early this year.'"

He chuckled.

"She sounds like a remarkable young woman."

"I thought so, Father Retramn."

"It required great strength for the two of you to act the way you did, more from her, I should think. You do pray for her, I hope?"

"Every night."

He paused and tapped his pencil, with which he never took a note, against the desk.

"You carry her picture, of course."

"I'm not crazy, Father Retramn."

"Would it be difficult if you did meet again?"

"Not after she's married, if she's happily married."

He nodded slowly.

"Now tell me about this other young woman. What is her name?"

"Irene."

"And where did you meet her?"

"At my great-grandfather's deathbed, the man who worked in the fields till he was seventy-five."

"Ah, and what was she doing there?"

I'll admit that I'd been savoring my reply to that question.

"She had come to take Pa to heaven. She was his wife."

He did me the favor of blinking.

"Tell me about her," he said, putting his pencil aside.

I told him about Pa's death and Irene's blink-of-an-eye appearances since then, including her outrageous appearance at my college graduation.

"I do carry *her* picture around. Our relationship isn't erotic."

I removed from my wallet the picture of Irene, just lowering her camera having snapped a picture of our family. I turned it over on the other side and showed a picture of her and Pa when they were both twenty, a copy I had made secretly.

He took the picture gingerly and quickly returned it.

"The young man is your great-grandfather?"

"And I look just like him, right?"

"Indeed . . . These blink-of-an-eye experiences are frightening?"

"No . . . Ma isn't a ghost. She's a real human person from the world to come. Sometimes I get upset and tell her to go away and leave me alone, but I apologize immediately because I don't want to lose her."

"Is she often here in the monastery?"

"Not often. Sometimes. You must understand that I see her for only a second or two, going up to receive Communion or walking along the lake. Then she disappears."

"What does she want?"

"To take care of me. What does any great-grandmother want?"

"Do you think you were supposed to see her there in her husband's death room?"

"Father," I said, impatiently, "I don't know how those people work. I don't know how God works."

"She always smiles at you?"

"Always, though sometimes it's a smile for a child who has been a naughty little boy."

"Did she like Kathleen?"

"I think so. Everyone in my family liked Kathleen."

"Do you think God has sent her as a substitute for Kathleen?"

"I don't think so. I don't know. I don't understand any of it . . . She's an attractive young woman, but she's my great-grandmother . . . You think I'm mad, don't you, Father?"

He sighed loudly.

"Certainly not, Herman. You may work too hard. However, you are the quintessential stolid, stable Russian German. Whatever else you might be, you're not crazy."

"I'm a sentimental romantic; Kathleen used to say that all the time."

I was conscious that, despite the storm and the cold, I was drenched with sweat.

"You dream of, er, Irene often?"

"Practically never. Kathleen, yes. Irene is real—or seems to be real."

"I see . . . Her assignment from . . . from the world to come is to watch over you?"

"She never says that. She never says anything. That's what she seems to be doing. That's what great-grandmothers do, isn't it?"

He rubbed his face.

"Oh, yes."

"That's what her daughter-in-law—my gramma—does."

"Surely."

We were silent.

"It is fortunate that I am your spiritual director, Herman. Most monks would call for a psychiatrist or an exorcist. I believe you are telling the truth. I don't think you're hallucinating. I am prepared to accept that your great-grandmother is watching over you. Presumably she'd be doing that anyhow because you look so much like her husband. What is most unusual is that you are able to see her, obviously with her consent. Such events are not unheard of in the history of Catholic mysticism though I have never read of one quite so whimsical as this."

"According to family folklore she was a very whimsical woman."

"Do you thank her after one of these glimpses?"

"No. I should, shouldn't I?"

"And God for sending her?"

"I'll do that too."

"Will that be all for tonight, Herman?"

He stood up and so did I.

"One more thing, Father. The first star dance experience was after I had made love for the first time with Kathleen."

He stood there thoughtfully, nodded his head, and murmured, "Why am I not surprised?"

I can't remember any dreams that night.

The next Sunday, Irene blinked in as I was coming out of the monastic church. She seemed to be smiling broadly. Then she blinked out.

At the end of our next session, when we stood up, Retramn shifted from foot to foot rather awkwardly.

"I did not mention the two women we mentioned previously, Herman. I do not want to intrude into your privacy. However, it was clear that you felt considerable release in being able to talk about them. If you ever want to discuss either of them again, please feel free to do so."

"I bumped into Irene—if you can call an eye blink that—after the monastic Mass on Sunday. She smiled approvingly."

"I daresay she would."

I continued to wonder whether she was merely a wish fulfillment or a pressure on some of my brain cells. Nonetheless, I thanked her and God for her protection. What else could I do?

Our numbers diminished over the winter. Mr. Sims left, much to everyone's relief. So did some of the gays and Hispanics and the "belated vocations." The monks' technique was, I began to suspect, to overwhelm us with academic work and thus to protect themselves with the argument that they were maintaining the standards of the past. A sponsoring bishop could hardly argue with that.

Of my friends only Dave Winter understood my passion for study.

"Why are you wasting your time on that stuff, Hermie?" Jock Binder asked in the rec room one evening. "What good will it do you as a priest? How many laypeople will ever ask you about Ephrem of Syria anyway? All a priest has to do is be nice to laypeople and never miss his day off."

Matt McLaughlin was silent as he always was. Jimmy Kerr and Jake Kolokowski agreed with Jock.

"Unless a priest reads a lot," I argued, "he won't be a good preacher. His mind and his imagination will just wither away."

"You don't need all that biblical criticism stuff," Jock continued the argument. "All you have to do is give a decent homily about the Sunday Gospel. That's all the people want."

"So what's the kingdom of heaven that Jesus talks about all the time?" I demanded.

"That's easy," Jimmy Kerr replied. "It's the place where we go when we die."

"No it's not. It's the kingdom of God's love present in the here and now."

Jock laughed. He almost sneered.

"That doesn't make a bit of difference to the laity. You just tell them how wonderful heaven is. That's all they want to hear."

It was a lost cause. My friends were prairie conservatives, inherently skeptical of ideas and militantly anti-intellectual. The only reason I was not that way was that I'd been raised differently. Even in Lincoln Junction, little more than a crossroads in the plains.

"Many of us have little respect for learning," John Horvath had said to me during the Christmas vacation. "We have little intellectual interest to begin with, and the culture of the seminary and the priesthood doesn't add much. We tend to be militant anti-intellectuals. Some of us think that if we read *Time* every week, that's enough. No wonder so much of preaching is bland and dull."

I resolved that I would never be part of that culture.

Two months later, on a false spring day just before Easter, the Archbishop, Monsignor Meaghan, and Father Peters descended on St. Clement's for a "visitation." It seemed that Mr. Sims had turned his notebook over to the Archbishop and that the whole seminary was in trouble. Rumors spread that he wanted the rector removed, the lay teachers either replaced or banned to college, and Father Retramn banished to someplace like Siberia.

I saw the three of them stride into the abbey, breathing fire—the lords of the Inquisition. A little later the rector and Father Retramn followed with the hesitant steps of those destined for an auto-da-fé. All we needed was a chorus singing the *Vexilla Regis*. A wide-eyed young monk came to tell us that classes were canceled for the day, but that the Archbishop would preside over the Eucharist at noon.

It was a strange Mass. The monks choir drenched the "visitation" trio in music, beginning with the usual *"Ecce Sacerdos Magnus"* which marked every solemn high entrance of a bishop. The monastery seemed to be celebrating a happy event instead of fighting to stay alive. The three inquisitors looked bored during the liturgy and yawned frequently. They must have risen early in the morning for their ride up here in the thawing snow.

The Archbishop delivered himself of his "stump speech" about the four "D's" which caused a certain amount of quiet sniggers from the back of the chapel where we were sitting.

The laity who regularly came to the noon Mass glanced at their watches frequently. I saw (or thought I saw) Irene walking to the altar to receive the Communion. She was wearing jeans and a heavy down jacket.

Did those in the world to come receive Communion? Did the blessed wear jeans?

She didn't blink in among those returning after Communion.

Had she taken the monastery under her protection too?

"What's happening at the abbey?" I asked one of the young monks after Mass.

"A lot of shouting," he said with a sly grin. "Meaghan is doing the shouting. Father Abbot is replying calmly.

That slimy creep Peters sounds like he's trying to make peace. The Arch isn't saying much of anything. I fear that Father Rector has lost his temper a couple of times."

"Retramn?"

"I'm only guessing, but characteristically he's probably laughing."

"Who's winning?"

"Herman, my boy," he said, though he was at the most a year or two older, "we've been fighting with bishops and archbishops ever since we came to Holy Hill a century and a half ago. We've never lost, and we're certainly not about to lose to this bunch."

The visitators departed in their massive Cadillac about four in the afternoon, as the sky grew dark. They seemed grim and determined as though they had a major victory.

Nonetheless, classes continued normally on the next day.

"You guys won," I said to Retramn at the beginning of our weekly conversation.

"You might say that . . . They had their chance to vent their anger. The abbot told them that the charges were false and that he would be delighted to close the seminary. It was a losing proposition for the abbey. If we were subjected to any further harassment because of the wild charges of a clearly unbalanced student whom we had not wanted to take in the first place, we'd do just that. Slippery Louie was terrified of what Rome might say if he shut down St. Clement's after all these years. Meaghan talked like he was willing to take that chance.

God protect us if he's our next bishop . . . Now, how are you sleeping?"

My seminary years flew by. I worked hard, learned a lot, prayed a lot, fought off exhaustion, and looked forward eagerly to ordination. Dramatic events were occurring all over the world. We watched in astonishment on TV as countries like Poland and Hungary and Czechoslovakia broke away from the Soviet Union, and East Germany fell apart. Then finally one summer while I was home, so did the Soviet Union itself. An expert from State U told us that it would be another century at least before religion reappeared in Russia. We learned later that it already had. I thought that it would be interesting to study the German families who had remained in Russia, some of whom had survived Stalin. I would not be the one to do it, however, because I had no plans ever to leave the state, much less the country.

Bumpkin. Peasant. Hayseed.

The first two summers I worked for a month as a catechist in a parish up near the northern border of the state. It was a poor farm community, but the people were wonderful. I had a grand time making up stories for them. I looked forward eagerly to an assignment in a parish of my own. At the end of my third year I would be ordained a subdeacon, make the promise of celibacy, and spend the summer and autumn as "my deacon year" experience at the same parish. Then at Christmas I'd become a deacon, the last step to the priesthood at the end of May.

At an alumni lunch at the end of April, a middle-aged

priest with dancing eyes and salt-and-pepper hair took me aside.

"Tom Donohue. Little Flower Parish. You're Hoffman, aren't you?"

"Yes, Father."

"I performed a wedding in the fall of a young woman with whom you went to school out in the Junction, gorgeous redhead, very poised and composed . . . Can't remember her name . . ."

I felt like someone had punched me in the stomach.

"Kathleen Quinlan was the only redhead in our class," I said, controlling my emotions.

"Yeah, that was it . . . Calmest bride I've ever seen . . ."

That was not my Kathleen.

"She was anything but calm at St. Killian's."

"She had high praise for you. Said you'd make a wonderful priest."

I permitted myself a laugh.

"I'm not so sure . . . Yet if Kathleen said it, by definition it's true . . . Was her husband a Catholic?"

"Hell yes, a mick from Cork City. Doctor. Funny, funny man. What was his name . . . Lemme see . . . Shannon, Liam Shannon. Good guy. They made each other laugh a lot . . . Great sign of a good marriage."

"I'm glad to hear it. Kathleen deserved the best . . . I didn't know she was back in Plains City."

"Some kind of job at University Hospital. We get a lot of marriages from the U. Santa Claus over there doesn't like to do them. Too much work. Rarely a bride as beautiful as your friend Kathleen."

"I can believe that."

The chaplain who had replaced John Horvath was one Sanford Clause, a man cordially disliked, I had heard, by everyone in the U. But unquestionably orthodox. Naturally, he was called Santa Claus.

Choking back tears, I eased out of the refectory and slipped down to the house chapel. Maybe God would help me organize my thoughts. That's what we Volga Deutsche did in times of emotional confusion: we organized our thoughts.

My strongest emotion was happiness for Kathleen. She had matured into a poised young woman and found a good husband, Irish like herself and with a gift of laughter. What more could I wish for my childhood buddy and teenage lover?

Yet there was a dark side to my reactions, anger, disappointment, frustration. Why couldn't she have waited till I was ordained, or at least become a subdeacon? What was the rush? Had she forgotten about me completely? No, she remembered me well enough to sing my praises to Tom Donohue.

I could have been that bridegroom. Maybe I should have been. Would I not have been a better spouse for this poised, laughing, gorgeous young woman?

Probably not, dammit.

Anyway. I had my chance and blew it.

Then I laughed at myself. What an idiot I was!

I apologized to God for being a goof. I had postponed my absolute, final decision about the priesthood till my retreat for the subdeaconate. Then I would have definitively chosen between God and Kathleen—though I now knew enough to understand that it was a false choice. I could marry and still be on God's side. Now she had preempted me, and I was angry at her for being more confident in my vocation than I was . . . How dumb could I be? She was supposed to sit around and wait for me and pass up a good man?

So I prayed to the Lord God for Dr. and Mrs. Liam Shannon that He would take care of them and protect them and grant them a long and happy life together.

I saw Father Retramn that night and told him the story, including my dark reactions.

He pondered me thoughtfully.

"So you think you should be immune to jealousy, do you? Russian Germans don't have such emotions, do they?"

That bubble burst.

"You have me cold, Father. My reactions are normal."

"She didn't invite you to the wedding, did she?"

"I guess not. Nor my family either. I would have heard."

"Do you think that was not a wise decision?"

"No, it was probably very wise, all things considered."

He said nothing for a moment.

"So she is back in Plains City? Will you try to find her this summer?"

I hadn't thought of that.

"I don't think so."

"Why not?"

"It would be kind of gauche, wouldn't it? Would her husband like to see his wife's old lover appear within a year of their marriage? She said Judgment Day because she knew we should avoid meeting each other until after we were dead."

"Perhaps."

"What do you mean by that, Father?" I said, my anger rising.

"I mean I think that it is evident that you and she will encounter each other sometime and will then try to straighten out what happened. Then, perhaps, only perhaps, you could become friends again, like you were in your grammar school days."

Then, without any warning, I sobbed. Tears poured down my cheeks. My chest heaved in and out. I pulled back just an inch short of hysteria.

"I don't think that would be a very good idea," I said, when I regained some self-control. "What would her husband think?"

"He would have to be part of the relationship . . . Forgive me, Hermie, for being facetious. I was speculating . . . It would not be a good idea, not now."

"Not ever."

"Some healing might be necessary . . ."

"I don't see how."

"Perhaps, yet God has His ways . . . Has your friend Irene weighed in with her reaction?"

"I don't believe in her," I said irritably. "She's a nuisance."

"Perhaps . . . Yet even if you do not believe in her, what do you think her reaction, might be?"

"That same goofy smile of approval, I suppose."

Despite Retramn's hint that he had changed his mind, I avoided University Park during the day I spent in

Plains City before my return to Lincoln Junction. Irene did blink in when I drove by the village limits—this time a young woman in slacks and a blouse carrying iced tea out into a wheatfield. Her smile seemed especially gentle. No one at home said anything about Kathleen's marriage, though I was sure they knew about it.

Emily Hirsch, a friend of Hildy's about four years younger than I, did mention her name when we were compiling a list for first Mass invitations.

"Are you going to invite Kathleen?" she asked innocently.

"No," I said flatly.

"It would be rude not to," she replied.

"*Ja, ja,*" Mama agreed.

"She didn't invite me to her wedding."

"You knew about it?" Hildy gasped.

"I heard about it. She could have found out where I was if she wanted me to be there."

"*Ja,* we will send her an invitation anyway," Mama said, settling the issue.

"Suit yourself," I said, washing my hands of all responsibility.

During my brief stay at the Junction, during which I worked in the fields with Papa, I felt haunted by two women, Irene and Kathleen. The former was a benign presence. The latter somehow oppressive. I was glad to leave for the north country and my deaconal assignment.

As I drove across the state and then north I understood. The family all wanted me to be a priest. Yet they loved Kathleen as an almost member of the clan and missed her. I should have understood that.

Some healing was necessary, Retramn had said. OK, I said to God—and to Irene if she were listening—if You want that, You have to make it pretty clear. Like hit me over the head with that.

Before I left for my assignment, the *Prairie Reader*, the local "underground" weekly, appeared with a story about "priests missing in action." They had checked assignments of priests in the *National Catholic Directory* and in the Archdiocesan Directory for the last twenty years. Fifteen priests had appeared in the list, then disappeared and later reappeared. They seemed to have changed assignments frequently. Frequently they were described as being "on sick leave." When presented with this list the Archdiocese had refused comment and warned that the *Reader* was risking suit if it published the list.

The paper was cautious in its speculations. "Might one not wonder," it said editorially, "what exactly was the nature of this mysterious sickness?"

"Most of us know what they are," John Horvath said to me my last day at Mass before I left on my assignment. "They're the ones who play with little boys or creepy teens. It's all going to explode someday soon. Then we'll really have trouble right here in Prairie City."

XVI

THE FARMLAND AROUND FORT SCOTT WAS NOT AS RICH
as our land out in Lincoln County, and the farmers hovered on the edge of poverty. They were pushed back
and forth across the edge by vagaries of the world
market. Yet I loved the little town and the parish of St.
Herminegeld. The pastor was an ancient Pole who was
glad to get summer help of any kind and let me do
whatever I wanted. "Young men work hard." He
sighed. "Sometimes old men do too."

Most of my work that summer and autumn—
allegedly a preparation for parish work after ordination—was with the kids and the teens. I tried to battle
with their profound ignorance of their faith (to which
they nonetheless strongly adhered) with stories and
games. They liked that, though I think they liked me
more than the stories and the religion. A priest must not
let his personality come between himself and the
Gospel, I kept telling myself.

I was also the best basketball player in the township,
so I enjoyed doing battle with the teenage boys. They
enjoyed every rebound they took away from me, which
wasn't very many.

The ancient wooden rectory looked as if it would be
blown away by even a small tornado (which it was a
couple of years later) or even a stiff winter breeze.
There was no air-conditioning, of course. And there
were so many crannies between the planks of the wall
that I knew my large and dilapidated bedroom would be

bitter cold during the winter. I thought that perhaps I should buy an electric blanket for the winter, then decided that it would be a sensual indulgence.

The shy and impoverished people of Fort Scott were not given to frequent picnics like my own clan back in the Junction. But they did have a Christmas party for me in early December when I returned to the seminary. It was a warm and cheerful gathering in the church basement, which smelled vaguely of cow manure. Irene put in a brief appearance, even quicker than a blink of the eye. I thought she had forgotten me.

"People like Deacon," said the pastor. "Is good."

It was. It was hard to say good-bye to them. I thought then that I could happily work at Fort Scott for the rest of my life.

Back in the seminary all the gossip was about the "anti-Catholic" *Prairie Reader*'s attack on the priesthood.

"All those guys were cleared by the shrinks and the cops," Jock Binder whined. "We have to stand by them."

"The shrinks and the cops have cleared Lucifer too," Matt McLaughlin said. "The Chancery had to send him away for a while to prevent a suit. But he says nothing happened."

No one among the divinity students had any doubt that Lucifer was innocent, though they themselves had given him the name.

"So," said Father Retramn, "you did not find Kathleen during the summer and autumn?"

"Didn't look for her," I replied.

"Hmm . . . You're inviting her to your first Mass, naturally."

"Nope."

"Is that fair?"

"She said Judgment Day."

"Is that not unnecessarily cruel?"

"My family will invite her."

"Why?"

"They love her, always have."

"I thought they wanted you to be a priest."

"Always have. They prayed me into it."

"They are not afraid that you might run off with Kathleen?"

"They might not trust me, but I think they trust her."

"I see . . . And your great-grandmother? What does she think of Kathleen?"

"I haven't the slightest idea . . . We never talk about her. Or about anything else. There isn't time."

"She's been around these last six months?"

"She's all over the Junction. She grew up there. So her good spirit is always around. She showed up at Fort Scott for the farewell party. That was all."

"You're sure it's your great-grandmother?"

"I think it's just my crazy imagination . . . Why did you guys ever recommend Lenny Lucifer for ordination?"

"You change the subject very abruptly."

"I worry about it."

"And you think that the *Prairie Reader* is anti-Catholic?"

"No."

"Then you're the only one of the seminarians who doesn't."

"Do you, Retramn?"

"I'm afraid that they are all too accurate in their speculations. The Archdiocese would be wise to read the signs of the times around the country."

"And stop covering up?"

"As for your friend, uh, Satan, you ought not to assume that because the Archbishop ordains a man we have recommended ordination."

"I see."

"The Archbishop," he said carefully, "seemed partial to Father Lyon . . . a man of great talent, he has often said."

"At tormenting people."

"So it would seem . . . Give my regards to Irene."

The sexual abuse problem was for me still academic. I could not imagine that I would ever be swept up in it.

As for Irene, she left me alone during most of my final year in the seminary. Nor did I think much about Kathleen. She was the past. Ordination was the future. I did not want anything to remind me of her.

In our Archdiocese, ordination always takes place in the Cathedral. We do our final retreat at the seminary, then are conveyed into Plains City on a school bus. The abbot himself was the retreat master. He was a fine preacher and offered us a splendid vision of the priest based on the Epistle to the Hebrews as reflected through the teachings of the early Fathers: "Our high priest is not one who cannot feel sympathy for our weaknesses. On the contrary, we have a high priest who was tempted in every way we are, but did not sin. Let us be brave and approach God's throne where there is grace. There we will receive mercy and find grace to help us just when we need it."

Jock, Matt, Dave, Jimmy, and Jake often dozed off. Their minds were on the ordination ceremony and the first Mass and the reception afterwards, on their family and friends, on the "happiest day in our lives" which even then was what we thought ordination would be.

Well, I didn't. I was stubborn enough to believe that it was only the beginning.

I thought a lot about Kathleen during those three days. Had she been a temptation? Or was she perhaps a grace? I had never thought of her as a grace. That was probably a dangerous thought. Jesus was tempted every way we were, Hebrews said to us. Was there a woman in his life who was a temptation? Would it have been a temptation? He had no vow of celibacy, did he?

It was an absurd issue, a side road down which there was no point in going because nothing was learned.

Friday morning after we came off retreat, we were bundled into the creaky old school bus and delivered in rush hour traffic to the Cathedral rectory, where we were assigned to the top floor to wait for our interviews with the Archbishop that afternoon and evening before our ordination the next morning. Technically we were still on retreat, but there was television and laughter, and drinking (not a lot), and joking with the Cathedral priests. I chatted with Monsignor Meaghan and Father Peters, the latter a lean, saturnine man with thin hair and a long face, a SherlockHolmes-looking character. It was difficult to imagine him as the victims' advocate who hoodwinked the families of victims into a lowball settlement. I wanted no part of any of them. Or of our Archbishop, who was a hollow man.

I was the last to be summoned to his study on the third floor of the rectory, a corner room overlooking the square, with the Mormon tabernacle directly across the way.

He did not look up when I entered the study, but read through my record as I stood awkwardly waiting for him to notice me. He was older than when I had first encountered him out in the Junction. The smell of powerful cologne permeated the room. A Waterford tumbler with some dark substance in it rested near his hand on a crowded mahogany desk. His hair was the same neatly coiffed iron gray that it had been in the Junction, though now it was clear that the color was not quite authentic. He would have been better-looking and more the prelate if he had permitted the hair to turn its natural white.

None of which was any of my business, I told myself as I waited.

He looked up at me.

"Ah, yes, Herman. Please sit down . . . I trust your pastor is well."

"Both pastors," I said, always the Volga troublemaker.

"Ah, yes, Monsignor O'Brien . . . I assume that he will not make the trip in here tomorrow morning to lay hands upon you."

"He will be here," I said, putting on my Gary Cooper

Plainsman persona.

"I'm delighted to hear it." He sighed. "The monks sent us an excellent report on you and your work. They seem to think that you've been well nigh a perfect seminarian."

"Then, alas, I must have deceived them."

Shut your mouth, you idiot.

"I hope not," he said with a yawn. "Monsignor Jablonski has submitted an excellent report of you from St. Herminegeld . . . That's a pretty forsaken place, is it not?"

"I enjoyed my time there. They're wonderful people."

"Indeed." He yawned again and replaced the papers in the manila folder.

"I hope you realize, Herman, that academic performance is not the only or the most important virtue in a priest . . ."

"Charity is the most important in a priest as in every Christian."

I was spoiling for a fight.

"Yes, of course." He sighed. "But you should never forget the importance of obedience. When I was a young priest, we all knew that the Bishop's will was the will of God. With all the change in the Church, many seem to have lost sight of that truth."

It was time for me to take cover.

"Yes, Your Excellency."

"Your parents are still alive?"

"Very much, Your Excellency, and my grandparents. They'll be here with a large family entourage."

I was not about to tell him that my great-grandmother

would surely be there too.

"Fine . . . Welcome to the great fraternity of the priesthood."

"We band of brothers," I said with only a touch of irony. "We happy few."

"Hmm, oh yes." He extended his hand. I took it, and that was that, as I often say.

It was not, I reflected in the dark, sepulchral corridor, that there was no there there in my archbishop. Only that there was very little there there.

He preached at the ordination Mass—interminably it seemed. He used his favorite theme of the four D's, maybe his only theme. He seemed to elaborate it at greater length on ordination day. I paid little attention to him, however. The stars slipped into the dank old Romanesque cathedral, danced above us under the dome, and, when I was prostrate in front of the altar, swirled down and enveloped me for the third time in my life. I floated through the rest of the Eucharist, riding on the waves of the Absolute. I barely noticed when priests laid hands on me, passing on the power of the priesthood. I was sure that Frank O'Brien and John Horvath must have pressed their hands firmly on my head, but I missed them both.

"Are you OK?" Dave Winter whispered.

"Fine," I said. "Never better."

I don't know what to make of that third encounter, any more than I did of the first two. Perhaps, I thought, just perhaps, someone is sending me a message.

The weather was perfect on ordination day, a gentle spring day in the prairies with the trees and the lawns on the square a promising green and gentle sky smiling down on us. A good omen? I wondered, as we progressed out of the Cathedral to the cheers of our family and friends.

The Lincoln Junction bunch was right up front, cheering more loudly than anyone else. I half expected accordions and beer and wurst. However, that exuberance would have to wait till we were safe out in the middle of the prairies. My parents, my grandparents, my Hildy and Franky, my cousins, my aunts, my uncles—were all sobbing with joy. Their joy and their tears captured me. I was sobbing as much as they were. A perfect day for the Volga Deutsche—enough tears to water the square for a week.

There was no grinning redhead to accuse me of sentimental romanticism. I had not expected she would be there. I did not intend to look for her carrot top as we proceeded into the Church and later, the oils of ordination still not dry on our hands, out into the square. Yet I could not help but search for her. Later I would rationalize that a relationship as intense as ours would of course force me to look for her.

However, it was not Judgment Day, only ordination day.

Irene, on the other hand, was everywhere, blinking in and out with her camera taking pictures. I wondered what kind of pictures a camera person from the other world might take. As far as I could tell, she was taking the same kind of snapshots that the others in the family were taking.

I turned my attention to the living and rejoiced with

them. I did not know what the priesthood would bring me, but I was happy for the opportunity to find out. I would never turn back, I promised myself.

And if I had known what would happen in my first year, would I have turned back?

No way, but I am glad I did not know that day what I know now about my first year in the priesthood.

The big news in the Archdiocese after the ordination ceremony was that the man who had succeeded John Horvath at Newman had been picked up by the State U police for engaging in a group grope with five freshmen during the Spring Fling. No one believed the charges. The cops and the shrinks had cleared him. He was on a long vacation in Italy and would return to his order for reassignment. Tony Calabrese had replaced him. Tony was, I thought, substantially to the right of Ivan the Terrible. He was just what State U needed.

Though it was time for the winter wheat harvest in Lincoln County, it was also festival time. The Russian Germans had a priest of their own, the first that anyone could remember. So he must be toasted, lionized, celebrated—complete with a full color picture on the front page of the *Lincoln County News*, the first full color that the distinguished paper (published in German as the *Lincoln Zeitung* till 1910) had ever carried. It bore some resemblance to me. I said Mass at a different church or convent every day of the week after the mammoth celebration on Sunday at high noon in St. Killian's. I drank beer and ate wurst and sang old German drinking songs or Bach cantatas every day.

We also sang the bittersweet melody that our ancestors sang when they were leaving home to migrate to Russia. It was so sad that we Russian Germans saved it for great celebrations.

Now the time and hour are here,
for us to move to the Ukraine.
The carriage is already standing in front of the door,
with wife and children we are moving.

Now the time and hour are here,
for us to move to the Ukraine.
The horses are already in their harness,
We are moving to a new country.

Now, dear friends, all of you together,
Give us your hands for the last time.
Don't make parting so difficult for us,
for we'll never again see one another.

And when we come to the high gate
we will raise our arms to God.
And sing loudly: Victory!
Now we are in the Ukraine.

Before the week was over I was exhausted, my stomach was in open revolt, and my patience was worn as thin as the upper stalk of a wheat plant.

However, the celebration was not for me or even of me. It was a celebration of the community by the community itself. I was merely the occasion of it. Therefore, I had to be charming and happy and poised and joyous. I tried hard and mostly succeeded.

"Ja, ja," Mama whispered to me at a picnic at River View, "you are a good sport, *mein Herman*. You do not spoil any of the fun by being tired."

"Ja," I agreed. "The people are entitled to a good time."

"Most young priests would not understand that."

She was probably right.

"Do you see a woman who is everywhere with a camera?"

"A stranger?" she asked in surprise.

"She looks kind of familiar, but not anyone we know."

Just then Irene blinked in behind us snapped a picture and blinked out.

Pest.

"Everyone is taking pictures."

"Yes, I guess so."

Later, I would go through the stacks of photos my family had taken in search of Irene. I found four such pictures. I asked my grandaunt, who would have been Irene's daughter, if she recognized this woman.

"Nein, little Herman. She is familiar. Yet I don't know her name . . . Perhaps long ago, but that cannot be. She is too young."

Ja.

So it wound down on Sunday with another big Mass at St. Killian's. The Monsignor preached, from a carefully prepared manuscript lest he wander. He was very good. The cheers after Mass were for him as much as for me. He referred to finding me and Kathleen when we were very young, practicing Bach in the auditorium, and how proud of his little saints he was. He said he had missed her at the celebration.

Not so young, Monsignor, and not really little saints either.

No one in the family mentioned his comment about Kathleen. She was history now, though not yet forgotten history. Perhaps she never would be.

Monday morning, Jock Binder woke me with a phone call at seven-thirty.

"You've been screwed, Hermie." He sounded jubilant. "They've sent you to Theodolinda. You must really have offended the Arch!"

"Theodolinda?"

"Yeah, that hoity-toity suburb across the river east of the city. Monsignor Flannery is a falling-down drunk and a nasty man. And guess who the other associate is—your old friend Lucifer."

"Sounds like an interesting place."

"You won't last a year."

"We'll see."

He was right, though I did not ask out of the place.

John Horvath was less than reassuring.

"They know Downtown what Flannery is and that they have to retire him. Lenny Lyon will be back in a tank somewhere soon for another go at psychic detox. You'll end up as administrator."

I did not find his prophecy appealing.

And it certainly wasn't accurate.

XVII

"WHOEVER THOUGHT THAT YOU WERE GAY, FATHER Hoffman?" the young psychiatric resident asked me at St. Edward's Mental Health Center.

I had been incarcerated there for four months and was beginning to pull myself together. It had taken me that long to recover from the trauma of being locked up in an institution on the order of my Archbishop. It was a savage blow to my self-esteem. I was not gay, I was not crazy, yet I had offered no resistance to what they had done to me.

Why not?

I don't know why not. I was an inexperienced young priest, accused of a terrible crime by my superiors and overwhelmed by the horrific crime I had observed but had not committed. Yet I am not proud of my behavior during my first year in the priesthood. I lost my poise. I permitted myself to be swept along by others. It took me three months to regain my self-possession and another three months to force them to release me. I did not act like a plainsman, a Russian German plainsman at that.

John Horvath would say to me before I went into exile the following summer that I was in trauma from the homosexual rape I had seen in the rectory.

"No one is so sophisticated about sex that an experience like that doesn't induce some post-traumatic stress. Then when your Bishop—that consummate bastard—locks you up, why wouldn't you be wiped out. I realize that shouldn't happen to a big tough Russian German from the Plains who might look like Wild Bill Hickok. But it did."

Now I'm prepared to admit that he might have been right. Or maybe there was another motive. It may have been immature of me to let them push me around or, perhaps, as I think back on it, I was being shrewd Volga Deutsche. Maybe I was waiting for the eventual day when I would get even. Which is what we Russian Germans do.

Anyway, when Dr. Straus gave orders to the hospital staff that I was to have no visitors and receive no phone calls, I dug in my heels, such as they were.

"I insist on the right to call my parents every week," I said.

He hesitated.

"Only if it's monitored."

"All right."

I was at least enough in possession to realize that the monitor would have to speak Volga Deutsch to know what I was saying.

"And a call to my classmate Father Dave Winter, to bring me books to read."

I was desperately clinging to my sanity.

"Young man," said Dr. Straus, "you are in no position to make demands. You're very sick. You will do what you're told."

"I will leave here unless you permit me to call Father Winter."

"We will keep you under restraint."

"That won't do any good."

"Very well. We'll monitor that call too."

"OK."

As soon as he and Monsignor Meaghan and Father Peters had left, I called Lincoln Junction on a phone from the admitting office. Fortunately, Papa was in the house and answered the phone. I immediately went into Deutsch and told him what had happened.

He was, as one might imagine, ready to assemble the clan and march on Plains City, perhaps to string up the Archbishop by his big toe.

I persuaded him that we're not quite ready for that. I wanted him and Franky and a few of the boys to go to St. Theodolinda, rescue my car and my belongings, and take them all back to the Junction.

"Especially my journal. You know what that looks like."

"*Ja, ja,* everyone knows. We'll find it, or we'll tear the rectory down."

They swept into Green Grove the next day and rescued everything, including the journal, which was just sitting on my desk, ready for Slippery Louie's storm troopers to confiscate it. They would have found my accounts of my relationship with Kathleen interesting though it would hardly fit their diagnosis, if they could translate my Germanic script and language. Heaven only knows, and I mean that literally, what they would have made of Irene.

However, on reflection I realized that they weren't smart enough to do that.

Dr. Straus prescribed medication for me to "calm me down." It must have been some kind of tranquilizer because I became very calm indeed. Not so calm, however, that I did not begin to realize, however dimly, that I was being drugged. So I faked taking the medicine. I'm not sure how long into my "treatment" I rebounded from the drug. However, after a time I took over ministry to my fellow inmates. St. Edward's was not a cuckoo's nest, but a clean and neat, albeit sad place, filled with pathetic people who were grateful for my daily greetings when I made my rounds through the hospital. Many showed up every morning for Mass. The nurse supervisor, a nun who ran the place in the absence of the invisible Dr. Geneva, didn't quite approve of that, but she wasn't sure how to stop me. With my reading and my care of souls, the bitter months of winter passed quickly. I remembered shivering in the bedroom at Fort Scott and was grateful that the rooms at St. Edward's were automatically sixty-eight degrees, never any more and never any less.

Irene was around some of the time. I'd glance out the window, and she would blink in walking up the steps to the mental health center. I'd see her in the usual twinkling in the visiting room next to the office. Once she was in nurse's garb and carrying a large bouquet of flowers. If I had told the residents about Irene, they might have locked me up permanently.

In response to the question from the resident about who suggested that I was gay, I said, "Off the record?"

"Sure." He shrugged. "My comments too?"

"Absolutely."

"Straus is a quack. He's not board-certified and

indeed never did a residency. Has a lot of influence with the Church though."

So I told him the story.

"Good God!" he exploded.

"That's what I think too."

"The other guy was the one they call Lucifer?"

"You got it."

"We had him here. Filled him with drugs. Calmed him down. Tried twelve-step therapy. The whole route. He didn't fool the residents much, but he fooled Straus, who was the attending physician. So they sent him back. We heard a few weeks ago that they had picked him up again and sent him out of the state. So they must know that you weren't the one . . ."

"I think they knew all along," I commented.

"What are you going to do about it, Father?"

"Get out, what else?"

"Just walk away?"

"No, I'll force them to let me out."

"How?"

I almost described the scheme that was taking place in my mind.

"You don't want to know."

"I'll make sure that your records show clearly our diagnosis, in case you ever need them."

"I can't imagine that I would, but thanks."

The next morning I told Sister to call Father Retramn up at St. Clement's and ask him to come to hear my confession.

"We have strict orders that you are to have no visitors," she said firmly.

"You cannot deny someone the right to go to confession. Father Retramn has been my confessor for four years."

"The answer is no." She pursed her lips.

"I think you'd better check with Dr. Geneva, Sister. It would not look good for the center if there was a charge that you denied a man the right to go to confession."

One rumor at St. Ed's was that Dr. Geneva, the distinguished psychiatrist who had founded the place, was dead. Others claimed that he was senile. Yet another, which I inclined to believe, was that he was sick of sick people.

"We'll bring in a local man."

"I am entitled to my own confessor. I demand to talk to Dr. Geneva."

"We may have to put you in restraints, Father."

"Before you do that, consult with Dr. Geneva. You're violating both civil and canon law."

"I'll consider that."

I knew that she would not bother the doctor—that was her mantra—but she would call St. Clement's.

The next morning I cornered her again after I had flushed down the toilet the double dose of tranquilizer she had prepared for me.

"When is Father Retramn coming to hear my confession, Sister?"

"Sometime tomorrow," she snapped.

So at eleven the next morning, Retramn, in his gray monastic robes, was waiting for me in the visiting room. We embraced.

"What have they done to you, Hermie?"

It was a rhetorical question. I'm sure that he, like every priest in the Archdiocese, knew a version of what they had done to me.

"It's a long story . . . I'm sure that bitch of a nun has the room bugged."

I turned on the television to confuse her, and told Retramn my version of the story.

We talked in whispers. No way she'd think of a sophisticated bug.

"We had heard up at the Hill that they had cleaned out St. Theodolinda, that old Flannery was in a nursing home and that Len Lyon was off in a treatment center in New Mexico. No one said anything about you."

"I disappeared from the face of the earth."

"They keep you in here much longer, and you really might go round the bend."

"Not the strong, stable plainsman from Lincoln Junction. I think they'll let me out eventually and tell me that I'm cured of my homosexuality, but that I'll have to continue my struggle . . . and would I mind going away somewhere for a time."

"Graduate school?"

"Probably, though that will increase my pride and indocility."

We both laughed.

"Exile, Hermie?"

"Off to Egypt till Herod is dead!"

"It's not fair."

"They'll destroy themselves, Retramn. They're in so deep now that they can't get out. There are suits all over the country. It's only a matter of time before some tort lawyer figures out there is a gold mine here."

"This could mark you for all your life."

"My family believes me. I think the people at St. Theodolinda would believe me too. I don't care anyway."

"What do you want me to do, Hermie?"

"There's a lawyer in town named Horst Heller, my college roommate and boyhood friend. He's at a firm called Gulden, Rivers, and Schultz. You stop in to see him and tell him the story. Tell him to get me a habeas corpus or something so I can sell this cheap hotel. All he'll have to do is to threaten to go to court or to tell the *Prairie Reader*. They'll let me out right away."

"How will you know that I've talked to Horst Heller?"

"Call my dad over in the Junction. I can talk to them every week, though she's listening in all the time." I gestured with my head towards Sister's office. "We talk *auf Deutsch*—Volga Deutsch."

"I'll do it. Call me when you get out."

I promised that I would.

"Now hear my confession, just so I'm not lying to her."

He did. There weren't many opportunities to sin at St. Edward's, save through anger at the people that put me there.

We passed by Sister as I showed Retramn the way out.

"It's a mortal sin, Sister," I said, "to eavesdrop on a confession. You are bound by the seal of confession just as much as Father Retramn is."

274

She turned away in a huff.

Gotcha.

The next conversation with my family, my father said in the tone of an archconspirator, "Horst says *alles gut*."

"*Ja, ja, alles gut.*"

A week later Sister pounded on the door of my room.

"Yes, Sister," I said meekly.

"Well, you're being released, Father. I can't say I'm sorry to be rid of you."

"To tell the truth, Sister, I won't miss you either."

"Pack your things. You must not keep Monsignor waiting."

I almost said that she belonged inside instead of at the door, but I remembered that I was a priest.

Monsignor Meaghan and Father Peters were waiting for me, both grinning broadly. They shook hands and congratulated me on my triumph.

"I still have to get my books," I said.

"We'll put your stuff in the car," Father Peters said, putting on his genial, con man voice.

I brought back two satchels of books to be returned through Dave Winter to the local public library and carried them out to the car, the usual huge Cadillac limo.

"A lot of books," the Monsignor said, trying to be genial.

"Intellectual pride," I said. "I've got one more stack."

I picked up a basket with a half dozen more books.

"Oh yes, Sister," I said as I passed by her office. "I stopped taking your medicine three months ago."

As the car drove away, Irene, bundled up in a beige coat against the March wind, blinked in and out at the gate of the mental health center.

"It's no small feat to cure oneself of homosexuality," Father Peters said, continuing in his advocate's modality.

"Let's get one thing straight gentlemen, I am not gay, was not gay, and was not cured of being gay."

An uncomfortable silence.

"Furthermore, you know as well as I do, that Len Lyon is back in treatment for the second time since his ordination. You know what happened at St. Theodolinda. You've known for a couple of months, probably knew all along. Still, you kept me locked up in that asylum. I'd probably be there till Judgment Day, if my lawyer hadn't threatened you."

Judgment Day—that was an interesting term wasn't it?

"Don't worry; I do not intend to make trouble for you. But I do want you to know that I am aware of the game you played, perhaps because the Archbishop could not believe that Lenny would go right back to his old tricks."

"Father Lyon is a priest, Father," Peters said piously.

"And I'm not?"

"It's a different situation."

"I won't argue the point."

The plainsman was back, with his six-shooters loaded.

Silence descended on the Cadillac.

In retrospect, it would have been wiser to keep my big peasant mouth shut. I was warning them that I might be dangerous.

My possessions were dumped inside the door of the Cathedral rectory and Father James "Josh" Reynolds, the Archbishop's new secretary, conducted me up to his study.

Josh, back from a canon law degree in Rome, was alleged to be a man with a great future. He was a little guy, five-three, five-four, with slick black hair, a ferret-like face, and a deep and ponderous voice, matched by his deep and ponderous style.

"The Archbishop is very eager to see you, Father Hoffman."

"I bet."

"He is proud of your triumph over, ah, sickness."

"I'm not sick, Josh, and never was. Except maybe from all the tranquilizers that Dr. Straus was forcing me to take."

That shut him up.

Put away your guns, Hermie. At least be civilized with the Archbishop.

"Father Hoffman, Your Excellency."

The scene in his plush study was almost exactly the same as the last time I'd been there not quite a year ago. He was not wearing the Roman collar, and his purple-tinged cassock was open at the neck. However, the red ruby cuff links on his French cuffs were the same. Or perhaps that was the only kind he wore. The same aroma of strong cologne permeated the room. The same glass of dark liquid rested at his fingertips. It was only an hour after dinnertime—lunch to most Americans. Already he needed a drink.

"Ah, Father Hoffman . . . Herman." He rose from the

chair and extended his hand. I accepted with about as much enthusiasm as he had extended it.

"Sit down, sit down," he said. "Please do."

I did.

"I see from the hospital . . . uh, mental health center reports that you made great progress. I'm proud of you. I hope and indeed am quite certain that you will continue to grow in virtue and self-restraint."

"Yes, Your Excellency."

"I think it possible"—he sat down and flipped open my dossier—"that it might do you good to get away from Plains City for a time, perhaps to obtain a larger perspective on life."

"Yes, Your Excellency."

"Perhaps in graduate school somewhere . . . History seems to be one of your favorite fields."

"Yes, Your Excellency."

"We would, of course, pay your expenses, tuition, whatever."

"Thank you, Your Excellency . . . The University of Chicago. I'd study immigration history. I was once offered a fellowship there."

"That means some kind of scholarship?"

"It might."

"Well . . . I'd rather have you attend a Catholic university . . . The Catholic University of America, perhaps . . . Yet if the University of Chicago is really interested in you, it would be wise, I think, to go there."

"Yes, Your Excellency."

"I'm sure my good friend Sean Cardinal Cronin would take good care of you . . ."

I doubted that the Cardinal of Chicago, reputedly a man of considerable intelligence and devastating wit, would admit to being a good friend of Slippery Louie.

"Yes, Your Excellency."

"Keep me informed through my staff of your requirements. I will, of course, write a demisorial letter to Cardinal Cronin, indicating that you're a priest in good standing of Plains City and asking him to find, if possible, a parish in which you will work on weekends. I will want to hear periodic reports of your progress. I expect you will live with your family out in, ah, Lincoln County until you leave for Chicago."

"Thank you, Your Excellency."

Off to Siberia with you, Herman Hugo Hoffman.

Well, only to the shores of Lake Michigan.

I stopped at the door of the office and turned to face him. He was writing a note to place in my folder.

"For the record, Your Excellency, none of this deceives me. You're sending me into exile, one that is not unwelcome perhaps, but exile just the same. I have spent the last half year in a mental institution under treatment for a condition which you know I do not have. If it were not for a tough lawyer I might have been there till Judgment Day. All of this because you and your staff mishandled badly the situation at St. Theodolinda parish in Green Grove. I am not going to run to the *Prairie Reader* with my story. However, this strategy of cover-up and deception will not work in the long run, perhaps not even in the short run."

Before he could respond, I closed the door gently, walked down the stairs to the street and out into the

Square. The plainsman exited the saloon and spun his two six-shooters into his holster. Jerk. A fierce wind was blowing in across the prairies. Another blizzard?

I didn't care. I was free again.

The long run was longer than I thought it might be, but it came eventually.

Horst Heller was waiting on the street, hands jammed in his coat pockets. My things had been loaded into his already crowded Buick.

"Hermie!" His open, boyish face erupted into a characteristic smile. "Climb in. I'm driving you out to the Junction."

"You don't have to do that. I can take the bus."

"I have to drive out there anyway. Jump in before the cops come and give me a ticket."

"Not with a priest in the car . . . Thanks for springing me."

"Only sorry I didn't know five months ago . . . Those creepy bastards. They wouldn't even listen to me till I threatened to go to the *Prairie Reader*. You have lots of grounds for relief against them, if you want to drag them into court."

He started the car.

"I don't want to, Horst. I'm going to the University of Chicago. I just want to get out of this madhouse before I become as crazy as they are."

"Probably a good idea."

"Why are you driving to the end of the prairies?"

He blushed.

"Well, I guess I'm getting married. Emily tells me I am, so it's true."

"Emily?"

"Emily Hirsch, you remember her?"

I whistled my approval. She had been a gorgeous blossoming beauty in eighth grade at St. Killian's when we graduated from Township, a sweet and intelligent child. And a protégé of Hildy on the summer basketball court who was now teaching at Township High.

"Sure do."

"I can't figure why I'm so lucky. She graduated State U year before last. I've been dating her off and on. She claims she seduced me. I have no complaint. She's studying law. She'll be a better lawyer than I am. You know what, Hermie, I don't much care . . . Hey, will you say the wedding Mass? I called Father John as soon as I knew they were letting you out. He said it would be wonderful."

"Does the bride approve, Horst?"

"Approve? She's worshipped you since fourth grade. It's lucky for me you're not in the competition."

"Not so. Emily always was a woman of intelligence and taste."

"I'll be very good to her, Hermie," he said reverently. "I mean through the rest of our lives. She deserves the best a man has to give. My best may not be much, but it all belongs to her."

"Emily is the lucky one, Horst. What's more, I'm sure she knows it."

"That's what she says."

XVIII

THE FUNNY-LOOKING LITTLE PRIEST IN THE CHICAGO Bulls jacket looked up at me, his kind blue eyes blinking behind thick glasses and his mischievous smile hinting at fun. He was an unprepossessing little man, the kind, as he would later say, you would not even notice if you encountered him on an elevator.

"Call me Blackie."

He was, among other things, the pastor of the Cathedral and the vicar for extern priests of the Archdiocese of Chicago, the man whom I would have to persuade that I would not be a threat to the city or the Archdiocese if I was permitted to attend THE University.

I had put in an enormous amount of work to get into his office at the Cathedral rectory, including a rough airplane ride (my first) from Plains City to Chicago O'Hare and a struggle through that surreal madcap place and a morning rush hour ride down the expressway.

However, the most difficult challenge had been persuading the Plains City Chancery to send the demisorial letter I needed. I had sent my letter of application to the Archdiocese along with my admission to the University of Chicago which my old friend Tim Goodwin had won for me. Tuition paid and a teaching assistantship with enough money to live on if I could find a rectory that would take me in. However, the secretary to the Cardinal replied and said that the Cardinal was duly impressed with my academic record and would be delighted to have me resident in the Archdiocese, but it would be helpful if his very good friend, Archbishop Simon Isidore Louis, would send a letter to Chicago testifying to my good standing and good repute. The letter should be sent to Monsignor John Blackwood Ryan, vicar for extern priests.

I forwarded his letter to my Archbishop, who did not acknowledge it.

I struggled all summer to pry the letter out of the house on Prairie Square. I decided that if worse came to worst, I would fly to Chicago and enroll in THE University, then deal with the Chicago Chancery. Finally, I was assured by Josh Reynolds, none too patiently, that Mrs. Fiorenze, the Archbishop's administrative assistant, was aware of the Archbishop's commitment to send such a letter and would do so in due course.

The wedding of Horst and Emily was a huge success. The latter had matured into a slender, lovely young woman with not only intelligence in her light blue eyes but a hint of wisdom.

"I know what a good deal I'm getting, Hermie. I'll never let him get away."

"To tell the truth, Em, I don't think there's much chance of him trying."

I worked in the fields with Dad and Franky harvesting the winter wheat, plowing the fields we would leave fallow for the year, planting the beans that would grow in other inactive fields, and, finally, sowing the spring wheat.

I worked out every day and played basketball in the schoolyard, prayed in the church, gossiped with Monsignor O'Brien (hale and hearty in his upper eighties) and John Horvath. The word in the diocese was that Downtown was utterly committed to Lenny Lyon. He had been cleared every time. The complaints came from families who intended to take a lot of money from the Church. The rumors about me were vague. There was no evidence that I had done anything wrong. I had been cleared of the homosexuality suspicion and had left the Archdiocese in anger, perhaps to go to school somewhere else. One theory said that I was too much of an intellectual for the prairies and another that I had a bit of a breakdown because of the false charges against me.

John and I were nursing bottles of beer on the front porch of the rectory, watching the August sun sink into the haze. The Monsignor was sipping on a tiny glass of Jameson's straight up (any other way, he insisted, was a sin against the Holy Spirit). I sniffed rain coming in from the Rockies. We could use some.

"Some of this will always stick to you as long as you are a priest in Plains City," John said thoughtfully. "Chicago is a nice place . . ."

"No, John. *Urbsincampuensis* is home. I won't be driven out of it by malicious clerical culture, not even when the big explosion comes over the sexual abuse folly."

"It should have come already."

"Out here in the prairies it takes us longer to get angry. And the crisis has settled down nationally. But it will arise again. So much bad has been done in so many places that our leaders will never be able to keep it quiet."

"You're not going to make a fight of it when you come back, Hermie, are you?" the Monsignor asked anxiously.

"I won't have to," I said, not knowing fully what that answer might mean.

"Do you ever see our old friend Kathleen around the city, Herm?" John asked innocently. "I hear she has a daughter now. A little redhead."

"Good for her," I said, with equal innocence. "I assume that she will be as spirited as her mother."

"The girl's father," the Monsignor added, "is some kind of head shrinker at University Hospital. Forget his name . . ."

"Shannon," I said evenly, "Liam Shannon. An Irishman of some sort."

And that, like I say, was that.

My two priest mentors did not want me to run off with Dr. Shannon's wife. Nor did my family. Nor did anyone else in the Junction. Indeed the *News* had printed this most recent triumph of the plains on its front page. Yet everyone somehow thought it would be nice if this favorite young couple of nine years ago could be friends again. In principle I thought that their hope might be valid. Neither one of us was the kind of person who violated vows, were we?

But she had said "Judgment Day." She had not invited me to her wedding. Nor had she come to my first Mass, despite the invitation my parents had sent her. The matter rested apparently where she wanted it. What if there should be a signal that she didn't want it that way anymore?

We'd have to wait and see.

"What did they say in Cardinal Cronin's office?" John asked, changing the subject.

"A woman speaking for Monsignor Ryan, or it may have been Father Ryan—she was a very young woman—said that I should just come, and they'd worry about the letter later."

"Sounds pretty flexible."

I sighed.

"I'm fed up with it, John. They played a dirty trick on me once. They might do it again."

"Excuse me." Monsignor O'Brien wandered off.

"I'll make a call or two and threaten to bring the matter up at the priest senate meeting. I don't think they'd like that."

"The Archbishop wants to get rid of me," I complained, "then he throws obstacles in my way."

"I bet he doesn't know anything about it. His secretary, Mabel Fiorenze, makes a lot of decisions without asking him . . . Ever have a run-in with her?"

"No."

"Well maybe she just doesn't like your German name. I'll see that something is done before it's too late."

Monsignor O'Brien drifted back on the porch, a refill in his shot glass.

"I thought it would be useful under the circumstances if I read this letter Frank Sheed sent long ago:

" *'We are not baptized into the hierarchy; do not receive the Cardinals sacramentally; will not spend an eternity in the beatific vision of the pope. St. John Fisher could say in a public sermon, "If the pope will not reform the curia, God will." A couple of years later he laid down his head on Henry VIII's block for papal supremacy, followed to the same block by Thomas More [when Sheed wrote this he was not then canonized], who had spent his youth under the Borgia pope, Alexander VI, lived his early manhood under the Medici pope, Leo X, and died for the papal supremacy under Clement VII, as time-serving a pope as Rome ever had.*

" 'Christ is the point. I myself admire the present pope but even if I criticized him as harshly as some do, even if his successor proved to be as bad as some of those who have gone before, even if I find the Church as I have to live with it, a pain in the neck, I should still say that nothing that a pope (or a priest) could do or say would make me wish to leave the Church, although I might well wish that they would leave.

" 'Israel, through its best periods as through its worst, preserved the truth of God's oneness in a world swarming with gods, and a sense of God's majesty in a world sick with its own pride. So with the Church. Under the worst administration we could still learn Christ's truth, receive his life in the sacraments, be in union with him to the limit of our willingness. In our awareness of Christ, I can know the Church as his mystical body, and we must not make our judgment by the neck's sensitivity to pain.' "

We were all silent for a moment.

"Good stuff," I said.

"I'll make a copy of it for you."

"I think I may have to read it often," I admitted.

The University of Chicago does not start its winter quarter till the first week in October. Incoming graduate students were urged to present themselves in the last week of September.

On the Wednesday of the third week in September, the phone rang.

"*Ja, ja,*" Mama said. "*Ja,* he is here."

"A priest for you." She handed me the phone.

"Yes?"

"Father Ryan here," the voice said.

"Yes, Father," I said. "This is Herman Hugo Hoffman."

"Interesting that you should call me just when I was trying to make a call to you."

"You did call me, Father."

"Remarkable . . . In any event, we have finally received a demisorial letter for you from a certain Mrs.—sic—Mabel Fiorenze. She avers that the Archbishop has instructed her to send this letter. It is highly irregular for an Archbishop to direct a secretary to write a letter to a Cardinal . . . Should I credit it?"

"I don't know, Father. She often acts on her own."

"Fascinating . . . I think Milord Cronin will also find it so . . . In any event by all means come to Chicago. I can see you Friday at three o'clock here in my office at the Cathedral. Would that be convenient?"

"I'll make it convenient, Father."

"Remarkable."

So I packed a suitcase for a couple of nights in Chicago, drove across the state to MacArthur International, and stumbled around the airport, trying to remember how I had navigated it with Kathleen so long ago. I managed to find my plane five minutes before takeoff. Bumpkin flies to graduate school at one of the world's great universities. Through a storm system that was spawning tornados to the south of us, as the pilot frequently reminded us. How could Kathleen have so lightly risked her life flying to Europe every summer?

O'Hare International Airport overwhelmed me. I thought of the herd of bison that had swept across the prairies at the same time my ancestors were planting winter wheat in times past. We Volga Deutsche do not take taxis. I searched for public transportation and found that I had to go to another terminal. I went in the wrong direction, retraced my steps, asked a black passenger agent how to find the train to Chicago.

She looked at me in bemusement.

"You mean the L, Father."

"If that's what they call it."

"You just go down that escalator right behind you."

"Oh . . . How do I get to Chicago Avenue and State?"

"That's the easiest thing in the world. You just ride downtown to Washington then cross over to the State Street Subway and then ride up to Chicago Avenue. You can't miss it."

Well, I could and did. But I finally managed to climb up the stairs at Chicago and State and looked around for a cathedral. I asked a cop where the cathedral was.

289

"New in Chicago, Father?"

"I'm a cowpoke from the plains, sheriff, but my six-shooters are loaded!"

The cop thought that was very funny.

"It's right behind you, Father."

"Sure enough."

At exactly one minute to three I was admitted to the cathedral rectory by a pretty Asian teen with a brilliant smile.

"I'm Father Hoffman to see Father Ryan."

"I'm Megan Kim, there are four of us, like four women named Megan, you know. Some people are confused by that . . . I'll tell Father Blackie you're here."

She showed me into a room that looked like a comfortable parlor in a private home. There were no pictures of popes or bishops on the wall. I heard her talking in the office next door.

"There's a tall young priest here to see you, Father Blackie. He's like totally cute."

What kind of Catholic establishment had I stumbled into—charming and intelligent teens at the door, all apparently named Megan; rooms that did not intimidate; priests named Blackie . . . The rules were being bent.

Megan showed me into an office piled high with computer output and decorated with several glorious sunburst paintings.

The funny little priest bounded to his feet, shook hands, removed some of the output from a chair, and informed me that I should call him Blackie.

"Not Ishmael?" I said as I sat in the chair.

"An educated plainsman? Remarkable . . . Yes, as in Boston Blackie or the Black Prince or Black Bart . . . and your proper name is . . ."

"Herman, though I'd like to use my middle name in Chicago. Herman Hoffman sounds like a Gestapo officer in a World War Two film. My parents told me that they always liked Hugh better."

"Huey it will be then . . . Though in truth you look more like a pleasant, blond Gary Cooper in *The Plainsman*."

I was in a strange wonderland that had nothing to do with the Catholic Church that I knew from my homeland.

"Volga Deutsche, naturally," he continued.

"Ja, ja," and I spoke in German, "five generations of wheat farmers out beyond the big river."

"Interesting accent, probably authentic like mountain folk talk authentic English . . . Ah, accepted at THE University with tuition and a teaching assistantship . . . You must try your German on the undergraduates . . . Small wonder. They must have looked at your credits . . . Remarkable . . . Good letter of recommendation doubtless . . . You will write on your own people, presumably?"

"I hope to."

"You will find THE University an interesting place. Unlike the clergy, they have the highest respect for intelligence. We could well afford to learn from them. Unfortunately, priests with grades like yours are often considered flawed, though not in this rectory."

"I have been warned many times of the dangers of spiritual pride."

"Much less common in the clergy than aecidia—pride over being a slug . . . If I may make a suggestion about THE University"—his blue eyes blinked—"they set much store not only in intelligence but in flair. Thus you must establish yourself early as a man who possesses flair. Turn in your papers a couple of weeks early, quote Max Weber or Ludwig Pastor or some such in the original German, with your quaint Volga accent, admit to being from the prairies, celebrate the agricultural accomplishment of your ancestors. A quarter of such discreet interventions and you will own the History Department."

"I'm not sure I could practice such . . . tricks."

"They only become tricks when you take them seriously . . . Now let's see . . . Indeed, there is this letter from your Ordinary's office, my very good friend the Most Reverend Simon Lazarus Isidore Louis, a.k.a. Slippery Louie."

"I take it 'very good friend' has a certain idiomatic meaning in Chicago, Father, er Blackie."

"You learn quickly. Here is his letter. I wait your considered reaction."

Dear Cardinal Cronin,

His Excellency Archbishop Simon Lazarus Isidore Peter Louis has directed me to write you with regard to a certain young priest of this Archdiocese who has begged insistently for permission to attend graduate school at some college in your city. We have finally acceded to his requests. It is true that Father Herman H. Hoffman is a priest in good standing of this Archdiocese, though we have found him on occasion to have inclinations to spiritual pride. Therefore, we recommend him to your attention with some reservations. Since we cannot at the present time afford to pay his tuition or expenses, we hope you will be able to find him a parish where he might make a useful contribution to the work of the Church.

Cordially yours,
Mabel Fiorenze
Vice Chancellor

I felt my face turn red. Before I could explode the ineffable Blackie commented, "It is not the offense of someone of that rank directing his secretary to presume to address a cardinal prince of the Holy Roman Church so familiarly. It is the hint that THE University can be adequately described as 'some college.' But tell me, Huey, why were they so eager to get rid of you and then to cut you off, so to speak, at the knees?"

I told him my story, as objectively as I could, including the Archbishop's promise to pay my expenses.

"Fascinating . . . Drugged and locked up in a cuckoo's nest . . . Alas, you are not the first whistle-blower to merit that fate . . . To change the avian metaphor a bit, the chickens will shortly come home to roost, and the American Church will face the worst crisis in its history."

"In our case, prairie chickens."

"Arguably."

He sighed loudly, as though he were about to experience an asthma attack. Later I would learn that it was a family trait, traceable to their west of Ireland origins and could mean anything or nothing, depending on the context.

"Let me make a second suggestion. I assume you will return to, ah, Lincoln Junction periodically in the course of your years at THE University? On one of those trips, you would be prudent to return to this St. Edward's Center and obtain, as is your right, the transcript of your treatment there."

"You would want to see it?" I asked uncertainly.

"Not hardly. You are patently a truth teller. However, it might prove useful in years to come to have such a record, especially since it is not unknown that chancery offices destroy records that might not serve their purposes."

"I will certainly do that . . . Then I have permission to live here in Chicago as a priest?"

He looked at me in confusion.

"Oh, yes. Patently . . . We will find you a parish, one that you will, I think, enjoy. Out of respect I clear such decisions with Milord Cronin who is wise enough invariably to accept my recommendation on such matters . . . You are flying back to bison land immediately?"

He glanced at my luggage.

"I thought I might go out to THE University tomorrow, then fly back to Plains City, pack my car, and drive back to meet the first day of class . . . Can you recommend a hotel at which I might stay?"

"You're in one such. Alas, we have all too many spare rooms available. Feel free to ask the good Megan to place a call to your family if you wish to tell them that you are now officially a Chicagoan. I'll drive you out to your parish tomorrow evening, so you can hear confessions, such as these might be, on Saturday and say Mass on Sunday. Milord Cronin will look forward to meeting you at supper."

He led me out of the office.

"Megan, Father Hugh will be staying with us for a few days. He'll be on the third floor . . ."

"Room Three-oh-four?"

"Indeed."

"You may want to rest your eyes a few hours before supper. Possibly there'll be a touch of refreshment in my room at the opposite end of the corridor at five-thirty, it has a splendid view of Chicago Avenue and the John Hancock Center."

I lay on the bed in my room but could not nap. There was too much noise outside, and I was too overwhelmed by the Archdiocese of Chicago. I felt I had passed through Alice's looking glass into a different world.

At 5:30 I walked down the corridor to Monsignor Blackie's room. I encountered a tall, handsome man in a gleaming white French-cuffed shirt, with thick white hair, bright blue eyes, broad shoulders, and a face deeply marked by character, both sadness and laughter.

"Sean Cronin, Huey. Welcome to Chicago."

"Thank you, Cardinal," I stumbled.

"I read the letter that my very good friend S. I. Louis directed his secretary to write to me. He shall receive an appropriate response. We'll take care of you while you're here—insurance and that stuff too. It's an honor to have you with us."

We entered Monsignor Blackie's suite. The Cardinal continued to talk as he opened a liquor cabinet and removed three Waterford tumblers.

"Blackwood has decided that you're going to live and work to the extent you can at St. Praxides." He poured a fair amount of Bushmills Green into a glass for the Monsignor and one for me and a tiny drop for himself. "It's one of the most unique parishes in our Republic, which the good people out there will be the first to tell you. It's what happens to the South Side Irish when they make a few dollars. It is especially noted"—he sat down and lifted his glass in a toast—"as the swarming ground for the Ryan clan. I defy you to figure out the intimate connections among them. However, I warn you that they think they are an ecclesiola, a church in miniature. If they see someone who could benefit from their help and protection, they will indeed take that person under their wing, *whether he or she wants that protection or not*. They're a little mad."

"I am, alas, the white sheep of the family," Blackie admitted, "the only normal one."

"So, Huey," Cardinal Cronin said, "welcome to Chicago! It's good to have you with us!"

"Failte and slainte!" Blackie agreed.

I could hardly believe that first day in Chicago—or the days and weeks and months afterwards. I grew up a little in my Chicago years, I think, because of the respect for intelligence at THE University and for wit at St. Praxides. I still can't quite believe the exuberance of that experience. I would later find in Chicago the same anti-intellectualism and capacity for denial that I had encountered in Plains City. Clergy are clergy everywhere. I often encountered a lifting of eyebrows when I told them where I was from and that I was studying immigration history at THE University; both the subject and the place were just a little bit suspect. However, I was never ridiculed.

Irene did not come with me, though when I returned home in the summer to visit the family and pore over the archives the Lincoln County folks had assembled through the years, she was often around. She never did give me the album of the pictures she had taken at my ordination and first Mass.

I think I matured in both my intellectual discipline and priestly skills in Chicago. I sang with the parish choir at St. Praxides. I bought an old accordion and taught the people German drinking songs, and they taught me Irish rebel songs and lullabies. They insisted that it was possible for me to learn how to hit an iron shot on the golf course and were correct. I resolved that I would be a once-a-week golfer in the years to come who could sometimes get into the low eighties instead of a more frequent golfer who might occasionally break into the seventies.

I followed Blackie's advice on how to cope with THE University. I even made up quotes from German historians that were approximately what they had said. I noted that the highest compliment you could pay to someone about the originality of his research findings was to say, "That doesn't surprise me." With little effort I had become a character on the Hyde Park scene.

The archives in Lincoln County contained enough material for a lifetime of research. Major history journals had accepted two of my articles even before I passed my Ph.D. exams.

For all the success, both academic and parochial, I remained intensely dissatisfied with myself. OK. I was a little bit better than a pedestrian parish priest and a competent student of archives. I would return to Plains City thirty years old with a sense of failure. I had not lived up to my ideals. I was not the kind of priest I should be. I had wasted many opportunities. I had let down two people who had trusted me, Kathleen Quinlan and Todd Sweeney. Without any resistance I had permitted the Archdiocese to imprison me and drug me.

I could do adequate parish work, sometimes more than adequate. I would continue my research. So what? Other priests had done that too. I wanted to be more. No, I had to be more. I didn't know what that meant, however.

Most of the time I did not think about Kathleen, though, occasionally, like the first night at the Cathedral rectory or on my trips to the Ryan compound at Grand Beach, I wished I could pick up the phone and tell her about what had happened.

Despite my Germanic melancholy (and we are far more global in our world sadness than the Irish), my four Chicago years were wonderful, even glorious. Bishop Blackie, as he had become, hinted to me that I might stay on in Chicago when I had finished my degree. I had come to love its beauty, its culture, and its vitality. I knew, however, that I must return. There was unfinished work back home, though I did not know what it was.

XIX

MONSIGNOR O'BRIEN DIED DURING THE FIRST SUMMER of my graduate work. The Archbishop sent word that because he had been called to Rome by the Holy Father, he could not be present but he "extended the sympathy and the blessing of the Most Holy Father to all the people of St. Killian's." Bishop Meaghan was busy administering the affairs of the Archdiocese in His Excellency's absence. Josh Reynolds was sent as the Archbishop's delegate. John Horvath asked me to say the Mass and preach. I argued that I should not and was overruled by the community. A large crowd of priests turned up in the Junction because everyone loved Frank O'Brien. Many a clerical eyebrow was raised when they saw that I was the principal concelebrant and not Josh.

I was so choked up that I didn't know whether I could begin my carefully prepared homily. Then, more reckless than prudent, I told the story about Kathleen and me singing Bach while the Monsignor had silently watched and wept at his multicultural parish. The parishioners laughed and sobbed because it was so typical. Not a single priest stirred. I sang a little bit of "O Sacred Head" then went on to the fifth chapter of the Epistle to the Hebrews about human priests. It was a good homily if not a great one. The congregation cheered and applauded, much to the dismay of the clergy.

I turned to the priests in the front pews in their white surplices. "Gentlemen, you must understand that the applause is not for an inadequate homily but for one of the finest priests Lincoln County has ever known."

Of all the priests present, only Dave Winter reacted to me after the burial while we were eating lunch in the same hall in which Kathleen and I had sung.

"Best funeral homily any of us ever heard, Hermie. Most of the guys won't tell you that. Never praise another priest because it might go to his head."

"I don't care one way or another."

Yet, in truth, I did care. I wanted the band of brothers to like me and respect me. Foolish hope.

"Was the girl in church?"

"Girl?"

"The one you were singing Bach with?"

"Oh, no, she moved away."

Two days after the funeral, John Horvath and I were sitting on the front porch as the rain clouds were rising in the west, glowering above the unseen mountains before they began their mad rush across the prairies.

"Is the sexual abuse scene quiet here?" I asked casually.

"Quiet, but not dangerous. It turns out that Dick Peters, 'I'm the victims' advocate, you can trust me,' has disappeared from public view."

"Oh."

"You know how much he loved working the African-American poor in that old parish by the rail yards? Well, what he loved the most, it seems, was spanking the bottoms of his black Mass servers."

"Vomit stuff!"

"Some of the parents tried to sue, but they don't have the money. The Archdiocese has filed a countersuit charging defamation and also blamed the parents for not providing adequate supervision for their sons. Then Joe Kennedy asked that the suit be dismissed because priests are independent contractors and not employees of the Archdiocese. The judge granted the motion. The parents didn't have the money or the will to appeal."

"The media?"

"The *Prairie Reader* reported it, of course, but as straightforward news, no editorial. The *Plainsman and Gazette* reported the dismissal in a three-line story on page thirteen. The TV stations ignored it. Everyone is afraid of the Archdiocese."

"The cases around the country were big news in Chicago. Every network did a special *Sins of the Fathers*."

John nodded.

"You know, Herm, I thought that they wouldn't get away with it. But I think they weathered the storm. The scandal has come and gone. The bishops think it's business as usual."

"I wonder."

"The guys are saying that it's all a crock of shit," John

went on. "They agree with Joe Kennedy that the victims and their families are just after our money. They're our enemies."

"That's what the guys would say . . . And your successor at Newman?"

"The word among the guys is that he was cleared by everyone, and that he's doing fine work out in California."

"Is he?"

"Not to my knowledge . . . The point is that Downtown thinks they've gotten away with the stonewalling and disinformation. Meaghan brags that we have the lowest per capita loss on these cases of any diocese in the country."

"Do you think the Church can permanently cover up the terrible things that have been done to kids and teenagers, the lives they've destroyed, the agony of parents . . . !"

"They're continuing to do it. Your friend Lenny Lyon has been sent off for another round of rehabilitation. No one seems to mind."

Somehow I didn't think it would be that easy.

There were no new scandals, however, when I returned from Chicago with my Ph.D. diploma under my arm (actually packed in my suitcase). I had sent a letter from Chicago to the Archbishop respectfully saying that I had completed my graduate work and earned my doctorate. I requested assignment to a parish. I enclosed offprints of my two published articles, fully aware that they might lead to another ferverino about the need for spiritual humility. I also called the Chancery and asked for an appointment to see the Archbishop and was informed that I would be put on the waiting list, but the Archbishop was very busy.

I settled in at Tom Donohue's parish near downtown to be prepared for my appointment, though I was not prepared to wait all summer. Dave Winter phoned and invited me to play golf with the "guys" on Thursday. I figured the Thursday golf game might symbolize my readiness to reintegrate into the Archdiocese, so I agreed. Our "regular" course was inside the city limits at South Park at the south end of the city, near the interstate bypass.

"You haven't changed much, Herm," Dave said to me.

"It's been only four years, five counting my time at St. Edward's."

"It seems like much longer. You're also the only one who hasn't put on weight . . . You must have worked out a lot in Chicago . . . play any golf?"

"No one loses weight on a golf course."

He chuckled.

"Especially when they have a couple of drinks and eat a big dinner at the Steak House after the game."

"Do they kill the steers there now before serving them?"

"Your mordant Volga wit hasn't changed."

"Got worse."

"There's something I have to tell you before we meet Matt and Jock . . . Everyone has strong opinions on it."

"Oh?"

"Lucifer is dying."

"Poor man," I said.

"In an AIDS hostel."

"I'll have to visit him."

"You'll be the only priest to do so . . . You see, he denies that he's dying of AIDS. Most of the guys accept that. If they see him in the hostel, they'll have to face the fact that, if he's not dying of AIDS, he's the only one in the place who isn't."

I thought about that.

"I don't understand, Dave, what the story is about Lenny. We called him Lucifer at the seminary with good reason. Why is everyone so eager now to deny that the title may be appropriate?"

"It's all part of the cover-up mentality. Lenny is the most blatant abuser in the Archdiocese. Yet the guys will tell you that he's never done any of the things of which he's been accused. They say he's dying because of terrible stress. He's been bounced around to treatment centers all over the country, in and out. He shows up in a parish and in a week or two the people find out who he is and complain to Downtown. So the Arch moves him on."

"I don't think what he has is curable, Dave."

"You're probably right." He turned into South Park.

The course was brown already, and it was only July. Nothing like the "Club" where I had played with the St. Prax people. Hard ground, long bounce on a drive. I should have a field day. That would show them.

Show whom? And what? Was I spoiling for a fight?

"The problem is"—Dave hesitated—"most of the guys kind of blame you for his run of bad luck. They

304

say it all started when you imagined that rape scene at St. Theodolinda."

"That isn't true," I said quietly. "He had already done time at St. Edward's before we were ordained."

"I know that, I know that, Herm. I'm just telling you what they're saying. It will not be easy coming back here."

"It will be difficult only if I let the 'guys' get to me."

Only Jock Binder and Matt McLaughlin were playing with us that day. Jimmy Kerr and Jake Kolokowski were too far out in the prairies to make it every Thursday.

Jock started in on the first tee.

"Hey, good to see you again, Herm. Finish in Chicago?"

"Yep."

"Where next?"

"A parish somewhere."

"The Arch will never give you a parish, everyone knows that."

"We'll see."

"Yeah, well, good luck . . . we play for money . . . five dollars a hole. Whoever wins a hole, everyone else gives him five bucks. The most you can lose that way is ninety dollars, the most you can win is two hundred seventy dollars. It's always a lot less. Then at the end we go double or nothing on the last hole. OK?"

"It goes against my Russian German instincts, but OK."

Jock had put on at least thirty-five pounds, Matt maybe fifteen. Dave hadn't changed much.

I drove last—275 straight down the fairway.

"Same old big drive." Jock laughed uneasily.

"Without the hook," Dave said in some awe.

To make a long story short, I won $270. I had three bogeys and one double bogey, but I won those holes too, and three birdies. First time I had cracked seventy-five. I would have been ten strokes higher at the "Club."

"You must have played a lot in Chicago," Jock admitted grudgingly.

"Not really. Some of my friends at the parish where I worked turned me over to their pro."

There was no talk of double or nothing on the eighteenth.

I rolled up the fives and gave them to Dave. "I'd put them in the poor box at my parish if I had one. So you put it in yours."

I was pretty certain that there would be no more golf invitations.

At supper (I had salmon that was not too dry) the talk turned around to Len Lyon.

"I talked to him on the phone the other day," Jock boasted. "He sounded great, much better than the last time. He says they're going to let him out in a couple of weeks. He doesn't belong in that terrible place."

"No one does," Matt agreed.

"Where will he go when they release him?" I asked.

"That's up to the Arch. Probably to the seminary, where he can recover completely."

Smart move.

"You did good, Herm," Dave said to me as we

pulled out of South Park.

"No return invitations, I suspect."

"You ruined Jock's little game."

"Give him a few days, and he'll deny that it ever happened . . . What will he do when Len dies of AIDS?"

"The story will go around that he had a stroke."

"It will all catch up someday."

"Do you honestly think so, Herm? They're still getting away with it."

"They're just digging a deeper grave."

"There's a parish I might show you, if you don't mind. No one wants it because they say it's not worth much. I think they're wrong. The personnel board can't give it away. You might be able to pry it away from the Arch."

"Sure, where is it?"

"St. Cunegunda in Prairie View. Nice little town. There's a development coming in. High-quality homes. Probably a lot of Catholics. No one Downtown seems to know about it."

It was night when we arrived on the hill above the little town. The ramshackle old wooden church and rectory seemed solid enough structurally. My family and friends could put in planks and add new paint and in a couple of days it would look great. Out to the west, spring wheat glittered faintly in the starlight. Beneath us the short main street with its single stoplight was already empty. The smell of wheatfields filled the air.

"Two interstate exits from State U, maybe two thousand people, half of them Catholic. Nice quiet Poles and Czechs and Germans, all of them hoping that the development comes through. Rumors that some of them want a Catholic school . . ."

"There'll be a lot of Irish . . ."

"The town has only a few years left, Herm. That's why the personnel board can't give it away."

We got out of the car and walked up to the church. Though it was made of wood, it was also the work of skilled craftsmen, the kind that Germans brought with them from Europe. The door was locked, but there was a light on in the church, which revealed the exquisite colors of the stained glass. A perfect immigrant church for a historian of immigration.

"Thanks, Dave, I'll take it."

"You'll have a struggle with the personnel board."

"I'll pry it out of the Archbishop."

"He won't want to give it to you."

"We'll see about that."

The next morning I walked over to the AIDS hospice, a run-down wooden apartment building in the poorest section of town. Depressing on the outside, it was even worse on the inside. But the workers were impressive.

"I'd like to visit Father Lyon," I said to the young white woman at the desk.

"You're Father . . . ?"

"Father Hoffman."

"I'm so glad you've come, Father. Priests don't seem to want to visit Father Lyon."

I was outfitted with surgical gloves and conducted to the room Lenny shared with another dying man. I was shocked when I saw him. It was hardly Lenny anymore, only a gaunt skeleton with a haunted face and grim eyes.

"Lenny," I said tentatively.

He looked up for a moment, peered at me, smiled a hideous smile, and extended his hand.

"Hermie!" he said in a dry rasp. "Great of you to come! Most of the guys can't take this place. Sit down for a moment."

"How you doing?" I asked, an idiot question.

"Not too bad, better now than last week. I hope to be out of here in a couple of weeks."

"They seem like good people."

"The best, kind and considerate, gentle . . ."

"Good deal."

"It's a little odd, you know. The Archdiocese couldn't find anyplace for me to recover, so they put me in here, though I don't have AIDS, never have . . . So anyway what's new? You're back from Chicago?"

"Yeah, finally finished up."

"Where to next?"

"Waiting for a parish."

"You'll have a hard time getting one. Those guys are really mean . . ."

"I'll get one all right."

"You better have something on them."

"They'll give me a parish."

"Yeah, hey, it's great to see you. Just like the old days at St. Theodolinda, huh? We had fun there, didn't we?"

"Sure did."

He closed his eyes.

"I'm falling asleep, Hermie, bad night last night. Come back again."

"I sure will."

The nurse at the door persuaded me to make the rounds of the hospice. I blessed people and heard confessions.

"Thank you so much, Father. It's good to see a priest. You're a sign here of God's forgiving love."

"That's what a priest should do," I said. "We try."

"I hope you'll come back."

"I will," I said. "What's your name?"

"Rosie."

"How much longer for him, Rosie?"

"Anytime. A week, two weeks at the most."

"I'll stay in touch with you about Father Lyon. As soon as I get a permanent address, I'll give you a phone number. When Father Lyon starts to go . . ."

"We'll call you."

"Any hour of the day or night."

"Yes, Father."

I walked out into the glare of the noonday sun. Dear God in heaven, why do You let these things happen? I know You don't have to explain. I believe that You know what You're doing. Yet so much suffering . . ."

God did not venture an answer. He never does, other than those He has already given.

Back at Little Flower—Tom Donohue's parish—I called the Chancery again about my appointment. I was told they knew where I was, and they'd call me.

I turned on my laptop and continued to work on an

article about the advance scouts that the Volga people had sent to check out the prairies.

That night I had supper with Horst and Emily Heller. They lived in a yuppie town house in the gentrified east end of Little Flower. Their two blond sons were polite and respectful, as befits the offspring of the Russian Germans. When the kids were in bed, we relaxed with a beer before supper. *Ja, ja,* Volga Deutsche drink beer (or schnapps) not cocktails or white wine. Both my friends seemed in excellent physical condition. *Ja, ja,* we Russian Germans believe in fitness, though we may have picked that up from the real Germans.

"You'd never guess who I bumped into the other day, Herm," Emily chirped brightly.

"Can't guess."

"Kathleen."

"Kathleen whom?"

Prig! You hide behind your pedantry to cover your anxiety!

"OUR Kathleen, who else? Kathleen Quinlan or Kathleen Shannon as she is now. We are both doing the marathon on Sunday."

"Kathleen runs the marathon?"

"Certainly! She was a great athlete, don't you remember?"

Horst didn't say a word or move a muscle.

"Softball and basketball," I said tonelessly.

"She was also in track at Township . . . Neither one of us will win the marathon. But it's a fun way of staying in shape!"

"And we run it in late June," Horst said, "because we

311

really don't want to avoid dehydration, which is part of the game."

His wife ignored him.

"She's more gorgeous than ever," Emily bubbled. "And very happy. She has two adorable little redheads and seems very much in love with her husband. He's Irish, you know. I mean from Ireland."

"Worst kind."

"And runs a psychiatry center at State U."

Eventually I would bump into her someplace. Long before Judgment Day. I would have to plan my reaction.

"Sexual abuse victims," Horst said.

The always effervescent Emily bounced up from her chair.

"Well, I'll go put the wurst and schnitzel on the table and let you two talk business."

"Will you watch the marathon?" Horst asked, raising a blond eyebrow.

"I doubt it."

The thought had occurred to me.

"Will they give you a parish?" He shifted to our business.

"They don't want to, but they will."

I handed him a copy of the letter from Mabel Fiorenze to Cardinal Cronin.

"This isn't what they promised you, is it?"

"The Archbishop promised me they'd pay my tuition and expenses."

"Possible breach of contract?"

"We could hardly sue them, Horst."

"We could whisper threats . . ."

"Maybe we will. Maybe I will when I barge in and demand to see him."

"Is there a parish open?"

"St. Cunegunda in Prairie View. It's a place the personnel board can't give away."

"Why not? There's a big development of high-quality homes going up out there."

"It has been delayed several times. I gather from Father Donohue that the Archdiocese has washed its hands of the project."

"They're crazy, Herm, totally crazy."

"No, Horst, just arrogant and dumb . . . So what's happening on the pedophile front?"

"Calm before the storm. Arrogant and dumb is right. They figure over there that since they've gotten away with stonewall and cover-up for four decades they can continue to do it. They don't see that the tort lawyers now smell the bacon. They're picking up big awards all over the country, and they're sniffing around here."

"Why aren't they worried?"

"They figure they control the courts, the media, and juries. No twelve people in Plains City will find against the Archdiocese."

"Aren't they right?"

Horst twisted in his chair.

"Herm, Em and I hang with our own kind—Yuppies who are solid Catholics. They don't like the smell. Even out in the Junction attitudes are changing rapidly. I'm not sure the Archdiocese would get the verdict out there, especially if the plaintiff had a good case."

I sighed, an imitation of Blackie.

"I visited Father Lyon this morning."

Horst blinked.

"That was awfully generous of you, Herm. How's he doing?"

"Dying," I said. "Doesn't have long. Still denies that he has AIDS."

"He's denied all his life, hasn't he?"

"Poor guy."

"It was good of you to visit him, Herm. I hear that the other priests avoid him. Are they afraid of catching AIDS?"

"No, they're afraid to discover that he's dying of AIDS. Even at his funeral they will deny it was AIDS and blame it on the stress I started."

"Idiots!"

"You've never known cops or doctors or lawyers or journalists who do the same thing?"

He shrugged his shoulders.

"A tort lawyer who picked up a big judgment in Michigan has been scouting out Plains City, Anton Vandenhuvel. Tough, tough man. He's particularly interested in the story of Leonard Lyon."

"He'll be dead."

"That won't matter. The suit will be against the Church. If you ask me, the Church will lose. Then the floodgates will open."

"Figures."

"And you'll be involved."

"Why me?"

"Gimme a break, Herm. You're the first whistle-blower in the Lucifer Lyon story. They locked you up and drugged you. You're a prime witness. That might be why they don't want to give you a parish, though they're not clever enough to think of that."

"Would I have to testify?"

He thought about it.

"I don't think Vandenhuvel would risk forcing you to appear as a hostile witness. It probably would be up to you."

"I see."

Emily called us to the breaded schnitzel and wurst.

Several days later I was watching the Plains City Marathon with Horst.

Emily and Kathleen were running neck and neck towards the finish line. They were wearing number patches around their necks and the minimal, tight-fitting running clothes that are permitted to women runners these days. Both of them were soaking wet. Kathleen saw me watching hungrily. Flashes of lightning exploded from her green eyes.

"It's not Judgment Day yet, you horny bastard."

One of the bolts hit me, and I screamed in pain.

I woke up, not at all sure that it all hadn't happened. For five minutes perhaps I thought that it had. Then wakefulness scattered the illusion. It had been, I had to admit to myself, a wonderful illusion.

XX

"FATHER HOFFMAN, THIS IS THE CHANCERY OFFICE calling."

"Yes."

"You have an appointment this afternoon, punctually at three with Father Reynolds. Father Reynolds is very busy. He should not be kept waiting."

"I'll be there."

I was, precisely at 2:58. I waited till 3:15, a delay that I had expected. At 3:10 I removed my laptop and began to work.

"Sorry to keep you waiting, Herman," Josh Reynolds said with an attempt at urbanity. "This place is a nut-house."

"I won't argue that," I said.

The damn plainsman again. I was looking for a fight.

"Congratulations on your doctorate."

"Thank you."

"Was it very difficult?"

"Yes, but I enjoyed it."

"It was very good of you to visit poor Lenny Lyon the other day."

"He's dying, Josh."

"I don't think it's quite that bad."

"He's dying of AIDS, though all the guys deny it, as he does. It won't be more than a week or two."

"I'm sure you'll be happy to know that the Archbishop wants you to teach at the seminary."

"No."

"No, you're not happy or, no, you won't obey?"

"No, both."

"Why not?"

"I don't want to."

"And why don't you want to?"

Josh was becoming flustered. Even though he was young and short, he had acquired enough power and enough ruthlessness that most priests feared him. I didn't.

"St. Clement's has a wonderful faculty whose talents are wasted on a student body that has no interest in the intellectual life. I don't want to fight that battle."

"Don't you think you owe the Boss something because of all the money we spent on your education?"

"You didn't spend a cent."

He seemed startled.

"We agreed to pay for your tuition and your expenses."

"As a price for my going into exile. You didn't pay the price."

I passed over to him a copy of Mabel's letter to Cardinal Cronin.

He glanced at it quickly and read it carefully.

"That woman keeps making trouble," he said, trying to bring me into the inside conflicts of the Chancery. "Believe me, Herm, I knew nothing about this. I'm sure the Archbishop doesn't either."

"Oh yes he does. Cardinal Cronin called him about it."

"Are you sure?"

"Absolutely."

I had not been present, but Blackie had, and he reported with great glee the conversation. Patently, as Blackie would have said, Slippery Louie had not passed the story on to his staff.

"What do you want, Hermie?"

"A parish."

"There aren't any available just now. If you were willing to wait . . ."

"St. Cunegunda in Prairie View."

"There's nothing there."

"A thousand Catholics."

"Down from two thousand ten years ago. The place is dying, Hermie."

"Maybe we can save it."

"Not a chance. That development will never happen. Never. We will have to merge the parish with St. Damian in West Town."

"Give me a couple of years."

He sighed.

"I'll see what I can do . . . Can I keep this letter?"

"Sure; I have other copies. The Cardinal was so amused by it that he sent copies all around the Chancery."

True enough. Blackie had made five or six copies.

Reynolds winced.

"Can you come back in a week?"

"No. I won't leave without a letter from the Archbishop appointing me as pastor of St. Cunegunda—pastor, not administrator."

"OK. I'll see what I can do."

Sensibly he would do his best. Unlike the Archbishop

and Bishop Meaghan and Joe Kennedy, Josh was not yet completely corrupted by Chancery office power. Given time, he would be.

I waited an hour, during which I worked on my article.

Finally, Josh returned, a letter and an envelope in his hand.

"I had to struggle for this, Hermie, but it has the Archbishop's signature and seal, so it's official." I was thereby appointed pastor of the parish of St. Cunegunda in Prairie View effective immediately.

"Thanks, Josh," I said.

"You may not be grateful when you get out there. The last pastor took off with a married woman from West Town. Still with her. The previous one was a drunk. Neither lasted more than two years."

The Archbishop's signature seemed unsteady. Was the tumbler of cognac empty?

That was not my concern.

"You don't happen to have set of keys, do you?"

Josh reached in the pocket of his vest and pulled out two keys.

"Your immediate predecessor threw these on the desk when he came in to tell us he was quitting. . . . I have no idea what the finances are like out there. We haven't had an annual report for five years."

"Thank you, Josh," I said wryly. "It sounds like fun."

"Good luck," he extended his hand tentatively.

"I'll need some of that too."

I drove back to the Little Flower rectory, accepted Tom Donohue's congratulations and loaded half my stuff into the Crown Victoria. It was rush hour, however, so I walked over to the AIDS hostel to see Len Lyon.

"Father is having a bad time of it," Rosie told me at the door. "He knows he will die soon and doesn't want to."

"How you doing, Len?" I asked in his room.

"Well, I've outlived the other guy." He gestured at the empty bed. "Private room till they bring in the next freak . . . What's new with you?"

There was not much left of him, less even than the last time.

"They gave me St. Cunegunda out in Prairie View."

"Hey, good deal! . . . What's out there?"

"An old church, an old rectory, a lot of history, and a nice view of the prairie."

"How many families?"

"Two hundred, two-fifty."

"Sounds like a lot of work . . . You'll stay in touch with me, won't you, Hermie? Everyone else seems to have lost interest."

"Every time I come into town I'll stop by."

"I'm getting better," he said, closing his eyes. "Never can tell, however, when I might take a turn for the worse . . . I'd like you to be here."

"I'll leave my phone number with Rosie."

"Thanks, Hermie. Means a lot to me."

Then he was asleep.

"Fall asleep on you?" Rosie asked at the reception desk.

"Yes . . . How long?"

"Couple of days at the most."

I wrote the phone number of my parish on a desk pad. "Call me, any hour of the day or night."

I added my cell phone number.

"Yes, Father."

I had a lot on my mind during the ride out to Prairie View. What kind of parish priest might I be now that I had full responsibility? What would happen to Josh Reynolds, who still retained some shreds of integrity in what was obviously a chaotic operation? Was the Archbishop a heavy drinker? What about poor Lucifer?

Lightbearer indeed. How did someone get that way?

The sun was setting when I arrived at St. Cunegunda, painting the old church with a swath of gold that transfigured its peeling white paint. The wooden steps were shaky, the door hung loose on its hinges, yet the structure seemed sound enough. I unlocked the door, fumbled for a light switch, and gasped with astonishment.

The woodwork inside, mid-nineteenth-century German, might have been in a museum. Statues, pews, decorations around the altars on either side, rococo trim of cherubs and seraphs, a very old altar rail—all were masters of a woodworker's art and craft. As were the stained-glass windows. Someone had lavished a lot of loving care and spent a lot of money on St. C, probably a long time ago.

No, I was wrong about the loving care. It was continuing. Someone had polished the woodwork, swept the wooden floors, dusted the sanctuary, lighted the sanctuary light.

I explored the sacristy. That too was freshly dusted, though it was very old. I looked at the vestments. They also were very old, a little tattered, but had once been expensive. I opened a closet door and discovered a long row of file cabinets. Inside were the archives of the parish, not only the sacramental record books—baptisms, first Communions, confirmations, marriages, deaths—but also file upon file of correspondence and newspaper clippings. Material for a doctoral dissertation. The parish had been founded in 1858—back when six-foot-high prairie grass had covered the plains. It must have been the first entry port for my ancestors. Prairie View in those days was a bustling market town that could easily have supported a church of three thousand people.

I walked back into the sanctuary and knelt under the statue of St. Cunegunda, the wife of St. Henry, the emperor of Germany, with whom she had an allegedly virginal marriage, though perhaps they were merely unable to have children.

Well, I said to her, a lot of people put a lot of love and devotion into this church in your honor. The Archdiocese has not treated them very well recently. We'll try to correct that. Help me to have enough sense to heal the wounds around here.

Then I felt my confidence ebb. I was merely celebrating my own victory over the Archbishop, poor man. I really didn't care much about the parish, past or present. It was just a place where I could show off my pastoral skills and win the acclaim of these people. I was seeking my own honor and glory, not God's. That would be a temptation against which I would have to strive all my life.

I apologized to the Presence who hovered in the church, turned out the lights, walked outside, and locked the door. In back of the church, I found the usual small cemetery that is customary in rural America. In the light of the full moon I saw that, like the church itself, the cemetery was carefully maintained, lawn trimmed, flowered borders, dates neatly painted on the wooden crosses—young men who had died in the eighteen sixties, still teenagers, casualties of the Civil War.

I prayed for them too and, romantic sentimentalist that I am, wept for them and their families.

The rectory, like the church, seemed structurally sound but frayed around the edges. The steps up to the porch were shaky, but the porch was rock steady. Inside, the house was clean, neat, and well dusted, as if they had been expecting a priest to show up. The bed in the pastor's room, as I assumed it to be, was freshly made. My parishioners might be obsessive-compulsives, but they surely loved this old outpost on the prairies.

I picked up the phone in the rectory office. It still worked. I called Lincoln Junction and told my parents about my good fortune.

"*Sehr gut,*" Mama exclaimed.

"*Ja, ja,*" Papa agreed. "Franky and I come out on Sunday, see what needs to be done."

I unloaded my stuff, dug out an alarm clock, and set it for 6:00. I would have to drive in before the rush and collect the rest of my things from Little Flower.

I expressed my thanks once again to the Lord on my

knees before I jumped into bed. I didn't deserve this place. I was grateful for it. I'd do my best. Please help me. I'll try not to create a kingdom of my own admirers.

When I was loading the car at Little Flower the next morning, Tom Donohue appeared.

"Great old parish, Herm! Congratulations."

"The rectory and the church were clean and polished," I said. "Even the phone worked. A lot of love for it out there. How could the Archdiocese . . ."

I paused.

"Tom, does the Archbishop have a problem with . . ."

"With the drink taken, as my kind would say?"

"Yeah?"

"It's a deep secret, which everyone knows. When he winds down at the end of the day, he sips a glass of cognac, maybe two. So he's usually out of it. Not drunk exactly but kind of dazed."

"He seemed to me dazed all the time."

"That's true. Place is too big for him. However, the end-of-the-day daze is more, well, more dazed."

My cell phone buzzed.

"Father Hoffman? It's Rosie. Father is dying. Can you come right away?"

"I'm at the parish. I'm on my way . . . Lenny Lyon," I said to Tom.

"Bring him through," Tom said grimly.

"God will have to do that." I removed my sick call set from the glove compartment of the car, dashed into the church to collect the Eucharist, and ran over to the hostel.

"This way, Father." Rosie was at the door to greet me with a candle. "He's the one screaming."

I rushed into the sickroom.

"Thank God, you're here, Hermie," he whispered. "I don't want to die, but I have to."

His body was wracked by a rasping cough.

"Not long, Father," Rosie whispered. "A few minutes."

Around me were a few of the staff members, rosaries in their fingers. Not nuns but playing the same role.

"I'm sorry," Lenny moaned. "God damn it, I'm sorry! I couldn't help it. I'm so sorry."

I went through the absolution and the anointing, gave him Holy Communion and the final blessing.

"Thanks, Herm." He sighed. "You're a good guy. I don't deserve a friend like you."

Then he closed his eyes for the last time in this world and died. His face relaxed and slowly the same smile appeared that I had seen on Pa's face.

I finished the prayers for the dying.

Out of the corner of my eye, I thought I saw Irene blink in and blink out. First time since I had returned to Plains City.

"Eternal rest grant unto him, O Lord."

"And may perpetual light shine upon him."

"May he rest in peace."

"Amen."

"Thank you, Father," the little band of Catholics in the room said in unison.

I folded my stole and put it in one pocket and the rest of my sick call kit into the other.

"He's gone home, guys," I said to the group, "where we will all join him eventually."

Irene blinked in and out again, this time with tears streaming down her face.

The blessed in the world to come don't weep, do they?

What did I know?

"Will you notify the Chancery, Father?"

"Certainly . . . Rosie, all of you are wonderful."

"Thank you, Father."

"He's gone, Tom," I said back at the rectory.

"He died in the Church?" he asked cautiously.

"Most definitely . . . Will you call the Chancery and tell them? I don't think they'd want to hear it from me."

"Sure, Herm. Right away."

I pulled up to St. Cunegunda, precisely at noon, dashed into the bell tower, which I had not inspected the night before, found the bell rope, and rang out the Angelus.

I remained in the church for a few moments to pray for the repose of the soul of Lenny Lyon.

"You fooled the demons, didn't You?" I said to the Presence.

I'm sure He didn't laugh. Fooling demons was an old game, I suspected.

Outside two young women, fourteen maybe, one blond, one brunette waited for me. They wore shorts and tee shirts which said PRAIRIE VIEW.

"Are you the new priest?" they asked suspiciously.

"I am. Father Hugh Hoffman . . . And you?"

326

"We're Megan."

"I'm Megan Green."

"And I'm Megan White . . . You're not going away are you?"

"I just got here."

They nodded solemnly.

"Our priests always go away."

"Every priest since 1858?"

"No."

"But ever since we can remember."

"Well, there's been a change. I'm staying."

"Great!"

Early adolescent grins replaced their solemnity.

"I bet you two want to work in the rectory," I said, "when you're not in school, answering the phone and the doorbell and being nice to people."

I was not about to fight Blackie Ryan's argument that all porter persons are Megan.

"Could we really!"

"Totally cool!"

"Look, you go into town and tell everyone that there'll be a parish meeting here at seven tonight. Tell your parents to come so I can ask their permission to hire you. OK?"

"Super."

"Totally good."

"Don't run away . . . Who keeps the church so neat?"

"Our mothers . . ."

"And Mrs. Kovacks."

"And Mrs. Palowkowski."

"And Mrs. O'Meara."

"Aha . . . well tell your mothers to tell the others that I don't want them to stop."

"Yes, Father!"

"Who works in the rectory?"

"Mrs. Smid . . . She used to be cook and house-keeper till the last priest ran away with someone else's wife."

"Look, kids, you don't have to worry about my doing that . . . Anyway, tell Mrs. Smid that I said that if she wants the job, she can have it back."

"Yes, Father!"

"And who takes care of the cemetery?"

"Mr. Korngold . . ."

"He rang the bells too . . ."

"He used to teach at State U . . ."

"Ask him if he'll ring the Angelus tonight and ring it again at six forty-five for the parish meeting!"

"Yes, Father!"

Then forgetting all their dignity as emerging women, they turned and ran down the hill to the town.

Back in the house, I unloaded my car, put away the groceries I had purchased on the way out, and called Father Abbot.

"I hear you gave the last rites to Len Lyon yesterday," he began.

"Word gets around . . . I have a parish now, St. Cunegunda out here in Prairie View. I need another priest on weekends. Could I borrow Retramn?"

"I'll have to ask him, of course. But he'll be delighted!"

Not a bad afternoon for my first day in the parish.

By the end of the day I had reactivated the parish council and the finance committee, rehired a housekeeper and cook, reinforced the women who had taken care of the church and the sexton (a retired professor of botany at State U), reestablished the parish choir, and signed on the two Megans.

"It'll be good for them," said Ms. Green.

"Keep them both out of trouble," said Ms. White.

"MoTHER!" exclaimed the Megans.

I had also raised the question of the time for daily Mass. I proposed 8:30. The people wanted 8:00 and so it was. For the weekend I proposed 5:00, 8:00, and 10:30. They agreed. I said a Clementine father would come to help on Sundays. I pointed out that my father and brother and craftsmen from Lincoln County would be ready to stabilize rectory and church, paint both, and install air conditioners in both buildings, but only after they had discussed the plans with the parish council.

Applause at the mention of air conditioners.

"They'll go in first thing," I said.

More applause.

"Right after the basketball and volleyball court in the backyard of the rectory."

Cheers from the younger generation.

"Who's going to pay for all this?" someone demanded.

"The crowd from Lincoln County wouldn't take a cent. They love to build things and rebuild old things. It keeps the heritage alive. I'll pay for the air conditioners and the sports stuff, at least until the finance committee sets up a budget."

"And your housekeeper and doorbell persons?"

Boos from some of the people.

"I had always intended to pay for them until such time as the finance committee decides it is able and willing."

I wasn't being reckless. Some of the people from St. Prax's had taken over my investments.

A man in a black suit, and vest, and rimless glasses walked back to the rectory with me.

"I'm Adam Kreisler," he said, "president of the Prairie View Bank. I'm not on the finance committee because there might be a conflict of interest. They'll tell you that the parish is more than able to pay for your staff. I think air conditioners are a nice gift."

"And the two courts?"

"Parish should pay for that too."

"OK. We'll see what they come up with."

Mrs. Smid and the Megans were already in possession of the rectory.

"Hi, Mr. Kreisler . . . Father Hugh, would you and Mr. Kreisler like some of our iced tea?"

"It's the coolest iced tea in the whole world."

"I'm sure we would."

"Be careful," Adam Kreisler said with a laugh. "Those two little charmers will take over the whole parish if you don't watch out."

"We could do a lot worse."

"I think you should know"—he took a single sheet of folded paper out of his pocket—"that there is a million dollars in a special account in the bank earmarked for the construction of a parish school."

I choked on my iced tea.

"We've been raising it here for twenty years. When your predecessor arrived it was only a half million. There was considerable conflict between him and the parish. So nothing was done."

"Was Downtown involved?"

"Not to my knowledge . . . I think they would have wanted the money too. His predecessor was not interested in the foundation or anything else, I fear. However, Monsignor Cafferty, who was here for thirty years, established a foundation to which people could leave money or make special donations. In subsequent years the foundation grew from a hundred thousand dollars to what it is now. Believe me, Father, the foundation is solid. No one can take money out of it for any other purpose."

"I see."

"It is invested now in a balanced account; even if the bottom falls out of the NASDAQ, as it well might, the foundation will still yield enough money each year to pay, along with tuition, for the budget of a Catholic school."

"Which one must build first."

"That's the important point in my visit tonight. Messrs. Regan and Healy, who are developing Prairie View Estates, are willing to fund the construction of such a school by the foundation. They feel it will attract many Catholic families to the development."

"They'll build the school for us, and the foundation will support it."

"Succinctly Father, that is the general idea."

"Megan!" I bellowed. "I've run out of iced tea."

"Just as soon as the program is finished, Father Hugh."

We both laughed. My help worked on their own terms.

"What are we waiting for, Adam?"

"For the parish to agree to it. The last two pastors wouldn't sign off on it."

"Does the firm . . . what's their name?"

"Regan and Healy."

"Why do they need me to sign off?"

"The land for the school is at the foot of the hill. While St. Cunegunda won't own it exactly, they want to know whether you will acknowledge it, teach in it maybe some of the time. They don't want to give us the gift and find that you will repudiate it."

"Fat chance," I said. "Can we meet them tomorrow?"

"I was about to ask that."

"I hope I am not the head of the foundation."

Adam Kreisler chuckled.

"Monsignor Cafferty thought of that too. You are ex officio a member but cannot be a chairman of the board."

Bishop Meaghan would be furious. Doc Collins, the superintendent of schools, would scream that it wasn't a Catholic school. That wouldn't make any difference. The developers' hunch was good: a Catholic school out on the edge of the prairies—Catholics with young families would swarm to it. The "publics" might even have to reopen their school in the town.

Everyone in the Church believed in Catholic schools,

they just didn't want to risk money and work building new ones.

That night as I was falling asleep, exhausted and happy about the success of my first day in my new parish, the phone rang—eleven at night.

"St. Cunegunda, Father Hoffman."

"Josh Reynolds here, Herm. Sorry to be late. I had a hard time sorting this out."

"OK."

"Is it true you, uh, attended at the deathbed of Lenny Lucifer this morning?"

"It is."

"Did he die in communion with the Church?"

"He did indeed."

"I'm happy to hear that of course. As you doubtless know there have been many complaints about him, many not true, some perhaps true."

"I am aware of that, Josh."

"Yes . . . There is concern down here that a public Mass and funeral will lead to considerable public comment, which we would rather avoid."

Just a new form of denial.

"I can understand that."

"We decided that a private Mass tomorrow and private interment in the priests' section of Holy Wood Cemetery might be the most prudent method for dealing with the issue."

"I can understand that."

"Therefore . . ."

"You want me to say the Mass, ah, preside over the Eucharist."

"For any number of reasons, Herm, not all of which entered the discussion down here."

"One pariah presiding over the obsequies of another?"

"I wouldn't put it that way . . . You did minister to him at the end, which was astonishingly generous of you."

"I don't imagine anyone else down there would agree, Josh. But yes, I would be happy to say the Mass."

"And go to the cemetery?"

"Certainly . . . Lenny, at any rate, will appreciate the irony."

"I would not be surprised . . . there will be only one family of mourners, his sister Lucy and her husband and children."

That would be messy.

"At Little Flower?"

"Yes, at nine. Father Donohue will assist you."

"OK. I'll be there."

"Finally, while we will send out no notification to the presbyterate, as you can imagine, the guys will find out."

"I'm sure they will. They won't like it, but Josh, you know what, to hell with them!"

And that, as I am in the habit of saying, was that.

XXI

"So what was Lenny's funeral like?" Retramn asked me on a warm October afternoon when State U was playing its hated rival U State (né State Normal School). The windows were open in the rectory to capture the Indian summer warmth. The aroma of Mrs. Smid's zwiebelfleisch floated around the rectory. Downstairs, the Megans were squealing with delight every time State U scored another touchdown against the infamous enemy. I had just showed him my plan for creating a master file of all the data from St. Cunegunda, including almost every issue of the *Plains Courier*, first on microfilm, then on two CDs. The *Courier* was a Catholic paper that sided with the populist political movements in the plains, including opposition to World War I. During the Depression it went under and was picked up as the official Archdiocesan paper, whereupon two things happened—a) it became dull and b) there were many pictures of the Bishop and eventually Archbishop in every issue. It was now run by the usual bunch of hacks the Archdiocese hired for every job. It had no archives.

My proposal to Tim Goodwin would be that they could bring copies of all our files over to the university microfilm library in exchange for the two CDs. How could he say no to that? Even the copies of the *Courier* would be worth the exchange.

"Are there other caches like this around the state?" Retramn asked.

"Out in the Russian German area, sure. Nowhere else that I know of. We owe all this to Monsignor Cafferty, who, back in the sixties, knew valuable material when he saw it."

"And set up an independent foundation for a Catholic school . . . Does Downtown give you trouble over it?"

"Letters from Bishop Meaghan instructing me to stop construction because they have not authorized the school."

"To which you reply?"

"That I am only a member of the board and have no control over what's happening."

"I always knew you were a troublemaker . . . I suppose your friend Irene still puts in an occasional appearance?"

"She loves the parish. Her grandparents were married here."

"You believe in her, do you, Huey?"

"I don't know that belief is the issue."

"Then what is the issue?"

"Why she shows up at all? . . . Like she was in the room when I was anointing Lenny Lyon . . . Crying like the sentimental romantic Volga Deutsche she is."

That's when he asked me about the funeral.

"Anticlimactic," I said. "His sister and brother-in-law and a solemn-eyed kid about ten years old. I preached on God's implacable love. It seemed to work. They were grateful at the cemetery. I don't know how much they knew about his life. I assume practically everything."

"Just you and Tom at the Eucharist?"

"Yes, and I went to the cemetery. And Irene, of course."

"Did they see her?"

"No one else ever sees her . . . Retramn, do the blessed in the world to come weep?"

"Why not?"

"Right, why not . . . Well I have to say the five-thirty . . . See you at supper."

"I'll ask you then about the other woman."

"Other woman?"

"The redhead."

"Oh, her!"

Retramn joined me at the back of the church after the 5:30 to greet the people. As always he was Continental in his courtesy and affability. No peasant from the plains, he.

As we walked back together, he observed, "Well, Herman, you certainly have your people charmed."

"The secret of success as a pastor, John Horvath once told me, is to succeed a bastard and smile."

"That may well be the case. The Catholic laity are in truth easily pleased when they encounter a priest who preaches a decent homily, greets them after Mass with a smile, and is good to kids. None of these require great skill, though in combination they seem to be rather rare. You do all those things well, yet their affection goes beyond gratitude for minimal pastoral competency."

"I'm a fraud, Retramn, a hollow man. I go through all the motions, but they don't mean much to God, who knows that there is no depth in my priesthood, no deep

337

devotion. In all things I fear that I seek my own image rather than His honor and glory."

"In one of those moods, eh? It follows that you're working too hard and need time off or at least time away from this dedicated and demanding parish. If God could speak up, She would wonder who you think you are to make Her judgments for Her."

"Same old Retramn . . . Still, if I feel like a hollow man, probably I am."

Ms. Green was waiting at the rectory to take her Megan home. The latter was not on duty that day but both the Megans tended to hang around the rectory when not on duty because, as they insisted, the boys left them alone there. I would call Ms. White around 9:00 when her daughter was through for the day.

We sat down at the table for our portion of zwiebelfleisch and noodles and beer. Mrs. Smid brought a small plate to the office for the faithful Megan.

"So what about the redhead?"

"I have not seen her or sought her out. Her husband is on the staff at U Hospital. I suppose I will bump into her sometime, someplace. We both will be awkward and polite. We won't say the things we should say and will think of them only later. It will not be a pleasant experience. As I am fond of saying, that will be that."

"I wonder . . ."

"She has two children, both redheads, and runs in the marathon."

"You watched her?"

"Certainly not!"

"Not even on television."

"When it came on in the sports report, I turned off my TV . . . Retramn, what do you expect of me? You want me to meet her and realize that we would not have been happy together? What difference does that make now? I do not grieve for her . . ."

He sighed, cut himself another slice of zwiebelfleisch, and sipped on his dark beer.

"It is a loose end in your life, Hugh. You will certainly not leave the priesthood for her. Presumably she will not leave her husband for you. It is still, however, a loose end."

"I'm not in love with her."

"Quite the contrary, Hugh, you are still in love with her and always will be . . . There are many kinds of love in the world. Perhaps it would enrich your life and hers if you could be friends again."

"You've changed your tune, Retramn."

"Perhaps because I understand you better."

"Look, why don't you go over to University Hospital and find her. Ask her if she would like to have lunch with me someday. For my own spiritual welfare."

"You are being absurd, Hugh, and also unnecessarily defensive."

"*Apfeltorte mit schlag* for dessert."

Again that was that. Our conversation turned to ecclesiastical gossip and the Archbishop's expectation that he was on the edge of being named to a cardinalatial see or summoned to Rome for a major Curial position.

Why is he bothering me about that? I asked the Lord God at my night prayers. Why does he probe the subject constantly? I shouldn't even ask that. He knows I'm not at peace on the subject. I never will be. Why doesn't he leave it alone? Does he not understand that twice, maybe three times, in my life, the woman swept me off my feet. And, to be fair, vice versa. Is there any reason, given my lack of spiritual depth, to think that it wouldn't happen again? At least it might happen again. I wouldn't trust myself near her. You alone know what she feels about me, and I don't want to find out.

I fell asleep with thoughts twirling in my head. If I dreamed about her, I cannot remember.

The next morning as I went over for Mass I wondered how old we would both have to be so that we would not be a threat to each other? Eighty-five, maybe.

In the beginning of November I drove down the interstate to State U, parked in a visitors' lot and trudged through an early snow to the history offices in the grimly inhuman concrete humanities building. I knew that Tuesday morning was Tim Goodwin's time in the office. I had not called for an appointment because I wanted to create the impression that this was a casual visit and not an occasion for a pitch that the University Library microfilm the St. Cunegunda archives.

"Is Professor Goodwin available?" I asked his secretary, who did not remember me.

"He's working on a paper for the meetings next month . . . Who should I say wishes to see him?"

"Hugh Hoffman."

"I'll tell him you're here, Mr. Hoffman . . . What do you wish to discuss with him?"

"Archives."

Tim exploded from his office, a featherweight boxer kind of man with enormous energy and great enthusiasm.

"Herm, you haven't changed a bit! Congratulations on your dissertation and your articles! Great to see you again! How long have you been in town? Are you teaching somewhere? Or in a parish? You're still a priest, aren't you?"

"That's permanent, Tim. I have a parish a couple of exits up the interstate, a town called Prairie View, where my Volga Deutsche ancestors stopped on their trip farther west. The parish archives are waist deep in nineteenth-century immigrant history."

"As rich as what you found out in Lincoln County?"

"In some ways richer. Would you believe almost every issue of the *Catholic Courier* from the very beginning!"

"How exciting!"

The secretary brought in a teapot and two cups. She had remembered that I drank tea in the morning.

"I'm sorry I didn't remember you, Dr. Hoffman; you still look like an undergraduate."

I thanked her for the compliment.

We talked about the parish archives. He seemed in sympathy with my proposal.

"How many other parishes might have the same or similar material, Hugh?"

"Not very many, I fear. In my first assignment over in Green Grove, everything had been destroyed, except the sacramental records. In some places even those have been burned in fires or irreparably damaged in a flood or a blizzard. The only reason we have this treasure trove is that Monsignor Cafferty, who became pastor in nineteen-sixty, knew that the material was valuable. There were not many like him."

"I understand, I understand . . . I can make a case to the librarian that there are state funds available for such work . . . You wouldn't mind if the two of us came over to look at your material?"

"I'd be delighted."

I gave him my card, which didn't mention my name, but only the parish phone and address. I also handed him copies of two papers, one already accepted and the other returned with a "revise and resubmit," which was very favorable.

"Four articles already . . . and your dissertation published in the spring . . . If you were a junior member of our department, we would have to vote on tenure early next year."

I laughed.

"Tim, I already have tenure."

"That's true." He laughed again. "However, you will continue your work in this field?"

"The *Catholic Courier* story alone is worth another book. It will show that the prairie German Catholics were on some occasions very radical."

"That would be quite an important contribution, though I do not doubt for a moment that it's true . . . You will have time to do this?"

"Tim, it's a small parish. Although there is a new development going in, it will still be relatively small.

I can do both. To tell the truth, I always hoped I could do both."

"The Archbishop didn't want you for his seminary?"

"He did, and I said no. I don't want to be too close to Downtown these days."

His eyes flashed.

"I think I can understand that . . . Hugh, let me make you a proposal . . . I'd like to sign you on as a professorial lecturer/associate professor in this department. We have one such non-tenure track position available, and you'd be a perfect fit . . ."

My heart beat faster, my stomach stirred uneasily. This was wonderful and quite impossible.

"It sounds great, Tim. I don't see how I could possibly do it. I have to heal our parish from the bitterness of the past several years. There just wouldn't be time."

"Sure there would be . . . You're what, fifteen minutes away on the interstate. One class each semester, a seminar in immigrant history in the second semester and a two-hour lecture in the first semester. We could pay . . . well, up to six . . . no, seven thousand dollars a semester and consider ourselves very fortunate at twice the cost. I'd have to speak to the dean and the provost. When I show them this material of yours, there shouldn't be any problem."

Tim's enthusiasm had always been dangerously contagious.

"I don't know . . ."

"The regents are always complaining that we don't do anything about the history of this state. Your work, at what I might call a bargain price, would answer them for a long time to come. It would, of course, delight your friends out at the far end of the state . . . Local priest to teach immigrant history at State U . . . Expert on Volga Deutsche."

All of that was surely true. An intoxicating idea, like a powerful jug of schnapps.

"I'll have to talk to the people in the parish," I said.

"Not the Archbishop?"

"That was in the old days."

"You will really ask their permission? Will it be a plebiscite?"

"I'll consult with the parish council and abide by their advice."

"I'll just assume that they will say yes and unofficially sound out the department, the dean, and the provost. I know what they'll say. We'll count on you beginning in January, unless your parish council doesn't realize that it's a bargain for everyone involved."

I had fantasized about the possibility of giving the occasional lecture at State U. A Catholic priest who was a passable scholar would be good for the image of the Church. I did not kid myself on the way back to Prairie View: I definitely wanted to do it—two hours a week plus a half hour driving back and forth, a little bit of extra reading. Many priests would spend more time in a week watching television. I might compensate a little bit for the idiocy of the Newman Center and improve the Church's image at University Park.

I would probably pick up some new pastoral work, but people who wanted to see me about religious problems could always drive up the interstate.

Perhaps I was kidding myself. Too many dreams had suddenly come true. Wasn't I pushing my luck? The "guys" would say that I was stealing time from my parish to make money at the U. Who cared what the "guys" said? What if there were a sick call? In the parish bulletin I listed my cell phone number. Anyone needing a priest in an emergency could always reach me in the classroom, which was closer than most golf courses . . .

What do You think? I asked the Lord before I fell asleep. Am I just thinking of myself, my own academic career, my own love for research? Am I being shallow, superficial, and selfish again?

I asked Retramn on the weekend. He seemed to be delighted.

"Congratulations, Hugh! What a wonderful development! It's just what you need—more work for your voracious appetite for work and an escape from the parish! By all means accept!"

"The Archbishop won't like it!"

"Don't tell me that makes any difference to you."

"I guess not . . . I'll have to consult with the parish council . . ."

"Sure you do. Present it to them as though it is something you think you shouldn't do. They'll argue you into it."

"I don't know, Retramn. People are very jealous of the time and attention of their parish priest."

"They've received more of that from you in the last year than your predecessors gave them in six years. You have to do it. For your own health and peace of mind."

345

I waited till after Christmas and a visit from Tim and Jim Farnsworth from the library. Both were astonished at my archives and assured me that they could start microfilming in mid-March. Tim presented me with a formal offer, signed by the provost—the same one that he had outlined to me in his office, except the salary had been raised to $7,500 a semester.

It was, as he insisted, a bargain for the department. They were paying new assistant professors $65,000 a year for four classes, twice what they would be paying me. With my publications, the new assistant would cost a lot more.

"I'll take it up with the parish council tomorrow night," I promised them.

I decided to lay it out straight and not follow Retramn's idea of letting them think I didn't want it.

As the meeting wound down and we were about to turn to fruitcake and coffee, I said, "There are two other issues about which I want to consult. As most of you know, I spent four years at the University of Chicago studying immigrant history. I wrote my dissertation on the migration of my own ancestors to places like Lincoln County. I've published a couple of articles on the subject. I've brought some offprints for you to read if you're interested.

"So I have a great interest, some would say an obsession, about archives. One of the first things I did when I came out here was to look at the archives of the parish, which, because of the wisdom of the late Monsignor Cafferty, are in good condition. They are, in fact, a gold mine for an historian, though, as you can imagine, much of the material is very old and very fragile . . ."

"We should have them microfilmed," Pete Reuter, the pharmacist insisted. "We can't let that kind of thing go to waste."

General agreement from around the table.

"How much would that cost, Father?" Ms. Green wondered. "I agree that it should be done. It's our story. I think we should be willing to pay for it. God has been very good to this parish."

"I can get it wholesale," I said with a laugh.

"Wholesale?"

"Free. The library at State U has the money to pay for a project like this. Jim Farnsworth, the director of the library, was out here last week and offered to do it . . . What we get out of it is a couple of CDs with all our records on them."

"Free?"

"Like totally free, as the kids would say, if you agree. I told Jim that I would have to consult with you."

"With us?" Adam Kreisler exclaimed. "Why, Father, why would anyone say no?"

"Look folks, the microfilm people from State U come up here and set up camp. The word gets around the parish that they're messing with our records. People will ask why weren't we told. You can say it was in the parish bulletin, that we approved it because we wanted to preserve the very fragile files."

"I mean," Megan's mother jumped in, "suppose there was a fire? Or a tornado? We should do it as soon as we can."

"Any objections?"

There were none.

"You're spreading the risk around, aren't you, Father?" Adam Kreisler said with a wry grin. "As an investment counselor I can understand that. No one can blame you alone."

"That's the advantage of democracy, Adam."

Then I told them about the offer from State U. They applauded, shook my hand, and said we ought to have another drink of Christmas punch to celebrate. I vetoed that. I didn't want anyone to bang into a light pole on the slippery hill.

"It's simply great news, Father," Adam said expansively. "A feather in the cap for St. Cunegunda. "Two and a half, maybe three hours once a week? Hell, most priests spend more time on television."

"Good to get away from us for a little bit of time," Flora Green said. "Did you really think we'd vote it down?"

"Time Catholics had a little influence down there. More power to you, Father."

"Yeah."

"Catholics are often very jealous of what a priest does with his time," I argued. "They get very upset if he's putting in time elsewhere."

"There'll be some begrudgers," Adam admitted. "No one can complain that you don't do the work of three or four priests here."

"You want to do it, Father?" Pete Reuter asked. "It's hard to tell whether you really want to take it on or whether you're hoping we'll tell you not to. Well, let me tell you, we won't make your decision for you!"

"Yeah, I really want to do it."

Applause.

"Did you think there was any chance we'd say no?" Maria Reuter, Pete's wife, asked as they left the rectory basement.

"I wasn't sure," I admitted.

She held the door open long enough for a searing blast of cold air to rush into our meeting room.

"Give us more credit!" She laughed.

"Thank you. I will."

Most Catholic laity, I told the Lord that night, would have done the same thing. This is a special time here; and they're feeling specially generous. Yet the secret about something like this is to ask them first instead of telling them afterwards.

He didn't agree, but He didn't disagree either.

On the morning of New Year's Eve I called Jim Farnsworth and told him the parish council was happy to approve the project. Then I called Tim and told him that I had already put my acceptance in the mail. Finally, I called Retramn and told him that I had the unanimous support of the parish council and had sent my acceptance to the department chairman.

On January 3, something happened to blight the promise of the new year, a sign no bigger than a man's hand (as the Bible says), a sign of a blizzard on a lovely crisp winter day.

I picked up the phone about 9:30.

"Horst Heller," my lawyer informed me.

"Horst! Happy New Year to you and the family!"

"Thanks, Hermie . . . I have news for you that might

not make you feel so happy . . . There's a woman lawyer from Chicago here who wants to talk to you. Name of Deirdre Delaney. She works for a very fast tort lawyer named Anton Vandenhuvel. He's thinking about involving himself in the Todd Sweeney matter."

"Oh."

"She's a straight shooter. I checked on her. She says they won't subpoena you unless you're willing. Wants to talk to you. Can I bring her out tomorrow, maybe one-thirty?"

The blue sky suddenly didn't matter.

"Why not?"

"Why not? I'll tell you why not: Downtown, for all its incompetence, still controls the criminal justice system and the media. They play hardball and think they're invincible. They could chop you up in little pieces and spit you out."

"Do I have to make a decision tomorrow?"

"No."

"Then bring her out."

Ms. Delaney was a trim, brisk woman in her middle thirties with a wedding ring and a large diamond.

"We haven't made a decision yet on the Todd Sweeney case, Father. I'm here to explore the scene, so to speak. We are aware that abuse is rife in this diocese. We are also aware that the playing field is anything but level. The Church firmly controls the courts and the media. If we subpoena you, you will have to testify. However, we do not want a priest as an unfriendly witness. If you tell me that you don't want to testify, we will give you a pass . . ."

"When will this happen, Ms. Delaney?"

"Two years, three years. Maybe."

"Well, the world might come to an end by then, and I won't have to decide."

Her smile was thin and cautious.

"May I ask you a few questions, in confidence, in the presence of your lawyer and without taking notes?"

"I guess so."

"Is it true you personally witnessed the late Father Leonard Lyon raping Thomas Sweeney, Junior?"

"Yes."

"Is it true that you reported this fact to his father, Dr. Thomas Sweeney, Senior?"

"Yes."

"And to Chief Emil Baker of the Green Grove Police Department?"

"Yes."

"And to the then Monsignor Theodore Edmund Meaghan of the Archdiocese of Plains City?"

"Yes.

"Anyone else?"

"Yes, the late Monsignor Flannery, the pastor of St. Theodolinda."

"And you were subsequently committed to the St. Edward's Mental Health Center for six months?"

"That is correct."

"For what purpose?"

"To determine whether I was a homosexual."

"Are you a homosexual, Father?"

"No."

"You know as a fact that Father Leonard Lyon was

subsequently removed from St. Theodolinda?"

"Yes."

"And was then assigned to other parishes in the Archdiocese?"

"Yes."

She paused.

"What will happen to you, Father, if we should subpoena you and you should testify?"

"The Archdiocese, Ms. Delaney, plays hardball. They would try to suspend me from the exercise of the ministry and remove me as pastor here."

"Can they do that?"

"Canon law will not permit it, but they will try just the same."

I had asked Blackie about that once. He had said that I could fight them all the way to the door of the papal apartment.

"How will your parishioners react?"

"As of this moment they would rally around me . . . Three years? I don't know."

"It's a very nice parish you have here, Father. I see foundations for new homes. Horst tells me you are planning to build a school."

"The foundation is in."

"You would put all that at risk, even though the alleged perpetrator is dead?"

"I would have to think about it . . . However, the real criminals are still alive and wearing purple buttons."

Horst winced.

I was being given a choice. I had no desire to be a hero. Yet . . .

XXII

THE REST OF THE WINTER WAS BITTER COLD. I FORGOT about the possible suit. If Anton Vandenhuvel was smart, he wouldn't take on Downtown. Despite the repair work the crowd from Lincoln Township had done, the rectory boiler could never get the heat much above sixty. The fireplaces were decorative, but I settled for space heaters. I made it to all my seminars at State U only because the interstate was effectively plowed. I was reminded occasionally of clinging to Kathleen on the road back from River View—and of her nipples outlined in lace.

That was long ago, and that was that.

I paid my respects to Tony Calabrese at the Newman Center, a courtesy call to tell him that I had joined the faculty in a non-tenure track appointment. Tony was a short, dark-skinned butterball who wore a cloak over his cassock as if he were a member of the Roman Curia. His hands were in constant motion as he talked.

"I'm afraid I can't authorize that, Father. His Excellency the Archbishop told me that he wanted a uniform Catholic voice on this campus."

I was stunned. Had the Vatican Council ever happened?

"You don't need to authorize it, Tony. The provost does that."

"Not if it's a Catholic matter. If I say you can't teach at this university, you can't, and that's final."

The immensity of his arrogance silenced me for a moment.

"What's more, if you persist in disobeying me, I'll have no choice but to delate you to His Excellency the Archbishop."

He did think he was a member of the Curia Romana. At least sixty percent of the students were Catholic. They deserved better. The Catholic laity almost always deserved better.

"Do what you have to do, Tony," I said with a shrug, and departed for the seminar.

Later in the week, Josh Reynolds called from Downtown.

"Herm, the Archbishop would prefer that you stop teaching at State U. He feels it's inappropriate."

"Sorry, Josh. No."

"No?"

"No."

"You are deliberately disobeying the Archbishop?"

"If he wants me to quit, I want a written order."

"Which you could post on the faculty bulletin board."

"Hardly, but I would show it around."

"All right, Herm." He sighed. "I'll tell the Archbishop."

No more trouble on that score, though Tony did denounce me from the altar at the Newman Center. Moreover, the next autumn, when the catalogue carried my lecture course he forbade Catholic students to attend it.

The seminar seemed to have been a success, a kind of glorified bull session about research design at which everyone had a good time and some of us might even have learned something. There were five students in the class. Three of them asked me to direct their dissertations. I agreed and warned everyone that I would chair no more than five at any one time.

"But, Hugh, most of the department don't chair any."

"Lucky them."

A little more work, but State U was fun. Not that the parish wasn't. Healy and Regan were, as they bragged to me, "a deluxe development firm." When their first five homes were sold that spring, the streets, trees, and grass were already in. All five families were Catholic and were delighted by the architect's drawing of the forthcoming St. Cunegunda School. They wondered about a high school.

I took heat from Downtown about the school.

"Bishop Meaghan, Herman."

"Yes, Bishop, congratulations on your promotion."

"I want that school canceled. Permanently. We can't afford to build new schools at the present time."

In bishopspeak "present time" meant "forever."

"I can't cancel it, Bishop. I'm on the board of the foundation, but I'm not the chair, and I can't control its decisions."

Technically that was true.

"Talk them into it."

"I'll relay your message to them."

"They may not like it, but we're the Church in Plains City. You got that?"

"I understand, Bishop. They are, however, an independently chartered group. Technically, you have no authority over them."

"Unless we approve it, you can't call it a Catholic school. You can't use the Saint's name."

I didn't believe that. They didn't own the good imperial saint.

"I don't want a single cent of our money to go into that place. I'll send out auditors every year to check on it."

"There's no parish money involved, Bishop, and there won't be."

"And I don't want you inside that building. If your foundation goes ahead with it, we may place the school under interdict."

I managed not to laugh at him. Sexual abuse he could keep out of the papers, but not excommunication, especially if the media could find canonists who would say that the excommunication wasn't valid.

"Yes, Bishop."

"If I find out that you're in the building, I'll remove you as pastor."

"Work on it hasn't even started."

"I'm keeping an eye on you, Hermie. I never did like you."

"Yes, Bishop."

I'd leave quietly. The people would put up a terrible fight.

Anyway, the "guys" had always figured that "Pot" Meaghan was a blowhard, lots of talk and no action. Like his boss, he hated making decisions because, if you made a decision, there was the risk you could make a mistake.

Construction began on the school in autumn, it would

be finished in a year and open the following year. New homes were popping up like dandelions. Young men and women were swarming to the parish dances held in a hall in the village with the weary parish priest in attendance. The same youngsters would play basketball and volleyball on the "courts" behind the rectory early the next morning, so said parish priest would not be able to sleep in.

I was uneasy about the lecture course. I had outlined it during my week's vacation in Lincoln Junction. I knew I was a good enough faker to talk forever around my outline. I also understood that the most important task of the lecturer is to entertain. If you cannot amuse the children with your jokes and your stories, you won't be able to hold their attention. Many of them will stay away from class and collect notes from the dogged few who do come and do take notes. When they learned I would grade them on a term paper at the end of the semester, there would be no reason at all to put in an appearance at class. So I would also require a one-page answer to a question at the end of each class to be submitted the following week—a hedge against the possibility that I might be dull.

I began with my thesis that I was a bumpkin, a peasant, a hick, the kind that would chew on a cornsilk if he knew where he could find one. I fell into my Volga Deutsche dialect and shouted *Achtung!* at them.

There were 150 people crowded into the classroom when I arrived, many of them undergrads, but also graduate students, faculty members, people who looked like staff.

"Someone thank Father Calabrese for me," I had muttered.

Much laughter.

"Actually, I'm not interested in heresy. I am interested in how religion became a way for immigrants to be both Americans and whatever else they were—Russian German in the case of my ancestors, some of whom were among the very first students here at State U. They drank their beer in German, Volga German. *Ja, ja, zum wohl!*"

Not very funny, but it had broken them up. So then I admitted what a bumpkin I was. They laughed because my delivery was droll. They were not quite sure whether I really was as much a hick as I claimed. The young women in the first row giggled all through class.

As I finished my prelude, I saw a familiar Cheshire smile in the back corner of the room on my right, a mischievous smile that said that everything I said was true.

Kathleen.

She wore a light brown business suit and beige scarf, all competent and efficient. Next to her was a slender, boyish fellow with pale skin, thick black hair cut short, and dancing blue eyes.

The most fortunate Dr. Shannon.

I skipped a beat, but no more than one. I knew that our reunion would be easy and pleasant—after thirteen long years.

I pushed on with the lecture. Most of the people in the room were taking notes, including some very senior members of the History Department, even Tim

Goodwin. If you're a plausible enough fraud, you can fool even the elect.

My thesis was that immigrants, despite their funny clothes and their stern facts and their poverty, were people just like us with the same hopes, same fears, same problems, and same joys as we had. If we wanted to understand them, we had to grant them that, then try to get inside their minds and hearts and strive to see their world as they saw it.

It was a good show. It was also true, though it took me a long time to understand it myself.

Needless to say, Irene was there, blinking in and out as she always did. She sat next to the giggly women in the first row and smiled, I think proudly.

Irene and Kathleen in the same room. Did they know about each other? Well, Kathleen did not know about Irene. However, Irene certainly knew about Kathleen.

What did my lost love look like? As far as I could tell, she was the same old Kathleen, yet not altogether. She was more relaxed, composed, even complacent. She had managed to achieve happiness without me. Shame on her.

As the lecture was winding down, I assigned the question of the week:

"*Ja, ja.* A single typed or computerized page. I'll read only half a page extra, and that only if the first page is brilliant. The question is tell me about your own immigrant ancestors, if you can, who they were, where they came from, what they wanted out of life. If you don't know anything about them, tell me about your grandparents and great-grandparents."

The undergrads were busy writing down the assignment, as if they couldn't remember a simple question till the day before the next class when they would sit down at the computer and write. Or maybe even the morning of the class.

Irene actually scribbled down the assignment. That, I thought, was pushing things a little too far.

I called for questions. A few kids were worried about the exact meaning of the assignment, as I had once worried. An older man wondered if immigration worked the same way in other countries. I told him that usually no one ever wanted to leave home, even if home were a very difficult place to live.

Then Kathleen's consort raised his hand.

"Doctor . . ."

That I knew who he was didn't faze him in the slightest. Kathleen looked up at him admiringly. I knew the expression.

"Well, Father, wouldn't it be hard for me to answer your question, because, sure, I'm first generation, and immigrant meself."

"Not from the Volga obviously."

The class leaned forward. I had encountered a worthy adversary. He wore khaki trousers and a spotless white shirt, no tie, no jacket. Boyish young doctor that you couldn't help but trust.

"What I wonder about, and meself being a head shrinker as you doubtless know, is what kind of stress it is to be a hyphenated American, especially if you have three groups to put hyphens between as you apparently do."

An Irish troublemaker. Kathleen had chosen well.

"*Ja, ja!* Out in Lincoln County we have no stress. We are Americans, as good as anyone else, maybe better. *Ja, ja, Herr Doktor!* We have no hyphens either. Only equal signs. To be a Russian German is a way of being an American, *nein?* Everyone has to be something!"

Kathleen was convulsed with laughter. Good Lord in heaven, it was wonderful to see her laugh again!

"Well, isn't there hope for me then, and meself from County Cork?"

"I can't say anything about Corkmen. They told me in Chicago that you folks talk with a potato in your mouth. But the Irish are different from the rest of the immigrants. Before they get on the plane or the boat to come over here they know already that they're better Americans than anyone else!"

Much laughter from my class as it broke up.

Dr. and Mrs. Shannon lingered in the background while I accepted congratulations from Tim Goodwin and my other colleagues and answered questions from students about their grandparents and great-grandparents.

If you have a quick head and a quicker tongue it is so easy to be an impressive faker.

Kathleen's voice wavered just a little when they were the only two left in the classroom.

"Father Hugh, I'd like to introduce you to my husband . . ."

I grabbed his hand and shook it.

"Dr. Shannon, 'tis good to meet you. May I congratulate you on your great taste in wives . . . And you, Kathleen"—I pecked her cheek—"on your exemplary taste in husbands, even if the poor man does talk with a potato in his mouth."

She blushed, lowered her eyes, and murmured, "Judgment Day comes early this year."

So, as was to be expected, Kathleen had the decisive word.

"How are your mother and father?" I asked, lest there be a dangerous lag in the conversation.

"They're fine." She fumbled in her purse, removed two plastic wallets of color photos and handed me one of them. "They're very happy together. I have two little brothers and a little sister. I'm very proud of them all."

"Only the older brother is a carrot top," her husband informed me, "and he doesn't live up to the stereotype, like some other people I might mention if I didn't care about getting in trouble."

"These are the pictures I really wanted to see," I said, removing the second wallet from her unprotesting fingers . . . "Liam Shannon, don't I know this little girl? Didn't I know her a long time ago?"

"That's Katie," Kathleen said, her eyes still down. "She looks like me, Hugh, but she's not like me at all. She's sweet and gentle like her father . . . This little punk, he promises to fit the stereotype of the spitfire."

"That's Billy," her husband said proudly. "He may play for the State football team in a few years. Isn't he a big guy now?"

Katie was seven or eight and Willie maybe going on four. She had a mystical little smile, he a huge grin.

"Congratulations to both of you," I said. "You should be very proud of them."

Kathleen recovered her composure.

"I'd love you to meet them, Father Hugh."

"Sure, would you ever consider coming to supper at our house? Herself makes good scrambled eggs."

"Wurst and beer is all we Russian Germans eat," I said.

"We'll sort out the schedule, and I'll give you a ring," Liam said. He and I shook hands again. I brushed my lips against Kathleen's lips. They tasted as good as ever, but it was like none of the kisses from long ago. We were now grown-ups. Mostly.

And that was truly that.

"Vintage Lincoln Township today, Father Hugh," she said, as we parted. "All you needed was an accordion and the beer."

Driving back to the parish, I thought about her. Her figure was undamaged. She ran in marathons and would be in good physical condition. She was more beautiful than ever, a few lines around her eyes and some smile lines at her mouth. Yet she was, as Tom Donohue had said, poised, composed, almost complacent. She was happy. You did a good job with her, Liam Shannon. Dammit, a better job than I could have done.

I hated to say that, even to myself. Yet it was true. God bless him, actually. As Father Retramn had often said, you have no business fighting the Holy Spirit.

And what about her comment as we parted, a final zinger from the sharpshooter. I was not the same old Lincoln Junction Hermie Hoffman. I had learned a lot at the seminary. I had learned a lot more and expanded enormously at Chicago. I had gone far beyond the hayseed I had been when we were lovers. I was the new, refurbished, mature, adult Hugh Hoffman, Ph.D. She acknowledged the change of names, but thought I was otherwise no different?

How come she thought I hadn't changed? She had changed a lot!

I had better stop trying to exegete what she had said and pay attention to the highway.

Her husband called several days later. He pronounced "Liam," I noted, like it was spelled "lim."

"Herself thinks that I'm the one who should invite you, Father Hugh. She thinks I might resent you."

"If it's as much as I resent you, then it's not worth worrying about."

"No human emotion," he said softly, "is ever free from its dark side. Yet she claims—and she's right— that you saved her until I came along and took over."

"I don't know, Liam. The older I get the more doubts I have about myself. I would have thought it was my family that provided a family for her when hers wasn't working all too well."

"She says it was you who brought her into that affectionate Deutsche family and protected her till you let her know that you wanted to be a priest, and then, as she said, she went to Palo Alto and became a virgin again."

I felt a strange pain in the very pit of my stomach.

"In your profession, you come to know how two people can view the same story from very different perspectives. Like in *Rashomon*."

"And both perspectives can be true . . . Look, Hugh, you both have more adult loves now, which neither of you will ever give up."

What does one say to that?

"I think that's obvious."

"May I quote you? She doesn't disagree, she just wants to be certain that you won't be embarrassed to come and have dinner and meet the rugrats."

"Not in the least."

"Good. One of us will be back with a couple of dates . . . And, as my County Cork mother used to say, 'We shouldn't be surprised that there are so many different kinds of love. God couldn't help Himself when He created love.' "

I sat back in my chair, stomach churning, throat dry, fingers trembling.

We're both grown-ups, we're both adults, we're not about to act like kids. Tell that to yourself over and over, and you might start to believe it. I went over to church to talk to God about it. I had the impression that the Presence was amused.

However, the matter was not settled. Three days later I received a letter on University Hospital letterhead, printed out on a Hewlett Packard laser printer.

Dear Hugh,

You must excuse the computerized letter. It's not a form letter that I send out to all my old lovers. However, I spoiled the versions of this I've tried to do in pen and ink with my tears. I pushed up the date of Judgment Day at Mass when that horrible little toad denounced you. I figured it was time for us Lincoln Junction folk to stick together. I also wanted you and Liam to meet. I knew you would like each other.

You looked surprised when I said that your wonderful performance was vintage Junction. All we needed was the accordion and the beer. You seem to have no idea who you were back in those days. Well, I'll tell you. You were a magic little boy, a magic teenager, a magic lover, and now a magic priest who has learned a lot but never forgotten where he came from.

Ja, Ja.

You saved me, Huey, from my anger, from my bad language, from my melancholy, from my temper, from my conviction that I was bipolar and would follow my poor mother into an early grave, from the absolute certainty that I could never give or receive physical love, from my near miss at ruining Dad's marriage and my own happiness. As I have told poor dear Liam many times, without you he never would have met me.

I know that's an image of yourself that you haven't acquired yet. I just have to tell you that it's who you are.

Did we sin when we made love? Liam says no one can commit a sin of the flesh until they're forty. He also says that no woman is really attractive till she's forty. He refuses to reconcile those two dogmas. However, I know what he means. I think we both should forget about it and get on with our lives. Whatever our hormones drove us to when we were kids, God has forgiven us and loves us now more than ever. Our hormones are never in complete control, but I'm not worried about the context we're in.

I'm afraid you might be. You might not want to be part of our family and I can understand that. I didn't want to take you away from God thirteen years ago, and I certainly won't do it now. No one can take me away from my poor, dear, long-suffering Liam. So I think, very tentatively, that it might be time for us to be friends again.

I don't want to discuss this letter with you for a long time, perhaps ever. There's too much of myself in it. However, if you're still willing to come to supper, next Tuesday at 7:00, please give me a call at 793-219-0900.

Love,
Kathleen

PS I made poor Liam read this. He's heard it all before.

I put the letter down. It was a love letter, a strange kind of love letter, but a love letter nevertheless. I would reread it and reread it over again. But not now. I picked up the phone and dialed the number.

"Dr. Quinlan."

A calm, professional voice.

"This is Dr. Hoffman."

"Hi, Dr. Hoffman . . . Did I surprise you?"

"No, I just assumed you'd pick up a doctorate in computer science in your spare time . . . At Leland Stanford

Junior Memorial University, I presume."

"Doesn't everyone? I had most of my course work done when we were married. Then poor Liam got the job over here and I tagged along and finished my dissertation, computer graphics in emergency medical care, if you'd believe. So they gave me my own little unit over here."

"And you've had two children and run in the marathon."

"Which I'll never win."

"I have read your letter, though so far only once."

"And?"

"I'll have to read it many more times."

"That's the way you Volga Deutsche are. Always looking for hidden messages."

"I'll accept your condition that you do not want to discuss it now . . . or perhaps ever."

"That's good."

"I have a different view of my own importance."

"I figured you would."

"So where do you live?"

"It's Three-twenty South Central Street, right near the hospital. Park in the driveway."

"I'll be there."

Catch of breath.

"We'll be happy to see you . . . Bring your accordion . . . I've told the kids about it."

"All right."

"Can I ask you a question, quite unrelated to supper?"

"Sure?"

"Who was the pretty woman in the first row the other

day, the one with the dress next to three kids about her age who were in jeans and sweatshirts? She looked kind of familiar."

Oh.

"That was probably Irene. She's from the Junction."

"All your Volga women look the same."

She sounded relieved. There would be some tricky waters to navigate.

And what would I tell her about Irene?

XXIII

"ARE YOU REALLY A PRIEST, FATHER HUGH?" KATIE asked me.

"I really am, Katie."

The Shannon kids were polite and respectful, but their eyes were alert and cautious. How could a priest who played the accordion and sang songs and told stories about Maximilian the Mad Monk and Erich the Eerie Anchorite possibly have gone to school with their adored mommy?

"A priest like Father Calabrese?" She was indeed a clone of the little girl who walked into our singspiel a quarter century ago, but, as her mother had admitted, a lot sweeter and more gentle.

Liam Shannon winced at Katie's question. His wife waited expectantly for my answer.

"I don't have a cape and I don't wear my Roman collar when I'm teaching at your mommy's university, and he doesn't play the accordion, but we're both priests."

369

"Different kinds of priests," Katie said wisely.

"Very different," I admitted.

"I'm glad," she said. "He makes Mommy and Daddy very mad."

"You want to know something, Katie?"

"Uh-huh."

"Sometimes he makes me very mad too."

She clapped her hands.

"Oh, good!"

A touch of the mother, however.

"Katie, what's that picture on the wall?"

It was computer output, a big explosion of light.

"My mommy made that," Katie said proudly. "It's God."

"God?"

"Well, it's what God looks like when He's making light, isn't it, Mommy?"

"It's how my computer thinks the Big Bang might have been, dear."

"Yes, Mommy."

"I think, Katie and Willie, that it's time to go to bed."

"Will you tell us a story, Mommy?"

The wild prayer of longing, a child searching for reassurance that all is right with the world.

"Father Hugh already told you a lot of stories, and you're falling asleep on your feet."

"Yes, Mommy."

Billy was so tired that there was no resistance left in him. Bed. Now.

"Maybe," I said, "someday you'll come up and see my church, and I can tell more stories about Max and

Erich and Lemuel X. Quicksilver, the man in the flying saucer who comes to visit me."

"Do you have your very own church?"

"It's real old and it's pretty and there's a bell inside it."

"Can we, Daddy? Can we?"

Liam lifted his eye to consult with his wife. She inclined her head.

"We'll see about it, kids. Now go to bed and hear all those wonderful bells ringing."

"Hug Father Hugh good night," Kathleen advised them.

"I love you, Father Hugh," the little clone said to me.

"Me too," Willie agreed.

"Bell," I said as they went upstairs, Kathleen holding their hands. "Only one old bell. Installed when the church was built in 1852."

"In 1852?" Liam said. "We have lots of churches like that in Ireland, but those who kick with their left foot own them."

"Civil War casualties buried in the cemetery behind our church. My crowd stopped there for a while before they went off to the far end of the state. Some of them are still around."

"She's beginning to relax. She wanted everything to work out perfectly."

"That's the way they are, Liam."

"Isn't it the truth? . . . Would you ever be playing golf?"

"Sometimes."

"Could I take you off to my club someday soon?"

"You could."

"Do you have a handicap?"

"Not really. I've played at a lot of different courses lately. I used to play every week with some of my classmates, but I've sort of lost the habit as I work in the parish."

"And would you usually beat them?"

"More often than not."

"Testosterone-driven male macho competition," Kathleen observed as she reappeared. "You were a big hit with the kids, Hugh, not that I'm surprised."

We ate crusted salmon for supper and drank white Rhone wine. We chatted first about Lincoln Township.

"I'd like to see it sometime," her husband said.

"I'll take you out there before winter starts," Kathleen promised. "Not much to see, flat country and Volga Germans who talk funny . . . And sing beautifully."

"Great meal, Kathleen," I said.

"I'm glad you liked it, Hugh. I was just not up to schnitzel and wurst tonight."

"I'll ask Mrs. Smid to make a real *deutsch* dinner when you and the kids come over to see St. Cunegunda."

"Now tell us about yourself, Hugh. We heard you were studying in Chicago. There was a touch of mystery about it."

"I'm sure there was . . . Liam, you administer a sexual abuse treatment center?"

"I try to. It's tough work."

"Any victims from the Archdiocese?"

He hesitated.

"None that Downtown sends us. I think they prefer St. Edward's. My impression is that they're covering up a lot."

"OK, let me begin my story by telling you I spent six months at St. Edward's while they tried to cure me of homosexuality. I was very heavily medicated for the first couple of months, then was smart enough to throw the pills away."

Kathleen cut off her laughter, acutely embarrassed by her outburst.

"I'm sorry, Hugh."

"Sure no one can *cure* homosexuality, can they now? Still I wouldn't be surprised if Bob Geneva is senile enough to try it, if Downtown told him to. Was there an attending physician?"

"Dr. Straus."

"I don't think I've ever heard of him."

"He's a family practitioner who also does 'counseling.' He clears everyone for the seminary by giving us a TAT and MMPI test. He signed me in for treatment of a personality disorder, complicated by homosexual inclinations. Horst Heller finally got me out after six months, then the Archbishop sent me out of town to study before I caused any more trouble."

"How did you cause trouble, Hugh?" Liam asked cautiously.

"Let me clear off the table, and I'll get the ice cream."

"Won't we be helping you now?"

"You will not!"

We did anyway.

"I do cook two nights a week," Liam whispered to

me. "And I'm a better cook, but she insisted on cooking for her long-lost love."

"Her very words?"

"Course not. You should know better than to take an Irishman literally . . . Tell me now, do you ever, on the odd occasion, break eighty?"

"It's the pretty odd occasion," I replied.

"Well now, we should have an interesting day of it."

Kathleen served us the ice cream, went upstairs to make sure her kids were still alive, and rejoined us at the table.

"You were about to tell us how you caused trouble for Downtown," she said.

"I witnessed a homosexual rape of a thirteen-year-old boy by the other associate pastor and reported it."

"You would, of course," Kathleen said, tears pouring down her cheeks. "Typical straight arrow Hermie."

I went through the whole story, including the death of Lenny Lyon at the AIDS hostel.

"Was he gay?" Liam asked.

"I think he was an equal opportunity tormentor. He was after a thirteen-year-old girl at St. Theodolinda too. I warned her off."

The three of us sat around the table in silence. I declined another dish of ice cream.

"You've deserved better of the Church, Hugh," Liam said sadly. "You're the kind of priest we need."

"Maybe you should have stayed in Chicago."

"This is my home, I'm not leaving."

"Typical," she said with a grin. "Does the Archbishop

know with whom he's dealing?"

"I don't think so."

"It's all over now, isn't it? I mean you have a parish?"

"I think so, Kathleen. They're a little afraid of me down there."

"As well they should be!" Liam said.

"I don't know about that, Liam . . . And there's always a possibility that the scandal will finally erupt. Downtown may have lost its control of the playing field, as has happened in other dioceses."

"You don't need that, Hugh!" Kathleen said, pounding the table.

"Well, I might get it anyway. I'm not afraid to fight Downtown. I've done it once, and I'll do it again if I have to. I have some friends elsewhere . . ."

Now, however, was not the time to tell them about Blackie Ryan.

It was a great relief to be able to talk to friends who understood and sympathized.

"Do you know Dr. Stephan McAteer?"

"Sure, don't I now? He kicks with his left foot, but he's a good man."

"He was one of the residents who treated me at St. Edward's. You might check out my story with him. Tell him I said it was OK to talk about it."

"I don't need to check it out!"

"You do too need to check it! The story is too incredible!"

"Well, if you say so . . ."

It was time to leave. It had been an exhausting day. The lecture always wore me out. The evening was

pleasant but difficult. It was time I returned to St. Cunegunda.

"Who is Irene?" Kathleen demanded.

"Irene?" Liam said.

"The woman I saw in the first row that I thought I recognized and you said was from Lincoln County."

"Irene would take up another hour. I can report on her
at St. Cunegunda a week from Sunday. I have a couple
of built-in baby-sitters on my staff. Mass is at ten-
thirty."

So I escaped their house without offering testimony
that would convince Liam Shannon that I was crazy.

Our golf match the following Tuesday was, as Liam
said it would be, a fierce contest altogether. All hor-
mone and machismo as Kathleen had disdainfully predicted it would be. We played practically even through
the whole course—after an eight o'clock tee off so I
could make my lecture and he could make grand
rounds.

On the eighteenth green I was lying seventy-five with
a three-foot putt. Himself was seventy-six with an
eight-foot putt. If I missed the putt, we could end up in
a tie. Take my girl would he?

"If you miss that putt, you friggin' gobshite, I'll
knock this one through the clubhouse window."

Ah, no. There were no attempts at false generosity
with your man Liam Shannon. I banished the temptation, glanced up at him, grinned, and drilled in the putt
without even looking at the ball.

"You're a nine-fingered shitehawk," he informed me
with a firm handshake.

"What's that?"

"I don't know." He sighed like Blackie Ryan would sigh. "But it sure sounds terrible. Here, let me sink me putt just for the sake of me tattered honor. And then we'll have a quick lunch."

He rimmed the putt. We walked silently into the clubhouse for our lunch as he mumbled and grumbled to himself.

"Tell me, Hugh"—he gazed levelly over his glass of iced tea—"if I should die, would you leave the priesthood to marry Kathleen?"

"No," I said firmly.

"OK. If the Church changed its mind and permitted priests to marry, would you then marry her, assuming that I had gone on to a better world?"

That was not a question I had ever permitted myself to ask and did not want to answer. Yet I knew the answer immediately.

"No."

"Why not?"

"Because I am a celibate priest," I said promptly.

"Why is that important?"

"I don't care what people say, it's an enormous help in working with people. I have the time and the energy to be more to them. They fill my life with joy that I would lose if I had a wife of my own."

"You're claiming that celibate priests are happier than married ministers."

"I guess I am."

He began to work on his soup.

"That's what I don't understand about you guys . . . I

377

don't mean you personally. The recent research shows that what you just said is true. It also shows that only thirteen percent of the married, mainline Protestant clergy are very satisfied with their family lives. Yet you don't seem to value what you have."

"We don't want to make invidious comparisons that will offend the separated brothers and sisters."

"Fine, but don't kid yourselves into thinking that a married Catholic clergy will be any happier than the Protestant married clergy is."

"Guys leave," I argued, as I slurped up the soup, "because they fall in love and want to marry."

"Would it surprise you, Huey"—he jabbed his soup spoon at me—"to know that the proportion of ministers who leave is higher than the proportion of priests—and they're married! Most priests who fall in love and still like priestly work, don't leave. Celibacy isn't the reason priests leave; the reason is that they don't like the work."

"Guys don't want to become priests anymore."

"Small wonder with so many of you sad-sacking around about how tough celibacy is. Why doesn't anyone say how wonderful it is to be a priest anymore?"

I put down my soup spoon.

"Probably because they heard so much of that before and are tired of it."

"Then don't blame me if you don't get many recruits."

"I guess you're right."

"Look, you still adore my wife, don't you?"

"Yeah. You know that."

"But you wouldn't marry her even if you could with the Church's blessing. Why?"

"Should she lose you, which God forbid, she'd need someone just like you."

"That dodges the question."

"OK, you win. Because I'd have to give up too much."

"The trade didn't seem worth it when you broke up, and it still doesn't seem worth it."

I sighed. "Don't tell her."

"Huey, boy, she already knows."

"I suppose she does."

"As she said to me when she told me about you before we were married, there's no point in fighting God. He holds all the cards."

Why didn't this discussion make me happy?

Because Liam Shannon was like a retreat master or a confessor. He was telling me truths I didn't want to hear.

"The guys don't understand that."

"That's because the guys and the whole Church are currently so fucked up, mostly because Rome sends idiots like Slippery Louie to Archdioceses like Plains City . . . Look, I'm not saying that the celibacy rule shouldn't be changed. I'm only saying on the basis of the evidence it wouldn't make much difference."

"It doesn't cause sexual abuse then?"

He began to eat his tofu sandwich.

"This guy who was at your first parish? Would marriage have made him any different?"

"You mean Lenny Lucifer? No, he'd humiliate his own children."

"There are all kinds of abusers, Huey, and they have one thing in common, arrested sexual development, whether they're gay or straight. You shouldn't ordain them, and you shouldn't reassign them to parishes. That's what it's all about. I see a lot of clergy in my work, one way or another. You guys have no monopoly on it. Married clergy or heterosexual-only clergy won't solve the problem at all, no matter what the media think."

"I hope you start saying it."

"I will when you get a new archbishop. This guy can barely read and write."

"Better the devil you know than the devil you don't know . . . you should start writing your book now."

"That's what our mutual friend keeps telling me. I guess I'll have to."

"And go on television the next time you're asked."

'We have the same kind of problem in Ireland. It's unleashed the latent anticlerical in all of us."

"The Curia blames it on American obsession with sex and the Jewish-owned media."

"Gobshites! Those theories don't account for the Archbishop in the Pope's own Poland who was forced to retire, or the Cardinal in Vienna who had terrorized a monastery when he was abbot there! It's a human problem, Huey. A sixth of all Americans, men and women alike, report sexual abuse before puberty. There are not enough priests to account for all of that!"

I found it hard to keep up with Liam's conversation.

It was like Bishop Blackie's only more so—allusive, indirect, filled with questions which need not be answered, rapid changes of subject, winks and nods, and the rolling of eyes. The Irish, as Blackie had once said, never mean what they say and never say what they mean. All of which is a little difficult for a bumpkin from the prairies.

I thought about asking him if he would give up Kathleen because he would be happier without her and the kids. I knew the answer—there is not the joy and the happiness in the practice of medicine that a priest can have constantly if he wants it by just being a priest to his people.

It was all so old-fashioned and out-of-date.

"The trouble with you guys," he said, as the waiter refilled our iced tea glasses, "is that you let the malcontents prevent you from realizing how goddamn happy you are."

"Guilty," I admitted.

We left the clubhouse, promising that we'd play again soon. It would be a while, I suspected, before my new friend recovered from his defeat. Golfers, however, always come back for more.

"Oh," he said as he opened the door to his Benz, "I checked with Steve McAteer. He told me that he was glad to leave St. Edward's. It's usually a good place. They help a lot of people. However, Geneva is terrified of Downtown. He'll do anything they say. He regrets what happened to you."

It was a very measured and cautious comment.

"Better late than never."

"He says he can't figure out what Downtown had against you."

"I'm a Volga *dummkopf,* as your good wife would tell you. I broke the code of silence without even knowing it existed."

XXIV

"An interesting love letter." Retramn passed Kathleen's letter back to me. "She's obviously a tough and intelligent woman . . . Mind you, she doesn't say anything I don't already know about you, Hugh."

We were in the minute sacristy of St. Cunegunda preparing for the 10:30 Mass at which our choir performed. Retramn would return to the rectory to eat his huge *deutsch* breakfast, and I would chant the Mass.

"She exaggerates the role I played in her life."

"What she's doing is describing her perception of it. That's what matters. However, she is, I suspect, basically accurate. You saved her."

"No."

"Yes, Hugh . . . You haven't argued with her about it?"

"Certainly not . . . she said in that letter that she didn't want to."

"What did you get out of the relationship?"

"I hadn't thought of that."

"I'm not surprised. Think about it."

"I'll try . . . Oh, yes, she sees Irene too."

"What!"

The poor monk's face fell off the edge of a mountain.

"I haven't told her that Irene is my great-grandmother."

"Her husband will want to lock you up . . . They're coming to this Mass?"

"So they said."

"I look forward to meeting her."

I tried not to distract myself during the Eucharist. No time for thoughts about what I had got out of the relationship.

After Mass I was at the door of the church like I always am, congratulating the choir, talking to the people, high-fiving the kids. It was a perfect Indian summer day—affectionately warm, the lightest of breezes, a last desperate promise that winter would not have the final say, not even out here in the prairies.

Kathleen was wearing a pale green spring dress that matched the ever-dangerous color of her eyes. The little clone was wearing a clone dress. Liam had actually put on a tie, as had Willie.

"Father Retramn," I said somewhat formally, "I'd like to introduce the Doctors Shannon, Liam and Kathleen, and their two perfectly behaved children, Katie and Billy . . . Father Retramn was my spiritual director in the seminary."

"That should have been an easy task, Father. Hugh must have been the perfect seminarian when he arrived. Everything that you'd expect of a young man the week before ordination. That's the way we grow them out in Lincoln Junction, *nein?*"

"Well, Kathleen," my monk friend joined the game, "we never did catch him doing anything wrong."

"Just like my computer never makes a mistake."

"Father," Katie said, coming to my rescue, "are you Maximilian the Mad Monk?"

"No, dear"—he patted her head—"he wears red robes, and I wear gray. I'm Erich the Anchorite."

"Oh! . . . Do you take care of Father Hugh?"

"I do my best . . . You look a lot like your mother."

"Everyone says that. Mommy says I'm a lot sweeter than she was when she was seven, going on eight, because I'm like my daddy."

"That's what mommies always say," her father observed.

"Most kids are like both their parents," I said. "Isn't that true, Billy?"

"I'm hungry!"

"Then let's go over to my house and have some breakfast."

"Lots of wursts," his mother promised.

The two young people dug into the food, Katie with cautious care, Willie with reckless abandon. Kathleen continued to cross-examine Retramn.

"I don't suppose that Hugh ever showed off in class, did he? I hope he gave up his Lincoln Junction habit of knowing more than the teacher—all the time!"

"Well, I can't say that, Kathleen. However, it is possible that he did that less as time went on. There were some of us who knew more about the subject matter than he did. Abbot Radbert, for example, was a little more up to snuff on St. Ephrem the Syrian than Hugh. Most of us didn't mind the interruptions, however, because the students couldn't care less about what we were teaching. Indeed, in the whole monastery, the only ones who care about the Sainted Ephrem were the Abbot and Herm, as he was called in those days."

"Some things never change." Kathleen sighed.

"Ephrem did all his writing in verse hymns that were sung by women. He was a very interesting man . . . Speaking of interesting men, Professor Korngold, who used to teach at your mommy's university, is about to ring the bells in the church. If you come over to the window, you can see him doing it. He takes care of our flowers too."

Our bell ringer always approached his task with sparkling eyes and a happy grin. He loved to wake people up. When the Angelus bell rang, we all stopped eating and said the prayer. Retramn bid us good-bye. He wanted to be back in the monastery for Vespers. Sunday Vespers, he always argued, was a critical component of monastic life. I walked with him to his car.

"She's a very interesting woman, Herm. I would have expected that. But she's a good deal more than I expected."

"To tell the truth, she's more than I expected."

"She will do you no harm," he said mysteriously as he entered his car.

That was something else to think about.

"Isn't he a grand man now?" Liam said. "And aren't you the lucky one to have him come every weekend?"

"He loves to come," Kathleen said. "I like him a lot."

"A man approved then," I said. "We'll keep him."

"Would it be all right if we come up here some of the time?" Liam asked. "I don't know whether we can make it every Sunday because of my schedule at the Center, but this is so much better than the Newman Center."

"Maybe my poor little Katie could make her first Communion here. I could instruct her, Hugh, and you could ask her all the right questions."

"I'd be honored to welcome her to the altar. I wouldn't dare reject her mother's answers."

The Megans came to take the children out to play.

"Now who's Irene?" Kathleen demanded. "I know her from somewhere, but I can't quite remember her. Did she go to school with us?"

"She's from the Junction all right, but she didn't go to school with us. Was she at Mass this morning?"

"I didn't see her . . . Does she come regularly?"

"She's pretty unpredictable."

"WHO is she?"

"You remember the old man we called Pa? My great-grandfather?"

"Sure! He was a sweet old man who told stories and gave kids chocolates."

"*Ja, ja*. Irene is his wife."

"His wife! Didn't you tell me when we were at State U that he had died? How could he have had such a young wife?"

"She died thirty years before him, when she was in her early sixties, don't you remember? I told you about her when we were having dinner one night at State U? Didn't I show you her picture?"

Dead silence.

"I think I tried to forget about her. I didn't want to

believe you . . . It was a strange night."

It was indeed. A night of sweet if unwise passion.

"You're putting us on now, aren't you?" Liam said with a shiver.

I removed my wallet and showed the photo snapped at my graduation.

"Isn't that the woman you saw in the first row of the lecture room?"

Kathleen looked at the picture and shivered too.

"Certainly is . . . But Hugh . . . ?"

I flipped over the photo and showed the photo of Ma as a young woman in 1920.

"Maybe the woman in the first picture is a descendent . . ." Liam suggested.

"I'm sure there are many young women in the Junction that share genes with Irene. But they didn't come into the death room to take Pa home, and they don't blink in and out at various occasions of my life, just as she did at my lecture the other day."

"Is she a ghost?" Kathleen asked, deathly pale.

"I wouldn't call her that. She's a benign presence from the world to come who for some reason has taken charge of me. I don't know why. I've learned to thank her. She has wonderfully expressive eyes; even in a blink you can tell whether she's pleased with you or not."

"And she takes pictures? She's holding a camera in this snapshot."

"I don't know why the blessed need to take pictures. But she does. I keep waiting for an album to show up."

"Who else sees her?"

"No one until you."

Liam entered the discussion.

"You seem quite at ease, Hugh, with this, ah, other-worldly visitor?"

I laughed.

"Whoever or whatever she is, Liam, she's not a bad person. In fact, she acts pretty much like a grandparent or a great-grandparent. I have the impression that she's spoiling me rotten."

"Why would God," Kathleen wondered, "permit someone like her . . . Now I'm being silly. Who am I to try to budget God's time?"

Liam drew his narrow black Irish forehead into a thoughtful frown.

"I have a suggestion to make," he said. "It's not based on Trinity College Medical School or St. Mary's Hospital in Castlebar or Stanford Hospital or anything I have learned as a psychiatrist. It's from the bogs of West Cork . . ."

Kathleen and I waited for the suggestion.

"I think," he went on slowly, "that neither of you will see Irene again. Or at most only very rarely. The good woman probably figures now that her work is done."

"What work?" I asked.

"Didn't she reckon that it was her job to take care of her favorite great-grandson until Kathleen and I came along to replace her?"

"How could I be her favorite great-grandson when she was dead before I was born?"

"If we accept the premise of this whole business, death does not make any difference."

The color had returned to Kathleen's face. She grinned.

"Liam, you're right as you always are. Hugh is our project now."

"If I don't see her again," I admitted, "I'll kind of miss her."

"That doesn't mean, Hugh, that she won't still be around."

"Not if you're Irish," Liam said, "and believe that the others are always with us."

"And you believe that?" I asked.

"I'm a physician and a scientist, Hugh and I'm also bog Irish."

I wrote that conversation down immediately after they left to return to University Park. I still don't know what to make of it. However, I'm not convinced that these two friends were wrong. I haven't seen Irene again, and I do kind of miss her. Kathleen says she hasn't seen her either. They have made me their project. They insist that I must not exhaust myself, that I must take time off, that I must permit myself to enjoy a vacation now and then, even if it is only to return to the Junction. I have yet to accept their proposition that I am more important to people than I realize. However, sometimes I do incline in that direction. They have yet to take over my life, but they certainly try to surround me with love and protection.

I had at least learned that one does not try to rearrange the crooked lines of God or to prevent God's Holy Spirit from blowing whither He (or She) wills. I also understand, without worrying about it much, that Kathleen will always be an important person in my life. What had I got out of the relationship in the past, as Retramn had asked me? Besides a temporary exciting bed partner. She had been someone to take care of and to talk to. Now she was taking care of me.

Humans, it turns out, are at their best when they're taking care of one another.

Katie made her first Communion at St. Cunegunda. I baptized their third child, Irene, in the parish church, yet another redhead. I figured that if the little girl's namesake was still on my case, we might catch some glimpses, as I poured water on the head of the grinning girl child. Neither Kathleen nor I saw any blinks. But both of us had the sense that someone else was with us around the baptismal font. Kathleen and Liam bought one of the new homes in Prairie View and will move in as soon as our school opens. Liam and I play golf often together, sometimes with Dave Winter. The matches are always close, and the victories about evenly divided. No, the truth is that I win more than I lose. When I win, Liam still suggests on the eighteenth green that I'm a nine-fingered shitehawk.

The Shannons lurk discreetly in the background. I did watch her run once in the marathon. It was not a sight to forget easily.

"Would you think, Huey," Liam asked me as she ran by us, "that she knows how beautiful she looks?"

"Yes," I said, "but no and yet finally yes indeed."

"Haven't you been associating too long with the Irish, lad?"

"Did your great-grandmother like to play with a

camera?" Liam, not nearly as spooked as his wife and I were, asked at our next supper.

"I thought of that too. When I was home last Sunday I worked around to the subject. Papa said, '*Ja, ja,* she loved to play with one of those little Brownies they had forty years ago. I always thought her pictures were pretty good, weren't they, Mama?'"

"Did they have any of her shots around?" Kathleen asked.

"A lot of them buried in a box in the attic. She had all the moves. I brought them over to the archives in the Junction."

And that was that.

I continued to work hard in the parish. The honeymoon with the people was over, but they still seemed to like me. My classes at State U were popular. I had taken on too many dissertations. I was still publishing an article or so every year. Kathleen and Retramn had joined forces in trying to slow me down, a most unusual alliance. The ensuing couple of years, after my great-grandmother decided I didn't need her protection anymore, passed quickly and happily. The cloud on the horizon no bigger than a man's hand seemed to become smaller, but it never did disappear.

Then one morning in February, in the midst of a false spring in which snowmelt rushed down the side of our hill towards the creek on the edge of town, Horst called me on the phone.

"Did you read the *Plainsman* this morning?"

"Yeah, did I miss something?"

"It's easy to miss. Page nine down in the corner."

I reached for the paper and fumbled for page 9.
Down on the inside corner was a single paragraph.

ARCHDIOCESE SUED

Anton Vandenhuvel, a lawyer from Columbus, Ohio, has filed suit against the Catholic Archdiocese of Plains City in the name of young men. The suit alleges that a now deceased priest of the Archdiocese sexually abused these young men. A spokesman for the Archdiocese declined to comment on the suit.

"Have you decided yet whether you are willing to testify?" Horst asked me.

"No."

"You've got time yet. They'll be taking the depositions in the autumn. Their strategy is to pry open the Archdiocese archives. I'm not sure the media will pay any attention to the whole business."

"It will be the first place in the country where they'll pass on such a story."

"You have a lot to lose, Hugh."

"You're saying that I should not testify?"

"No. Emily and I have two kids in Catholic schools. We're worried about them. As your lawyer I have to warn you of the risks you take."

"Thanks, Horst. I'll be back to you."

"What could you lose, Hugh?" Kathleen asked later that week at supper in a comfortable French restaurant down the street from their home in University Park, not the same one where we had consumed a bottle of

Barolo so long ago.

"The parish anyway, the respect of priests and people in the Archdiocese, I might have to leave town . . ."

"Downtown can't take the parish away from you, can they?" Liam demanded. "Surely you have some rights in the matter?"

"Technically, they can't. They couldn't suspend me either. They don't know much canon law down there, though they pretend to. I could fight them and probably will. It'll be a long, drawn-out process, as will the civil suit. Parishioners out here don't like controversy. Everyone will say that I'm betraying a dead colleague. I don't know. I might have to go back to Chicago, where I'd be welcome."

"It would serve them right!"

"It's home, Kathleen."

"Will the plaintiff's lawyers make you testify?" Liam wondered.

"Yes and no. They'll subpoena me but only if they're sure I won't be a hostile witness."

"Only if they're sure you'll tell the truth."

"That's right."

"Do you have a choice, Hugh?" Tears were forming in her huge green eyes.

"I don't think I do."

In saying that I realized I had to do it.

"We'll stand by you," Liam promised.

They both embraced me.

That clinched what I had to do.

The subpoena came in the autumn. I was summoned Downtown. The Archbishop, Bishop Meaghan, Father

Reynolds, Joseph Kennedy, and Dr. Straus were convened around the Archbishop's desk (on which no cognac glass was visible). I was placed in a single (wooden) chair facing them. There were no stars on the wall, only portraits of popes, but it was a star chamber just the same.

The Archbishop began the trial.

"I am very disappointed with you, Father Hoffman. After all I've done for you personally, I would not expect you to betray us. I feel betrayed by this subpoena."

"Archbishop, I did not issue the subpoena. The court did at the request of an attorney."

"But you accepted it."

Bishop Meaghan joined the assault.

"We have no intention of permitting you to get away with this disloyalty. If you give testimony to these fly-by-night tort lawyers, we will suspend you and remove you from your parish."

"Pot" Meaghan had been superintendent of schools. He had a reputation of knowing "where the bodies are buried." A man without any hint of subtlety or sensitivity, he had brutally closed schools, especially in the small towns out in the prairies. He had become Vicar General and Bishop because he knew the Archdiocese well enough to tell the Archbishop where the towns were and where the money was.

"Father Reynolds will tell you, Bishop, that canon law does not permit you to do either in these circumstances. I will fight both penalties and appeal any decisions you might make all the way to Rome. And I will

394

fight publicly. As a citizen of the state I have the duty to reply to a subpoena."

Josh didn't say anything. Doubtless he had made the case. The Bishop was bluffing.

Joseph Kennedy was next in line, a tall lean man with the face of a hawk and the voice of a bullhorn.

"I warn you that if you repeat your frivolous charges against the late Father Leonard Lyon, we will bring a defamation suit against you."

"You surely don't believe, Mr. Kennedy, that you can file suit against testimony I might give in a deposition?"

"We might ask the court for a psychiatric examination. We would argue that you are deranged on this subject."

"You've gone that route before, Doctor."

Now Josh Reynolds delivered his line.

"It's hard for us to understand why you would want to attack another priest, especially a dead one."

"I witnessed a rape at St. Theodolinda rectory, Josh. I am not attacking anyone. I am simply telling the truth under oath."

"You're being disloyal to the priesthood and the Church." The Archbishop actually raised his voice, so his words came out as a squeak.

"The clergy and the laity will drive you out of the Archdiocese," "Pot" Meaghan thundered, his baritone anger an off-key antiphon to the Archbishop's squeaky tenor.

"I won't go."

"You will not change your mind?" Counselor Kennedy demanded.

"No, sir."

Perhaps I should have kept my mouth closed. Nonetheless, as I rose from the chair to leave their star chamber, I seized the last word.

"All of you know that the charges against poor Lenny Lyon are true. In the past you have been able to sweep these charges under the first available carpet because you controlled the courts and the media. If you look around the country, you will see that those days are over. You'd be much better advised to seek a settlement with the plaintiffs than risk a long court battle. Moreover, you will not intimidate me. As I said, I will fight you all the way to the Throne of Peter, not a good place for a fight, Archbishop, if you expect to go to Philadelphia."

"You shouldn't have said those terrible things, Hugh!" Kathleen protested, as I called her from my car as I drove back to Prairie View.

It was a pro forma protest.

"I'll call the zoo and see if other female leopards are changing their spots."

So we had the deposition at Horst's law office, Ms. Delaney representing the plaintiffs and a Ms. Irma Young, a child just out of law school, representing the Archdiocese. Silently.

She said to me when the deposition had adjourned, "A priest would never do such terrible things, Father!"

"I was there, Counselor, and you weren't."

XXV

ARCHBISHOP SPEAKS OUT ON SUIT

Breaking his silence on the charges against Plains City priests and the hearing before Judge Sturm on Friday, Archbishop Simon Isidore Louis said last night that he is astonished by the viciousness of the attack on the Church and the priesthood. "We have our procedures for dealing with charges of sexual abuse, and I think we've done pretty well with them. We've made a few mistakes, but I think we've rectified them. No one grieves more than I do when a child is hurt. Yet I also grieve when a priest is falsely accused, especially when he is dead."

Asked if this was a reference to the suit against the Archdiocese, which charges Father Leonard Lyon with serial pedophilia, the Archbishop replied candidly, "I don't want to judge specific cases, but my heart breaks when I hear a priest has attacked the virtue of another priest who is no longer with us. Father Lyon may have made some mistakes, but I have always felt that he was cleared both by the police and our psychological team . . . I blame the lawyers and the media for the current situation."

Would he excommunicate Father Herman H. Hoffman for testifying against the Church in the ongoing hearing before Judge Arthur Sturm?

"Well, it does seem to me that Father Hoffman is violating canon law. He has in fact committed a delict. There are, I am told, automatic penalties for doing that."

About the rumors that he might be transferred to Philadelphia, the Archbishop chuckled. "I told the Holy Father the last time I spoke with him that I wanted to stay right here in Plains City for the rest of my life."

He also expressed complete confidence that the Archdiocese would be vindicated in the hearings this morning.

"It's all just a tempest in a teapot," he said.

THE TODAY SHOW

COURIC: Dr. Shannon, you're the director of the Center for the Treatment of Sexual Abuse Victims at Plains State University. Are you familiar with the suit against the Archdiocese charging repeated sexual abuse by one of its priests?

SHANNON: I am in a general way. I would not want to comment on it specifically.

COURIC: In general, do you think it is credible that a priest could have been imprisoned in an asylum because he reported a case of abuse in his rectory?

SHANNON: (his brogue grows thicker as he talks) It wouldn't be the first time, Katie.

COURIC: Why is there so much sexual abuse in the priesthood, Doctor?

SHANNON: We treat a lot of victims at State, Katie.

Only a small number have been attacked by priests, no more than by clerics of other denominations or men and women in other professions that work with children—teachers, coaches, Scout leaders. The problem is not that there is a lot of abuse—though one case is too many. The problem is that the Church has been trying to cover it up for a long time.

COURIC: Why does it do that?

SHANNON: To protect its reputation, to guard its finances, to shelter priests.

COURIC: Why does it reassign priests who have been repeatedly charged?

SHANNON: Probably because they have so deceived themselves as to believe that the man is innocent.

COURIC: Is that really possible?

SHANNON: It would appear so, but that doesn't make it excusable.

COURIC: Has the Archdiocese ever consulted with you, Dr. Shannon?

SHANNON: It has not, Katie Couric.

COURIC: But you're internationally known in the field?

SHANNON: Sure, ma'am, you must have kissed the Blarney Stone in my native Cork . . . I feel certain that the Archdiocese of Plains City had confidence in its own consultant.

COURIC: Who is only a family practitioner.

SHANNON: (a quick wink of the eye) Sure, don't they sometimes know more than all the rest of us?

COURIC: Do you think it likely that Plains City will become another Boston?

SHANNON: Judging by what I read in the papers, it seems very likely. Maybe worse.

COURIC: Has the problem become public recently because the Church is ordaining homosexuals?

SHANNON: Most of the men recently charged were ordained a long time ago, before this alleged change occurred. Most child abusers are not gay and most gay men are not abusers. The problem is an underdeveloped and twisted sexual maturation.

COURIC: Do you think, Dr. Shannon, that if priests could marry, the problem would be solved?

Shannon: I do NOT. There may be good reasons for priests to marry, but sexual abuse isn't one of them. It's a syndrome that's deeply rooted in a personality disorder, a sickness that, as far as we now know, is incurable. A married abuser is still an abuser. He may victimize his own children. It is atrocious to blame the present problem on celibacy.

COURIC: And who would you blame it on, Dr. Shannon?

SHANNON: And isn't that evident, Kate Couric? Stupid bishops and their incompetent staff.

COURIC: Are we likely to get different kinds of bishops?

SHANNON: Ah, lass, if I were a betting man, I wouldn't bet on that at all, at all.

COURIC: Dr. Burke Crawford, a psychologist who used to be a priest, has said about the case in Plains City that sometimes a victimizer fantasizes that someone else has committed his crime. What do you think of that theory?

SHANNON: Katie, if we were back on my farm in Cork, I could tell you an appropriate word, but here on family television, I'll just say it's nonsense.

LOCAL NEWS ON KOPC

ANCHOR: As Plains City prepares for the continuation of hearings before Judge Arthur Sturm this morning, police are searching for the vandals who damaged the new school at St. Cunegunda in Prairie View last night. Members of the school foundation estimate that twenty thousand dollars' worth of damage was done to the school. Kenneth Moran is chairman of the school foundation. Our Jerry Osterreicher spoke with Mr. Moran early this morning.

OSTERREICHER: Mr. Moran, do you have any idea of who vandalized your school?

MORAN: Good Catholic laymen, no doubt, who were offended by Father Hoffman's telling the truth under oath yesterday.

OSTERREICHER: Do you blame Father Hoffman for what happened?

MORAN: Certainly not. He's a brave and honest priest. We blame the corruption at the Archdiocesan Chancery.

OSTERREICHER: Will you have increased security tonight?

MORAN: It's not clear whether the county or the state police will protect us. In any case, we will have plenty of our own here. I defy the vandals to try again.

OSTERREICHER: There it is, Jenny. Out here in Prairie View they are very much on the side of their pastor.

ANCHOR: However, elsewhere in the Archdiocese there are other opinions. KOPC *Instant News* spoke with Father Joachim Binder, who attended seminary with Father Hoffman. Steven Suarez has that story. Steven.

SUAREZ: Jenny, Father Binder spoke harshly of his classmate. We asked him if he thought Father Hoffman had a future in Plains City.

BINDER: Hermie has always wanted to be different. He should return to the University of Chicago, where people appreciate intellectuals. All we need here is good solid parish priests who say Mass and take care of their people. Now that he's turned against the Archbishop I don't think my fellow priests are prepared to put up with him. He should leave town on the first plane. There's no one who priests despise more than a disloyal priest.

SUAREZ: Father, do you think there will be more violence at St. Cunegunda school?

BINDER: I don't approve of the violence, but I can understand why the laypeople are angry. I'm sure there'll be more.

SUAREZ: So, Jenny, things look grim for Father Hugo Hoffman as he prepares for what will surely be a harrowing cross-examination by the Archdiocese's brilliant lawyer, Joseph T. Kennedy.

ANCHOR: Thanks, Steve. KOPC has just caught up with Father Hoffman as he enters the Prairie County Courthouse. Good morning, Father.

HOFFMAN: Good morning, Jenny.

ANCHOR: You look remarkably relaxed for a man who has a harsh ordeal ahead of him.

HOFFMAN: I have a secret, Jenny.

ANCHOR: Could I ask what it is?

HOFFMAN: You could ask, but I'm not telling.

ANCHOR: Your classmate, the Reverend Joachim Binder, has just told KOPC that you should leave town on the first plane.

HOFFMAN: Did he? Well, I'm not leaving Plains City on the first plane or the last plane . . . Now I have to get into the courtroom.

ANCHOR: Will the school still open in the autumn?

HOFFMAN: It will.

ANCHOR: Father Hugo Hoffman, live from Prairie Square. I must say that he does not seem very worried.

(PRINTED IN THE *PLAINS CITY PLAINSMAN AND GAZETTE*)

(PARTIAL TRANSCRIPT OF HEARING *IN RE THOMAS PATRICK SWEENEY VS CATHOLIC BISHOP*; SUPERIOR COURT OF PRAIRIE COUNTY, JUDGE ARTHUR STURM PRESIDING. MS. DELANEY FOR THE PLAINTIFF, MR. KENNEDY FOR THE DEFENDANT, MR. HELLER FOR THE WITNESS.)

KENNEDY: Now, sir, I'll begin by asking you how much you have been paid for this testimony.

DELANEY: Objection, Your Honor. The question is

gratuitous and irrelevant.

JUDGE: I'll permit the question, Counselor. I want to know the answer.

HOFFMAN: No one has paid me anything.

KENNEDY: Do you expect me to believe that?

DELANEY: Objection.

JUDGE: Sustained.

KENNEDY: All right. Was any offer made to pay your expenses?

HOFFMAN: I was asked if I had any expenses for my testimony. I said that I did not.

KENNEDY: But you were asked about expenses?

DELANEY: Objection! Your Honor, defraying the traveling expenses of witnesses is common practice in suits like this. I don't understand what the point in this line of questioning is.

JUDGE: Come now, Ms. Delaney. Counselor is trying to impugn the motivation of your witness. I sustain your objection and direct you, Counselor, to change your line of questioning unless you have evidence to show that the witness is not telling the truth.

KENNEDY: We will reserve the right to present such evidence later, Your Honor. Now, Father Hoffman, is it not true that you visited the late Father Lyon in his final illness?

HOFFMAN: Yes.

KENNEDY: Why did you visit him?

HOFFMAN: I had heard that few priests had visited him.

KENNEDY: Was that the only reason?

HOFFMAN: Yes it was.

KENNEDY: It was not to gloat over his sickness?

DELANEY: Objection, Your Honor. Snide and irrelevant.

JUDGE: Sustained. Counselor, you're on dangerous ground.

KENNEDY: Is it not true that you administered the Last Sacraments to Father Lyon?

HOFFMAN: Yes, on the third time I visited him. I had instructed the hostel staff to call me when he seemed to be entering his last agony.

KENNEDY: Did he at any time admit that he was a child abuser?

HOFFMAN: I won't answer that question.

KENNEDY: I insist you answer it.

DELANEY: Your Honor, I can't believe that counsel for the Archdiocese is trying to force a priest to violate the seal of confession.

JUDGE: I can't believe it either, Ms. Delaney. However, both of us heard it with our own ears, didn't we? Joe, what the hell is the matter with you?

KENNEDY: Are you claiming priestly privilege, Father Hoffman?

DELANEY: I continue my objection, Your Honor. The seal of confession is more than just a priestly privilege.

JUDGE: Sustained. Leave it, Joe. It's an improper question and an improper line of discussion.

KENNEDY: Your Honor, I believe it is proper. Witness claimed to have given Father Lyon the last rites of the Catholic Church. He told the Archdiocese that Father Lyon died as a member of the Church and later said Father Lyon's funeral Mass. Does that not say something about the state of Father Lyon's soul on his deathbed? How could witness have given absolution to Father Lyon unless he either admitted or denied to the end that he was an abuser?

JUDGE: Sounds to me, Joe, like you're trying to abolish the seal of confession. Drop it.

KENNEDY: I reserve the right to appeal that decision, Your Honor.

JUDGE: Noted.

KENNEDY: Now, Father Hoffman, you swore under oath on Friday that you are not a homosexual, did you not?

HOFFMAN: Yes, sir.

KENNEDY: What if I told you that we have expert evidence that you are?

HOFFMAN: I would say that the evidence is wrong.

KENNEDY: You have admitted that you were confined some months at St. Edward's mental institution.

HOFFMAN: St. Edward's Mental Health Center.

KENNEDY: I have here, sir, a letter from Dr. Robert Geneva, the distinguished director of St. Edward's Mental Health Center. Would you read it aloud, sir?

HOFFMAN: Your Excellency, Dr. Michael Straus has asked me to write to you about the conclusions our staff made as a result of our treatment of Father Herman Hugo Hoffman of the Archdiocese when he was a patient at this center. I consulted Father

Hoffman's records and determined that we did indeed conclude that Father Hoffman was homosexual in orientation and tended to have fantasies about others engaging in the homosexual actions that he himself desired to perform himself.

DELANEY: Objection, Your Honor. Counsel has not submitted this evidence prior to the hearing. We would demand to see all of Father Hoffman's records before permitting that letter to be entered in evidence.

HOFFMAN: Horst . . .

HELLER: May I approach the court, Your Honor?

JUDGE: Who are you?

HELLER: I am Horst Heller, Father Hoffman's attorney, and I have here copies of the medical records from his stay at St. Edward's Mental Health Center.

JUDGE: Those records are supposed to be secret, young man.

HELLER: Father Hoffman gave me permission to reveal these copies, which he obtained several years ago should the question arise about his treatment at St. Edward's.

JUDGE: Very well, let me see them.

KENNEDY: Objection. Those records may be forged, Your Honor.

JUDGE: They look fine to me. Seal on every page. I'll look through them . . . Witness, why did you seek these copies?

HOFFMAN: Against the day when something like this might happen.

JUDGE: How provident of you . . . Father, did you know that you were drugged during your months at St. Edward's?

HOFFMAN: Only for the first few months. It takes us Russian Germans a while, but we finally figure things out. So I threw them away during the last three months.

JUDGE: How did you feel during the first three months?

HOFFMAN: Tranquil, Your Honor, very tranquil.

JUDGE: You're a dangerous man, Father Hoffman.

HOFFMAN: Yes, Your Honor.

(Judge leafs through documents.)

JUDGE: Bailiff, will you ask one of your assistants to go out to the mental health center and attach copies of Father Hoffman's records. They should also attach the person of Dr. Robert Geneva and bring him to this courtroom, in restraints if necessary . . .

KENNEDY: Your Honor, I object to this whole interruption. I do not see the point in it. Surely Dr. Geneva's letter is enough proof that the defendant has committed perjury . . .

JUDGE: Counselor, you raised the issue of his treatment at St. Edward's. I have documents here that present a very different picture of that treatment. Someone may well have committed perjury, but I don't think it was Father Hoffman. Now be quiet while I check this sheaf of records.

JUDGE: Let me rehearse for the record a document at the end of this file. It is signed by three psychiatric residents then on the staff of St. Edward's. It reads: "It is clear from tests and from our observations that Father Herman Hugo Hoffman is a healthy, heterosexual young priest of considerable zeal as displayed by his work with the patients here. We objected to the medication he was given and suspect that he simply stopped taking it. We also recommended his release several months ago, but both the director and Dr. Michael Straus, the admitting physician, rejected our recommendations." It's signed by three men with M.D. after their names and their license numbers.

JUDGE: Order in the court, I will have order.

JUDGE: Witness, do you know whether any of these men are present in this jurisdiction at the present time?

HOFFMAN: I believe that Dr. McAteer is on the staff of the medical center at State U.

JUDGE: Bailiff, would you send another one of your henchmen out to the medical center and ask Dr. McAteer to come to this courtroom immediately for the sole purpose of testifying to the validity of these records.

KENNEDY: Your Honor, I fail to see what relevance all this has to do for the purpose of my cross-examination of the witness.

JUDGE: Counselor, your line of questioning raised the issue of the defendant's sexual orientation. I have two records of his treatment at St. Edward's Mental Health Center. One of them has to be perjured. There would appear to be prima facie evidence that the Archdiocese has committed the felony of misprisioning perjury and indeed has conspired to misprision perjury. If it has, I will notice the State's Attorney and the respective professional organizations. I will also convene a hearing tomorrow morning to consider contempt of court citations against the Archdiocese, including the Archbishop, the Vicar General, Dr. Straus, and Dr. Geneva to answer such charges. I will instruct you to deliver all such persons into this jurisdiction tomorrow morning at nine A.M., or I will send my bailiffs to attach their persons.

KENNEDY: Your Honor, this is an outrageous violation of the separation of church and state. We will appeal . . .

JUDGE: No, you won't appeal, Joe. You can't appeal a contempt citation until it is issued.

DELANEY: Your Honor, Dr. McAteer is here already.

JUDGE: Were you waiting in the wings, Doctor?

MCATEER: No, Your Honor. I was in my office across the square. My assistant told me you were looking for me. I figured I had better come over right away, lest your bailiff would have to attach me.

(Dr. McAteer is sworn.)

JUDGE: Just a couple of questions from the bench, Doctor. Is this your signature on this document?

(Judge hands witness a document.)

MCATEER: Yes, Your Honor. It is.

JUDGE: Will you look through this file of papers

410

and tell me whether it appears to be a fair copy of the records of Father Herman Hugo Hoffman.

(Witness scans files.)

MCATEER: Yes, Your Honor, it would appear to be.

JUDGE: Can you tell me, Doctor, the difference between the practice of the representatives of the Archdiocese in this case and that of the former Soviet Union in dealing with internal dissidence.

MCATEER: St. Edward's, Your Honor, is an excellent institution. It was only in cases in which Downtown was involved that such things happened.

JUDGE: By "Downtown" you mean the Archdiocese.

MCATEER: Yes, Your Honor . . . we repeatedly told the director that Father Hoffman should be released. He procrastinated.

JUDGE: Thank you, Doctor. You may go back to your patients. We may want to talk to you again. It won't be necessary to come in a rush. Mr. Kennedy, I am astonished and shocked both by the brutality and by the crudity of the behavior of the Archdiocese. I am also astonished and shocked by the stupidity of this letter. I will not issue my contempt citations, however, until tomorrow. If you do not deliver the persons I have instructed you to deliver, I will attach their persons and imprison them for contempt of court, no matter how high their ecclesiastical dignity.

KENNEDY: We'll appeal all of this . . .

JUDGE: You're welcome to try. Do not misunderstand my seriousness, Mr. Kennedy. If His Excellency the Archbishop is not here at nine o'clock tomorrow morning, I will not hesitate to have him dragged into this courtroom. Now, where are we . . . Witness, you may step down. I do not think we will need you any further at this hearing. You have behaved with dignity, and restraint, and, if I may say so, courage. I still have some hope for the Catholic Church.

Ms. Delaney, with regard to your petition to enjoin the Archdiocese to release to you the records of the response of the Archdiocese to the various charges against the late Father Lyon, I will obtain these and other files this afternoon and determine whether they should be released to you and to the public. At the moment I incline strongly in that direction. The public has a right to know what chicanery goes on across the street.

DELANEY: Thank you, Your Honor.

JUDGE: Mr. Kennedy, I am directing my bailiffs to go across the street to the Chancery and collect all files on sexual abuse cases in the Archdiocese—all of them. These are to be delivered to this courtroom by the end of business today. I warn all Church officials here present that I expect full and immediate cooperation. I can sentence any or all of you to an unlimited term in the county jail if you do not cooperate.

Now we will adjourn for an hour to await the arrival of the unfortunate Dr. Geneva.

XXVI

I SHOOK HANDS WITH DR. MCATEER AND HORST ON THE way out.

"Our guy was great on *Today* this morning, wasn't he?" I said.

"Too bad that gorgeous fire-eater wife of his wasn't on camera with him."

"I agree," said Horst. "Hermie, we've won."

"It's not over till it's over, Horst."

I pushed through the crowd of reporters in the corridor. The woman from the *National Catholic Inquirer* asked the only question I could not ignore with a "no comment."

"Wasn't that a very homophobic session, Father?"

"Homophobic?"

"Shouldn't you have come out of the closet and admit you were gay to make common cause with persecuted gays and lesbians of this country? Didn't you engage in gay bashing in there?"

"No, ma'am. I don't think you can find a single word that I said to support such a claim."

"It wasn't what you said, it was what you seemed to accept."

I struggled for an appropriate answer.

"If you're seeking gay bashers, you should look at the Archdiocese."

Blackie was waiting for me outside in my Crown Victoria.

"First time I ever had a bishop pick me up anywhere."

"I will drive up to the stoplight and we will then change places. I do not want to convey you to Portland, Oregon."

When we had made the change, he relaxed.

"I have enough trouble driving around Chicago . . . You did very well in there. I think one could arguably say that you creamed them."

"It was your idea back in Chicago that I get the records."

"Possibly . . . I have already communicated by cell phone with Milord Cronin. It is safe to say the Slippery One will not be translated to the City of Brotherly Love. I also suspect that the Holy See will accept his resignation sooner rather than later. They will not delay as they did, with unfortunate results, in Boston."

"Will you be flying home tonight?"

"Milord Cronin wants me to stay around a little longer to see which way the dust settles."

On the car radio we heard that poor Bob Geneva had appeared in the courtroom in shackles and weeping, having fought his hysterical way through swarms of media waiting for him outside the courthouse. Judge Sturm gave him a very hard time.

"I was just doing a favor for the Church. Monsignor Meaghan called to ask me if I would write a brief letter summarizing my memory of the Hoffman case. I wrote down what I thought was the truth. I did not look at the files. I am director of one of the largest mental health centers in the state. I have no time for files."

"You did not know that Dr. Straus ordered heavy sedation medication for Father Hoffman?"

"No . . . no. I do not have time to monitor every treatment in our facility."

"Do you admit that you permitted the Catholic Church to submit to this court a letter with your signature that is totally at variance with the clinical records of the hospital?"

"I did not know that. I was doing only what the Church asked."

"You can say that, Doctor, when you are released from the two weeks in county jail to which I am sentencing you for contempt of court. You can say that to the grand jury that I presume the State's Attorney will convene. You can tell that to the state medical board when it revokes your license."

According to the radio reporter, Dr. Geneva collapsed on the floor of the courtroom and sobbed hysterically. Judge Sturm snapped at his bailiff, " 'Incarcerate this man.'

"Bishop Meaghan was asked when leaving the court whether the Archdiocese would accept the subpoena for all its sex abuse files. He replied, 'Everyone knows that Art Sturm has been acting senile recently. I have instructed our security guards to repel any attempt of bailiffs to enter the Chancery office. We will not cooperate with this farce. I warn Judge Sturm that Catholics will not forget this assault on the Church and its leadership on election day.' "

"Ah," said Blackie, "I am always reminded of the saying that those whom the gods would destroy, they persuade to dig their own holes."

I did not know what to expect when we pulled up to the

parish. Hundreds of people milled around cheering and shouting encouragement. I had to make a speech from the porch, like an old-time political candidate making his acceptance speech from a front porch without a megaphone. Blackie characteristically disappeared.

"I hope I didn't let you down today," I began.

"No! No!" they shouted.

"I am grateful for your support during all the publicity these past few weeks. I also ask you to pray for our poor Church, which faces many troubles in the weeks and months ahead. Never put your faith in us poor priests. Always cling to God's love for us and the beauty and goodness of the Catholic heritage."

After I had shaken hands with all of them, I entered the rectory. Blackie was chewing on a wurst bun, sipping from Meganesque iced tea and entertaining the two Megans, about to become high school seniors, with stories about his Megans.

The young women hardly noticed me when I came in.

"Oh, hi, Father Hugh."

"Nice going today."

No match for the celebrity from out of town.

"I'm going upstairs to work on my lecture for tomorrow and call my parents."

"OK. . . . Oh, Father Horvath will be here for supper. We told Mrs. Smid."

"The doctors too."

"Ah, the fabled Kathleen."

"She's really cool, Father Blackie."

"Just like one of the kids."

Before supper my guests and I sat around the parlor

and watched the news on the large-screen TV the Shannons had left there at Christmas without asking me or, indeed, telling me.

We had congratulated Liam on his *Today* show triumph.

"See," his wife said, "I told you that you were sensational."

There were dramatic shots of Dr. Geneva being dragged out of the courtroom in shackles as he sobbed hysterically, of uniformed bailiffs contending with Chancery office security guards until Josh Reynolds waved the guards off and led the bailiffs inside, of the bailiffs lugging large cardboard boxes across the square to the courthouse, of a glowering Bishop Meaghan shoving TV cameras out of his way and pushing reporters of either gender aside as he stalked out of the courthouse.

They found Tom Donohue, who announced that there was going to be a meeting the following evening at his rectory of concerned priests who would demand a complete review of Archdiocesan policies in sexual abuse cases. A lay professor at State U called for the formation of the VOTF (Voice of the Faithful) group, which had emerged in Boston. A recently ordained priest, though older than me by at least ten years, in cassock and biretta, warned in apocalyptic terms that the Church was locked in combat with demons who were trying to destroy it. I was the chief demon.

"They were fair to you, Hugh," Liam Shannon said, "for a change. I assume they quoted the judge correctly?"

He and his wife had come directly from the airport, exhausted by the overnight trip to New York and back. Herself's eyes were shining. She knew victory when she saw it, even if I didn't.

"I don't know," I admitted. "I wasn't listening too closely."

We were at the supper table, devouring zwiebel-fleisch mit wurst.

"Verbatim," Blackie said. "I think you will experience a quick metamorphosis from a disloyal priest to a folk hero."

"That's what he is, Father," Kathleen said, "a blond Gary Cooper riding in from the plains, six-shooters in both hands."

"Arguably an excellent metaphor," Blackie admitted. "Smiles a little more than the late Mr. Cooper."

"You're Mary Kate's little brother, aren't you?" Liam said.

"That allegation has been made on other occasions."

"So you're the legendary Bishop Blackie Ryan."

"Arguably, but it would not suit our purposes if my presence became public knowledge."

"Mary Kathleen Ryan Murphy is one of the best in our trade."

"So I am told. Also her long-suffering husband Joe, who is regrettably from Boston. . . . Speaking of which, John Horvath, I would ask a very great favor."

"Sure."

"Do not attend that meeting tomorrow night or any subsequent meetings. It would not help the cause if a close personal friend and onetime parish priest of

Father Hoffman were seen as an activist in demanding the resignation of the Ordinary of this troubled place."

I tried to figure out what Blackie was scheming. He can be opaque when he wants to.

"OK, Bishop. That's probably good advice."

"Call me Blackie."

"What will the endgame be, Bishop Blackie?" Kathleen asked.

"Oh, the final endgame is evident. The Archbishop will submit a resignation to Rome, which will promptly accept it."

"How soon?"

"Three months. I think we can assume that, no matter how disorderly the Chancery office records might be, they will contain damning information. The media will scent blood and turn on the Archbishop. There will be new revelations every day. The level of anger and embarrassment among the laity and the clergy will rise. The Archbishop has neither the stamina nor the intelligence to withstand it. Then there will be a new archbishop, who will have a lot of healing to do."

"They generally deliver a diocese from Annas to Caiaphas, from one idiot to another," John Horvath said sadly.

"Patently. Sometimes, however, they make mistakes. In any event, our local folk hero cleric is now pretty close to untouchable, even, Kathleen, for a Volga Deutsche from the prairies."

"I've had to keep him out of trouble most of my life," Kathleen said. "It's a little easier these days because I have a shrink who lives with me and is a big help in dealing with folk heroes. . . . By the way, I presume that you came home from court this afternoon and worked on your lecture for tomorrow?"

"I did."

"I knew it!" She waved her hand. "You see, Bishop Blackie, that's what folk heroes from Lincoln Junction do!"

"In my role as your future parish priest, Kathleen, I am using my authority to send you and your husband back to University City. You're both so tired you can hardly see."

"We took a cab from the airport. Would you ever, Father Pastor, see if you can find one for us?"

"I'll drive them home," John Horvath said, "then come back here for the morrow if I may. I want to see the next chapter."

"Capital," Blackie agreed, as if he were in charge of my rectory. "I'll join you. I believe that Father Pastor has a class to meet tomorrow."

Liam and his wife both embraced me, glad that the worst seemed to be over. Kathleen's hug sent a rush of hormones into my bloodstream. That happens sometimes.

The hug wiped out dreams of the courthouse scene.

"Interesting people," Blackie murmured as he disposed of his second dish of German chocolate ice cream. "They do indeed represent the Holy Spirit with great skill."

"I'm lucky."

"Patently. . . . I would adjure you, Huey, in the bowels of the Lord, as we used to say, that you stay away from the media. They will be waiting for you at the doorstep tomorrow morning and the entrance to your classroom in the afternoon. Be nice to them, smile, and say at the present moment you don't want to comment. Later on, when so tempted, you might call me and ask what I think."

"I never argue with a vicar for extern priests."

The media did indeed wait in the morning and in the afternoon.

In both places I was asked if I were thinking of leaving the priesthood. Apparently someone had started the rumor.

"With the help of God and the Blessed Mother, no way, no never."

My students applauded me.

"Not bad for Volga Deutsche," an African-American kid announced.

Blackie had been right as always: I had become a folk hero. I must be careful to prevent it from turning my head.

The report from him and John Horvath seemed to confirm how bad things were in the Archdiocese. Judge Sturm sentenced Bishop Meaghan and Joseph Kennedy to a month in the county jail for contempt of court and Dr. Geneva to two days. Josh Reynolds received a suspended sentence of a week, depending on how efficiently he provided the Chancery files.

Two hotshot corporate lawyers were there to appear for the Archbishop. They weren't much help because Slippery Louie was not functioning too well. He repeatedly rubbed his forehead in confusion.

"I can't find definitive proof, Archbishop," Judge Sturm said at the conclusion, "that you were part of this conspiracy, though it would seem to me that as the man responsible for an important Archdiocese, you are almost completely out of touch with what your staff does. Personally, I think your Chancery office is steeped in both dishonesty and incompetence."

"Fair enough," I said to John. "Poor Slippery Louie should have never given up his place in Bemidji."

"He always pretends he doesn't know what's happening. The reason is that he doesn't want to know. So people like Straus, and 'Pot,' and Peters knew that their job was to protect him from controversy. It worked for a long time."

"The times are a-changing," Blackie mused.

I drove him to the airport.

"Presumably you will keep me informed," he said, "and will come to Chicago in the near future to thank Milord Cronin personally. You could bring along your new parishioners."

John Horvath drove back to the Junction. The next day, the *Plainsman and Gazette* carried a front-page editorial.

CATHOLIC CRISIS

It will be no secret to regular readers of this paper, that we have opposed tort suits by buccaneers from out of state against the Roman Catholic Archdiocese of Plains City. Surprised by the events of the last few days, we must change our position. The credibility of what Catholics call with some affection "Downtown" has been savaged. While we are inclined to believe that Judge Arthur John Sturm may have gone too far, he is nonetheless a devout, practicing Catholic. We must assume that he is pretty close to the truth when he says that recent revelations indicate that Downtown is not only corrupt but incompetent.

The Archdiocese needs to recapture its credibility. The Archbishop needs to apologize. He needs to make all sexual abuse files transparent. Priests with past records of abuse need to be replaced. A new staff needs to be appointed. In the absence of quick attention to these reforms, the Vatican needs to find Plains City a new Archbishop.

This paper also hails the singular courage and integrity of Father Hugh Hoffman. As Judge Sturm remarked, a church that can attract such a priest still has strong resources.

The Archbishop did issue an apology, which continued to blame the mistakes on his staff. He admitted that he should have devoted more attention to the processes that his staff had followed in the past.

The *Plainsman and Gazette* rejected the apology. "The Archbishop had to have known about the suffering of victims and their families."

The expensive PR people that Josh (now Acting Vicar General) had hired tried again with a press conference, which would begin with the Archbishop reading an abject apology that his flacks had written. However, he read it so poorly that the journalists concluded that he had never even glanced at it before the press conference. The media folks tore him to pieces during the question period. He even asserted that if it hadn't been for Father Hermann Hoffman's betrayal of the priesthood, the whole sad story would not have become public, and the Church would not have suffered irreparable harm.

That night the Plains City Priest Association voted to demand his resignation and sent copies of their demand to the Papal Nunciature in D.C. and to the Congregation for the Making of Bishops in Rome. Slippery Louie went into hiding and was not seen for weeks. The Church continued to function, which as Tom Donohue said, proves that it really doesn't need bishops. Eventually the hate calls from my fellow priests became less frequent. I even got some friendly calls, mostly from the members of Tom Donohue's group.

The next week Blackie returned for dinner at the Shannon house with an invitation for Liam to serve on the National Review Board for the Protection of Children and Young People, which, as he put it, in a moment of inattention, the hierarchy had established to make sure that the bishops kept their word on sexual abuse. Hardly had he ensconced himself on the couch when Katie climbed up on one side and Billy on the other. Irene toddled over and raised her hands, demanding a place on his lap. Rita, the normally exuberant chocolate retriever puppy, curled up quietly on the floor in front of him. It was a scene I had often witnessed before. Without being asked, Blackie began to spin out stories about two magic princesses named

Katie and Irene and a prince named Billy and a friendly dragon called Rita, who was also part unicorn.

Finally, he called time-out.

"A certain mother wants her children to go to bed."

"How do you know what my mother wants?" a sleepy-eyed Katie demanded.

"I have vast experience with reading the minds of mothers."

Reluctantly, the foursome headed for the stairs, their bemused mother following them.

"A brilliant trick altogether, isn't it now?" Liam observed.

Blackie sighed loudly.

"Won't your sister, Mary Kate Murphy, be on your frigging committee? Isn't she at the top of our profession of cranks, crackpots, sorcerers, and necromancers?" said Liam.

"Although usually people suggest that I'm her brother, it would seem to many that putting her there would have been a power play too vast even for Milord Cronin."

At supper—poached John Dory which himself had prepared for us with his own hands—we continued the discussion.

"The commission will have trouble," Blackie said. "The abuse crisis is out of the media temporarily. Some of the bishops think that the storm is over and they can go on pretty much the same way as always. Hence there is no reason to pay attention to a group of pushy laity who have no authority whatsoever under canon law."

"They can't think we'd let them get away with it, can they now?"

Liam had not formally accepted the invitation, but he was already part of the group.

"You know what was said of the Bourbons?"

"They never learn anything, and they never forget anything?"

"Indeed."

"I may have remarked"—Liam changed the subject—"that I cooked this delicious white fish with me own hands? All me wife did was to set the table!"

"And buy the fish," Kathleen added with the amused laugh that mothers reserve for impossible but adorable boy children, "and the potatoes and the vegetables and the ice-cream dessert and make the salad and open the wine."

"Sure, aren't women much better at that sort of thing than we are?"

It was Kathleen's turn to change the subject to more serious matters.

"Won't these terrible things ever stop, Bishop Blackie?" she asked. "The lives of innocent children ruined, good priests like Hugh punished for telling the truth, incompetent men appointed bishop?"

"Isn't your man making great progress now, Hugh?" Liam interjected. "My man," in this instance, was Todd Sweeney, now a patient in his center. For an Irishman, I had learned, "your man," could mean almost anyone. It was your job to figure out who it was from the context.

"Arguably"—Blackie sighed again—"we can mini-

426

mize the harm done by those with arrested sexual development. Unless and until the Lord God decides to replace us poor priests with seraphs, we'll continue to make a mess out of things."

Kathleen refilled my glass of white Châteauneuf du Pape with the affectionate smile I had seen often in the last couple of years. It said, "We're still lovers, *dummkopf,* and we always will be, though it's a different kind of love now, maybe better."

The smile always confused and disconcerted me. As Retramn said when I worried about it, "Confusion and disconcertment are part of life, as hard as it might be for a Volga Deutsche to understand."

"So," Blackie continued, as Kathleen poured the wine into his empty glass, "you must put your faith in God and in the Lord and His Blessed Mother and our whole glorious heritage and not in us poor priests, even if we are bishops and popes."

"In the meantime," I broke into the conversation, "continue to raise hell with us for our sins and mistakes."

"Arguably that's what the laity are for."

Kathleen, her face glowing, her green eyes radiant, raised her glass in a toast.

"All the priests I know," she began, "have been good priests. Even the poor dolts over at Newman since John was sacked are good men, though clueless. Otherwise, the priests I know have been better than we laity deserve, even our poor straight-arrow Volga German here. So, gentlemen, I toast the good priests and their hard work. God send us more of them."

"The sooner the better," her husband agreed.

I raised my glass of Châteauneuf in response. "And to the Catholic laity, who are better Catholics than we are . . . As they should be."

Then, on a September morning when our school opened for the first time (with Katie and Billy as students), I read a single sentence on the AP line, which I pick up on the Net.

> New bishop. Father John Horvath, parish priest of Lincoln Junction, has been named Archbishop of Plains City, succeeding Most Reverend Simon Isidore Louis, who has resigned.

And that was that.

Tucson–Chicago

END NOTE

Like all humans, all of us priests are sinners. Which of us are the worst sinners we must leave to God to judge, and it's not at all clear that God engages in invidious comparisons. "Sinful priests" means simply "human priests." However, in this story, with its variegated collection of priests, those who might seem to be the worst sinners are not the predators possessed by their own uncontrollable urges, but other priests who know about what the predators have done and remain silent or even defend them out of mistaken loyalty. And still worse are the bishops and bureaucrats who hide the truth, then reassign these desperately ill men to other parishes, where they can continue to destroy the lives of children and young people.

The ending may be untypically happy. Usually, as Father John Horvath says (ironically), they replace an idiot with another idiot. With some wondrously happy exceptions, the Vatican is unwilling to appoint competent, intelligent, and sensible men to American dioceses. It does not seem to ask too much of the Roman Curia that they improve the quality of the kind of bishop they send to the American Church. I suspect that the idea hasn't occurred to them, despite the crisis caused by the sex abuse scandal.

So in order of responsibility for the crisis—the abusers themselves (who are developmentally arrested men and not totally responsible), priests who persist in clerical culture denial, bishops who reassign abusers, and the Curial dicasteries who appoint such bishops.